TH_
ARCHIE
GOODWIN
FILES

THE ARCHIE GOODWIN FILES

EDITED BY MARVIN KAYE

WILDSIDE PRESS

THE ARCHIE GOODWIN FILES

For more information, contact:
Wildside Press, LLC
www.wildsidepress.com

ACKNOWLEDGMENTS

THANKS TO the officers and Steering Committee of The Wolfe Pack for permission to select and republish contents of *The Gazette,* contents of which are property of the Pack.

Thanks to all its editors over the years, in chronological order: Lawrence F. Brooks and Patricia Dreyfus, John McAleer (Consulting Editor), Ellen Krieger, Ettagale Blauer, Susan E. Dahlinger, Bill DeAndrea, Sarah Montague, Alexandra Franklin, J. G. O'Boyle, Henry W. Enberg II, Beverly Norris, Joel Levy, Sandy Olubas (Associate Editor), Joe Sweeney, Carol Novak (Web Master), and Jean Quinn. The City Editor, of course, has always been Lon Cohen.

I am deeply thankful for the aid and support of Barbara and Rebecca Stout, the late John McAleer and his son Andrew, and owner of New York City's splendid *The Mysterious Bookshop* Otto Penzler.

Inestimable thanks to Steering Committee member Kevin Gordon for allowing us to use his splendid self-portrait of Mr. Wolfe and his Neronian Still Life for the covers of this book.

Anyone wishing to purchase prints of them should get in touch with The Wolfe Pack via its web site:

http://www.nerowolfe.org

Thanks to the following Wolfe Pack members for contributing titles to this anthology — Tenby Storm for *Wolfe Tracks,* and Dr. B. T. See, of Singapore, for *Nero Wolfe Redux.*

Special thanks to Wolfe Pack former Treasurer Saralee Kaye for support and assistance, and love and thanks to my college roommate and pal Dave Ossar for first introducing me to (actually, *insisting* that I read) Nero Wolfe, and to the late W. S. Baring-Gould for his book, *Nero Wolfe of West 35th Street.*

N. B. — *The Archie Goodwin Files* was originally intended as a continuation of *The Nero Wolfe Files.*

Parenthetical editorial commentary in the ensuing articles were written by whichever editor was then in charge of The Wolfe Pack's publication, *The Gazette.* It either appears without indicated authorship, or with the appendage " — ED.") Any comments by myself end with " —MK.")

CONTENTS

III. The World of West 35th Street

IV. Nero Wolfe Redux

WOLFE TRACKS

ARTICLES about Nero Wolfe outnumber all other subjects in *The Gazette;* my untrimmed list of possibilities for this section was originally three times its present size. The majority of the selections began as speeches at the annual Assembly on the afternoon of the Black Orchid Banquet: Marina Stajic's *The Black Mountain Revisited* (Summer 1990, Volume VIII # 3), Jeannie Thelwell's *The Legal Wolfe* (Spring 1984, Volume III # 2), Emily Mikulewicz's *The Forensic Wolfe* (Summer 1990, Volume VIII # 3), Ettagale Blauer's *Wolfe and the Post Office* (Fall 1990, Volume VIII # 4), Gahan Wilson's *Mr. Wolfe's Nose* (Spring 1989, Volume VII # 2), and Maggie Goodman's *Stout on Stage* (Fall 1990, Volume VIII # 4). Wolfe Pack members who were there remember the fascinating information — and the laughs — conveyed in their presentations. It happens every year!

The question of Nero Wolfe's birth, parentage and early history has been argued eloquently and often in *The Gazette* and elsewhere, notably in W. S. Baring-Gould's "official biography" *Sherlock Holmes of Baker Street*, which first proposed the often-accepted theory that Nero Wolfe is the offspring of Sherlock Holmes and Irene Adler (from Dr. Watson's story, *A Scandal in Bohemia.*) Rex Stout neither confirmed nor denied the possibility, nor have his daughters Barbara and Rebecca, nor any other member of his family, which led to a song parody at a Black Orchid banquet. Oren Dalton's discussion of this topic from Volume IX # 3 (Summer 1991) of *The Gazette* is one of the most thoroughly reasoned ones to appear in its pages.

Joel Levy wrote his article about who was or had ever been married in the West 35th Street brownstone and its irregulars for the Autumn 1986 *Gazette* (Volume IV # 4), whereas in Volume IX # 3 (Summer 1991) Jerry Edwards tackled the touchy issue of law-breaking in the line of duty by Archie and Mr. Wolfe.

While I regret not including the (hopefully) amusing and informative debate between me and Werowance Jonathan Levine concerning whether Mr. Wolfe's beverage of choice is beer or wine (Werowance Emerita Ellen Krieger, also the late Henry Enberg, pawkily suggested Classic Coke!), two of Mr. Wolfe's other greatest passions are represented here: orchids, as expounded by Charles E. Burns in the Fall 2000 *Gazette* (Volume XVI # 2), and books, by Larry Brooks in the Premier Issue (Winter 1979).

The section begins and ends with poetic encomiums to Mr. Wolfe by Andrew McAleer and Kevin Gordon, whose splendid Still Life and portrait of The (literally) Great Detective grace the covers of this volume.

— Marvin Kaye

A NERONIAN CLERIHEW

by Andrew McAleer

Nero Wolfe is our king sleuth,
Who consumes beer while questing truth.
And when Cramer feeds him hooey,
Wolfe shuts his eyes and says "Pfui."

[*Author's note: As we know, Rex had a great devotion to Sherlock Holmes, and much like the debate, "Are we Sherlockians or Holmesians?" are we devotees of Wolfe, Wolfeans or Neronians? Edgar Award winner William L. DeAndrea reminds us in his* Encyclopedia Mysteriosa *that we are "Sherlockians" if we reside in the United States and "Holmesians" if we are British. Still, while Holmes fans can take delight in knowing their identity, how are Wolfe Packers to cope? Are we Wolfeans or Neronians? Fortunately, I did pose this question to my father and he informed me that Rex preferred Neronian. In Stout's own words: "I don't use the word 'Wolfean' . . . It's what I would call one of those clumsy words. Some words, I don't know why, but they're clumsy, and that's that. 'Neronian' is all right. I don't mind that. Neronian has a flow to it."* (Royal Decree, *John McAleer, Pontess Press, 1983 p.38) Accordingly, I dedicate the above clerihew to my father and Rex — Neronians to the end!*]

NERO WOLFE — MONTENEGRIN OR AMERICAN: A PARADOX

by Oren Dalton

Wolfe's early history supports an apparent paradox. On the one hand, he states unequivocally to the FBI that he was born in the U.S. On the other, the allusions to a Montenegrin birth are many. This is inconsistent; it creates a paradox.

(1) If we choose the Montenegrin birth we are forced to a single conclusion: in *Over My Dead Body,* Wolfe lied to FBI-man Stahl. This creates enormous problems; the consequences of this are bad, irrespective of Wolfe's motives for lying. Stahl is trying to obtain background on a murder involving a pair of Montenegrin girls with possible international implications. Wolfe, practicing genius, chooses to tell a lie to the FBI about a subject which can be readily verified or discredited. In aid of what? In a fit of petulance Wolfe tells the one sure lie guaranteed to focus unfriendly government attention on him.

When the government wants to know why he lied, what does Wolfe answer? "I didn't like you?" Wolfe in the throes of a truculent eccentricity jeopardizes the entire bastion he has constructed on West 35th Street by stamping his not-so-dainty foot and declaring, "I don't like you!" That's not from the ratiocination of a genius; it's the yapping of an utter idiot.

As if this weren't enough, in the same interview Stahl asks Wolfe if he has ever been married. Wolfe stammers, says one thing, changes his mind in midsentence, refutes his statement and is finally rescued by Archie. (Check the text around p. 15 in *Over My Dead Body.*)

Having made one anti-survival lie, which could be easily refuted, apparently without a quiver, Wolfe is now confronted by a second choice. Obviously, he doesn't want to answer Stahl's question, so now is the time, if ever a time there was, for a good convincing lie. Moreover, this one should be difficult to refute.

But this time, our little grey cells are expected to swallow the spectacle of a Wolfe who wasn't able to tell an easy lie. (If you thought that was a wild metaphor, wait 'til you hear about "Parsnips do not a prison make nor iron bars a summer." Don't ask me. That's exactly the way it was told.) My little grey cells can swallow a lot of things, but this isn't one of them.

Stahl reappeared in *The Black Mountain* for essentially the same reasons as he did in *Over My Dead Body*, and the meeting was far from cordial. However, despite provocation, Wolfe did not lie to Stahl. He did what he usually did: he withheld information. That's a big difference. A lie to Stahl is a lie to the reader; withholding information, whether the reader is privy to it or not, preserves the integrity of Wolfe's world.

There is a more subtle objection to a lie to the FBI. Step out of the world with Wolfe in it for a minute and into the one with Rex Stout in it. Then ask: If Wolfe was born in Montenegro, then why in time did Stout kill off Vukcic and then send Wolfe galloping back to Montenegro? On sober reflection, *The Black Mountain* is not needed. To the contrary, it is an embarrassment.

(2) Assume Wolfe did not lie to the FBI in the person of Stahl. Some incredible and sticky problems are smoothed. Some new ones are created: we have a paradox. We've been lulled into the belief that Wolfe was born in Montenegro. In Stout's world the conflict needs to be resolved and Stout sets out to do it. Now it is vital to get Wolfe into Montenegro and onto the Black Mountain. There is only one possible event of sufficient force to pry Wolfe from NYC into Titograd neé Podgorica: the murder of Marko Vukcic.

This wasn't a last-minute plan, either. Notice how *Over My Dead Body* merges into *The Black Mountain* with scarcely a ripple. Other than a few concessions to the passage of time, it is as if we passed from one book to the other in an unbroken progression. Carla was single in *The Black Mountain* and she was single in *Over My Dead Body* — except she had been married and widowed. Here she is: back in the same ebullient state she had been in before she became a widowed matron. Stahl was the same FBI man except he was slightly older and had more authority. *Over My Dead Body* introduced the play and *The Black Mountain* is here to carry the drama to its conclusion.

In Stout's world, it is my opinion that *Over My Dead Body* and *The Black Mountain*, if not written back-to-back, were jolly well conceived together. They fit together almost seamlessly. Stout held back on publishing *The Black Mountain* for at least one very good reason: he didn't want to kill off Vukcic any sooner than he had to, of course, but of equal importance, he had to build a believable and convivial, even intimate, relationship between Wolfe's ménage and Vukcic. He did this through Rusterman's. Rusterman's quickly assumes considerable importance and its owner calls Wolfe "Nero." This intimacy, not particularly apparent in early books, is principally developed between *Over My Dead Body* and *The Black Mountain*. Here is an open question: Did Stout make a provision in his will, say, to have *The Black Mountain* published if he couldn't do it personally? 70/30 says he did. *The Black Mountain* may not have been published until after 1950 but I feel confident that at least an outline existed long before then.

Does *The Black Mountain* resolve the paradox concerning Wolfe's birth? The answer is a resounding and very satisfactory "yes!" It also resolves some other seemingly unconformable relationships. For example, ask yourself this: why did Wolfe ride in rigid fear in the back of his car, which Archie called "eccentric"? Yet when he went after "Z" he did not display this fear. (I argue this deduction this way: "Z" clearly knew Wolfe's habits. He had demonstrated this knowledge on several occasions and he was certainly aware of this Wolfean proclivity. If the new man in his organization had shown such a tendency [Wolfe rose high in the organization, remember] especially after Wolfe had disappeared, it is possible, indeed probable, that "Z" would have noticed. And you can bet Wolfe knew it. Could Wolfe have gritted his teeth and covered up his phobia? If it was a genuine phobia, probably not. Fortunately, at this time, Wolfe had no fear of riding in an automobile. Isn't that nice? It's all explained by *The Black Mountain*.)

At this point I stop pursuing this line of reasoning. I have thirty to forty pages which do explain it — containing many redundancies. The grammar needs tightening, too, but I want to present the conclusions (which the editor has probably already guessed) as a *dénouement, a la* Wolfe.

Under my assumption, Wolfe didn't lie to Stahl. Did he ever directly lie to the reader and/or authority? Yes, for several reasons. But in all cases but one, they were jokes, conversational gambits; they were there to add verisimilitude to the narrative and were sooner or later resolved. They can be dismissed. The notable exception concerns Wolfe's marital history. But when this one does arise, whistles go off and bells ring. Wolfe stammers and contradicts himself in a most unWolfean manner (though not unlike Conrad's Wolfe in the late unlamented TV series.) And Archie comes charging in like the White Knight, and deflects the conversation into safer channels. One time of note was during the catechism with Stahl in *Over My Dead Body*. I only have two references (not including the one where Wolfe claimed to be a poisoned husband) but I think there were three.

If we assume that baby Wolfe was born in the U.S., I favor the theory that Wolfe lived in the U.S. for six to eight years if, for no other reason, the ability to master a spoken language, without an awkward accent, is virtually confined to the prepuberty years and especially those of the first half. (Coincidentally, there is a very good recent article on just that subject by Richard P. Meier, "Language Acquisition by Deaf Children," *American Scientist*, Vol. 79(1), Jan-Feb 1991, pp 60-70.)

Wolfe was also a master of Montenegrin. This assumption isn't based on thin air; I base it on the seemingly effortless way he convinced local Montenegrin authority, in *The Black Mountain*, that he was a returning native son. He also convinced a farmer and aroused suspicion here and there that he might be a government spy. Later he spoke Montenegrin to the guerrillas in the hills — the same language but likely to be slightly different in idiom and accent.

Accepting Wolfe's dual linguistic achievements and accepting, as a hypothesis, that he was born in the U.S., what is the most likely series of events? There are a large number of possibilities, but I assume that Wolfe's father was a Montenegrin and his mother an American; I'll ignore other possibilities. Am I justified in this? Is there anything in the core *Corpus* to sanction it? You can bet your blue-eyed bippy there is. I'll introduce it later.

Based on many considerations, not only in the core *Corpus* (i.e., those books that Stout, himself, wrote) but the *Corpus* as a whole, the broadest time limits for Wolfe to have left the U.S. could have varied from infancy to young manhood. Although possible, is it likely Wolfe's parent(s) would have travelled the ocean before an infant was a year or two old? Most likely not, so the lower limit would not be too far out if it is raised to two years. And what about the upper end? Could he have been eighteen to twenty-two, say, before moving to Montenegro? First off, Wolfe was an "agent" as we know, but not for Montenegro.

Before this, he had to have had time to become embroiled in some sort of idealized politics. But prior to this he, with young

Marko Vukcic, herded goats and explored a fort on the Black Mountain. And he learned Albanian. (I would guess it was during this period.) But there is also the consideration of language fluency which must have occurred at a young age. All of these things mitigate against Wolfe having moved to Montenegro much later than puberty. Surely he wasn't older than fourteen. Based on these considerations, a very good estimate, as good as 90% to 98% probable, is that the age limits when Wolfe left the U.S. would be two to fourteen.

The derived limits, two to fourteen, are broad. You may not like them, but based on what I've said so far, there is little justification to narrow them. Please note: there is nothing in the core *Corpus* that make other limits impossible. You or I could devise quite easily a scenario where Wolfe didn't arrive in Montenegro until he was twenty-two years old, but it would be highly improbable. But we have to start somewhere and, as we accumulate facts and interpret them in their most likely context, we can rule out the improbable events. We choose a sequence of events that seem most likely and then assign some probability measure to the result with the reasons why. But the measure has to reflect equally likely, less likely and even not impossible events.

There is nothing in the core *Corpus* about Wolfe's mother. There is nothing specific about her during his formative years, and as far as the core *Corpus* is concerned, her life could have varied from dying in childbirth to becoming a grandma. Fact: Wolfe had a mother but it is not known if she went back to Montenegro with him. There are only two possibilities: either she did or she didn't. A 50% probability either way. If a possibility is rejected, a cogent reason is needed for jettisoning it. (Below I give a reason for changing the odds to 51% for.)

Here's the drill: assume the following three postulates whether you believe them or not:
1. Wolfe had a mother.
2. Wolfe was born in the U.S.
3. Wolfe left the U.S. and went to Montenegro.
Q: Did Wolfe's mother go to Montenegro?
Sub-Q: If so, was it before Wolfe, with Wolfe, or after Wolfe?
Answer to Q: Since there is no enlightenment in the core *Corpus*, as a first cut, estimate the probability to Q as 112 for and 112 against. Now the conditional probability for Sub-Q given that Q is yes, I would estimate is 98% for. This isn't in the core *Corpus*, it's based on my assessment of human nature.

Although her fate appears to be undecidable, we can infer something about Wolfe's mother and decrease the odds (though not eliminate them) against her dying during childbirth. Under the assumption of Wolfe being born in the the U. S., we can assume that she taught her son English, but most importantly, she taught him American English, not British English. Nowhere in the core *Corpus* does Wolfe speak British English. That is, unless we allow the feeble possibility that Archie replaced all Wolfe's British witticisms with their American counterparts. There is no suggestion of such a thing and I consider its probability so low that it's uninteresting. (This, of course, does not mean he didn't understand British English. He may well have. We know he knew and liked "sennight" which I consider essentially British. But is it?)

Everything in the core *Corpus* suggests that Wolfe spoke accentless American English. I will assume it with a very high probability: 99%, essentially a sure thing. He knew idiomatic American English and also used certain somewhat prim expressions. "Idiomatic," of course, is not to be confused with "slang." This suggests two sources: (1) someone who knew the language well and loved it, and imparted it to the learner; and (2) a peer group. The first person was surely his mother. True, it is not impossible that an aunt, a priest or a kindly bricklayer taught English to Wolfe. There are a myriad such possibilities but we can fix on just two: his mother or not his mother. If it wasn't his mother is there any other likely candidate? Remember, his father was Montenegrin and far from home. This is contestable, but I give his mother a probability of about 96%.

Since a peer group clearly aided Wolfe in learning American English and such a peer group has little effect until two and a half to three and a half years old, and since it is unavailable in Montenegro, he must have been near it at least until four and very likely until five or six. Did Wolfe have an accent? From all indications, little or none. This is why I favor the assumption that Wolfe's environment was an American town or city to at least four and most likely five or six years old.

The most probable age limits for Wolfe's move to Montenegro are now five to fourteen years, and I'm going to give it a probability of, say, 88%.

Had Wolfe been as old as fourteen he would have had little time to herd goats on Black Mountain (or master Montenegrin and learn Albanian) before more violent events occupied him.

Also the description of the way he and Marko climbed through the old fort sounds like the antics of young boys. There are other considerations. For one, there is Wolfe's own "as a boy." As another, from the reading and movies I've seen, it seems that Eastern European mountain-goat-herders are usually boys whose ages are in the range of six-twelve years. Put all this together and isn't it reasonable to assume a probability of about 80%-88% that Wolfe was herding goats between the ages of six and twelve years and, concomitantly, left the U. S. just prior to that time? My prejudice for the goat-herding is six to eight years with a mean of seven, but I can't seem to justify narrowing the five-twelve range further. Is there a good reference? I would like to know it.

Did Wolfe's mom accompany him and his father to Montenegro? (His father went back. He had to have, based on the above hypotheses.) I don't know. If she were alive she probably did. In that era a woman followed her man no matter where he led. (In this era they don't!) On the other hand, perhaps she died. This could even be the impetus for Wolfe's father to return to his homeland. There is one very tiny ray that suggests she may have been alive and, ipso facto, accompanied them to Montenegro. When Wolfe remembers herding goats on the Black Mountain, it seems to me there is an undercurrent of pleasurable nostalgia; no sense of sorrow for a dead mother. Assume this nudge is worth a probability of 1%. Did mom then accompany Nero to Montenegro? 51% says "yes," 49% "no." Flip a coin.

Why assume that a Montenegrin man married an American woman? From *The Black Mountain*, of course. As soon as Wolfe and Archie stepped onto Montenegrin soil, in that wonder book, until they left, it was Alice-in-Wonderland time. Into this dreamscape one of the first things Wolfe did was to introduce Tone Stara. Wolfe tells how, because of its poverty, men used to leave Montenegro for other countries where they worked for most of the year, and then returned home with their earnings. (This was a common practice everywhere, including my own family.) Now Wolfe becomes a man who left Montenegro for the U.S. Only he didn't return the following year. He married there, became well-off, and now is returning to Montenegro with his son, who, coincidentally, speaks English and is to be taught Montenegrin. Wow! During this dream-time could part of the "phoniness" Archie claimed in his (unprecedented) preface which left us glassy-eyed, be that Wolfe was dramatizing his own history? Is this an epidemic of "like father, like son?" It has to be! It is the first thing that gives any rationale to Archie's mind-numbing preamble and Stout's writing the book at all. On a less exuberant note, it fits so well; it complements and makes good sense with many other suggestive incidents.

Please note that other than being an American (and, probably teaching her son English) Tone Stara's son's mother is not alluded to in the core *Corpus*. The same is true of Wolfe's mother. Again, it's possible that either, or both, died in childbirth; the core *Corpus* is silent on that issue. Also note that Tone Stara's son's mother didn't accompany them to Montenegro. Does this mean, to strengthen the similarity, that Wolfe's mother didn't accompany little Nero? I don't see why it should have any bearing on it at all. The similitude isn't perfect. For one thing, Archie is considerably older than Wolfe must have been.

THE BLACK MOUNTAIN REVISITED

by Marina Stajic

[Marina Stajic, Ph. D., is Director of the Forensic Toxicology Laboratory at the Office of the Chief Medical Examiner, City of New York. She
has spoken twice at Wolfe Pack. events. — MK]

I WAS quite flattered, not being expert on Nero Wolfe, when
Miss Ettagale Blauer asked me, at the suggestion of Henry Enberg, to speak here today. After I had graciously accepted, my
first thought was, "What on earth do I tell these people about
Nero Wolfe that they already don't know?" Then I realized that I
probably do have one advantage over you all. I am sure that I
have been to Montenegro more times than all of you here together in this room. As Miss Blauer said, that is due to the fact
that I was born and raised in Yugoslavia.

We all know, of course, that Nero Wolfe was *not* born in Yugoslavia. I'm not saying this because I think that he was born in
Trenton, New Jersey, of dubious and questionable parentage, as
some people would have us believe. [*A reference to the theory proposed in W. S. Baring-Gould's* Sherlock Holmes of Baker Street
(Bramhall House, New York, 1962) *that Wolfe was the offspring of*
Holmes *and* Irene Adler. — MK] He was simply not born in Yugoslavia because at the time he was born, the state of Yugoslavia
did not exist. But he and I do come from the same part of the
world, about four hundred miles apart. We come from what
would be in today's Yugoslavia, diametrically opposite corners
of the country — I from the northwest corner, Wolfe from the
southeast portion of what is now Yugoslavia.

Judging by the way Archie Goodwin was talking in *Over My
Dead Body*, I suppose that he would have called Nero Wolfe a
Balkan. I want to make it clear here that I am not a Balkan, since I
come from north of the Dunav (Danube). As you may or may not
know, the rivers Dunav and Sava (the largest Yugoslav river)
form the northern border of the Balkan peninsula. So, if you

travel through Yugoslavia and you meet someone like me from north of the Dunav, it is considered an insult if you call them a Balkan, since that will mean that you consider them uncivilized or at least primitive. You certainly don't want to insult any Yugoslav and, especially, you don't want to insult a Montenegrin.

Yugoslavia, as you probably know, is a country of many nationalities and many ethnic groups (today 20 million Yugoslavs use two alphabets, embrace three religious faiths, speak three native languages, and many other languages). When I was a child, these groups were called minorities, but not any more. They are now called ethnic groups, because in Yugoslavia there are no minorities, only majorities. Montenegrins are famous for being brave and very active warriors throughout their long history. It is true, however, that in peace time, they will go to great efforts to avoid any kind of physical exercise, and so appear lazy. Montenegro is the smallest of the six Yugoslav republics. It is only about 5,000 square miles in area. It is one of the poorest and least developed parts of the country and has been so since antiquity. Probably because of the mountainous terrain, it is very hard to have any kind of agriculture. It is even hard to raise cattle, and goats and sheep are therefore raised throughout the land. In the old days, a major industry was foresting. That is how Montenegro got its name in the first place. The Venetians named it so because it was so heavily wooded, mainly pines, that approaching from the sea it would actually look black. Those same Venetians later cut down most of the trees, and today Montenegro is really more of a "white mountain" because it is composed of "carst" which is a kind of limestone. From Archie's description you know that Montenegro is a very rocky and desolate place. Due to always having had poor economic conditions, Montenegrin men did traditionally leave the country and went elsewhere to find work. Large groups went to the United States in the Nineteenth and Twentieth Centuries and there was a large contingent that went to Montana, working the mines there. Once they returned, whatever money they had made was considered a large fortune.

As I said earlier, I can't tell you very much about Nero Wolfe, but I was hoping to give you at least a bit of information about the history of Crna Gora (pronounced "tsrna gora") or as you would call it, "Montenegro." I wanted to go briefly over several centuries of life in Crna Gora before Nero Wolfe was born there. Further, I was hoping to introduce some other famous

Montenegrins to you. The part of the country that is Montenegro today was settled by the Slavs back in the Seventh Century and evolved from the independent province named Zeta. Zeta is named after a major river in that area. In the Twelfth Century, Zeta was incorporated into the Serbian Empire. Therefore, modern Montenegrins are really Serbs. They are Serbian orthodox by religion. They speak Serbo-Croatian. They use the Cyrillic alphabet, an old Slavic alphabet ascribed to Saint Cyril and currently used in a modified form by Russians, Bulgarians, Serbs and other Slavic nations. Montenegrins are proud of their origins and always refer to themselves as Montenegrins. This year (1989) marks the six hundredth anniversary of the fall of the Serbian Empire. Montenegro was the only portion of the Empire that retained its independence when the rest was conquered and occupied by the Turks, probably due to the nature of the mountainous terrain. The Montenegrins believe that they were not conquered by the Turks because of their bravery and their quality of fighting. This is probably true to some extent. If you do travel to Yugoslavia, I would not recommend fighting with any of them. The highest mountain in Montenegro is not Lovæen (pronounced "Love-chen"), which is 5,737 feet high. The highest mountain in Montenegro is actually Durmitor, which is 8,274 feet high. Lovæen appears higher since it rises directly from sea level by the Gulf of Kotor.

The Montenegrins love to listen to epic folk poems that celebrate their great glories from the past. There are people who do this almost as professionals. They tell the epic poems using an instrument named "gusle." It is a stringed instrument, probably descended from the Greek lyre. It has only one horse-hair string, sometimes two, so you can imagine the awful sound it makes when scraped by a bow, accompanied by a sort of chanting. The older Montenegrins still regard a pistol as a part of their national costume. Of course, people like this would consider the birth of a son as a great event, because we have here a future warrior. If you ask an old fashioned Montenegrin how many children he has, the answer is likely to be, "I have three children and one daughter."

After the Fifteenth Century, Montenegro was forced to recognize the Turkish sultan's rule. It was around this time that the ruler of Zeta Ivan Crnojeviæ established his capital in a remote village in the mountains. The name of the village was "Cetinje" (pronounced "tset-in-yeh") which remained the capital until

1918 when Montenegro was absorbed into Serbia and became part of Yugoslavia. Due to the fact that one of the sons of Ivan Crnojeviæ adopted the Islamic faith, Montenegrins drew a special privilege during the 500 year Turkish occupation of the other Slavic parts of the Balkans. During the Sixteen and Seventeenth Centuries they were also able to develop their autonomy. The political climate in those days led to the formation of tribal life and tribal organizations. These survived in Montenegro much longer than in any other Balkan nation, except for Albania where they are still quite strong.

Following the alliance between the Montenegrins and the Turkish overlords, Montenegro was ruled for many years by bishops. They had a dual role, they were both heads of the church and heads of state and because of this were called Prince-bishops.

Montenegrins continued to fight throughout their history defending their independence against Turks and Albanians. In 1711, Prince-bishop Danilo Petrovic the First (Danilo was, as you may remember from *The Black Mountain*, a very popular and common name in Montenegro) established an alliance with Peter the Great from Russia against the Turks. From then on ties with the Russians became traditional and almost all Montenegrin rulers went to "big brother" for aid. In 1767 a man by the name of Stepan Mali (the British Stephen the Small) showed up out of nowhere. He claimed to be the Russian Czar, Peter the Third. If you remember, Peter the Third was the husband of Catherine the Great. He was assassinated and that was how Catherine became the Empress of Russia. Montenegrins were so credulous that they easily accepted this imposter Czar and at a tribal assembly proclaimed him the ruler of Montenegro. He actually did a good job. He reduced the blood feuds that ran rampant among the tribes in those days. He established a court of law. He built roads. He even conducted a census of the population. The Russians were not happy with this state of affairs and their imperial court sent a special envoy to expose him. The Montenegrins refused to renounce the imposter Czar. Finally, he was assassinated by the Turks and the Venetians in 1774, upon which Montenegro again engaged in wars against the Turks. When Napoleon invaded Russia, the Montenegrins, of course, fought the French. I'm sure that to this day they believe Napoleon froze in Russia because they were fighting the French in the Adriatic.

The most notable Montenegrin (other than Nero Wolfe, of

course) to achieve international fame was Prince-bishop Peter II, Petrovic-Njegoš(pronounced "Petro-vish-Nye-gosh"). He became Prince-bishop at the age of seventeen and ruled the country from 1830 to 1851 when he died at the tender age of thirty-eight. He is also considered one of the greatest Yugoslav poets. His most famous work that has been translated into many languages is the epic in verse, "Mountain Wreath." This poem became the unofficial Bible of the Montenegrins. In the old days, the true Montenegrin would know the whole thing by heart and quotations and phrases of the "Mountain Wreath" have become part of everyday speech. People have called Njegoš the Serbian or Yugoslav Shakespeare. He is not nearly as prolific as Shakespeare, but he has the same significance in Serbian and Yugoslav literature. During his reign, Njegoš stabilized the political situation in Montenegro, obtained increased aid from Russia, organized the courts, established a national Senate and the first Parliament, and organized the first elementary school and the first printing house. (By the way, the first printing press in the Slavic region was established in Montenegro back in 1493, of course with Cyrillic type, but it was operated only for six years.)

Njegoš also introduced the first taxes in Montenegro. Until his time, the Prince-bishops ruled Montenegro out of an old monastery in Cetinje that was built in 1483. After a prolonged visit to Russia, Njegoš built a new palace, which at the time was considered a very tall building — it was five stories high. What was really important, however, was that next to his bedroom was a billiards room. He was a passionate billiards player, and when he had a chance he played the game with his guests. Because of this, the whole building became known as "The Billiards." If you go to Cetinje today, you will find it is still called that. Now you can see that Nero Wolfe comes from a long tradition with this game.

Njegoš, by the way, was buried by his own wish at the very top of the mountain, Lovæææn, in a small modest chapel. Some hundred years later he was moved to an imposing mausoleum, a little bit further down the road.

In 1878, at the Congress of Rouen, Montenegro was doubled in size, but because of continuing problems with the Albanians the frontier was not settled until 1880. Eventually, Podgorica (pronounced "Poed-goritsa"), which is today Titograd and is twenty-five miles from the Adriatic coast was acquired by Montenegro. Nero Wolfe was born and raised during the reign of the first and last king of Montenegro, Nikola I Petroviæ. During his fifty-eight year government, Nikola did transform the small principality into a sovereign European nation. He succeeded his uncle, Danilo II, who was assassinated in 1860. Nikola came to the throne as a "Prince" and in 1910 proclaimed himself "King." He was educated in the West and tried to westernize his little Balkan country. This was no easy task, although he did succeed to some extent. He continued to support Serbia during the first two years of World War I, but in 1916 he concluded a separate peace with the Austro-Hungarians and promptly went into exile in Italy. After the defeat of the Austro-Hungarian army, Serbs occupied the territory which was Montenegro and, after a national assembly, Nikola and his dynasty were formally deposed. At that point Montenegro was absorbed into Serbia and became a part of Yugoslavia in 1918. King Nikola died in France in 1921 and was buried in Italy. Allegedly, he wished to have his remains moved to Montenegro when it became a kingdom again. Now, just a few months ago, his remains were moved to Montenegro, although it is not a kingdom yet.

As far as recent history is concerned, in 1941 Montenegro was occupied by the Italians. Once again, the Montenegrins used their fighting skills, this time as partisans. They formed some of the toughest elements of Tito's army. Communism had become popular in Montenegro back in 1918 because of Montenegrin's love of things Russian. The Montenegrins were a special brand of communists though, since there was no proletariat. There were also no real workers, so it was not a typical communist profile. Under the new Constitution of Yugoslavia, Montenegro became one of the six republics. At that time, Podgorica was made the capital. Shortly after that it was renamed Titograd. That is what I call it, though Nero Wolfe adheres to the old name.

Speaking of old and new names . . . originally, there were thirty-five tribes which allied to form Montenegro. Even today, any Montenegrin can tell you from which tribe he comes. I strongly suspect Nero Wolfe comes from the tribe of Crnojeviæ, one of the most prominent tribes of Montenegro. "Crno" means "black" in Serbian. His last name, then, would have been Crnojeviæ. A common Montenegrin first name is Vuk. "Vuk" in Serbian means "wolf." There is a strong reason to believe that the birth of the future armchair warrior was preceded by that of a male child who did not survive infancy. Often, after the loss of a male child, the next son would be given the name Vuk (or some equally "scary" name) to ward off the evil spirits. During the immigration process to his adopted country the man who entered this world as Vuk Crnojeviæ became Nero Wolfe.

I have reread *The Black Mountain* recently in preparation for this talk and I must say that Archie Goodwin's description of Post-World War II Montenegro is rather accurate. It is amazing that things haven't changed significantly since Archie wrote about his adventure. Of course, the coast has been built up for tourist reasons. And I must say, not because I come from Yugoslavia, that the Adriatic coast is one of the most beautiful coasts in the world. The twenty-five miles of the coast belonging to Montenegro are the most gorgeous part. If you are planning a trip that way, I would be happy to give you some suggestions as to your itinerary.

You would fly to Dubrovnik, which is not Montenegro, but Croatia (at this point you will be as close to Montenegro as Rex Stout ever got). From Dubrovnik, by land, you would go south, down the coast, to Budva (pronounced "bood-va"), have a drink at St. Stephen's Island, and on to the beautiful bay of Kotor (pronounced "kaw-ttor"), and climb the Black Mountain. I recommend that you take the old narrow road to Cetinje, which is a quaint town and combines eastern and western civilizations. During the reign of King Nikola many palaces were built to house various consulates. The King built himself a palace that is known as the Blue Palace because it was painted blue. He built a theatre and many other buildings. You will also see a typical Montenegrin house (which is part of a museum now) from the first part of the Nineteenth Century, and which looks very much like the home in which Vuk Crnojeviæ, later known as Nero Wolfe, was born and raised. From Cetinje, if you really must, go to Titograd. Please don't expect too much; you will be terribly disappointed. The only reason for going there is to drive through the mountains that are truly breathtaking in their beauty.

If you still want to follow in Wolfe's footsteps, you can work your way back to Antivari, which is now called Bar, and from there you can take a ferry across the Adriatic to Bari, Italy, and from there I hope you can find your way home.

I would like to thank you for having me here. I was glad to become reacquainted with Nero Wolfe. He and I have much in common. We both love beer, I make my living cooperating with law enforcement people, we are both naturalized citizens, and we both make our homes on the island of Manhattan. [*This talk was given in 1989 when Montenegro was still one of six Yugoslav republics and Podgorica was known as Titograd before it became Podgorica again. — Marina Stajic]*

NERO WOLFE AND ARCHIE GOODWIN, CRIMINALS

by Jerry Edwards

[N. B.: *This article contains "spoilers" of the plots of the Nero Wolfe novels*, Fer-de-Lance, A Family Affair, *and* Gambit— MK]

WHILE MANY would consider it sacrilege to call Nero Wolfe and Archie Goodwin criminals, crimes committed by them directly or as accessories appear in most, if not all, of the *Corpus*. It is understood that they could not be prosecuted most of the time, but they do commit the crimes. Any crimes mentioned herein will be from the standpoint of a layman, since I am not in law enforcement.

Many crimes are an integral part of the story and are among my favorite scenes from the *Corpus*. Holding federal officers at gunpoint and making threats against them in *The Doorbell Rang* is a criminal scene that seems to be a favorite of Wolfe Pack members. The strong arm tactics in Nunn's Garage by Archie Goodwin and others in the employ of Wolfe in *The Golden Spiders* is my favorite "good guys versus bad guys" scene. Archie Goodwin's shenanigans with counterfeit money with the knowledge of Wolfe, in *Homicide Trinity* ("*Counterfeit for Murder*"), was about the closest they came to paying for their crime.

My favorite of all crimes is when Nero Wolfe was guilty of "harboring a fugitive from justice" by hiding Clara Fox in the long box of osmundine from Lt. Rowcliff and his search warrant (*The Rubber Band*). "Suppression of murder evidence" occurred in *A Family Affair* when the slip of paper with Orrie Cather's name on it was found in Lucille Ducos's book by Archie and Saul Panzer and was kept from the police. There are many other examples of the crimes mentioned above, but these provide a good cross-section from the *Corpus*.

There were several deaths to which Nero Wolfe contributed

as an accessory. Arnold Zeck's death in *In the Best Families* is one of the best examples. In *Fer-de-Lance*, Archie Goodwin confronts Nero Wolfe in the last two pages: ". . . You killed him." Wolfe replies, "E.D. Kimble was killed by the infant son whom he deserted sitting on the floor among his toys in a pool of his mother's blood . . . Manuel had tried to kill his father. By an accident beyond his control the innocent Barstow was killed instead. Evidence that would convict Manuel of murder was in my possession . . . If I had permitted you to . . . deliver him . . . he would have gone to the chair . . . a bitter and defeated man . . . and his father equally bitter and no less defeated . . . You would encompass the entire complex phenomenon by stating bluntly that I killed E.D. Kimble."

In *A Family Affair*, Nero Wolfe and his agents set up circumstances for Orrie Cather's suicide. As Cramer stated on the last page, "And you killed him. Your men killed him on your order." Nero Wolfe answers, "I won't challenge your right to put it like that . . . If it pleases you to say that I killed him, I won't contend . . ."

In *Gambit*, Cramer confronts Wolfe, ". . . Avery stuck a gun in his mouth and blew the top of his head off . . . Are you satisfied? Are you?" Wolfe replies, "Yes, I'm satisfied. You will be, too, when you cool off. You have been delivered from the ignominy of convicting an innocent man, and from the embarrassment of arresting a guilty man who couldn't be convicted."

There are several other examples of Nero Wolfe's contributions to death — *Some Buried Caesar, Death of a Doxy*, "*Instead of Evidence*," and *Too Many Women*. In most cases, the end result was to achieve justice because there was no evidence to prove the known guilt.

While I generally agree that these crimes are a necessary and often unavoidable part of the story, there is one instance that I have trouble forgetting or forgiving Wolfe's actions. In one of my favorite books (*In the Best Families*, chapter 13, paragraph 7), Wolfe states:

> I met people and I engaged in certain activities . . . With my two invaluable assets, my brains and my important debtor, and with a temporary abandonment of scruple, I made a substantial impression in the shortest possible time, especially with a device which I conceived for getting considerable sums of money from ten different people simultaneously, with a minimum of risk . . . I have been placed in charge of the operation here of the device

which I conceived and used in Los Angeles.

My concerns about this crime is that, granted that Nero Wolfe is fighting for his life and his way of life, nowhere else in the *Corpus* does it state that Nero Wolfe made amends or even tried to make amends for the "temporary abandonment of scruples." Since Wolfe is not a millionaire it is unlikely he has the funds to make amends. Of all the crimes Wolfe committed this is the only one I cannot excuse him for, and one that I like him less because of his actions. I would be interested in any opinions of other members of The Wolfe Pack on how they feel about this crime.

THE FORENSIC WOLFE
by Emily Mikulewicz

AS A member of the medical profession, when I see or read about something happening to someone, I usually think, "How can we help this person?" So, for example, when Bertha Aaron is strangled with Wolfe's tie in his office ("*Eeny, Meeny, Murder, Mo*") and discovered not five minutes after Archie has left her, rather than watch Archie put fluffs of carpet in front of her nose, I'd like him to loosen the tie and get on with some CPR (Cardio-pulmonary-resuscitation). Likewise, when Vincent Pyle in "*Poison á la carte*" reports vicious stomach pains and collapses, he is taken upstairs and what primarily happens is messages go back and forth about how ghastly he is. I'd see him whisked off to the hospital and treated aggressively. But, of course, if these things did happen, we'd have three or four pages of a treatise on the treatment of strangulation or poisoning and we might save these people from dying, which we really don't want to do. So it's really all right with me if they drop like flies, though some of them don't appear to need to.

The next interesting thing one might ask is, "Why do they die?" or "How do they die? So I thought I'd look into some poisons and diseases that appear in the *Corpus* to discover how these people actually die. Take cyanide, for example — take it and "Hey, presto," you're dead. There has to be some mechanism for changing a living person into a dead one.

I mentioned in choir practice one evening that I was working on a talk on cyanide, arsenic, and so forth. It turned out that one of the altos was a sort of physiologist. She started speaking about cyanide to me in a language I didn't understand. She proceeded each Tuesday, thereafter, to give me lessons and even brought in a chart. Her chart was about four feet by three-and-a-half feet. It looked like the subway maps of five or six cities superimposed on one another, in print the size of the telephone book. It was a busy chart. She told me that what went on in the chart is what goes on in the cells of the body. The whole effort is to keep the cells alive by providing them with oxygen. Well, when cyanide is introduced into the system, as it is frequently in Wolfe's books, it blocks the process right before the oxygen is produced. Cyanide disrupts the whole business and, of course, that's the end of that. What happens to these people, then, is that they die of asphyxia, a lack of oxygen. The reason it happens so fast is the effect on the oxygen-producing process is immediate. You don't have to wait for it to be absorbed through the intestinal tract or carried in the blood to some specific place. It effects whatever cell it touches. So Faith Usher (*Champagne for One*) drank champagne with cyanide in it and died in eight minutes, which is about average. These people tend to turn blue, usually about the lips first and then to the nail beds. Cyanosis is the symptom of turning blue due to a lack of oxygen.

I found out some interesting things about cyanide. It exists in sprout kernels, and cyanide is released when they are digested. Seeds of apples, cherries, peaches, and plums release cyanide when they are in contact with some digestive enzymes. This happens only when the seed cover is broken by chewing — swallowing seeds whole is harmless.

Poisons are measured (and I'm going to try to say this without laughing) in mouse-lethal-doses (MLDs). And that is, of course, how much it takes to kill your average mouse. Two MLDs of cyanide will render a person immediately unconscious. There will follow convulsions and death within one to fifteen minutes of inhaling or ingesting the cyanide.

Arsenic is another poison that Rex Stout used on his victims. Vincent Pyle ate some with fish and was dead within an hour ("*Poison á la Carte*"). Again arsenic attacks on the cellular level, interfering with cellular metabolism. This same lady explained to me with her chart how arsenic attacks the structure of proteins so that they can't link together. It effects the integrity of protein structure so that things get a little runny and mushy. It is most unpleasant and death comes from circulatory collapse. When arsenic is ingested, the stomach becomes inflamed and the arsenic is absorbed into the blood stream. The blood cells break down and can't do their oxygen-carrying bit. The whole circulatory system collapses. And that, as they say, is the end of that. By the way, arsenic is also highly carcinogenic.

Nitrobenzene is another poison that Rex Stout used, at least in his books. You'll remember in *The Red Box*, Perrin Gebert, getting into a car, spilled a saucer of nitrobenzene on himself. It absorbs very quickly, the way cyanide does. It is also called

Essence of Mirbane or an imitation Oil of Bitter Almonds. It works slightly differently from cyanide but, nonetheless, polishes one off right away. It acts through an unknown intermediary to change the hemoglobin of blood into methemoglobin that cannot carry oxygen. And there you are, cyanotic again. You'll notice that the policeman investigating Gebert's death said there was a factory worker who died in an hour after spilling some nitrobenzene on himself. And the policeman at the Gebert car got a little on his hand or breathed some fumes and he was in the hospital with a blue face and purple fingernails. And now, we know why.

In *"Cordially Invited to Meet Death,"* Bess Huddleston dies in a particularly unpleasant way as far as I'm concerned, of tetanus. Tetanus is a disease produced by a microorganism, Clostridium (syn. Bacillus) tetani, which looks a little like tennis rackets. The symptoms of tetanus are produced by a toxin created by the bacilli in a wound. Huddleston was cut with some glass and treated with so-called iodine that was really a fluid laced with tetanus bacilli. Three days later she developed symptoms (stiffening of the jaw) and three days later she was dead. That's about par for the course. To give you an idea how virulent it is, purified tetanus toxin contains 20 million MLDs per milligram. The average pill of aspirin has three hundred milligrams of drug in it. So tetanus means business. What happens with tetanus is that there is an infection at the site of the wound and the bacilli begins producing toxin. This travels through the lymph or blood system to the spinal cord and nervous system. The toxin glues itself onto the nerves and blocks the inhibiting response at the myoneural junction, the junction of muscle fiber and nerve. At this junction there are usually some "red lights" that say to the muscle, "Don't do anything, muscle, this nerve is not really talking to you." The toxin of tetanus destroys these "red light" inhibitors, and all the impulses from the nerves are acted upon by the muscles. That is why these people get muscular spasms. I remember treating someone with tetanus as a student nurse, lo, these many years ago. We tiptoed past the room, and I mean tiptoed. We kept the blinds down and the door closed. We tried to keep the patient as quiet as possible and nobody disturbed him because the slightest stimulus of any sort triggered all those spasms. When the muscles of respiration are involved, you're in deep trouble, and people frequently die of respiratory failure. Interestingly enough, most people who have tetanus die of kidney failure.

Because of the really ceaseless activity of skeletal muscles, there is a lot of protein going through the kidneys and they can't handle it. The treatment of tetanus today is different from when Archie originally wrote. Just as with strangulation victims and today's CPR, which has only been around for twenty-five years, today's treatment for tetanus is to put the patients on ventilators, paralyzing them with drugs and treating the original infection, killing the tetanus bacilli so they can't produce any more toxin. We also can neutralize the poison with antitoxin causing the toxin to fall off the nerve cells and wash away. And people can survive, although the mortality rate is fifty percent.

Anthrax is another disease that Stout used in the *Corpus*. The Bacilli Anthracia look like little rods and come in chains. They hunker in the soil as spores waiting for a victim to come along. As spores, they can exist for a long time. The infection comes by entry of these spores into injured tissue. Cattle can eat them and they pass harmlessly through, unless the intestinal tract of the cows has been disturbed by some injury such as eating spiny things or thorns. People get anthrax if a wound is exposed to the anthrax spores. In the blood plasma of animals dying of anthrax, for a brief time there is something called a lethal factor. It is not very well known what this is, but that's what Monte McMillan said (*Some Buried Caesar*) when he committed suicide by giving himself an injection of 5 cc's of the blood from his diseased bull. The lethal factor wiped him out in twenty minutes.

What snake bites don't do to you is not worth talking about. Snake venoms, in research I did, show up as so awful it's no wonder the fellow died there right on the golf course (*Fer-de-Lance*). Fer-de-Lance is actually the name for a variety of Central and South American pit vipers that are all related to one another. There is not one in particular that is called Fer-de-Lance. There are three ways snake venoms get at you. They can be neurotoxic, that is, there are some that attack the nervous system. They also can be hemotoxic in two ways: the first is to attack the blood protein, destroying its integrity; the second is to cause blood clotting in what is called disseminated intravascular coagulation. Now it used to be thought that snake venom caused people to bleed to death by anticoagulating them. What actually happens is that the venom causes clotting to such a degree that all the clotting mechanism is used up at the injury site, and the rest of the blood becomes unclottable. Thus people will sometimes bleed to death within their tissues.

There is another chemical compound mentioned in the Wolfe books. It causes profound biochemical and morphological changes of the liver, brain, gut, heart, endocrine system, bone, blood, and muscles. It causes inadequate nutrition and sleep disturbances. It effects insulin secretion. It causes gout, pancreatitis, and cardiomyopathy. It's not coffee, it's alcohol. And, of course, our beloved detective exhibits none of these symptoms, although he imbibes alcohol to excess. I spoke to the substance abuse chairman at our hospital and asked, "What do you think about five quarts of beer a day for forty-one years?" And he said, "It's not compatible with life." But, of course, that is one death that we are glad didn't take place.

[*This little tidbit was written by Ms. Mikulewicz for the Nero Wolfe Assembly in 1986. The lost tape was recovered and delivered to the editor of* The Gazette *by the Reverend Fred Gotwald. Emily is, for those of you who don't know her, a Head Nurse at the Englewood Hospital in New Jersey.*]

THE LEGAL WOLFE

by Jeanne E. Thelwell

When I was asked to speak on Nero Wolfe and the courts, my first thought was, if I try to go through all seventy-two stories to find the few times that Nero Wolfe actually gets near a courtroom I am going to get cross-eyed. This was followed by the equally horrifying thought that I would then be expected to be clever about them in public. This always gives me stage fright. When I first mentioned this to my friend, Carol Brener, of Murder, Ink, she said: "How can you have stage fright? You are a trial attorney!"

The difference, of course, is that when you try a criminal case, you can be reasonably sure that when you walk into a courtroom, you know more about what happened in that case than anyone, with the possible exception of the Defendant. That is a very different situation than having to expound your views to a group of people, most of whom know more about the subject than you do.

I started thinking about why I read Nero Wolfe novels. I think it's because, over the years, Nero, Archie, and Fritz have become old friends. I have a way of writing myself into the books I read, and I escape into them whenever the world becomes a little bit too cruel.

You may not realize how hard it is to write yourself into a book when the basic environment in that book is hostile to you. I have my name tag from a Black Orchid Dinner, the one at which Marjorie Mortensen inscribed the tags with quotes from the Wolfe books and, where she could, made the quotes appropriate. My tag reads: "I haven't included a sample of some questions asked by an assistant D.A. I've never seen before because they were so ridiculous, you wouldn't believe it."

I considered the possibility of collecting all the samples of vituperation Wolfe gives assistant D.A.'s, but it was too painful. This is one thing the Wolfe books have in common with *Kojak*. Interesting D.A.'s are either venal, political, or stupid.

I had the further problem in writing myself into these books because I am a woman, and a woman D.A. is about as close to being a non-person as I can imagine to Nero Wolfe.

A few years ago, Dilys Winn approached me about writing a piece on a D.A.'s idea of a good mystery story. (You get to see I'm considered to be something of a one trick pony). It eventually was published in *Murderess Ink*, and I now get what, to me, is the unprecedented pleasure of being able to quote myself in public.

I said: "Let's consider the more typical blunders of mystery writers. A Great Detective, in collusion with a member of New York's Finest (who ought to know better) coerces a murder suspect into his office. After a grueling cross-examination he manages to extract a confession without which he couldn't prove a thing. Dandy, but oh my! All I can see is days and days of hearings to determine whether the confession can be introduced at trial as evidence against the alleged Perpetrator. I'm afraid the Great Detective, much as he would resent the insinuation that he was an agent of the police, would have to do a lot of courtroom testifying — something he rarely deigns to do in fiction."

I didn't choose to identify the Great Detective in my article although I'm sure everyone knew who I was talking about. Later I concluded: "Would that we all had the acumen of the Great Detective. And would that he had our kind of respect for human rights."

That may sound a little bit petulant, but there it is.

When I was in law school, I was in an organization that ran mock trials for students to practice being Perry Mason. For one of my trials I wrote a program based on *Champagne for One*. It was a fiasco. In point of fact, as in most mystery novels, you could never convict anyone on the evidence collected in any of the Nero Wolfe stories.

While I was thinking along these lines, I started wondering what it would be like if I were trying a case and had Nero Wolfe as my witness. Anyone who has done any criminal work will tell you that the hardest part of the case is dealing with your witness. They either don't want to tell the story at all, or they only want to tell it their way.

In order for you to understand the situation better, I am going to give you an outline of the criminal justice system as it functions in New York City. To borrow a phrase from *TV Guide*, I think we can say it functions with an air of spontaneity verging on chaos!

When someone is arrested in New York, they are brought before a judge of the Criminal Court for arraignment. That is to say, they are informed of the charges against them and their right to have an attorney. They enter a plea — guilty or not guilty — and the court makes a decision about bail — whether or not to release the accused into the community pending trial.

As a matter of practice in New York, almost every judge will remand a murder defendant — will put them in jail without bail.

Another little quirk of the system is that when a defendant is in jail, because bail hasn't been set or because it has been set but the defendant can't raise the money, or because he has been remanded, the prosecution has seventy-two hours to have him indicted. That means you have to get all your witnesses to a Grand Jury of twenty-three people who listen and determine whether there is a reasonable cause to believe the defendant committed the crime with which he is charged. I don't know if any of you have ever seen a Grand Jury waiting room, but the mere prospect of Nero Wolfe standing in a hallway for two and a half hours, waiting to be called to tell his story, fills me with horror.

Due to the crowding in the criminal justice system, it is very common for criminal hearings or trials to take place at 111 Centre Street, which was built as a civil court building. With a civil proceeding, the witnesses do not have to be sequestered, they can be present in the courtroom during the trial. This is almost never true in a criminal case. Since this building was designed to handle civil cases, there are no witness rooms. That means that the witnesses sit on radiators in the hallway until they are called to testify. Not a good prospect for Nero Wolfe!

In the courtroom, it's no better. I barely sit in the chair they provide for me and, although I am not slender, I wish to go on record as saying that I weigh nothing near two hundred and seventy pounds! In fact, there is only one chair in the entire room that could possibly accommodate Wolfe, and I don't think the judge would appreciate the idea that he lend Wolfe his chair during the proceedings.

All of the proceedings in a criminal case are recorded. There is a court stenographer with a funny little machine which types hieroglyphics. Sometimes what the machine is typing is gobble-dygook but usually it comes back something like the testimony to the jury.

It is a very difficult job being a court stenographer, the witnesses don't speak loudly enough or they interrupt each other, or a dozen other things. I have had visions of pages of my testimony going by the boards as the reporter tries to figure out how to spell

"Pfui."

Problems aren't confined to the courtroom. Frequently you bring a witness in for a morning session and find that he has to be there for the afternoon as well. The City of New York, in its bountiful fashion, remunerates witnesses for their time and lunch — a total of $4.50 a day. I'm not sure I could live on $4.50 a day, let alone Nero Wolfe, but this leads me to the question of where I could send Nero Wolfe for lunch in the Chinatown-Little Italy area when he has forty-five minutes to eat — and he'd better not have any beer with his lunch!

There are all sorts of possibilities: There is Luna's, my favorite cheap Italian restaurant where they throw the food at you. There is Forlini's which, at the lunch hour, resembles the Grand Central Station on New Year's Eve. There's Chinatown — envision Wolfe eating his Mooshu Pork and spilling the vegetables all over his yellow tie. And finally there is the Greeks — that great New York institution, the Greek diner where the meal of choice is a cheeseburger and Pepsi!

I have no doubt that the upshot of all this is that Mr. Wolfe would have his lunches catered by Fritz. Then the problem would arise: where would Wolfe eat his lunch?

Usually, the only place to put your witnesses is in my office and, if the witness is being cross-examined, you are forbidden to speak to him. So I face the prospect of one-half of my office given over to a gourmet meal with a large, belligerent, hostile man who can't talk to me, but who will undoubtedly talk above me.

I was in Law School when I read my first Nero Wolfe novel and I've always been amazed by the little things that happen which make lawyers cringe, much subtler things than forcing confessions, burglary, coercing and that sort of thing. These we take as given, and we try not to know they exist.

You may remember that one of Inspector Cramer's favorite ploys is to threaten to arrest Nero Wolfe and Archie as Material Witnesses. Well, that sounds good, and when I wrote the script for my mock trial, I had someone arrested as a material witness. I had never looked at the statutes in New York pertaining to material witnesses. You wouldn't believe what you have to go through to get a material witness warrant! I suspect that Wolfe and Archie are a lot safer than Inspector Cramer would like them to believe when he threatens to take them in,

On the other hand, once he got them in, it would be a lot harder to get them out than Nat Parker allows them to believe.

Nero Wolfe in Riker's Island comes to mind as the topic of a wonderful short story.

I'm convinced Nero Wolfe in court would end in contempt citations, not excepting a citation for the D. A. who saw fit to put on the stand a man determined to fence with the D. A. It would probably also end with a number of acquittals as juries became more and more incensed by the hostility of Mr. Wolfe, who would undoubtedly be unpleasant sitting on the witness bench.

The reason mystery stories almost never present enough evidence to convict a killer, and the reason no one really minds is that mystery stories and the Criminal Justice System are about two totally different things.

Mystery stories are about right and wrong, about finding disorder caused by a character, identifying that character, and restoring order. The Criminal Justice System is about social regulation, so things aren't in favor of right and wrong, things are stacked to prevent someone from going to jail for a crime he didn't commit. The Criminal Justice System has as an underlying philosophy: the idea that we would rather have a lot of people who committed crimes walking free than have anyone in jail who is innocent — and that system is entirely unacceptable in any mystery story. The one thing a mystery reader demands is final order. He must know that the cause of the disorder has been isolated and removed. The Criminal Justice System asks for no such thing. It is designed to justify giving society control over another human being's life, not removing — once and for all — something that destroys the symmetry of the system.

It's much easier to write a mystery story that will leave the reader sure that the person who is identified as the villain actually committed the crime, gives the reason, and tells the reader that it's over. And if Wolfe can keep his client out of it, manage to collect his fee, and convince Inspector Cramer to arrest someone, or convince the guilty party to blow his brains out — so much the better. It's much easier than convicting people, let me tell you!

When you read a mystery, you are satisfied, completely, and utterly satisfied. It makes you feel good. Eden is back to its pristine state and order has been restored. That's why, apart from an occasional cringe, The Legal Wolfe — illegal as he may be — leaves me comfortable and satisfied in a way my job never did. Because, when I finished with my job, I was almost never sure that order had been restored. (*Jeanne E. Thelwell is a lawyer and a former assistant district attorney for the County of New York. She does not ask dumb questions.*)

LOVE AND MARRIAGE

by Joel Levy

THE VIEWS of Nero Wolfe on the feminine gender are relatively well-known, but an investigation of the realm of marriage in the *Corpus* has not yet been performed. In the first place, whether Wolfe himself ever married is still a question open to debate. In addition, the marital status of his closest associates illustrates some interesting trends.

First, with respect to Wolfe himself, Bernard DeVoto explores this issue rather thoroughly in his 1954 essay ("Alias Nero Wolfe," *Harper's Magazine*). He refers primarily to three key exchanges in the *Corpus*, one with the G-man, Mr. Stahl, and two with Archie Goodwin. In the first (*Over My Dead Body*), Stahl asks the key question in a manner which suggests that he expects a positive answer: "What about your wife? Weren't you married?"

Wolfe's response is at first negative, but then takes an unusual turn: "No. Married? No. That was what . . ." This exchange appears to indicate that Stahl has gathered some background data suggesting that Wolfe was, in fact, married at an earlier time. And despite Wolfe's initial categorical "No," there is that dangling comment which suggests that the specific concept of marriage in its accurate, legal terms might not be precisely applicable to his unique case.

The issue is further clouded by his exchanges with Archie in *Over My Dead Body* and in a related discussion in *The League of Frightened Men*. In the former instance, Wolfe remarks to Archie that he has "skedaddled, physically, once in [his] life, from one person, and that was a Montenegrin woman." It may very well be that this "skedaddling" was done when, on a mission to Hungary, this woman threatened his life. This fits rather neatly with the story to Archie in "League"; Wolfe "knew a woman in Hungary whose husband had frequent headaches. It was her custom to relieve them by the devoted applications of cold compresses. It occurred to her one day to stir into the water with which she wetted the compresses a large quantity of a penetrating poison . . . The man on whom she tried the experiment was myself." Since there is no evidence that Wolfe was deliberately lying on this occasion — there simply seems no point to it in the context in which this story is related — it can be assumed that Wolfe was, in fact, married to a Montenegrin woman from whom he later fled in mortal fear of his life. DeVoto does not come to this seemingly obvious conclusion. He appears not to want to conclude that Wolfe could ever have been married.

That Wolfe was apparently married early in his life — I would suggest that he was still in his teens when this event took place — is supported by later references. In a number of places in the *Corpus*, Wolfe notes that his added physical bulk and attitude towards females have been "donned" as it were, as a defense against any further emotional involvement with these "viperous creatures." Further, as he notes in *Fer-de-Lance*, "As I have remarked before, to have you [Archie] with me like this is always refreshing because it constantly reminds me how distressing it would be to have someone present — a wife, for instance — whom I could not dismiss at will." These remarks appear quite natural coming from a man whose very existence was threatened by a wife at a young age.

Wolfe is not, of course, totally immune to the charms of the females with whom he comes in contact. Proving that the best route to Wolfe's heart is through his stomach, his encounter with Maryella Timms in *"Cordially Invited to Meet Death"* provides some startling breaks in his "cloak of immunity." She begins by introducing the concept of adding pig chitlins to corned beef hash, an idea that so enthralls Wolfe that he writes to his fellow gourmet, Professor Joseph Martingdale at Harvard, about this development. Later Archie enters the kitchen only to find Maryella "standing beside [Wolfe], closer to him than I had ever seen any woman or girl of any age tolerated, with her hand slipped between his arm and his bulk . . ." This familiarity is apparently tolerated only because Maryella has "had a suggestion" regarding mock terrapin. Finally, Archie enters the kitchen again after the case's dénouement, only to find Maryella again in a position of familiarity in the haven of Wolfe and Fritz Brenner.

We might now turn our attention to the marital status of Wolfe's associates — which might reflect or clarify Wolfe's attitudes. After all, with the constant reminders that a woman is not to be tolerated in his house, one would think that he might even avoid those men who had succumbed to the potential perils of marriage.

His closest companion, of course, is Archie Goodwin. Archie

has not only never married, he has shown remarkable resistance to this state. Although he has had a variety of experiences with several women, his long-lasting liaison with Lily Rowan represents the epitome of a male/female relationship for him. Archie explains that both he and Lily are totally pleased with their relationship, and would never dream of ruining it by turning to marriage. (According to Ken Darby, Archie and Lily finally did change their minds and marry.)

Fritz Brenner is another constant associate of Wolfe's with whom he shares a great friendship and mutual affection. Although clearly a life-long bachelor, there is no doubt regarding his "fundamentals" and Fritz offers on at least two occasions to assist Archie in the handling of woman visitors. Thus, although his interest in females appears real, there is no record of any significant liaisons with females — not even on Sundays, which he has free normally.

The final permanent member of Wolfe's household is Theodore Horstmann, about whose personal life we know so little. We know he frequently visits his married sister in New Jersey, but there is little data regarding his own marital status in the past. However, according to Archie Goodwin, as related to Ken Darby (*The Brownstone House of Nero Wolfe*), Theodore was initially hired at the suggestion of G. M. Hoag. Hoag's story, in turn, was that Theodore "had just lost his wife — and most of his interest in living." Although he does seem to have regained his interest in living, as long as it involves his beloved orchids, the sour disposition to which Archie refers frequently could be a lingering consequence of his wife's death.

Wolfe's closest friend was Marko Vukcic, and there is a great deal of evidence regarding his attitude towards love and marriage. First, he had been married to Dina Laszio (nee Rossi) at one time. Further, there is some evidence that he was married at another time since he is referred to later as a widower. His intense interest in females persists throughout his life as evidenced by the testimony of his employees following his death (*Might as Well Be Dead*). Apparently Wolfe's mistrust of females was not shared by his boyhood friend.

We might now turn our attention to Wolfe's professional associates, beginning with the operatives who assist him in many of his cases. Clearly, two of these men were married. Fred Durkin was married to a lady of Italian descent, Fanny (*Fer-de-Lance*), and had four children — at least one of whom presented some problems (his daughter Elaine admits in *Please Pass the Guilt* that she smoked grass). Orrie Cather married the stewardess, Jill Hardy (*Death of a Doxy*), although this relationship apparently did little to curb his wandering amorous adventures. Although there is little information on Johnny Keems's personal life, several references note that he was married before his untimely death in *Might as Well Be Dead*.

The most confusing aspect of my research is the almost universal reference to Saul Panzer as a bachelor. Although this is clearly the case in the early and later portions of the *Corpus*, solid evidence for Saul being married appears in two references. In "*Bullet for One,*" which occurs in 1947, Archie says to Wolfe, "You're prejudiced about marriage . . . Look at Saul, staked down like a tent but absolutely happy." Then, in the next year ("*Door to Death,*" 1948), Archie needs to reach Saul and says: "So when I learned that Saul wasn't home but was expected sometime, I gave his wife the number and told her I would wait for a call." These references are clear and unambiguous evidence that Saul Panzer was married shortly after the War.

It is apparent, however, that by 1954 this marriage was over. Archie and Wolfe go to Saul's apartment (in "*The Next Witness*") to avoid Cramer and Stebbins, and the description of the apartment plus Saul's actions as host omit any reference to a wife. (In an interesting aside, I might note that Archie refers to the poker-playing sessions at Saul's place being held on Saturdays during this period, although later in *The Final Deduction* and elsewhere, the game was changed to Wednesday nights.) Archie provides a clinching bit of evidence that the marriage is over in "*Fourth of July Picnic*" (1956), when he points out that Saul "lived alone on the top floor . . . of a remodeled house on 38th Street . . ."

It would be interesting to speculate on when, precisely, Saul acquired his wife and how or why she disappeared. From his personality alone, a divorce would seem unlikely, but her death by misadventure or a failure of health is left undisclosed.

Aside from the residents of his household and his close business associates, Wolfe has others who are especially close to him. From the law side there are Fergus Cramer (once identified as L.T.C.), clearly identified as being married in several references; George Rowcliff (identified as J.M. Rowcliff in *Please Pass the Guilt*), married to Diana, brother of Dennis Copes, who causes him severe embarrassment; and Purley Stebbins, about whose marital status there isn't a single clue.

Three other people figure in many cases and appear to have special relationships with Wolfe: Edwin Vollmer, his doctor; Nathaniel Parker, his lawyer; and Lewis Hewitt, his friend and fellow orchidologist. Vollmer is identified as a widower in a number of settings. The status of Parker is not referred to directly, but may be solved by identifying the relationship, if any, between Nathaniel Parker, who was Wolfe's lawyer from 1950 (*In the Best Families*) to 1977 (*Murder in E Minor [by Robert Goldsborough* — MK]), and Henry George Parker who was Wolfe's lawyer from 1946 (*The Silent Speaker*) to 1953 (*The Golden Spiders*). At this point it is probably wise to pause for a moment to address the identity of Wolfe's lawyers.

An analysis of the *Corpus* reveals that Wolfe's lawyer in 1935 and 1936, at least, was Henry H. Barber. There is no reference to any other lawyer acting for Wolfe or Archie until 1946. From here there exists a problem in the minds of some, but not in mine. Barber had obviously volunteered to serve in the Army, and unfortunately was killed in action.

Wolfe was led to the firm of Parker and Parker by this event, since Henry George Parker was Barber's attorney and executor. Henry George Parker, the father of Nathaniel, started this firm, probably around 1905. He was to be head of the firm until his death in 1954, at the age of seventy-four. Wolfe enjoyed his services after Barber's death until 1953, although he had been acquainted with his son, Nathaniel, in a professional capacity since 1950. Although reasonably pleased with the services of the "old man," it was clearly Parker senior's bright and able son who performed in a totally satisfactory manner for both Wolfe and Archie over the next twenty-seven years. It appears clear, therefore, that Henry George Parker was married and the father of Nathaniel. Unfortunately, no direct clues whatever are to be found regarding the marital status of Parker, Jr. On the other hand, indirect hints suggest that he was single — these hints stemming from his attentions to several clients which suggested relationships beyond the purely professional.

With respect to Lewis Hewitt, there is some evidence that he was married at some distant time in the past. In Ken Darby's collection of edited stories of Archie Goodwin (*The Brownstone House of Nero Wolfe*), Archie notes that he called Hewitt regarding a gardener (a job which would eventually go to Theodore Horstmann), "but when Mrs. Hewitt answered, he [Wolfe] made me hang up. Very petty." If we can trust Mr. Darby's accuracy in transcribing Archie's notes, this would certainly clinch the thesis that Hewitt was married during the early 1930s. However, the close relationship which developed between Hewitt and Wolfe, resulting in Wolfe dining at Hewitt's home on Long Island several times a year, probably intimates that Hewitt lost his wife. It is inconceivable that Wolfe would spend much time in a home at which a female played a predominant role.

And so we come to the end of this little discourse. Of the fourteen friends and associates of Wolfe discussed herein, ten are or have been married, three probably were not, and there is no evidence on one. Despite Wolfe's own frequent feminist diatribes, therefore, considerable evidence exists showing this to be a posturing designed to hide some other inner feelings. At the very least, having a wife did not make it necessary for Wolfe to distance himself from a male associate.

Further, there is strong evidence that Wolfe was married. If this assertion is unpalatable, there is another source which suggests very strongly that Wolfe, in his youth, was very attracted to females, a feeling that was probably reciprocated. This additional evidence stems from the strong "vibrations" described by Archie in *Murder in E Minor,* when Wolfe meets Alexandra Adjari, the ex-wife of Milos Stefanovic (aka Milan Stevens). At their meeting after many years, Wolfe looks at her "with an expression I'd never seen him wear." Alexandra who is a woman of great beauty and elegance, provides several hints of Wolfe as a young man who was physically and personally attractive to the opposite sex.

After Wolfe takes Alexandra to see the orchids, Archie reflects: "She and Wolfe went back a long way, and the relationship obviously hadn't been a casual one. Well, I'll be damned . . . I thought I had . . . learned everything I was going to know about Nero Wolfe, but here was something new. I smiled . . ."

NERO WOLFE: LOGOMACHIZER

by Lawrence F. Brooks

". . . the book came. I read it last night."
"Why did you read it?"
"Don't badger me. I read it because it was a book."
The League of Frightened Men

Nero Wolfe likes food and orchids, but he spends most of his time reading: his real passions are written and spoken words. He wakes up at about eight in the morning, eats breakfast — either in bed or at table by the window — drinks his hot chocolate, and scans the two newspapers — the *Times* and the *Wall Street Journal* [*The Silent Speaker*] — Fritz has brought up on the tray. "He won't read lying down" [*The Final Deduction*], so he moves to his second favorite chair, where he holds the newspaper unfolded at arm's length. He occasionally peruses a book from the rows of shelves in the bedroom before dressing. Then, at nine, he goes by elevator to the plant rooms to join Horstmann for what Archie calls ". . . real work . . . the thousand chores that orchids take" [*Corsage*].

In the first few hours of his waking day, Mr. Wolfe utilizes what he calls "man's three resources: intellect, imagination and muscle" [*Pleases Pass the Guilt*]. He reads to exercise the intellect, eats to stimulate the imagination, and works in the plant rooms to toughen the muscles that allow him to move as gracefully as he does. At eleven he descends to the office where he sits in his favorite chair (rated ¼ ton), changes the orchid in the vase on his desk, reads the mail and greets or growls at Archie. "The current book lies on the desk, at the right edge of the pad, in front of a vase of orchids" [*The Final Deduction*]. If they are working on a case, Archie may goad Mr. Wolfe into discussion, but Nero Wolfe would rather read: he will gladly read until 1:15, when Fritz announces lunch. Immediately after coffee at 2:15 or so, Mr. Wolfe returns to the office and the book. "According to him the best digestive is a book because it occupies the mind and leaves the stomach in privacy" [*The Final Deduction*]; "the only civilized way to spend the hour after lunch is with a book" [*Champagne for One*].

Nero Wolfe prefers not to detect — it's too much work — and does so only for money or vanity; thus during nominal office hours — 11 to 1:15 and 2:30 to 4 — he plays with words, reading, logomachizing with Archie, or doing the *New York Times* Double-Crostic, the crossword in the *Observer* or the *London Times*. The second two-hour session on the roof with the orchids starts at four in the afternoon. At six, Mr. Wolfe gravitates to the office, Archie, and the book. Naturally, he is subject to interruption while he reads — Fritz needs guidance in the kitchen, Archie wishes to report, a client has the temerity to ring the doorbell, Inspector Cramer bulls his way in, or whatever. Even Archie often finds it difficult to recall Nero Wolfe from the world behind the printed page [*The League of Frightened Men*] and some of his most delightful exchanges with Mr. Wolfe ensue when he tries. After dinner, about nine, Mr. Wolfe returns to the office and the book . . . often three books at once, which annoys Archie because it seems "ostentatious." Mr. Wolfe has been known to stay in the office reading until two a.m. [*If Death Ever Slept*] — waiting for Archie to come home — but he usually goes up to his room at eleven, taking a book. He falls asleep somewhat later; Archie dares not wake him by one a.m. [*A Family Affair*].

Thus, we see Mr. Wolfe treats with words six to eight hours a day, while he tends plants only four hours, and eats or helps cook at most four and one-half hours (except during a relapse, when all bets are off). Archie accuses Nero Wolfe of having read ten thousand books [*Before Midnight*], which as we shall see is a fairly accurate guess. Mr. Wolfe reads slowly [*And Be a Villain*] and thoroughly ["*Before I Die*"] remembering easily a fact read ten years before ["*The Zero Clue*"]. Of his at least seven languages (Serbo-Croatian, Albanian, Hungarian, Italian, French, Spanish, English, perhaps Czech), English surely is not his first. Nero Wolfe was born in Montenegro, c.1896. (We must go by the rule of best evidence: Mr. Wolfe points out to Archie the house where he was born near the Black Mountain and the Albanian border in Montenegro [*The Black Mountain*]; Mr. Wolfe says he is a natural-ized citizen ["*The Cop-Killer*"], not born in the United States [*Too Many Cooks*]. He quotes the Constitution at length to Archie [*The Black Mountain*], easier for a naturalized citizen required to memorize it.) He lies to Mr. Stahl of the F.B.I. [*Over My Dead Body*] to annoy — he adds "my temperament would incline me to resent and resist any attempt by any individual to inquire into my personal history..." [*Over My Dead Body*]. The F.B.I. surely knows the answer, thus Mr. Wolfe doubly resents the question. He enjoys and savors the English language with the passion of a convert: "he knows more words than Shakespeare knew" [*Please Pass the Guilt*]; "a word he didn't know invariably got him" [*Too Many Cooks*]. He reads only "two hundred or so books ... in a year" [*Plot It Yourself*]. With Mrs. Lloyd Bruner's $100,000, he could accept no jobs for six months — "read a hundred books ... Paradise." If Nero Wolfe reads an average book in four or five hours, two hundred books, along with magazines, puzzles, discussion and detection represent a good year's work. Thus 10, 000 in his lifetime is reasonable.

The old brownstone contains only a few thousand books — about 1200 in the office [*Gambit*], a few dozen in Mr. Wolfe's bedroom [*Before Midnight*], some in Archie's room (his own) [*"Christmas Party"*], 294 cookbooks in Fritz's basement room [*The Father Hunt*] (289 in 1965 [*The Doorbell Rang*]), perhaps a few more on the roof in Horstmann's room. Mr. Wolfe keeps those books he likes, the others vanish (to the public library [*The Mother Hunt*]). Murger's, an extremely well-stocked bookstore [*The Rubber Band*] only a few minutes away [*The League of Frightened Men*], where either Mr. Murger or Mr. Ballard toils from 8:30 in the morning [*The Rubber Band*] until late at night, Monday through Saturday [*The League of Frightened Men*], supplies Mr. Wolfe's literary needs. Murger's delivers the books to the house, leaving Archie free to pick up items for the kitchen.

Bookshelves line the walls of the office, extending to the high ceiling, with cabinets and files below, storage above. The Webster's Second rests on a stand to the right of Mr. Wolfe's desk. This is the fourth copy; the others wore out. Three lights illuminate the bookshelves. Mr. Wolfe uses a set of library steps to reach the upper shelves easily — he stands five feet eleven and moves easily despite his bulk. The books seem to be grouped roughly by subject, but the collection is eclectic. The newspapers, the *Times* (not the copy from the bedroom), the *News*, the *Gazette*, the *World-Telegram*, the *Wall Street Journal*, and others from time to time stay out on the shelves for a few days: a cabinet below contains five weeks' back *Times*. Mr. Wolfe keeps a selection of magazines on the table near the big globe [*Before Midnight*], flipping through several at a time after dinner, "allotting around twenty minutes a week for looking at advertisements" [*Before Midnight*].

Archie can best describe Nero Wolfe's method of handling books. Mr. Wolfe appreciates a fine book, like his English edition of Spenser [*The League of Frightened Men*], and thinks enough of books as physical objects not to throw one at Archie despite extreme provocation [*The Second Confession*]. He burns Webster's New International Dictionary, unabridged, third edition, only "because it threatens the integrity of the English language" [*Gambit*]. (Archie Goodwin's literary agent, the late Mr. Rex Stout, felt the same way about Webster's Third, but in an interview with Michael Bourne, reported in *Corsage*, he says that he merely gave his copy away.) From this action we may infer, as Mr. Wolfe has implied in his statements, that he has more reverence for the contents of a book than for the object itself. Thus to Archie's description:

> I divide the books Nero Wolfe reads into four grades: A, B, C and D. If, when he comes down to the office from the plant rooms at six o'clock, he picks up his current book and opens to his place before he rings for a beer, and if his place was marked with a thin strip of gold five inches long and an inch wide, which was presented to him some years ago by a grateful client, the book is an A. If he picks up the book before he rings, but his place is marked with a piece of paper, it is a B. If he rings and then picks up the book, and he had dog-eared a page to make his place, it is a C. If he waits until Fritz has brought the beer — and he has poured to pick up the book, and his place is dog-eared, it's a D.
> — *Plot It Yourself*

Only five or six books a year rate an A, and he often changes from a marker to dog-ears halfway through a book.

Nero Wolfe's library contains the A's, perhaps a few B's. Archie notes for us some books in the collection and we may deduce others. Books play major roles in many of the cases: Mr. Wolfe accepts several clients based on their literary output and several clients' books are represented on the shelves. He shows an amazing range of literary knowledge, demonstrating familiarity with subjects divergent enough to suggest self-education rather than attendance in the halls of caliginous academe. In the first case Archie records, that of the patricidal Manuel Kimball [*Fer-de-Lance*] Archie recalls one statement in which Mr. Wolfe mentions Gibbon, Ranke, Tacitus, Greene, Galba and Vitellius:

one or all of these authors might rank the shelves. A "fat red copy" [*Fer-de-Lance*] of *Who's Who in America* is there, but the only other book mentioned, Professor Gottlieb's *Modern Crime Detection*, isn't — "a book," Mr. Wolfe explains, "that an intelligent criminal should send as a gift to every detective he knows."

As the Paul Chapin case opens [*The League of Frightened Men*] Nero Wolfe examines photographs containing snowflakes in a book sent to him by a friend in Czechoslovakia. We know this book rates at least a B — he puts in a marker when he sets (it) down — but probably not an A as Archie does not describe the marker as ebony (gold comes later). If the book was sent from Czechoslovakia. it would not likely be available in New York. Further, it would have some association for Nero Wolfe. The famous Czech photographer Josef Sudek. whose works were unobtainable in the United States in 1935, fought on the Italian front in 1915, as might Mr. Wolfe. Is not this book, then, one containing photos by Sudek — perhaps the catalog to the 1933 shows at Krasna Jizba, Prague? The solution of the case itself depends on Nero Wolfe's analysis of Paul Chapin's books (he reads all five by Chapin and one by Andrew Hibbard) after finishing *The Native's Return* by Louis Adamic and *Outline of Human Nature* by Alfred Rossiter. He quotes Nietzsche, looks up a poem in his volume of Spenser, explains Buddha and the art of writing to Archie, suggests an article on the philosophy of railway timetables to Byron, the magazine editor, recites a bit of Romeo from Shakespeare, shows familiarity with Harun-al-Rashid, and finally elicits from Paul Chapin the fact that he, Nero Wolfe, will die ". . . in the most abhorrent manner conceivable to an appalling infantile imagination . . ." [*The League of Frightened Men*] as the leading character in Chapin's next book. Paul Chapin's book featuring Nero Wolfe deserves a place in the library.

During the affair of Llewellyn Frost and the red box [*The Red Box*] Mr. Wolfe reads the *Seven Pillars of Wisdom* by T. E. Lawrence for the third time. He has four translations of the *Iliad* including Fitzgerald [*A Family Affair*], thus he must have T. E. Lawrence's translation of the *Odyssey* (the 1932 Bruce Rogers edition, naturally). The library also contains a copy of *Metropolitan Biographies* (ordered from Murger's for use in the Lord Clivers matter, a strange case which sees Mr. Wolfe reciting Hungarian poetry in the dining room to a woman — Clara Fox) [*The Rubber Band*], a copy of *United Yugoslavia* by Henderson [*Over My Dead Body*], *Pilgrim's Progress*, *The Essays of Elia*, autographed books by Franz

Boas [*Too Many Cooks*], a dozen volumes of Lindenia [*The Silent Speaker*], and a book of lyrics by Oscar Hammerstein [*Murder by the Book*]. Mr. Wolfe checks a clue in his copy of *Mathematics for the Millions* by Hogben, and even analyzes three years of the Dazzle Dan comic strip in the *Gazette* [*"The Squirt and the Monkey"*].

Nero Wolfe dramatizes his decision to travel to Yugoslavia to avenge Marko Vukcic by moving a half-read copy of *But We Were Born Free* by Elmer Davis from the desk to the book shelves [*The Black Mountain*]. On the way to Yugoslavia he quotes Tennyson, but reads nothing until he solves the case. He then buys "a few dozen books" in Italian for the sea voyage home on the Basilia. (He and Archie use the names Carl and Alex Gunther on board). When he visits Montana, he changes the rules, bringing along four books (*Man's Rise to Civilization as Shown By the Indians of North America from Primeval Times to the Coming of the Industrial State*, by Peter Farb, *The First Circle* by Alexander Solzhenitsyn, and two others) [*Death of a Dude*]. He always takes a good supply of books on pleasure trips: at Pratt's he reads "one of the books we had brought along" as the saga of Hickory Caesar Grindon unfolds, at the trout lodge in upstate New York he tries *Power and Policy* by Thomas K. Finletter [*"Immune to Murder"*]; on the way to Kanawha Spa [*Too Many Cooks*] he shuts out the perils of rail travel with *Inside Europe* by John Gunther. At the Spa he reveals his knowledge of the poet Paul Lawrence Dunbar; when Paul Whipple shows surprise, Mr. Wolfe chides, "I am not a barbarian."

The *Pour Amour* contest [*Before Midnight*] keenly tests Nero Wolfe and his library. He dog-ears a copy of *Beauty for Ashes* by Christopher LaFarge (a novel in verse), finishes *A Party Of One* by Clifton Fadiman, "quotes verbatim a bill which he said had been introduced into the English parliament in 1770," then with the help of *Letters of Dorothy Osborne to Sir William Temple, Casanova's Memoirs*, his remarkable memory and perhaps *Montaigne's Essays* (one of the books in the bedroom) solves the puzzles and the case.

He knows Latin [*"Immune to Murder"*], and is familiar with Rochefoucauld [*Might as Well Be Dead*], Keats, [*The Doorbell Rang*], John Webster's *The Duchess of Malfi* [*Too Many Clients*], Simone de Beauvoir [*A Family Affair*], Eratosthenes, Pericles, Lycurgus [*Trio for Blunt Instruments*], Ben Franklin, Thorstein Veblen [*A Right to Die*], Thales of Miletus [*Death of a Doxy*], Seneca [*A Family Affair*], and the Bible (he has nine copies, four in

English, 5 in foreign languages) [*Please Pass the Guilt*].

The variety of Nero Wolfe's `current books,' the books kept on the desk, reflects his eclectic tastes. A sampling over the years includes *A Secret Understanding* by Merle Miller [*Might as Well Be Dead*], *The Fall* by Albert Camus ["*Fourth of July Picnic*"], *World Peace Through World Law* by Grenville Clark and Louis B. Sohn [*Champagne for One*], *Inside Russia Today* by John Gunther ["*Method Three for Murder*"], *An Outline of Man's Knowledge* ed. by Lyman Bryson [*Too Many Clients*], *The Lotus and The Robot* by Arthur Koestler [*The Final Deduction*], *African Genesis* by Robert Ardrey [*Gambit*], *Travels With Charley* by John Steinbeck [*The Mother Hunt*], *Silent Spring* by Rachel Carson [*The Mother Hunt*], *The Rise and Fall of the Third Reich* by William L. Shirer ["*Kill Now — Pay Later*"], *My Life In Court* by Louis Nizer ["*Murder is Corny*"], *William Shakespeare* by A. L. Rowse [*A Right to Die*], *The Minister and the Choir Singer* by William Kunstler [*A Right to Die*], *Science, The Glorious Entertainment* by Jacques Barzun *(Jacques Barzun is the only member of The Wolfe Pack whose books are recorded to have been read by Nero Wolfe.)* [*A Right to Die*], *The Treasure of Our Tongue* by Lincoln Barnett [*The Doorbell Rang*], *Invitation to an Inquest* by Walter and Miriam Schneir [*Death of a Doxy*], *The Jungle Book* by Rudyard Kipling [*Death of a Doxy*], *Incredible Victory* by Walter Lord [*The Father Hunt*], *The Future of Germany* by Carl Jaspers (an advance copy) [*The Father Hunt*], *History of Human Marriage* by Westermarch [*Please Pass the Guilt*], stories by Turgenev [*Please Pass the Guilt*], *The Palace Guard* by Dan Rather and Gary Cates [*A Family Affair*], *Special Report* by Herblock (inscribed) [*A Family Affair*], and *The European Discovery of America (Southern and Northern Voyages)* by Samuel Morison [*A Family Affair*].

The fact that Nero Wolfe's library included a copy of the late Richard Valdon's *His Own Image* [*The Mother Hunt*] helped Lucy Valdon when she desired to trace the mother of the baby abandoned on her doorstep — this and her way with words. When she displayed feelings identical to Mr. Wolfe's on the subject of lawyers, the combination was a hit. Without the literary tie, however, she might not have gotten an appointment. In *The Doorbell Rang*, Mrs. Bruner asks Nero Wolfe if he has read *The FBI Nobody Knows*: he answers curtly, "yes." When she says she sent out ten thousand copies of the book, he exclaims, "Indeed," his brow up a full eighth of an inch — his equivalent of leaping from the chair. Mr. Wolfe takes her case also. Phillip Harvey, author of

Why the Gods Laugh, calls for an appointment while his book, marked with a gold strip, occupies Mr. Wolfe's attention. Harvey receives his appointment quickly. The case involves plagiarism and Nero Wolfe's analysis of the authors' styles provides the solution [*Plot It Yourself*].

". . . He is a man with a special and educated fondness for words" is said not of but by Nero Wolfe, regarding the first Mr. Thomas Yeager [*Too Many Clients*]. Mr. Wolfe later calls this man "an imbecile." Erudition alone does not suffice to impress Mr. Wolfe. He respects efficient functioning and ordered reasoning. Archie aside (he meets unique Wolfean criteria), Saul Panzer probably comes closest to enjoying Nero Wolfe's full approbation. When Mr. Wolfe takes refuge in Saul's apartment ["*The Next Witness*"] he rates the living room with its big chair and wall of bookshelves "satisfactory" ("I congratulate you"), and says please when he asks for beer.

"Which he loves most, food or words, is a tossup" says Archie of Nero Wolfe. Orchids Mr. Wolfe merely "likes . . . he gets some special kind of kick from color" [*Corsage*]. Words win forks down. You can use words to describe food, but you can't argue with a taste. It's there or it isn't. Food provides Nero Wolfe with the fat he uses "to insulate [his] feelings" [*Over My Dead Body*] and the energy to read. As a tactile, in the ultimate analysis, rather than intellectual phenomenon — food is in the same category as orchids: after words.

Mr. Wolfe has the final word in a conversation with Inspector Cramer (the last recorded) [*A Family Affair*] "I'm not going to tell you what I intend to do. Actually I don't intend to do anything. I'm going to loaf, drift, for the first time in ten days. Read books, drink beer, discuss food with Fritz, logomachize with Archie. Perhaps chat with you if you have occasion to drop in." Thus, Nero Wolfe's ideal existence: nothing about eating, no reference to plants, just a book, lots of beer and a good discussion.

[N. B.: *Logomachize means to contend with words.* — MK]

A PROFUSION
OF ORCHIDS

by Charles E. Burns

DID YOU ever wonder why Nero Wolfe spent four hours every day of his life in his rooftop plant rooms? And, aside from searching for mealybugs and annoying Theodore, exactly how he spent those four hours?

You might think it's because orchids are so exotic, so rare, and so fragile that they need his constant care. Well, they're certainly rare in the heart of New York City. But did you know that in the realm of flowers, the orchid family is the largest in the world, with somewhere between twenty and thirty thousand different species? This means that one out of every fifteen flowering plants is an orchid. Just as homo sapiens may be the end of Darwin's theory of evolution (and Nero Wolfe may be the most sapient of all) the orchid family must be the latest in plant evolution. And, it may be no coincidence that Darwin wrote an entire book on orchids.

Still, orchids are rare for their breath-taking beauty, their never-ending varieties, the fact that most are grown in the tropical rain forests, and perhaps because they are the most difficult plants to grow from seeds. Even in their natural habitat, they must have exactly the right type of soil, pH, and the presence of certain fungi. Against all odds, orchids do their best to assure propagation of the species by producing seeds in the millions. But they have very little in the way of food and must depend on the fungi to provide proper nourishment for germination. In this symbiotic relationship, they co-exist and grow in trees and underground, sometimes for as long as ten years. Eventually, proper roots appear and the plant sends a green shoot to the surface. Later, more leaves appear and at last the orchid is ready to flower. But a plant dug up from the wild and transplanted into a garden will invariably die. And orchids should never be picked — they make poor cut flowers, anyway. In Ireland, picking orchids is illegal; all are protected by law. Incidentally, the name orchid comes from the Greek. It means "testicle" — as, underground, many orchids have two round tubers. So, if you're ever in Crete, never compliment a gentleman on his orchids — it just might prove embarrassing!

Orchids can be grown from seeds. But they must have carefully balanced nutrients, all under aseptic conditions, as well as proper temperature and humidity. It helps to determine their original habitat, not only the country of origin but also the climate and elevation. Even if all these elements are perfect, it takes from three to five years for a plant to flower. Aha! I'm beginning to see how the plant rooms are not merely a horticultural showpiece — but how Wolfe keeps busy with the potting room, the cool, moderate, and tropical rooms, the fumigation room, heating and air conditioning systems on the roof top! And I'm reminded of one of the most frightening plots that climaxed with ciphogene in *Black Orchids*.

In this country, orchids were originally rare and expensive. They first gained popularity as a corsage for those beautiful gals at the Junior Prom. But growers here went through some difficult economic times. The florist business was hit hard during the late 1960s when corsages began to go out of style. (I wonder what ever became of that beauty I took to the Prom!) Then, in the 1970s, overnight airfreight put orchids within economic reach from Holland and South America. The Boston Flower Market, second largest in the world, soon featured international orchids barely less fresh than those grown in the Boston area. Then, in 1971, OPEC and the oil embargo sent fuel prices skyrocketing. Since orchids need a lot of heat, many regional growers failed.

Still, those who persevered developed modern cloning of plant tissue and other means of speeding up the propagation of orchids from seed to flowering plant. They also began shipping plants back and forth to Hawaii where one year of Hawaiian sun speeds up the growing process to two years.

Commercial growers have now spent years developing orchids suited to home growing — and the plants are reasonably priced. You may not be able to afford a rainbow of 10,000 orchids but you can brighten up your home with orchids by using reasonable care. First, be sure your florist picks from a genus that is suited to the climate in your area. Here in the northeast, three of the most popular are the Moth Orchid (phalaenopsis), Dancing Ladies (oncidium), and Tropical Lady Slipper (paphiopedilum). Tell your florist where you will place the plant and the usual temperature. Orchids are adaptable to almost every place in your home — from the basement under grow lights to hanging plants to window sills. Your plants will bloom from ten to twelve weeks. After they bloom, maintain them with good light and water. With proper care, they can live for thirty years before they stop blooming.

I have always been fascinated by Nero Wolfe's love and care for orchids — enough so that I have researched several sources for this article. However, I hasten to admit that I am far from being an expert and the color of my thumb is anything but green. Still, I can take some solace in the fact that the only thing Rex Stout knew about orchids when he began writing the Nero Wolfe series was what he had gleaned from one 1927 volume on the subject. And his first exposure to orchids was on a Caribbean cruise where he saw "a profusion of orchids." They must have made an impression! This article may explain why, though an expert horticulturist, he never had much luck with orchids. And why his favorite flower was — the iris! [*Q.V., Archie Goodwin's Annual Iris Inspection.* — MK]

WOLFE AND THE POST OFFICE

by Ettagale Blauer

I HAVE often been struck by the high regard that Wolfe has for the United States Post Office, an opinion not shared by anyone else I know. In one tale after the other he employs the Post Office to carry his draft notices to various suspects, commanding them to appear in his office for one of his inquisitions. These marching orders seem to be received minutes after they have been issued. It is equally startling that almost everyone turns up. The suspects and other assorted characters never have other plans, and only once in my memory has someone refused to play.

Given my experience with the U.S. Post Office — the letter that took a week to get from West 25th Street to West 57th Street, and the catch phrase of our time, "The check is in the mail" — I decided to take a hard look at the role played by the U.S. Post Office in the *Corpus*. Since I started with the premise that postal service had declined precipitously since the books were written, certainly the earlier ones, a scientific test seemed in keeping with the spirit of the project. To that end, I mailed letters to family and friends selected for their geographical diversity. Each person received two copies of the same message, both mailed at the same time. One was sent from the General Post Office on Eighth Avenue and 33rd Street; that's the main post office in New York City. The other was sent from a post box on Eighth Avenue and 27th Street, my neighborhood. It's just a short walk from Wolfe's own West 35th Street. It gave me momentary pause when I thought I had missed an opportunity to mail the second batch from the post box nearest Wolfe's own address. That, however, would have been sea mail, since as everyone who has walked along West 35th Street knows, the addresses given for Wolfe's brownstone put it somewhere in the Hudson River.

I asked each recipient to note the day and, if possible, the exact time the letters were received, and this information duly made its way back to me. The mailing went to both the East and

West sides of Manhattan, also to Brooklyn; Demarest, New Jersey (a small town that evidently has a direct line, if not to God, then to the General Post Office in Manhattan); Camden, Maine; Tamarac, Florida; Blair, Wisconsin; Denver, Colorado; and Los Angeles, California. East, West, North, and South, the bases were covered. The letters were mailed on June 30, 1986. The G.P.O. batch was deposited at 6:00 pm, and the mail box lot five minutes later. Gleefully, I awaited the returns.

But I found that Murphy's Law has a direct corollary: "If everything is expected to go wrong, it surely won't." The Post Office, in a display of efficiency not seen before or since, delivered most of the letters post haste (excuse the pun). The letters mailed at the G.P.O. were postmarked June 30th, the day I mailed them. Those in the post box, July 1st. That was expected since hardly any mail boxes in Manhattan provide for pickup after 5:00 pm, even on a weekday, which this was. The mail that had been deposited at the G.P.O. at 6:00 in the evening was delivered within the city the next day, even to Brooklyn, and even to Demarest, New Jersey. I have been advised by my resident correspondent in Demarest, Emily Mikulewicz, that the mail service to Demarest is always this good. She doesn't know why — it just growed that way. In each of these instances, to New York, Brooklyn, and New Jersey, letters dropped in the post box were received just one day later. This is logical since they weren't even picked up until the next morning.

As the distances grew, however, the efficiency of the postal service diminished roughly in inverse proportion and much more than I expected. The mail to Florida took two days from the G.P.O. and three days from the post box. Maine was a puzzler. Both letters were received together three days after they were mailed. They must have been held for the pony that carried the mail from Portland to the little town of Camden.

Moving well beyond these environs, it took only three days to reach a very rural area of Wisconsin, a location comparable to Lily Rowan's Montana ranch. It took the same three days to Denver and to Los Angeles (this was from the G.P.O.). The post box mail took five days to Wisconsin and California. The one that renewed my faith in my theory was the post box sample to Denver. That one arrived on July 8th, eight days after it was mailed, and five days after the one sent from the G.P.O. The pony here must have been plumb tuckered out.

While grousing to some friends about the rapid delivery to

the Metropolitan New York area addresses, I was advised that I had inadvertently speeded things up by typing the envelopes. That was only fair since Archie always typed Wolfe's letters. But the Post Office now has machines that can scan and sort typed addresses, while it still requires people to read those that are handwritten. That also sounded reasonable, so that last week I sent another mailing to the original recipients, this time with addresses handwritten. I had scarcely returned from the mail box, when Emily called to say that hers had arrived in Demarest the next morning. (Laughter, as usual, rang over the phone.) Likewise the recipient on the Upper West Side, our Werowance. California called in to say that his arrived three days after the posting, which was better than the first mailing from the post box. I stopped taking phone calls. The slogan chiseled above the glorious front portico of the G.P.O. needs to he amended. "Neither rain, nor snow, nor dark of night, nor Ettagale's miserable handwriting shall keep these couriers from the swift completion of their appointed rounds."

But these delivery achievements would still have been woefully inadequate for Nero Wolfe, who used the post office more in the nature of a messenger service than as mail delivery. In seven of the stories, Wolfe's reliance on the post office is absolute, and absolutely justified. Only once did I find a reference to poor mail delivery. And that, not surprisingly, was in his last book, *A Family Affair*, published in 1975. Going through the mail, Archie says, "The letter from Hewitt about an orchid was mailed last Saturday. Six days from Long Island to Manhattan, forty-two miles. I can walk it in one day."

It was a very different matter in the beginning, the very beginning, with the publication of *Fer-de-Lance* in 1934. In that story, on a Friday, Wolfe instructs Archie to place ads (sorry Mr. Wolfe, advertisements) in local newspapers to find someone who saw Manuel Kimball land in a pasture. The following Monday, by 8:30 am, Archie had already collected more than twenty answers to the ad, and is tooling his way up to Hawthorne to question one of the respondents.

The ad had been seen and answered, and the answers mailed and delivered to the various newspapers, and then sorted into the sender's postboxes. And all this between the time it appeared in the Saturday papers and Archie's visit to the newspaper Monday morning. I know that people were much more inclined to take pen in hand in 1934 when telephones were not universally available, but to get responses from rural towns in upstate New York, picked up and mailed, and ready for Archie Monday morning? Pfui. There are plenty of mail boxes in New York City that offer no pickup after one o'clock Saturday and none at all Sunday. But, of course, in those less efficient days before ZIP mail and Federal Express, and kamikaze bicycle messengers, the post office diligently delivered mail to the door several times a day.

In *The Rubber Band*, published in 1936, Archie types a letter for Hilda Lindquist to the Marquis of Clives. It's Sunday evening, and Wolfe tells Archie the letter should be written and posted with a special delivery stamp before the morning collection. Clives has the letter in hand when he turns up in Wolfe's office Tuesday morning. These tight schedules are one of the unsung hallmarks of the stories. They merely follow the Aristotelian unities of place and action. The post office played a vital role in enabling Wolfe to follow that schedule. His use of special delivery also depends on the addressees being home to receive the mail. Obligingly, they always are. For if they were not, and another try was required later, Wolfe would have been hard pressed to gather the suspects in the office for one of those tidy summings up or summing ups, as you prefer.

In *The Silent Speaker*, published in 1948, the post office nearly becomes a fourth operative for Wolfe. On a Tuesday morning, at ten minutes to nine, Fritz comes down with Wolfe's breakfast dishes. He also has a note for Archie, telling him to arrange for Del Bascom to be present for a meeting with Saul Panzer and Bill Gore at 11:00 am. They arrive promptly and are waiting for Wolfe when he comes down from the plant rooms at 11:00 am. Archie is shooed out of the meeting, but informed at lunch time that reports from Bascom were to reach Wolfe unopened. One chapter later, Archie says (the next day, Wednesday), "Here come the envelopes from Bascom." There were four in the morning mail, three in the one o'clock delivery, and in the late afternoon nine more arrive by messenger.

There are several mysteries here. How were the operatives employed by Bascom, who could not have received their marching orders until after the meeting with Wolfe that concluded at lunchtime Tuesday, able to do their investigating and write their reports and mail them so that they could be received next morning? Later that same Wednesday, Wolfe prepares to return Mrs. Bootie's check, by mail of course. After signing and blotting his signature, Wolfe says, "You'd better take this to the post office. I suspect the evening collection from the box doesn't get made sometimes." How does the great detective know this? Archie says that although it was only a ten minute walk to the post office, to Ninth Avenue and back, he was in no mood for walking. So he drives there! So Wolfe has moved the post office one avenue block over to bring it closer to the brownstone. But clearly it's the General Post Office they're talking about since it's the only one in the neighborhood and the only one that is open twenty-four hours a day.

In *"The Gun with Wings,"* published in 1950, Margaret Mion and Fred Weppler turn up in Wolfe's office on a Sunday afternoon. According to Archie they leave two hours later. Following up on information they have given him, Wolfe sends letters to the suspects, inviting them to a session of questions and answers. While Archie is complaining about the veracity of the clients, Wolfe says, "Shut up. Your notebook. These letters must go at once." And right on schedule, Monday evening, the six invited guests all show up. Three of them were so punctual that Archie says, "right on the dot of nine o'clock." He and Wolfe hadn't even finished their after dinner coffee in the office. Still, I must confess that all of the above is certainly possible. After all, I too was able to send mail and have it delivered the next day in the Metropolitan area.

And when Wolfe was delivering his billets doux, he could rely on two and more mail deliveries a day. But it is when he expects the same service from clear across the country that my credulity reached the breaking point. I accept murder, deceit, blackmail, and everything Stout dishes up, but not one-day mail service coast to coast. It is 1951, and the story is "Murder by the Book." Archie has gone to Glendale, California, to see Len Dykes's sister, Mrs. Clarence (Peggy) Potter. Together they send a letter to Mr. James Corrigan at the law firm where Dykes had worked. At 3:23 pm, Archie calls Wolfe from a telephone booth and tells him that he has just put an airmail stamp on Mrs. Potter's letter and dropped it in the slot at the Glendale Post Office. The next morning at 9:30 am (Glendale time — in New York it is 12:30 pm), Archie recalls, "At the Glendale Post Office they had told me that the letter would make a plane that would land at LaGuardia at eight in the morning, New York time. So it should be delivered at Madison Avenue any time now, possibly right this minute, as I stretched and yawned." By Archie's calculations, the letter would arrive at LaGuardia at 8:00 the following morning, and be delivered in Manhattan the same day. Corrigan takes a few hours to think about what he's going to do, for it isn't until nearly two in the afternoon (California time — in New York it's 5:00 pm) that Mrs. Potter calls Archie and says that Corrigan has just called her, responding to the letter. At this juncture, even the airlines are put on Wolfe's schedule. Corrigan tells Mrs. Potter that he is taking a plane in New York and he'll get to Los Angeles at 8:00 in the morning. Bear in mind that this is 1951, just a few years after the close of World War II. Passenger planes were few and far between, and with propeller planes, flying times were very long. The Red Eye had not yet made its appearance, yet that's just what Archie is describing. Corrigan would surely have had to land once along the way for refueling and the flight would have taken at least ten hours. Yet there he was in Los Angeles at eight in the morning. He leaves later the same day at five o'clock, with Archie snaring a seat on the same plane, an idea he realizes was not such a good one shortly after the plane takes off. After all, Corrigan might he the murderer.

Archie spends a long sleepless night, reaching the office just shortly before Wolfe's morning session with the plants. At 10:30 am, Archie is shaving when Corrigan calls. The members of the law firm make an appointment for eleven o'clock. That same evening after dinner, Corrigan calls. During the conversation, Corrigan is apparently shot to death. The real dénouement comes for me with the morning mail, which Archie is looking through the next day at 8:55 am. In it, he reports, is an envelope postmarked Grand Central Station, midnight. That lengthy explanation so thoughtfully provided to Wolfe by the murderer is vital to solving the case. Once again, the incredible efficiency of the post office enables Wolfe to pull a case out of the fire. If Rex Stout were still writing today, I predict Federal Express would displace the U.S. Post Office in the crucial role of summoning suspects, delivering ultimatums, and moving plots along to their inevitable conclusions

[ED. — This entertaining article was presented by Ettagale at the 8th annual Nero Wolfe Assembly in New York, 1986.]

MR. WOLFE'S NOSE

by Gahan Wilson

GOOD EVENING. It is nice to be speaking to you again. The last time I spoke to you was in the afternoon preceding the first annual Black Orchid Banquet in 1978, when many learned dissertations were being shared.I was, at that time, considerably more Wolfean than I am at present, since I had, I am proud to say, actually achieved the lowest weight estimate concerning the great man, and had entered that glorious area where the guessings hover around the 1/8th of a ton mark; that is to say, I sported a full 250 pounds. I apologize to you for my present, shrunken condition. All I can say in atonement is that I have done what I could to make up for it by consuming large quantities of the magnificent meal we have shared together, and I hope you've done the same.

My speech of 1978 was a modest, but heartfelt tribute to some of the marvelous characters which Archie and Mr. Wolfe have encountered in their interestingly combined careers. I seem to recall also that I gave an especially affectionate salute to the consistently misunderstood Inspector Fergus Cramer, which I was gratified to detect brought a tear to the eyes of those more sensitive souls among the audience.

The centerpiece of my offering, however, was a little review of the continual pantomime which goes on between Archie and Mr. Wolfe throughout their adventures. It has often struck me that these unspoken exchanges between the two friends are somehow their most eloquent. Though Nero Wolfe is certainly one of the most effectively verbal men who ever lived, I think he never makes it clearer just what he is — if you know how to read him, which Archie certainly can — than when he is entirely silent.

Is there anything in this world more ominous, for instance, than the whole bulk of Nero Wolfe gone totally still? And, very much on the other hand, is there a sight on this whole earth more heartwarming, more gladsome, than Nero Wolfe pulling the folds of his cheeks a little from the corners of his mouth in the fond belief that he is smiling?

I'll freely admit that this part of my 1978 presentation was unabashedly theatrical; some have been kind enough to tell me it even verged on the dramatic. In any case, I did my very best not to hold back a thing as I portrayed Mr. Wolfe surrendering to his emotions via his well-known silent whistle . . . I gave an unabashed, perhaps even slightly melodramatic, performance of the great detective making a tiny circle with the tip of his forefinger in order to demonstrate uncontrollable rage bordering on the amok . . . and I did not neglect to attempt an impression of his lip motions, both in and out, which he employs when he has engaged his genius at full throttle . . .

I would do all of these again for you gladly, and more besides, but the sad truth is I cannot exercise any of these satisfactorily because of my regrettable loss of weight. The simple fact is — that though I am certainly not totally devoid of the commodity — I currently lack the sufficient fat required.

Of course this put me in a quandary, one might even say it put me into a pickle. When Ellen Krieger wrote me a yellow letter asking me to speak at this august occasion, it was highly pleasant to accept her flattering invitation. It was more than that, it was delightful.

But, since my unfortunate loss of bulk ruled out a rehash of my previous discourse, what was I to speak about? I knew I had to choose with care because I would be in a company of scholars, of people singularly well informed upon any topic within the greater topic.

My first thought did have a certain novelty: 1 hit upon the notion of delivering a little speech on the subject of Nero Wolfe as an enthusiastic advocate of the healthy life. Though the theme did run sporadically through the stories, I was not aware of any previous student singling it out for a special examination. There was, of course, plenty of material, starting with the deservedly famous "javelins," the dart game taken up by Mr. Wolfe when he started brooding on the possibility of his being overweight, a line of thought rather cruelly derided by Archie as being, "about the same as if the Atlantic Ocean formed the opinion that it was too wet." Mr. Wolfe pursued the game with commendable enthusiasm until, one day, as a result of Archie being rude to him, he let his whole handful of darts fall to the floor, and, so far as I know, he never picked them up again. The pursuit of the healthy life forms the basis of one of my favorite episodes of all the accounts which have been left to us. This is the one wherein Archie returns to the brownstone in 1942 as a brand new major of United States Army Intelligence only to find nothing in the cupboard but a dish of oranges and six cartons of prunes. Theodore explains to him that Mr. Wolfe and Fritz were out exercising (only they call it training) on a pier over by the river. Theodore explains the pier with, I think, one of the funniest lines Rex Stout ever wrote: "Mr. Wolfe obtained permission from the authorities to train on the pier because the boys on the street ridiculed him."

All this was most encouraging, and I was well launched into the enterprise, when I suddenly remembered something that the great detective had said. This was something which a body of listeners as fiendishly well informed as yourselves would be sure to remember, something which firmly and mercilessly undermined my entire thesis. When a singularly irritating doctor accused Mr. Wolfe of being grotesquely overweight, his response was crisp and clear: "Death, sir," he said, "will remedy that."

So much, I thought, for health.

Then the subject for my little talk came to me, and when it did, I was amazed I hadn't thought of it before — I would tell you about the time I met Rex Stout. I am a very lucky fellow in that I have a number of things I can call to mind which never fail to cheer me up, no matter what. Just the thought of them makes me feel better. They are a collection of little triumphs, of things I actually did right, and a small, very precious number of these things are tied in with Mr. Nero Wolfe.

First and foremost amongst these latter items is, of course, the proud knowledge that I designed the little silhouette logo which is used by the Wolfe Pack. And I would like to take this opportunity to thank you all personally for using it these many years. I can't tell you how much pleasure it's given me to see it regularly printed in *The Gazette*, and emblazoned on all those swell, yellow T-shirts.

The second Wolfean thing that never fails to make me happy is that William S. Baring-Gould's *Nero Wolfe of West 35th Street* leads off with a quote from an article I wrote — anonymously. For I was one of the editors of the magazine it appeared in, and I already had another article in that publication, and I didn't want to appear to be abusing my position, which, of course, I was. The article was in a long-defunct magazine called *PS*. This is the only time I've brought my authorship of this article up in public, so far as I can recall. I can think of no better place to speak of it than here at a Nero Wolfe banquet, and no better people to tell it to.

If the name of the magazine, *PS*, conveys nothing to you, you are not alone. *PS* had, perhaps, one of the most unfortunate names in the history of periodical publishing in that it conveyed nothing much at all to anybody. It conveyed, for example, nothing to the people who ran the newsstands and they never knew where to put it. Sometimes they mixed it in with the sports magazines, sometimes they inserted it in amongst the movie stars' confessions, and once I came across it shuffled between two publications on astrology.

I could not blame the newsstand people for this, though, of course, I wanted to. Even the name *PS* conveyed very little to me, and it still does convey very little to me, and I helped make the thing up.

The quote Mr. Baring-Gould used from the magazine was from the introduction to an interview I did with Rex Stout way back in 1966, up in Brewster, New York, in his home called High Meadow.

High Meadow was very unbrownstone, very un-West 35th Street. I remember a quote from the *New Yorker* writer, Sheila Hibbon, who worked with Mr. Stout in preparing the cookbook that was printed with *Too Many Cooks* and was eventually transformed into *The Nero Wolfe Cookbook*. [*Barbara Burn was the ultimate editor of the cookbook.* — MK] She hated the place because it was deep in the country, and she hated the country. The second time she had to go there, in the late Fall, she expressed her relief by saying: "Thank God all these damned leaves have fallen down and you can finally see the sky!" But though High Meadow was un-urban in the extreme, it was entirely Nero Wolfean in that it was a civilized, even luxurious little world. It was carefully guarded from the big, not to say pleasant, outer world.

Inside there was one comfortable room after another, and the place was full of cozy corners. Mr. Stout, who was, of course, a marvelous host, graciously showed me things like a pot of flowers — I forget just what kind of flowers they were, but I'm sure they weren't geraniums — that he claimed he'd kept living for ten years past all scientific expectations. He showed me drying herbs he'd festooned the ceiling of his sweet-smelling garage with, and he showed me fine, old books and many other lovely things. But, outside, the building was an odd, concrete structure, very efficient looking, solid, built like a U-shaped bunker. Though it was supposed to be based on the romantic-sounding palace of the Bey of Tunis — which I suspect was really more a fortress — I must admit it struck me as being maybe a teeny bit grim, and even a little bleak. It had a distinctly military feel to it, and I noticed Mr. Stout had seen to it that the place occupied commanding ground atop a hill. Any untoward attack from Brewster would be repulsed easily. Nero Wolfe would have liked that.

Rex Stout himself was every bit as impressive as I'd hoped he would be, and that, of course, was a great relief since Mr. Stout has been, for many years, one of my heroes. You don't meet heroes lightly, especially if you've only met a few previous heroes. He radiated intelligence and great personal strength, but he never tried to bully me with it, and I don't believe it ever crossed his mind to do so. I give him the highest compliment I know when I say I think it is possible that he may have come as close as any person I've met to actually having been that rarest of creatures, a fully adult human being.

I was sorry about my reaction to Stout's beard. Many unkind things had been said and printed about Mr. Stout's beard, the most famous of which is that it appeared to be "a wishy washy thing stolen off a billy goat." I would have liked to have set the record straight about that beard, to have said glowing complimentary things about it, to have compared it with the beards worn by biblical patriarchs and the manes worn by lions. But the facts were against me and, being a responsible journalist, I could not. I am sorry to report that the beard fully justified its severest critics.

The interview went very well from the start. I asked him architectural details about the brownstone and learned he'd sketched a crude map of the first floor in response to readers' inquiries. I pleaded for it and he dug it up and handed it to me, and we gave it its first popular printing. I asked him about the routines of a group of people I was curious about and cared very much for, such as Fritz and Theodore and Saul. From the way the expression on his face changed and the way he started to answer the question, it slowly dawned on me that I was apparently the first ordinary reporter to ask him specific questions about the actual stories.

I remember asking him what restaurant inspired Rusterman's. If any of you have a copy of the magazine or the interview itself — I lost mine years ago — I'd love seeing it because I can't remember the name of the place. It seems that it was a swank restaurant of long ago New York which Stout had passed by enviously as an ambitious, but poor young man.

His opinions were just as interesting and individual as Mr. Wolfe's, but of course that came as no surprise to me, nor would it have to you. He thought Thomas Mann was a boring stuffed shirt and would soon become forgotten, and he thought Lewis Carroll was an unappreciated genius and that the Alice books would be increasingly respected by the literary establishment as the years went by. He paused and actually turned pale when I pointed out that J. Edgar Hoover was a regular patron at one of New York's finest restaurants. "My God!" he cried, "I'd hate to think he actually had a palate!"

I was delighted with the number of times he took me totally by surprise. For example, I asked him what did Archie look like? Not, I hoped, like Lionel Stander? "No," Stout told me, "if he looked like any movie actor, he'd look a little like Humphrey Bogart." I admit I was shocked at first with the Bogart notion, but I've played with it through the years, and I've slowly come to see what he meant. There would indeed be a Bogartian look about the eyes, and the mouth is certainly right.

The biggest shock of all, though, and I still suspect he may have been putting me on, came when I asked him how he went about plotting a story. How about *The Doorbell Rang*, for instance? It had only just come out and was delighting the critics and public alike and was, hopefully, infuriating the above-mentioned J. Edgar.

His incredible answer was that he really hadn't plotted it at all. He had only — as was, he swore, his regular practice — prepared a list of the main characters along with a brief, biographical sketch of each, and got clear in his mind a very rough notion of what he wanted to do with the book. In this case, it was to beat J. Edgar Hoover over the head with it. That, he swore to God, was it.

"Well what about the famous bullet?" I asked him. Surely you had planned all that!"

"No," he said, with a very convincing look on his face, "It was a great surprise to me when it was found and I hadn't the slightest idea what it signified, nor what it would lead to."

For me, personally, the most rewarding moment of the whole interview came when I asked Mr. Stout about Nero Wolfe and the way he looked. There were no surprises, by and large — no pun intended — until I asked him about Nero Wolfe's nose. I had always imagined it as a Roman nose, a kind of Sherlockian beak.

There was a longish pause, and I realized that Stout was studying me with a bemused expression.

"It is," he said thoughtfully, "very like your nose."

He paused, still studying the center of my face carefully, and then he nodded.

"Yes," he said, "it is exactly like your nose."

And that is the third Wolfean thing that always makes me happy whenever I think of it.

STOUT ON STAGE

by Margaret Goodman

THIS TALK is what is known in primitive television as a "spin-off." Two years ago, I spoke at the Assembly on the subject of Nero Wolfe and the performing arts (see *The Gazette*, Volume VI, Number 3). Today, I've been asked to focus a little more closely just on the area of the theatre and, because I am an actress-singer by profession, to comment on the theatrical references in the *Corpus* from my specialized point of view. As I observed during my earlier address, it seems appropriate for a body of work largely set in New York that the largest number of references with respect to the arts are to the legitimate theatre. The wonderful growth of regional theatre notwithstanding, and in spite of the defensive protestations one might hear from Chicago and Los Angeles, New York is still *the* home base of theatre in America. That's why young actors whose primary goal is theatre, as opposed to film and TV, still come here from all over the country. There is still only one Broadway.

So today I'm going to examine references to the theatre from the *Corpus* a little more closely to see what further nuggets we might turn up. Beginning with playwrights as I did before, there are nine allusions to Shakespeare (I had counted them as eight before, but there are two different ones in *Please Pass the Guilt*, both to *Macbeth*). I confess that the picture here is a little ambiguous, especially with regard to Archie's knowledge and familiarity with Shakespeare. On the one hand we have Archie commenting in *Please Pass the Guilt*:

> As for me, my chore wouldn't wait — or I didn't want it to. As someone said, probably Shakespeare, "twere better done' and so forth.

This quotation undoubtedly drifted into his subconscious from Dr. Vollmer's reference earlier in the same case to the "Lady Macbeth syndrome." I reread this several times to see if it's meant to be ironic, but I don't think so, though I'm open to disagreement. Now "If it were done when 'tis done, then 'twere well it were done quickly" is a child's play quotation to pinpoint for any Shakespeare buff, so the obvious conclusion is that Archie's not one! And since Archie never mentions actually attending any Shakespeare performances or relaxing with his copy of *Titus Andronicus* while waiting for Wolfe to come down from the plant rooms, it comes as something of a surprise when in another case he shows an intimate knowledge of *The Merry Wives of Windsor*:

> Archie: Incidentally, I'm glad to learn they're called prat-terias because Pratt owns them. I always supposed it was because they're places where you can sit on your prat and eat.
> Wolfe: I presume one ignorance cancels another. I never heard "prat" before and you don't know the meaning of "ipso facto." Unless "prat" is your invention.
> Archie: No. Shakespeare used it. I've looked it up.

Shakespeare's Bawdy, a wonderful reference work that I rely on, discusses "prat" only in *Merry Wife of Windsor* and does not mention Shakespeare's use of the word in any other play. In an explanatory note, however, it tells us that prat (is) buttocks in "cant and low-slang" so, naturally, we would not expect Wolfe to know the word. Obviously neither Wolfe nor Archie is a connoisseur of the great traditions of slapstick, since "pratfall" is, of course, a commonly known derivation. Because this familiarity with Shakespeare is in *Some Buried Caesar*, which takes place in 1937, and seems to have faded by *Please Pass the Guilt* in 1969, the obvious explanation is an all-too-familiar one to most of us: Archie had a great Shakespeare course in high school, still fresh in his mind in 1937, but hasn't looked at the plays since!

Wolfe, on the other hand, though he can never bring himself to leave the brownstone to attend the theatre, does, apparently, take an academic interest in the Bard. In *A Right to Die*, for example, Archie tells us that he is reading *William Shakespeare* by A.L. Rowse. Now this immediately caught my attention since A. L. Rowse is something of a controversial figure. I quote from *Current Biography*: Rowse has published several controversial literary biographies, beginning with *William Shakespeare: A Biography* (Macmillan, Harper, 1963). That book incorporated his solutions of several long-standing mysteries, including the dating of the sonnets and the identity of the man to whom they were addressed . . . His findings brought opposition from literary scholars, who objected to his application of historical method to their province. But the book sold well.

Twenty years later, in 1984, Rowse became much more famous for his modernized versions of the Shakespeare canon, which substitutes contemporary words for those in the original, which he contends will make the plays more understandable to today's audiences. One can only imagine with delight what Wolfe's reaction would have been to this! I had great hopes when I noticed in my notes a reference to Congreve. Aha, I thought, maybe Archie is a devotee of Restoration comedy. Alas, I quote in full from *Champagne for One*:

> Archie: The idea is that it will buck the girls up, be good for their morale, to spend an evening with the cream and get a taste of caviar and sit on a chair made by Congreve. Of course . . .
> Wolfe: Congreve didn't make chairs.
> Archie: I know he didn't, but I needed a name and that one popped in.

In fact, of the ten playwrights, both real and fictitious, referred to in the *Corpus*, only one does Archie quote with confidence, and that is George S. Kaufman. That is not surprising, since I can think of no works of the theatre that seem to me more compatible with Archie's character, taste and personality than the comedies of Kaufman and Hart. I quote first from *Three Doors to Death*:

> A dozen pink dogwoods in bloom, in big wooden tubs, were scattered around on Monday, the day I arrived, but when I went to the lounge at cocktail time on Wednesday they had disappeared and been replaced by rhododendrons covered with buds. I was reminded of the crack George Kaufman made once to Moss Hart — "That just shows what God could do if only he had money."

I compared this with the account given in Howard Teichmann's biography, *George S. Kaufman, An Intimate Portrait*:

> Moss Hart's delight in spending money never went unnoticed by Kaufman. When his collaborator bought an estate near the Kaufman place in Bucks County, rebuilt it, put in a swimming pool, and surrounded it with hundreds of freshly transplanted trees, Kaufman took note. "This is what God could have done if He'd had money," he said.

Archie's use of the quotation could scarcely be more apt.

Finally, Ruth Hazen, whom I must thank for helping me with research for this speech, turned up a wonderful reference which I should have caught and didn't near the end of *The Black Mountain*. Archie and Wolfe have an appointment with Richard Courtney at the American embassy in Rome. Their business successfully concluded, Courtney says:

> And now I hope you won't mind if I ask for a favor from you. After I told Mr. Teague, the secretary, that you were coming here this afternoon, he must have spoken of it to the Ambassador, because he told me later that the Ambassador would like to meet you. So if you can spare a few minutes, can I phone?"
> Wolfe was frowning. "She's a woman."
> "Yes, indeed."
> "I must ask your forbearance."

Our ambassador to Italy from 1953-57 was Claire Boothe Luce. The wife of Henry Luce, founder and publisher of *Time/Life*, etc., she had been an actress, an editor of *Vogue*, the managing editor of *Vanity Fair*, a congresswoman from Connecticut from 1943-47, and was the author of several successfully-produced Broadway plays, including *The Women* in 1936, which was made into an extremely successful and much-revived movie, and is still included in many basic anthologies of American plays. Only Wolfe would dismiss such a dazzling overachiever with "She's a woman." One must remember, though, that she was not only a woman, but also a Republican!

As I observed in my earlier article, Broadway and off-Broadway actors and actresses occur frequently as characters in the *Corpus*. Throughout, there is a certain element of cynicism about the sincerity, not to mention emotional stability, of those of us who act for a living. In *Where There's a Will*:

> May smiled at me. "My sister is always teetering on the edge of things, more or less. I doubt if she could be a good actress if she weren't. It seems that artists have to. It used to be attributed to the flames of genius, but now they say it's glands."

In *"Murder is No Joke"*:

> Actresses should be seen and heard, but not touched . . . She quit *Thumb a Ride* abruptly some months later, and the talk was that she was an alto and done for.

Frequently there are assertions that actors are always on-stage, always acting.

In "*The Next Witness*":

> Of course, she was acting, since actresses always are, but the glamour was turned off because the part didn't call for it. She was playing a support for a friend in need, and kept strictly in character . . .

In "*Disguise for Murder*":

> Up in the plant rooms Malcolm Vedder had caught my eye by the way he picked up a flowerpot and held it . . . He was an actor and had had parts in three Broadway plays. Of course that explained it. No actor would pick up a flowerpot just normally like you or me. He would have to dramatize it some way, and Vedder had happened to choose a way that looked to me like fingers closing around a throat.

In "*Counterfeit for Murder*":

> Ferris turned a hand over. . . "I was too sentimental, I always am . . . Also I am too sensitive. I couldn't hear the thought that the knife I had sliced ham with had been . . . " He finished it with a gesture, an actor's gesture.

As an actress, how do I plead? Is this a legitimate accusation? Well, yes and no.

Leaving aside the question of whether it is personally applicable, a judgement I leave to others, I have to say that I have known actors of two extreme types: one type is, indeed, as alleged, always "on" — especially when in the presence of a large group of people. The other type is entirely the reverse: offstage they practically disappear, and one can hardly believe the transformation that takes place when that person steps onto the stage or in front of the camera.

We are also accused, not only of acting ourselves, but of trying to direct other people. Also in "*Counterfeit for Murder*":

> Tammy: Oh, well. What do you care? Why don't you ask me what I want?
> Archie: I'm putting it off because I may not have it.
> Tammy: That's nice. I like that. That's a good line, only you threw it away. There should be a pause after off. "I'm putting it

off . . . because I may not have it." Try it again.

Now I would contend that this exchange is exceedingly unlikely in New York City, even as long ago as 1960/61 when
"Counerfeit for Murder" takes place. "Line readings" are an an-
achronism in the contemporary professional American theatre
and have been at least since I entered the business almost thirty
years ago. In community theatre, yes. In bad stock companies,
yes. In England, even at the highest levels, yes. But a young,
impecunious New York actress who undoubtedly studies with
Uta Hagen, the late Lee Strasburg, or any of the various offshoots
of the Stanislavsky "Method" school — never! Of course, it's possible that she hasn't studied at all and has only acted in bad stock
companies, so the point is definitely arguable. But, I confess that
it strikes me as something a non-actor would invent.

All in all, I think Mr. Stout gives us a pretty hard time. He
does seem to be aware, however, that research and observations
are a part of our equipment. Again, in *"Counterfeit for Murder"*:

> Wolfe: What were you doing around the docks?
> Paul Hannah: I was looking and listening. In the play we're
> doing, *Do As Thou Wilt*, I'm a longshoreman, and I want to get it
> right.

References to this kind of research, I must confess, always
leave me feeling that I have led a deprived life as an actress. Historical research, of course — endless hours of it. This last summer, in preparation for doing *(The) Lion in Winter*, I read four
biographies of Eleanor of Acquitaine plus countless chapters in
various books on English and French history. This is a need that
has arisen frequently in my professional life and, fortunately, I
love libraries. But I keep hearing of other actors and actresses
who spend months living in bordellos, schools for the deaf,
prisons, mental institutions, Indian reservations, and Olympic
training camps. Roles demanding research of this kind never
seem to come my way, and I don't know whether to feel thankful
or cheated!

Another type of preparation is alluded to in *Death of a Dude*:

> She forked a bit of meat to her mouth and started to chew.
> She often did that; she might get a part in a play with an eating
> scene, and mixing chewing with talking needed practice. An ac-
> tor can practice any time with anybody, and most of them do.

While this particular description seems a bit unkind to me, I must admit that most actors, myself included, are guilty of this, consciously or unconsciously. I tried to think of examples from personal experience, and the "practice" which I have engaged in the most often, going back to my high school days, is an acting exercise which I invented for myself. I have never named it before, but I will call it now the "As If" exercise for purposes of this paper. I learned at about the age of fourteen or fifteen, while attending an all-girls Episcopal boarding school, that I could do all kinds of illegal things if I just looked as if I had been given authority to do them. Being a rather straitlaced soul by nature, I hasten to assure you that these escapades did not take any of the lurid forms that may now be occurring to you.

But I did become quite adept at things like walking around the dormitory halls at will during study period, just by doing it boldly and with authority. Later I expanded this technique when, as an impoverished singing and acting student, I learned to walk into theatre and opera performances without a ticket or move from the rear balcony to the front of the orchestra with my best "if you don't know who I am, you should" expression. My all-time triumph was getting into, and remaining at, a totally sold-out Metropolitan Opera performance of *Turandot* with Brigit Nilssen and Franco Corelli, without any ticket whatsoever. Somewhere in my late twenties, I believe, I abandoned this technique as being a form of petty larceny excusable only for the very young!

There remain several assorted allusions to the theatre which, for various reasons, intrigued me enough to inspire further research. The first is in *Over My Dead Body*, in which Archie makes the comment, "She has a nice voice, but she talks like Lynn Fontanne in *Idiot's Delight*. Now since both Lynn Fontanne and *Idiot's Delight* were before my time, I wasn't sure just what Archie meant by this, so I decided to try to find out. I quote from Brooks Atkinson's review in *The New York Times* of March 28, 1936:

> As the spurious Russian, Miss Fontanne also puts on the flamboyant mantle, enjoying the bombast of her accent. If it is not unmannerly to say so, perhaps she enjoys it too much, for the space she takes makes the character a little irritating and also delays the show.

I think you'll agree that this adds wonderfully descriptive detail to our initial picture of Carla Lovchen!

Another set of details which sparked my curiosity were the two real (and still existing) theatres that are mentioned. What was playing at them? In the case of the Longacre, referred to in *Might as Well Be Dead*, we already know that it was *The Lark*, starring Julie Harris, and my phone call to *Playbill* confirmed that. It was indeed playing at the Longacre in April 1956. That left the Majestic Theatre. In *"Method Three for Murder,"* what show would Phoebe Arden have seen in September 1959 if she had met Mrs. Irving as supposedly arranged instead of being murdered. Does anyone know? (Time for answer.) *"The Music Man,"* which ran for 1375 performances and won the Tony for best musical in 1958 over *"West Side Story."* (Those were the days!)

Finally there is a line in *Where There's a Will* that struck me, as an actress, as so odd that it launched me into an all-out research project at the Lincoln Center Library, eventually getting all the librarians in the theatre division eagerly involved. That is the description of April Hawthorne as "the only actress, alive or dead, who has played both Juliet and Nora." Now my instant reaction to that was 1) it's not true: I know that Claire Bloom had played both parts, and 2) 1 would be willing to wager that DOZENS of young actresses had played both parts. Lengthy research at the library did yield the fact that, in addition to Claire Bloom, both Eva LeGallienne and Julie Harris have played both of these roles in major productions. This left me with lists of several hundred actresses, alive or dead, who have played either Juliet or Nora but, as certain as I was in some cases that they must have played the other role *somewhere*, I could not come up with any documentation supporting this thesis. If anyone can think of any possible use for this information, I'm sure I could go through the *Players Guide*, write all of the living actresses and ask them if they didn't indeed play the other role in stock somewhere. I can only assert that I'm sure I would end up with an even longer list. Nevertheless, this would be irrelevant. *Where There's a Will* takes place in July 1939, so in spite of the fact that there are three famous actresses that *we know of* who have played both roles, we can't, in all fairness, count either Claire Bloom or Julie Harris, since their performances were after 1939. But we can count Eva LeGallienne, who did Juliet in 1926 and Nora in 1934, so I rest my case: Archie was wrong!

As a closing note, it doesn't take an actress's eye to spot the most heartbreaking lines on the theatre in the *Corpus*. I quote from *"The Next Witness"*:

Having paid $4.40 or $5.50 several times to see her from an orchestra seat, I would have appreciated this free close-up of her on a better occasion . . .

Last week I paid $29.00 at the half price booth to sit in the rear balcony of the Martin Beck Theatre. I think I'll stop here before I start crying.

(NOTE: All of my dates are based on those given in "A Chronology of Crimes" in the premiere issue of *The Gazette*.)

[ED. — *The Gazette is very pleased to reprint this sparkling, witty speech by my favorite actress. She delivered it in December, 1989, at the Nero Wolfe Assembly.]*

A TRIBUTE TO NERO WOLFE

by Kevin Gordon

We honor here a man tonight
Whose eccentricities delight
The members of this esteemed Pack
In hardcover and paperback.
   From nine to eleven and four to six
   No flummery is allowed to mix
   With Cattleya or Cymbidium
   While Theodore is upstairs with him.

In custom chair the great man sits
As beer is served by loyal Fritz.
It takes more bottles than just one
To quench a seventh of a ton.
   The peephole, globe, and yellow chairs
   Are more than his artistic flairs.
   Each object in that hallowed room
   Help guarantee some scoundrel's doom.

A woman's tears are sure to vex
As fire did to Nero Rex.
And even though he's very Stout
He'll rush to take the quick way out.
   None but Archie has possessions
   Or the requisite discretion
   To keep the great man at his task
   So that in solvency they'll bask.

To some his pose may seem a pout,
As lips push out, pull in, push out.
But when that mouth starts its protrusions
The case is nearing its conclusion.
   So, without a "Pfui" or "Confound it,"
   Let NERO WOLFE know he's surrounded
   By those who think he's uppermost
   In offering this heartfelt toast!

GETTING
THE GOODS
ON GOODWIN

Articles in *The Gazette* about Archie Goodwin are far fewer than those concerning Nero Wolfe. This is understandable for two reasons. Wolfe is so colorfully idiosyncratic there are many things to discuss about him and his interests. The other reason is Archie's unwillingness to talk about anything other than the cases and his efforts keeping the big man on track. Nevertheless, it is Archie's viewpoint that has made the *Corpus* the most popular mystery series in the English language other than Sherlock Holmes. One *Gazette* article says that men admire Archie and women love him, and that is certainly true at The Wolfe Pack. One of the most popular guests ever to appear at one of the Pack's annual Assemblies was Tom Mason, who did a splendid job portraying Archie in the film version of *The Doorbell Rang*.

The evolving characteristics of the relationship between Archie and Wolfe are eloquently discussed in *Archie Goodwin: Pragmatic Picador*, which appeared in the Spring 1984 *Gazette*, Volume III # 2.. The article, excerpted from *Rex Stout*, published that summer by Frederick Ungar Publishing Co., New York, was written by David R. Anderson, at that time an assistant professor of English at Texas A & M University.

Archie's Birthdate appeared in the Fall 1988 *Gazette,* Volume VI # 4, and was written by Joel Levy, who was at that time the *Gazette's* editor. The preceding issue, Volume VI # 3, included the first installment of Henry W. Enberg's *The Daughter Hunt* (elsewhere this volume) and *Gentleman Don Juan,* a discussion of Archie's ongoing interplay with distaff clients and, of course, Lily Rowan, by one of the Pack's most prolific authors, the Rev. Frederick G. Gotwald. A significant aspect of Archie's romantic as well as professional life was to go dancing at the Flamingo Club with Lily Rowan and certain clients, so I have appended to the Rev. Gotwald's "Don Juan" article a second one he wrote for the Fall 1990 *Gazette,* Volume VIII # 4: *Nightlife a la Flamingo,* in which he both cites references from the *Corpus* pertaining to the Flamingo and reveals the location of the historical namesake for Archie's favorite night spot. And to round out the discussion of the opposite sex, I've included the amusing *Archie Goodwin and*

THE *Woman*, which though it did not appear in *The Gazette* was one of the most popular speeches at an early annual Wolfe Pack Assembly. One of the Pack's charter members, Saralee Kaye, was until recently its Treasurer. [*Yes, we share the same last name . . . and also our wonderful daughter Terry!*— MK]

Archie Goodwin once wrote an article about orchids, but the Fall 2000 (Volume XVI # 2) *Gazette* shows he is familiar with irises, as well. This is especially interesting in light of Charles E. Burns's orchid article in the preceding section of this book. Burns also contributed an enthusiastic overview of baseball in the *Corpus* in *The Gazette* for Fall 1991, Volume IX # 4.

This section ends with a toast to Archie by The Pack's beloved Tenby Storm, who after Henry Enberg died, inherited the unenviable task of preparing Neronian quizzes to perplex members and guests at the annual Black Orchid Banquets.

ARCHIE GOODWIN: PRAGMATIC PICADOR

by David R. Anderson

"Fundamentally I'm the direct type."
The Red Box

"If he has his rules, so do I."
The Second Confession

"Outside this house Mr. Goodwin is me, in effect— if not my alter ego, my vicar."
Gambit

With the possible exception of Holmes and Dr. Watson, Nero Wolfe and Archie Goodwin form the most successful partnership in crime fiction. As with Doyle's detectives their partnership is both domestic and professional, with the difference that the Wolfe novels tend to emphasize the domestic as much — if not more — than the professional side of their relationship. With their interest in menus, schedules, and family bylaws, the Wolfe novels depict not only the pursuit of crime but also the alternative to the morally disordered world of crime: the excessively ordered world of the brownstone on West Thirty-fifth street. That order depends as much on Archie Goodwin as it does on Nero Wolfe.

Wolfe, especially in the early novels, is a romantic. Archie, by contrast, is a realist. Wolfe's province is phenomena; Archie's is facts. Wolfe is subtle; Archie direct. Wolfe's rhetoric verges on pomposity; Archie's slang is concrete and street-wise. Wolfe knows who Thales of Miletus was, knows the difference between the philosophies of Plato and Protagoras, knows all about crisis intervention in modern psychotherapy. Archie knows who the Mets are, what Off Track Betting is, where to get pass keys made illegally. This fundamental division of labor enables Wolfe and Archie together to form a complete detecting team, and Archie knows very well how the labor is divided:

> Aside from my primary function as the thorn in the seat of Wolfe's chair to keep him from going to sleep and waking up only for meals, I'm chiefly cut out for two things: to jump and grab something before the other guy can get his paws on it, and to collect pieces of the puzzle for Wolfe to work on . . . I don't pretend to be strong on nuances. Fundamentally I'm the direct type. (The Red Box, p. 180)

Archie makes this point repeatedly, although in slightly different words, throughout the Wolfe novels, but especially towards the beginning of the series when the characters are getting established. Many of his self-revelations occur in comments about food. In *Fer-de-Lance*, Archie misses one of Fritz's special efforts; the next morning Fritz describes what he missed: "I was only politely interested," Archie reports, "yesterday's meals never concern me much." In *And Be A Villain*, Wolfe and Fritz are arguing over whether horse mackerel is as good as Mediterranean tunny fish for vitello tonnato. Archie listens briefly, until "The argument began to bore me because there was no Mediterranean tunny fish to be had anyhow." In the same trilogy — this time in *In the Best Families* — Archie elaborates punningly on that view: "I fully appreciate, mostly anyhow, the results of Wolfe's and Fritz's powwows on grub when it arrives at the table, but the gab often strikes me as overdone." As a man of action, Archie is not interested in hypothesis or theory, not interested in the unretrievable past or the uncertain future. He is interested in what is on the table, in detecting as well as in dining. He is, as he puts it in *The League of Frightened Men*, a swallower; Wolfe is the taster.

Archie's directness springs partly from the attitude that motivates him to detect in the first place. Wolfe pursues criminals to make money, a fact he frankly acknowledges in *Too Many Cooks*, though in the same breath he reminds the reader that he is an incurable romantic. The thrill of the chase motivates Archie, a fact emphasized by his response to the end of Wolfe's relapse. *Fer-de-Lance*: "I was excited all right. I shaved extra clean and whistled in the bathtub. With Wolfe normal again anything might happen," and later, "Fifty grand, with the Wolfe bank balance sagging like a clothesline under a wet horse blanket, and not only that, but a chance of keeping our places on the platform in the biggest show of the season." When Helen Frost walks in with an important news item in *The Red Box*, Archie's "heart began to beat, as it always does when we're on a case with any kick to it and any little surprise turns up." In *Please Pass the Guilt*, Saul Panzer appears on the doorstep with a look on his face that clearly tells he has cracked the case. Archie opens up the door: "It's moments like that that make life worth living, seeing Saul there on the stoop." Where Wolfe's interest in a case is partly financial, partly romantic, and partly intellectual, Archie's is visceral. As befits the master of fact, the man of action, for him the appeal of detection is direct and concrete. Archie feels it in his pulse. No doubt it is this extraordinary bond between a case and his own physical state that makes Archie so direct. In fact, he must restrain himself, he is so energized:

> Although I keep it down as much as I can, so it won't interfere with my work, I always have an inclination in a case of murder to march up to all the possible suspects, one after the other, and look them in the eye and ask them, "Did you put that poison in the aspirin bottle?" and just keep that up until one of them says, "Yes." As I say, I keep it down, but I have to fight it. (*The Red Box*)

It is as though Archie craved the physical sensation of hearing that "Yes." The same is true of that suspicion Archie harbors — though he knows it is false — that if you look hard enough at a group of murder suspects you can pick out the murderer. It never works, but he keeps trying.

Wolfe likes a case with complexities. Archie, a great one for the obvious, does not. "I like a case you can make a diagram of," he reports in *And Be A Villain*. It is not that he objects to complications per se; he simply prefers the direct approach to the circuitous one:

> . . . if you're out for bear it seems silly to concentrate on hunting for moose tracks. Our fee depended on our finding out how and why Orchard got cyanided by drinking Madeline Fraser's sugared coffee, and here we were spending our time and energy on the shooting of a female named Beula Poole.

"I am methodical by temperament," Archie complains elsewhere, and he makes a point of saying that he likes to see plans carried out when they've been made (*Some Buried Caesar*). This characteristic serves Archie well as narrator. Wolfe, who closes his eyes and flashes all over a case, all over its facts and phenomena, would be neither prepared for nor disposed towards ordered, detailed narration of a case. That would be like requiring Velasquez to explain how he painted drapery. Archie, however — direct, concrete, methodical — makes an ideal narrator. In watching him come to grips with the case and with Wolfe's artistry, the reader comes to grips with a case as well. Archie is not dull-witted in a Watsonian way; he's simply another sort of detective with another cast of mind than Wolfe.

As the man whose province is facts, Archie periodically punctures Wolfe's romanticism. These occasions — normally comic ones — help keep Wolfe honest. They also keep the Wolfe series active and energetic. Wolfe tends toward laziness; its parallel quality in the moral world is complacency. Fritz once commented to Archie that Wolfe would "do nothing without you to *piquer*" (*The Final Deduction*). As picador, Archie keeps Wolfe both physically and mentally alert In Fer-de-Lance Wolfe explains why he allowed E. D. Kimball to be killed. The explanation requires half a page and includes such rhetorical end-runs as "a substitute for fate," "judicial murder," and "the entire complex phenomenon." "I will take the responsibility for my own actions," Wolfe concludes; "I will not also assume the burden of your simplicity." Archie's reply deflates Wolfe's balloon:

> If [the murderer] had been arrested and brought to trial you would have had to put on your hat and gloves, leave the house, walk to an automobile, ride clear to White Plains, and sit around a courtroom waiting for your turn to testify. Whereas now, natural processes being what they are, and you having such a good feeling for phenomena, you can just sit and hold your responsibilities in your lap.

By mocking Wolfe's diction, Archie exposes its underside. Stout is not criticizing Wolfe; he is merely dramatizing the confrontation between a realist and abstractions. In doing so he reveals not only the character of the realist but also the depth of the understanding between his two main characters.

That exchange, though significant, was not particularly amusing. This next one is, in an ironic way. Wolfe and Archie are discussing the taste test that has been arranged for Les Quinze Maitres and Mrs. Laszio's report of an attempt to murder her husband in *Too Many Cooks*. Wolfe is uneasy. "I came here to meet able men, not to see one or more of them murdered." Archie is not fooled: "You came here to learn how to make sausage." He remembers the conversation with Berin on the train and won't let Wolfe get away with ennobling his own mission. Occurring in the same novel with some of Wolfe's most romantic pronouncements — for example, "The guest is a jewel resting on the cushion of hospitality" — Archie's sardonic realism surely nudges the reader when he hears those grand words. It preserves the thematic direction of the series, for as the remaining novels gradually show, Wolfe's idealism is fated to suffer a severe blow.

Because Archie Goodwin narrates the Wolfe novels, the reader sees all the action through his eyes and with his help evaluates all the characters and themes. In fact, Rex Stout himself once observed, "It's Archie who really carries the stories, as narrator. Whether the readers know it or not, it's Archie they really enjoy." Being the direct type helps him to fulfill the role of narrator. As he repeatedly remarks, Archie has a straightforward kind of mind. He prefers things clear, direct, methodical. This quality inspires confidence; a reader expects such a narrator to be reliable because of his directness. Archie capitalizes on this fact throughout the Wolfe novels. In *A Right to Die* he states, "I never, in these reports, skimp any step that counts, forward or backward. If I score a point, or if I get my nose pushed in, I like to cover it." In *A Family Affair*, the most intensely personal of their cases, the one where a participant-narrator would be most likely to fudge his account, Archie repeats his assurances: "I try to make these reports straight, straight accounts of what happened, and I'm not going to try to get tricky."

In *Please Pass the Guilt* he reminds the reader again: ". . . in these reports I don't put in stunts to jazz it up, I just report." But Archie's reliability is not really at issue in the point of view of the Wolfe novels. Stout never uses his narrator to offer ambiguous or contradictory versions of reality. Archie's importance as a narrator comes from the values he imposes on the Wolfe saga. It comes as a surprise that Archie, despite his fierce pride, his antiauthoritarian kink, and his roving eye for women is in fact quite rule-bound. He lives by a strict code which he continually alludes to in his reports of Wolfe's cases. His code pervades the novels, giving them an ethical dimension, just as the tension in Wolfe between the romantic and the realist does.

In fact Archie shares that conflict. Where Wolfe is a romantic who constantly brushes up against the real, Archie is a realist who constantly brushes up against the romantic. In *Too Many*

Cooks he points out to Wolfe that the real point of the journey was to learn to make sausage. But in the same novel he comes up with this effusion: "You might have thought we were bound for the stratosphere to shine up the moon and pick wild stars." In *Over My Dead Body*, Archie permits himself this fancy description: "It was ten to five, and a dingy November dawn was feebly whimpering 'Let there be light,' at my window." Certainly these two passages do not earmark Archie as another Wordsworth, but they show in him an imagination and a verbal fancy which are the bridges to another world beyond that of sidewalk and alleyways.

For the most part, though, Archie resists the transcendental. The best example of this trait is his distrust of the pastoral. In *Too Many Cooks* he reacts this way to the sublime West Virginia mountains:

> I strolled along carefree. There was lots of junk to look at if you happened to be interested in it — big clusters of pink flowers everywhere on bushes which Odell had said was mountain laurel, and a brook zipping along with little bridges across it here and there, and some kind of wild trees in bloom, and birds and evergreens and so on. That sort of stuff is all right, I've got nothing against it, and of course out in the country like that something might as well be growing or what would you do with all the space, but I must admit it's a poor place to look for excitement. Compare it, for instance, with Times Square or the Yankee Stadium. (p. 40)

This is the realist, the man of action, the direct type who craves excitement from the pursuit of crime. Such a person, one expects, when he does talk about rules will discuss them with a sharp focus on the concrete, the actual. In Archie's case, exactly that happens.

On the surface his rules are comic. In *The Second Confession*, for example, he plays off Wolfe's corpulence: "If he has his rules, so do I, and one of mine is that a three-by-four private elevator with Wolfe in it does not need me, too, so I took the stairs." In *The Doorbell Rang*, Archie turns interior decorator: "I have a test for people with rooms that big . . . the pictures on the walls. If I can tell what they are, okay. If all I can do is guess, look out; these people will bear watching." *Death of a Doxy* sets down another rule — very practical but not comic: "Because of a regrettable occurence some years back, I made it a hard and fast rule never to go on an errand connected with a murder without a gun." In *A Family Affair*, Archie introduces another rule: "No hat before Thanksgiving. Rain or snow is good for hair." Like Wolfe's inflexible plant schedule and dining hours, these rules are funny because their propagators hold to them so tenaciously even though the rules themselves are trivial or comic or cranky. Yet like Wolfe's rules, which are part of his attempt to impose some regularity and order on careless, scattered reality, Archie's rules point to more important considerations, for many of them are both serious and significant. In *Fer-de-Lance*, Archie's mock-Puritanism was comic. But another rule is not. He explains that Wolfe had a warning bell installed at his bedroom door not out of cowardice but out of his "intense distaste for being touched by anyone or being compelled without warning to make any quick movements." The question of cowardice arises because "ordinarily if I have cause to suspect that a man is yellow as far as I'm concerned he can eat at another table'." In *The Red Box*, Archie slaps Assistant District Attorney Matthias R. Frisbie for calling Wolfe "underhanded." "In a way I suppose it was all right, and of course it was the only thing to do under the circumstances, but there was no deep satisfaction in it . . . It had been a fleeting pleasure to smack him . . . but now that it was over there was an inclination inside of me to feel righteous, and that made me glum and in a worse temper than before." *And Be A Villain* offers another rule: "Money may be everything, but it makes a difference how you get it." In *A Right to Die*, Wolfe has all the members of ROCC at his office after dinner, but none will accept a drink at first. Archie points out: "It couldn't have been because of my manners, offering to serve people of an inferior race. First, two of them were white, second, when I consider myself superior to anyone, as I frequently do, I need a better reason than his skin."

Archie is a moralist. His rules, expressed or implied, comic or serious, articulate an ethical position. Wolfe, who cannot suppress his belief in an ideal order, tries to achieve that order in part through the constraints of his own schedule. Archie — less imaginative but more realistic — feels that ideal order only intuitively. He compensates for that fact by imposing it more strongly on his own life. Believing perhaps that "the rules you make yourself are the hardest to break" (*Death of a Doxy*), he constructs a world of action as firmly bound by rules as Wolfe's contemplative world is bound by his timetable. Archie's method — more concrete and more practical than Wolfe's — ultimately serves the same purpose: to impose an ideal order on messy experience.

In *Fer-de-Lance*, Archie assures Sarah Barstow, "you can regard me as Nero Wolfe." Twenty-eight years later in *Gambit*, Wolfe assures Mrs. Blount, "Outside this house Mr. Goodwin is me in effect — if not my alter ego, my vicar." These two statements suggest one reason for the close bond between Wolfe and Archie. Wolfe never leaves the house on business, so in order to do any detecting he needs an extension of himself to go around for him. That accounts for Archie's phenomenal memory, too, for it enables Wolfe to hear as well as see events at which he is not present.

But the two statements just quoted hint at a far more important link between Wolfe and Archie than the one required by the mechanics of the detective novel. In an important way Archie is Wolfe's alter ego, not merely his vicar. On the psychological level, their bond rests quite simply on mutual trust and respect. Wolfe explains it in *Too Many Women*:

> Archie, if I need to tell you, I do, that I have unqualified confidence in you and am completely satisfied with your performance in this case as I have been in all past cases and expect to be in all future ones. Of course you tell lies and so do I, even to clients when it seems advisable, but you would never lie to me, nor I to you in a matter where mutual trust and respect are involved.

"Respect" is the key word here. Archie needs to have Wolfe's respect and the satisfaction of having earned it; Wolfe's pride is more absolute, a combination of confidence and self-satisfaction. Their mutual pride is their strongest bond, the point at which they merge and their personalities become one. Mortified at having allowed Clyde Osgood to be murdered in the very pasture he was guarding in *Some Buried Caesar*, Archie puts his finger on the link:

> You're accustomed to feeling pleased because you're Nero Wolfe, aren't you? All right, on my modest scale I permit myself a similar feeling about Archie Goodwin. When did you ever give me an errand that you seriously expected me to perform and I didn't perform it?

In *Fer-de-Lance*, when he momentarily suspects that assistant district attorney Derwin has tricked him, Archie groans, "If I let a third-rate brief-shark do that to me I'd never be able to look Wolfe in his big fat face again." In *The Second Confession*, after Louis Rony switches glasses and gives Archie a drugged bourbon, Archie - still hung over - vows, "He would pay for that or I'd never look Nero Wolfe in the face again." As Wolfe explains to the Sperlings later, "Mr. Goodwin was mortified, and he is not one to take mortification lightly." But Wolfe, too, feels the prick of pride. In *A Family Affair*, he informs Cramer, "I intend to find the man who did it and bring him to account, with the help of Mr. Goodwin, whose self-esteem is as wounded as my own." In giving instructions to Orrie, Saul, and Fred, he vows, "I would like to come out of this with my selfesteem intact." And in the pessimistic mode with which this novel ends he tells Cramer, "Archie told me what Pierre had said when he arrived . . . Perhaps it was my self-esteem that made me give that item too little thought; Pierre said I was the greatest detective in the world. All is vanity."

But Wolfe and Archie are united by more than a shared sense of pride, just as more than pride motivates their pursuit of crime. Archie is Wolfe's alter ego in another important respect: their shared values. In *A Doorbell Rang*, Wolfe needs to play both ends against the middle. To satisfy Cramer, he needs to identify the murderer of David Althaus and to hand him over; to satisfy Mrs. Bruner he needs to identify the murderer, and, if he was an FBI man, not to hand him over. As Archie points out, "Cramer wouldn't like that, that's not his idea at all. Neither would you, really. Making a deal with a murderer isn't your style." Wolfe grunts. "I don't like your pronouns." Archie's reply is important: "All right, make it `we' and `us.' It's not my style, either." In *Death of a Doxy*, Archie again has to revise his pronouns. Speaking of Orrie Cather, who is being held for the murder of Isabel Kerr, he comments, "While he is no Saul Panzer, for years he has come in very handy for you — okay, for us." Forced by circumstances — Wolfe won't leave the house, Archie is not a genius — they function as one detective, one person. As a corporate personality they share the same dominant personality trait — pride. As a corporate ethical center they share the same "style." This is the depth and strength of their bond.

In the first Wolfe novel, where he and Wolfe still seem to be getting to know each other, Archie feels dissatisfied by the conclusion of the case. Wolfe permits a man to be murdered at the end of *Fer-de-Lance* just as he permits the murderer to kill himself rather than surrender to the police. This upsets Archie, who rejects all of Wolfe's self-justification at the end of the case. This sort of conflict occurs rarely in the novels. Normally Wolfe and Archie reach instinctive and unanimous agreement over the moral issues of any event. In *A Family Affair*, as soon as Archie and Saul identify the murderer, they know what must happen; the only question is how to make it happen. In *Death of a Doxy*, when Orrie has been named as a murder suspect Wolfe declares that if he is guilty they should not intervene — "Sympathy with misfortune, certainly, but not contravention of Nemesis" — and no one demurs. Later in the novel, Wolfe, Fred, Saul, and Archie display unanimity on the subject of blackmail. Wolfe and Archie agree on other subjects as well. In *The Doorbell Rang*, they agree about the FBI's overreaching its prerogatives. In *The Second Confession*, they both condemn communism. In *Too Many Cooks* and *A Right to Die*, both despise racism. Perhaps the best measure of their concord appears at the end of *The Red Box*, two years after *Fer-de-Lance*. There, too, Wolfe allows the murderer to commit suicide. Instead of protesting, Archie sits quietly, marveling at the murderer's composure in swallowing poison before a crowd of unsuspecting observers.

And so in the end, Archie proves both very like and very different from Wolfe. He possesses a different case of mind from Wolfe's, preferring the direct to the subtle, the concrete to the ideal. Insofar as he and Wolfe rub up against each other, these differences produce comedy, as they do when Archie deflates Wolfe's rhetoric or chastises his inactivity. But these differences, far from driving the two characters apart, actually bring them together, for it is through these differences that Wolfe and Archie complement each other. Underneath them rests a broad base of similarity. Wolfe and Archie share tremendous pride, a force that motivates them to pursue some crimes and, once they have begun, to solve others. That pride is the twin of a shared moral code which operates in the ethical sphere as their pride does in another sphere to hold Wolfe and Archie together. In their shared obsession with rules, timetables, schedules, Wolfe and Archie attempt to recreate in the messy real world the ideal order they envision. Their obsession reinforces their solidarity and gives their quest substance and meaning.

ARCHIE'S BIRTHDATE
by Joel Levy

The year of Archie Goodwin's birth is not agreed upon by scholars.

Although the day of his birth is definitely October 23 (*The League of Frightened Men*), the year of his birth has caused some confusion. The mystery, however, is easily solved from four clear references in the *Corpus*. In *The Red Box*, Archie describes his coming to work for Wolfe after killing two men while working as a guard on a New York pier. Several other sources can be used to set this year as 1927 [see, especially, "A Biography of Nero Wolfe's Early Years (1896-1933)" by Reverend Frederick G. Gotwald, in *The Gazette*, Volume V1, Number 2].

Further, in two instances Archie gives his age unequivocally. In *The League of Frightened Men* he says he is 25 years old, and in *Over My Dead Body*, he says he is 29. Finally, Archie says he graduated from high school at age seventeen, tried college for two weeks, and then went to New York. Using these dates a table can be set up which clearly sets forth major events in Archie's life.

CHRONOLOGY OF MAJOR EVENTS
— ARCHIE'S LIFE

1938

    Nov - Archie is 29 when *Over My Dead Body* occurs
    Oct - Archie's 29th birthday

1934

    Nov - Archie is 25 when *The League of Frightened Men* occurs
    Oct - Archie's 25th birthday

1927

    Dec - Archie goes to work for Wolfe

Oct/Nov - Archie goes to New York; gets job on pier
Oct - Archie's 18th birthday
Sep - Archie enters college; quits after two weeks

1927

June - Archie graduates from high school

1921

Spring - Wins spelling contest in Zanesville, OH

1916

Summer - Gets first shiner in Ohio creek

1909

Oct - Born on 23rd in Chillicothe, Ohio

The fact that *The League of Frightened Men* and *Over My Dead Body* both occur in November means that these cases occurred shortly after Archie's birthdays for those years. Archie's description of graduating from high school, trying college, and going to New York to work at the pier is so unequivocal that it is obvious these events occurred within a short span of time. After killing the two men on the pier (presumably during an attempted robbery), he is recommended to Wolfe for a job, does it successfully, and is then hired by Wolfe. Once again it is clear that these events take place sequentially, with no major intervening intervals of time. It is clear, therefore, that Archie's life is as shown in the table. He goes to work for Wolfe at age 18, during the last days of December, 1927. The exact day is not precisely known, although Frederick Gotwald likes to think of it as Saturday, December 31.

The dates in 1916 and 1921 are also clearly defined by Archie, strengthening the conclusion that he was born in 1909, approximately 13 years after Wolfe (the author shares with Frederick Gotwald the belief that Wolfe was born in Montenegro in 1896).

This age difference, although never specifically mentioned in the *Corpus*, seems logical. When Archie's age is frozen at approximately 34 years by Stout, Wolfe's age is likewise frozen and by his attitudes and behavior in the books published after the mid 1940s, he can easily be placed in his late 40s.

I hope this little treatise clears up the mystery of Archie Goodwin's birthdate. Other opinions are welcomed, of course - with substantiating background and evidence.

GENTLEMAN DON JUAN

by the Reverend Frederick G. Gotwald

If the truth were to be told, men envy and women adore Archie Goodwin. Archie's "handling" of the opposite sex brings respect from males. And what feminists think of him is best voiced by Marion Wilcox (from "A Meeting of Minds," *The Gazette*, Volume 1, Nos. 3 & 4). "To me, he is very elegant and polished and man-about-townish . . . I expect Nero Wolfe and Archie to stay as they are, ageless. And Archie to remain his usual suave self. Even when he is drinking a glass of milk at the kitchen table."

Since Archie finds his encounters with females so intriguing, and since he is given to describing and analyzing these events, it might be worthwhile to learn from this Gentleman Don Juan: Gentleman, since he never loses his respect for the ladies and Don Juan, since he evidently has a way with them. Nero Wolfe is a genius, yet even he acknowledges Archie as an authority on women under thirty-five years old. This article, then, is an exploration into Archie and "his women."

The first thing one notices is that Archie never loses control of himself in the presence of feminine wiles. There might be two reasons for this caution: one, he has been burned once before, and the other, he is more interested in his work. In *Fer-de-Lance*, he confides the painful experience: ". . . the only girl I had ever been really soft on had found another bargain she liked better."

In *The League of Frightened Men*, he explains the other reason. "Take the women I meet in my line of business . . . I never run into one . . . without letting my eyes do the best they can for my judgement, and more than that, it puts a tickle in my blood. I can feel the nudge on the accelerator But then the business gets started . . . and I guess the trouble is I'm too conscientious. I love to do a good job more than anything else I can think of, and I suppose that's what shorts the line."

Archie says of Nero Wolfe that he was elegant with women but that he had some sort of perverted idea of them that he never could understand. Women to Archie are a delight to the eye, a challenge to repartee, a dish to be savored, but also a trap to be avoided. He is as gallant as Wolfe is elegant with them. Both tend to hold women at a distance with their defenses against getting too involved, and both with good reason. Archie with his once broken heart, and Wolfe with a woman who tried to kill him with a poisoned compress for his headaches.

Archie enjoys playing with the girls he meets. Not in the sense of *Playboy* magazine, which is concerned with exploitation of the feminine, but in the joyful fun of childhood games. A classic is the fun he has with the purple-eyed Constanza Berin (in *Too Many Cooks*), who is foreign born. In proving that he is a detective, Archie shows her a fishing license from Maine. She asks, "And that Maine?" And Archie has a field day. "We have two kinds of detectives in America, might and main. I'm the main kind. That means that I do very little of the hard work, like watering the horses and shooting prisoners and greasing chutes."

Archie is taking advantage of her. Being a foreigner, she doesn't catch the pun to know that he is kidding. Archie's conversation is typical to American courting. Nothing said is to be taken seriously, and the more outrageous the patter the more prestige to the speaker. Archie is a champion in his patter with females (and males, for that matter). He is thoroughly enjoying the company of Constanza until he makes the complicated discovery that he was jealous of a blue-eyed athlete looking at her ankles.

Archie analyses the situation. "I pulled myself together inwardly, and considered it logically: there was only one theory by which I could possibly justify my resentment at his looking at that leg and my desire to make him stop, and that was that the leg belonged to me. Obviously, therefore, I was either beginning to feel that the leg was my property, or I was rapidly developing an intention to acquire it. The first was nonsense; it was *not* my property. The second was dangerous since, considering the situation as a whole, there was only one practical and ethical method of acquiring it." Archie reveals some old fashioned virtues and what feminists would consider some old-fashioned male chauvinism as well.

Both Archie and Nero Wolfe avoid marriage because of the commitment implied: "for better for worse, for richer for poorer, in sickness and in health, to love and to cherish, till death do us part." Wolfe has said about the advantage of having Archie with him, that it is refreshing to be constantly reminded how distressing it would be to have someone else present - a wife, for instance - whom he could not dismiss at will.

Archie does have a "playmate," however, in the presence of Lily Rowan whom he meets in *Some Buried Caesar*. Their relationship has qualities of affection, independent equality, playfulness, mutual respect, and enjoyment. The usual courtship patterns of male assertiveness and female submission are often reversed. Lily, surprisingly, is more frequently the assertive one with Archie being standoffish. Their meeting in the evening where Archie is guarding a bull in a pasture is instructive.

Lily tries to creep up on Archie and catch him unaware, but fails. She says, "I didn't realize it was so dark; I thought my eyes would get used to it. I have eyes like a cat, but I don't think I ever saw it so dark. Is that your face? Hold still." Archie tells us she put out a hand, her fingers on his face. "For a second I thought she was going to claw, but the touch was soft, and when I realized it was going to linger I stepped back a pace and told her, 'Don't do that, I'm ticklish.'"

Archie invites Lily for lunch the next day explaining, "You'll do fine to pass away some time, just a pretty toy to be enjoyed for an idle moment and then tossed away. That's all any woman can ever mean to me, because all the serious side of me is concentrated on my career. I want to be a policeman." Later, sitting on a running board, Lily says, "You can't do any work on your career, here on a lonely road at night. Come and play with one of your toys."

This rendezvous, instigated by Lily, is a beautiful example of the "mating dance" patterns between two young adults in the pre-WWII period. The half-serious, yet teasing conversation lets each partner know where the other stands without too much deep commitment. Archie even comments on their game. "The dangle-it-then-jerk-it-away is no good until after you're positive you've got the right lure." Lily shows she wants to be more serious with the invitation, "Let's get acquainted, shall we?" Their relationship develops over the years into a long term agreement of affection with no strings attached. It doesn't get to the point of living together as many couples did in the post-Vietnam period, but it has the same spirit of individuality and independence.

Archie does sometimes meet his match. In *Where There's a Will*, Naomi Karn is as intelligent and perceptive as he is, but we'll let him tell the story of their first encounter:

I looked at her. There was no indication whatever of any strain of baby doll in her that I could see. She was . . . something new in my experience . . . None of her features would have classified for star billing, but somehow you didn't see her features, you just saw her. As a matter of fact, after exchanging only a couple of sentences with her, I was sore. During the nine years of detective work I had polished up my brass so that I regarded a rude stare at any human face nature's fancy could devise merely as a matter of routine, but there was something in Naomi Karn's eyes, or back of them, or somewhere, that made me want to meet them and shy away from them at the same time. It wasn't the good old come-hither, the "welcome" on the door mat that biology uses for tangle-foot; I can slide through that like molasses through a tin horn. It wasn't something as feminine as that, it was a woman letting a man have her eyes, but it was also a good deal more - like a cocky challenge from a cocky brain. I knew I had looked away from it, and I knew she knew I had, and I was sore.

It's too bad that this interesting relationship had no time to blossom since Naomi Karn was to be strangled with her blue linen wrap. The same thing happens with another woman who might have been Archie's match for brains and courage. Wolfe leaves a note for Archie on his return from driving this woman to her apartment (*The Silent Speaker*):

> Archie: Do not communicate further with Miss Gunther except on my order. A woman who is not a fool is dangerous . . .
> — NW

Phoebe Gunther, who has won the respect of Nero Wolfe, is bludgeoned to death on the brownstone stoop with an iron pipe. Both Wolfe and Artchie put their heart into getting revenge.

Do women come between Archie and his boss? A number of times. The first (in *The Rubber Band*) is when Clara Fox so enchants Wolfe that he, for safety's sake, allows the unprecedented (to this point in the *Corpus*) occasion of having a woman sleep under his roof. He even offers her Archie's handsome silk pajamas, a birthday gift from his sister in Ohio. And in the most unusual event of all, Ms. Fox breakfasts with Wolfe in his bedroom. But both lose her to an Englishman, Francis Horrocks.

Among the other times, there was also Mira Holt ("Method Three for Murder") who became Archie's client after he quit his job with Wolfe. It happened on the steps of the brownstone, and

Wolfe was soon involved since a dead body was found in a taxi in front of the house. Wolfe's way of winning Archie back was to say, "I do not accept your headstrong decision that our long association has ended, but even if it has, your repute is inextricably involved with mine. Your client is in a pickle. I have never tried to do a job without your help; why should you try to do one without mine?" They then share the client and split the fee.

In *The Mother Hunt*, Archie comes closest to the comfortable and settled relationship of marriage without it happening. In the seven weeks that it took to solve the client's problems, Archie gets quite familiar with the wealthy socialite Lucy Valdon, a baby, a town house apartment, and a country estate at the beach. In fact, he plays house. Not with Lucy, but with Nero Wolfe in her house when they are forced to seek refuge from Inspector Cramer. But Archie's ardor wanes when dancing at the Flamingo is interrupted by a concern for the baby's temperature.

Archie has one conviction about women. There are some of them that are witches with an inexplicable influence over men. He meets one in *If Death Ever Slept*. Otis Jarrell, one of the world's richest men, raves before Wolfe, "Get that snake out of my house." He is referring to his daughter-in-law Susan. Archie goes to live in as Jarrell's private secretary, Mr. Green, and experiences her influence:

> I'll tell you exactly how it was. I wasn't aware I had moved until I found myself halfway to the door . . . I realized I was being pulled. I went and stood in the doorway and considered the situation. I started with a basic fact: she was a female squirt. Okay. She hadn't fed me a potion. She hadn't stuck a needle in me. She hadn't used any magic words, far from it. She hadn't touched me. But I had come to that room with the idea of opening her up for inspection, and had ended by springing up automatically to follow her out of the room like a lapdog, and the worst of it was I didn't know why . . . I am not willing to be pulled by a string without seeing the string . . . I had an impulse . . . to pack up and go home and tell Wolfe we were up against a witch and what we needed was a stake to burn her at ...

Archie and his women. They are a parade of fascinating creatures and Archie's delight in playing, working, exploring, examining, understanding, challenging, romping, managing, and teasing them fills the Wolfe saga with a joy of discovery of the difference between men and women. Vive la difference!

NIGHTLIFE à LA FLAMINGO

Archie's favorite rendezvous for dinner and dancing was the Flamingo Club. Until recently this was thought to be a place invented by Rex Stout's fertile imagination, but an amazing clue discovered in Lewis A. Erenberg's *Steppin' Out*, about New York nightlife, revealed that there was a Flamingo Club in the city in the mid-1920's. But where it was located is the question.

The New York Public Library's microfilms of telephone directories for Manhattan revealed "The Flamingo, 140 Macdougal, Spring 4013" in May of 1923. A foray into Greenwich Village uncovered a sign stating "RECEIVING AND SHIPPING 136-140 MACDOUGAL ST."

The site of the former Flamingo Club is now the New York University School of Law at Washington Square, directly opposite the Provincetown Playhouse and the Cafe La Lanterna di Vittorio, which features espresso and pastry. The law School was constructed in 1953 and it is the wonder of the *Corpus* that Archie was still able to enjoy the Flamingo long after it had disappeared. But such is the stuff of memories, the flavor lingers on long after the actual enjoyment.

A search through *Variety* found a vague reference to the "Flamingo cabaret." As *Variety* explained, "any restaurant or other public eating place offering dance music as part of its service is classed as a cabaret and taxed at 3 cents on a dollar earned." May of 1923 was a tough summer in which to open. *Variety's* headline read, "Cabaret Business Bad — Talent and Bands Cheap." Greenwich Village was also a hard place to open a "nice cabaret" for the Village had a bad reputation: [*The source of the below quote is presumably from the Erenberg book. — MK*]

Echoes of the raids by the police in Greenwich Village still come forth. The raid wherein voting girls were placed under arrest without their parents having been aware of their Village association may lead to a cleaning up in the Village that will not stop at the dumps. The conditions there are amazing for the lure that "Greenwich Village" has to the silly girl throughout the country. It's not unlikely the few genuine artists living in the Village will shortly leave for a cleaner habitation . . . If the youth escape the joints they must fall in with the short-haired women and lisping men.

Earlier in the year, it was noted that the Triangle Club had opened in Greenwich Village to run a month in a reconstructed basement on Seventh Avenue between 11th and Perry Streets. Only members and guests were admitted. This must be the idea that the Flamingo Club employed to keep out the riffraff in the honky-tonk atmosphere of the Village. It also kept the Flamingo out of *Variety*'s headlines. Rex Stout in the 1920's was living at 11 West Eighth Street in the Village, an affluent businessman with his Educational Thrift Service in 432 cities and thirty states.

Asked by John McAleer what he missed most at the age of 88, Stout replied: "Moving around on my feet, theatre, concerts, ballet, meeting new people, ball games at the park, sex and baked beans." This was his life then, when he ran the ETS almost as an avocation on his way to collecting a kitty of $400,000 so that he could give up the business world and get down to writing. Nero Wolfe and Archie Goodwin came into existence in 1933.

The Flamingo, as it was referred to by Archie, appears in seventeen of the adventures. Its first mention is in "Cordially Invited to Meet Death," where Archie is given the assignment to get better acquainted with Janet Nichols, secretary to Bess Huddleston, who reminds us of that other famous party arranger, Elsa Maxwell. Archie says, "I was wrapping my tentacles about Janet, coaxing her into my deadly embrace." He took her to a baseball game and was pleased to learn that she knew a bunt from a base-on-balls. "Friday evening we went to the Flamingo Roof and I learned that she could dance nearly as well as Lily Rowan." The Flamingo Club starts with roof dancing similar to the Starlight Roof at the Waldorf-Astoria (alias The Churchill in Archie's accounts).

In the following year (*Not Quite Dead Enough*), Archie invites Ann Amory, "Say we go somewhere and dance." To Ann's question of where, he says, "Anywhere. The Flamingo Club." She turns out to be a pretty fair dancer but not much at bending the elbow. But then, Lily Rowan showed up . . . I'll let Archie tell what happened next.

I think she was going to smack me. Anyhow, it was obvious that she wasn't going to care what she did, and intended to proceed without delay, so it was merely a question of who moved first and fastest. I was out of my chair, on my feet across the table from her, in half a second flat, with a gesture to Ann, and Ann passed the test, too, a fairly tough one, with flying colors. As fast as I moved she was with me, and before even Lily Rowan could get any commotion started we had my cap from the hat-check girl and were out on the sidewalk. Ann's reaction was a chuckle, "My lord, she was jealous. Lily Rowan jealous of me!"

Sergeant Dorothy Bruce in "Booby Trap" (1943) gets taken to the Flamingo for a night of dancing. So it isn't until "Bullet for One" (1947) that Archie reports a nice evening with Lily: a show and the dance band at the Flamingo where they went to get better acquainted. Archie don't get home until after three o'clock, the closing time for all cabarets. It's good to know that Archie and Lily have made up.

Lily Rowan also finds the Flamingo her favorite spot for an evening's entertainment. In *In the Best Families* (1950), Archie, looking for Lily by telephone, dials the Troubadour Room of the Churchill and then, next in order of priority, the Flamingo Club, where he finds her. By 1956, in *Might as Well Be Dead*, we find that Lily has her own table. Archie is only a half hour late in joining the party. The usual routine was to dance for a couple of hours until the floor got too crowded, move to Lily's apartment and then get home around 3 a.m. By the time of *The Doorbell Rang* (1965), it has become a Saturday night ritual to be with Lily at the Flamingo.

The Flamingo also features performers with its dance band. In "Die Like a Dog" (1954), Jewel Jones tells Wolfe, "Yes, I sing in a night club, the Flamingo, but I'm not working right now."

Other patrons of this night spot, it turns out in *Prisoner's Base* (1952), include Sarah Jaffee who goes there with Wolfe's favorite lawyer, Nathaniel Parker. Besides dancing at the Flamingo with Archie, Lois Jarrell has been there for dinner and dancing with a group in *If Death Ever Slept* (1957). Archie is envious: "Wish I had been there." Lucy Morgan in "Poison a la Carte" (1958) admits that she had gone dancing with the murdered Vincent Pyle at the Flamingo two years before.

The Flamingo casts such a spell that in "Christmas Party" (1956), Archie agrees to do Margot Dickey the favor of getting a forged marriage license for her and him so that she can flaunt it in front of Kurt Bottweill who has been promising to marry her. She hoped this would get him to set the day, but it only got him murdered. Dinah Hough, who came to the Yeager "bower of carnality" in *Too Many Clients* (1960), believes that she can induce Archie into giving her an incriminating umbrella by the suggestion, "take me to the Flamingo and we'll dance . . . dance till they close." Coincidentally, her husband, Austin Hough, is a professor of English Literature at New York University, which is around the corner from that night spot.

A number of recognitions takes place because the Flamingo is a popular place to be seen. In "Blood Will Tell"(1962), James Neville Vance recognizes Archie because he had been seen at the Flamingo. Even Archie recognizes Althea Vail, in *The Final Deduction* (1961), not only because he has seen her picture in magazines and newspapers, but because he has seen her in the flesh at the Flamingo. In "Death of a Demon" (1960), Ann Talbott is able to confirm Archie's identity, "I've seen him at the Flamingo."

There is no photographic record of the interior of the Flamingo. I imagine it to look like the uptown El Morocco, which is expensive and ritzy.

It is most fitting in *A Family Affair* (1974), Rex Stout's last work, that the Flamingo gets a salute by Archie. "I was in the office, having just got in from taking Lily Rowan home after a show and snack at the Flamingo."

This night club is a legendary place in Archie's favorite sport, dancing with pretty girls and one of three places where he entertains Lily Rowan. Some day, when we least expect it, the Flamingo may come to light to our satisfaction.

(A word of appreciation to my niece, Anne Fry, who lives in Manhattan and who participated in this search for the Flamingo.)

ARCHIE GOODWIN AND THE WOMAN

by Saralee Kaye

It's been nearly twenty years since I first discovered — and fell in love with — Archie Goodwin, upon reading my first Nero Wolfe book, *The Doorbell Rang*. Over the years, of course, I've read all of the Wolfe books, and still find Archie a highly appealing character. Most of all, I suppose I'm attracted to his sharp, quick wit. Then there is the way he handles Wolfe — the psychology he uses to prod him into action. Above all, I suppose, his virtual unattainability is one of his most maddeningly attractive features.

However, he has one quality that has always bothered me. He has a habit of sizing up women physically, as soon as he meets them — not merely a "She was tall and slender" or "She was young and wide-eyed" sort of description, but a purely subjective one in terms of what is or isn't appealing to Archie Goodwin.

For example, here's a partial description of Gwenn Sperling in *The Second Confession*: "She was not an eye-stopper, and there was no question about her freckles, and while there was certainly nothing wrong with her face, it was a little rounder than I would specify if I were ordering a la carte."

Or take this description from *If Death Ever Slept* — he meets Mrs. Trella Jarrell and says, "There was a shade too much of her around the middle and above the neck, say six or eight pounds. She was a blue-eyed blonde and her face had probably been worthy of notice before she had buried the bones too deep by thickening the stucco. What showed below the skirt hem of her blue dress, from the knees on down, was still worthy of notice."

Now this was my overall memory of Archie's assessment of women, but upon doing some research, I found that actually Archie's tastes changed and broadened over the course of time, and these subjective descriptions become less frequent as years pass. Also, his attitudes loosen, as can be seen in *The Mother Hunt*, where he has probably the most passionate relationship with a woman in any of the books. Here's a case where he starts by being very critical, but softens as he gets to know the woman better.

Lucy Valdon appears in the very beginning of Chapter One. The doorbell rings, and he goes to the door and looks through the one-way glass panel, and he sees "a face a little too narrow, and gray eyes a little too big, and a figure a little too thin for the best curves." (So far, not so promising.)

In Chapter Two, Lucy says to Archie, "And upstairs, when you were looking at the baby, I nearly called you Archie. I'm not trying to flirt with you. I don't know how to flirt."

Archie tosses it off with one of his witticisms, but in Chapter Ten he says, "Her arms went around my neck, and she was against me." And later, when they're sitting on the couch, she says, "What you said about mixing personal relations and business relations, you know that's silly. We've been doing it for nearly a month, and here we are. I started the first time you were here, exchanging sips with you, and telling you I wasn't trying to flirt with you. Why didn't you laugh at me?"

Archie makes a flip remark, and she says, "I honestly thought I wasn't trying to flirt with you. How can you stand a woman as stupid as that?"

And Archie says, "I can't. I couldn't."

Since Archie meets and describes so many women throughout the *Corpus*, I wondered whether it might be possible to find out if there was an ideal woman who might have more of a chance with him than any other.

I figured the most obvious place to start would be with Lily Rowan. Oddly enough, Lily wasn't much help. There are only a few brief descriptions of Lily that include only a general mention of her blue eyes and blonde hair, but nothing of the close scrutiny he gives to other women.

I did notice one general pattern — timing is of some importance. Archie seems to become less romantic as a case progresses, as in this excerpt from *The League of Frightened Men*: "I'm funny about women. I've seen dozens of them I wouldn't mind marrying, but I've never been pulled so hard I lost my balance. I don't know whether any of them would have married me or not, that's the truth, since I never gave one a chance to collect enough data to form an intelligent opinion. When I meet a new one, there's no doubt that I'm interested, and I'm fully alive to the possibilities. And I've never dodged the issue, as far as I can tell, but I never seem to get infatuated.

"For instance, take the women I meet in my line of business — that is, Nero Wolfe's business. I never run into one — provided she's not just an item for the cleaners — without letting my eyes do the best they can for my judgment. And more than that, it puts a tickle in my blood. I can feel the nudge on my accelerator. But then, of course, the business gets started, whatever it may happen to be, and I guess the trouble is, I'm too conscientious. I love to do a good job more than anything else I can think of, and I suppose that's what shorts the line."

I figured I had my work cut out for me, after reading that passage. Nevertheless, I decided to concentrate on specific physical features, beginning with hair, and try to determine if Archie has any preference in color or style.

In *Might as Well Be Dead*, Archie expresses the opinion that ". . . a headache is much harder on a blonde than on a brunette. Some brunettes are actually improved by a mild one." (I'm still trying to decide what he meant by that.)

Archie was rather taken with a woman in "Immune to Murder." She was "small and dark and dainty, with sleepy dark eyes and silky black hair." In *Champagne for One*, he was favorably impressed with Rose Tuttle, who sported a pony tail. And in *The Father Hunt*, Archie describes Amy Denovo as being "easy to look at." He mentions, among other things, her "dark brown hair was bunched at the back." Dark brown hair seems to have somewhat of an edge. In *Where There's a Will*, Archie makes several critical observations of Naomi Karn, among them: "She was dark rather than light, but she wouldn't have been listed as a brunette. None of her features would have classified her for star billing."

When it comes to noses, Archie seems not too particular. He makes very few references. He says of Evelyn Hibbard in *The League of Frightened Men*, "Her nose was too pointed," and in the same book, he describes the straight thin nose of Mrs. Loring A. Burton. This is a favorable observation, because he says, "I suppose Mrs. Loring A. Burton wasn't at her best that evening, but she could have slipped a few more notches and still have been in the money. A glance was enough to show you she was quite a person."

By far, the most important feature to Archie is a woman's eyes. In *The Silent Speaker*, he meets a woman named Hattie Harding and says ". . . she had skeptical, competent dark eyes which informed you with the first glance that they knew every-thing in the world." And in "Cordially Invited to Meet Death," Archie says of Beth Huddleston, "She was one of those people who don't look much like their pictures in the paper because her eyes made her face, and made you forget the rest of it when you looked at her. They were black and bright, and gave you the feeling they were looking at you when they couldn't have been."

But Archie is not partial to dark eyes only. In *Too Many Cooks*, he comments on a woman: "From the back, her neck looked a little scrawny, but when she turned to us, she had smooth white skin and promising blue eyes." And in "Bitter End," when Fritz was out of commission with the grippe, Archie answered the doorbell and was pleasantly surprised to find a woman whose "eyes were a kind of chartreuse, something the color of my bath-room walls upstairs."

Just to round out the color scheme, in *And Be a Villain*, Archie describes Madelyn Frazer thus: "Her gray-green eyes didn't give the impression that she was measuring me, though she was prob-ably was, and I sure was measuring her."

When Archie eyes a woman, he takes in her size and shape, and doesn't overlook her legs in the process. When he tells Theo-dore about Carla Lovchen, Wolfe's adopted daughter, he says, "There's a female immigrant downstairs who wants to borrow a book. She is twenty-two years old and has fine legs." (That, of course, is from *Over My Dead Body*.)

Archie has a definite preference for slender women. He is not pleased by even a few extra pounds, it seems. In *And Be a Villain*, he says of Mrs. Michaels, "There was nothing snappy about her appearance. The mink coat and the dark woolen dress made visible when the coat had been spread over the back of the red leather chair unquestionably meant well, but she was not built to cooperate with clothes. There was too much of her, and the distri-bution was all wrong. Her face was so well padded that there was no telling whether there were any bones underneath, and the creases were considerably more than skin deep. I didn't like her." And in "Before I Die," when he meets Violet Angelina Sally, he notes that she "has a nice long flow to her body."

And yet, paradoxically, he has a keen eye for a few extra pounds and will on occasion tolerate such "imperfection." Eleanor Gruber is a case in point in *Murder by the Book*. "She was the kind you look at and think she should take off just one or two pounds, and then you ask, where from? And end by voting for the status quo."

It seemed to me that a search for Archie Goodwin's perfect mate should include not only physical attributes, but behavioral aspects as well. A woman who may be Archie's physical ideal could enhance her chances in a few ways, behaviorally. For one thing, she could show up on time. Archie was careful to put Helen Lugos, a secretary in *Please Pass the Guilt*, in the back row chair in the office because "that was where I could see her best and oftenest without turning my head much." Yet in a later chapter, Helen comes to the office and Archie observes, "I was supposing she would be strictly punctual, maybe even a couple of minutes early, but no, she *was* female. She came at 6:18."

Along with being punctual, a serious contender should like to dance, do it well — and bring a certain attitude to it. In *Champagne for One*, although Archie finds Rose Tuttle pretty enough, he says, "As a dancing partner, Rose Tuttle was not a bargain. She was equipped for it physically, and she had some idea of rhythm — that wasn't it. It was her basic attitude. She danced cheerfully, and of course that was no good. You can't dance cheerfully. Dancing is too important. You can be wild or solemn or gay or lewd or art for art's sake, but it can't be cheerful. For one thing, if you're cheerful, you talk too much."

But if cheerful is bad, solemn is not a good substitute. Comparing Helen Yarmis to Rose Tuttle, he says, "Helen Yarmis was better, or would have been if she hadn't been too damn solemn. We would work into the rhythm together and get going fine, when all of a sudden, she would stiffen up and was just a dummy making motions."

Later in the same chapter of *Champagne for One*, Archie runs into Celia Grantham. Referring to a previous date with her, he says, "She was a good dancer, very good, but she was also a good drinker, and along toward midnight, she had raised an issue with another lady, and had developed it to a point where we got tossed out."

His best dancing partner, in that very same chapter, is definitely Faith Usher — a woman towards whom he first felt brotherly. "She had perked up some, too, with her face muscles relaxed, and in spite of the fact that she got off the beat now and then, it was a pleasure to dance with her."

No doubt, Faith Usher was also *young*. As I said in the beginning of this discussion, I first discovered Archie some twenty years ago, and his references to older women didn't phase me at the time. Consider this example from *And Be a Villain*, in which Archie describes Madelyn Frazer — "With no makeup on it at all, it was quite possible to look at her face without having to resist an impulse to look somewhere else, which was darned good for a woman certainly close to forty, and probably a little past it, especially since I personally can see no point in spending eyesight on females over thirty." And in *The Second Confession*, he says this of Connie Emerson: "She couldn't have had more than four or five years to dawdle away until her life began at forty, and was therefore past my deadline."

Archie does become a little more flexible as time passes. Remember his relationship with Lucy Valdon in *The Mother Hunt*? Lucy was already twenty-six — four years short of his deadline, and it didn't seem to matter at all.

Now the question is, can we find that perfect woman for Archie? We know she should be under thirty — early twenties, to be safe. She should be a good dancer who relaxes with the rhythm and doesn't talk or drink too much. She must be slender, although a few extra pounds are all right, in special circumstances. Her eyes — so very important — should be dark brown or black — or blue, or gray-green or chartreuse, and her hair should definitely be brunette — although silky black hair is terrific, and blonde is good, too . . .

So it seems impossible to nail down *The* Woman for Archie, which is why he remains unattainable. He's captivated by a huge variety, and fatally attracted to none. Nowhere can this be seen better than in *Too Many Women*. Archie is on the job in the stock department of a company that has "hundreds of desks and girls at them. One good glance, and I liked the job. At least half a thousand of them, and the general overwhelming impression was of clean, young, healthy, friendly, spirited, beautiful and ready. I stood and filled my eyes, trying to look detached. It was an ocean of opportunity."

I may have approached this whole notion from the wrong angle. Perhaps I should have tried to find the perfect match for Nero Wolfe. After all, in researching Archie's likes and dislikes, I also learned a lot about his employer's preferences, too.

A woman just might stand a chance with Wolfe if she can cook chitterlings, use no obscenities, does not have a pug nose, has shapely legs, *never* cries, and can appreciate a good meal, for he cannot abide women who are slim merely because they never eat.

And a woman could do worse — Nero makes a good living, has a fabulous brownstone, a live-in gourmet chef, and a breathtaking array of orchids . . . and to top it all off, he's not so bad in the back seat of a car, either. According to Lily Rowan in *In the Best Families*, "He has a flair."

ARCHIE GOODWIN'S ANNUAL IRIS INSPECTION

by John McAleer

When I was visiting Rex Stout in High Meadow, Danbury, Connecticut, Rex gave me a dozen rhizomes from his prize collection of magnificent irises, all graduated by color.

After consulting Rex and Ruth Stout (one of the world's leading authorities on gardening), I transported the precious booty back to Mount Independence, my home in Lexington, Massachusetts. Taking care to follow Rex's and Ruth's planting instructions, I cultivated a special garden bed for my future crop. Some three decades later the irises still flourish and annually offer a generous variety of beautiful colors. The spring of 2000 was no exception, as I was favored with a wonderful selection of yellow and rich purple flowers.

I'm a fair gardener, yet I can't take full credit for the success of the irises. Note the June 5, 2000, carbon copy of the following memorandum sent to me from Nero Wolfe's office.

MEMORANDUM

DATE: June 5, 2000
TO: Nero Wolfe
FROM: Archie Goodwin
RE: Prof. John J. McAleer's Iris Bed Annual Inspection

Pursuant to the request of your colleague, Rex Stout, to make an annual on-site examination concerning the iris rhizomes he placed in the custody of Professor McAleer of Lexington, Massachusetts, I am happy to report another bumper crop year.

Subject continues to maintain irises in a satisfactory way.

In total, I counted eight yellow and five deep purple flowers and document same for file. The overall body of the plants is hearty and without any signs of infection or relevant insect invasion.

Your concerns, nevertheless, that these irises will need to be thinned again this year proved not to be unfounded and subject states that he will separate rhizomes, as their condition indicates, in late August or no later than Labor Day, unless instructed otherwise. I have long found subject to be true to his word and give even odds that he will, in a satisfactory way, not inconsistent with Mr. Stout's instructions, carry out this task.

Petal contour and structure, pistol, stamen, and moisture consistency would survive Theodore's scrutiny. There is a small issue concerning the tertiary leaf on number seven which would best be addressed under separate cover, but preliminaries suggest Mrs. Thrips's (subject's neighbor) yellow lab. Thrips made privy of my supposition. Received acid response. The mandated leash law, rigidly enforced, will bring her back into line in short order.

Soil sample obtained. Sample for pH integrity sealed and forwarded to usual lab vendor, Bonner & Fox Technicians, accordingly. My soil visual noted nothing remarkable and expect favorable finding despite Thrips event.

You may report to Mr. Stout that the irises in Professor McAleer's care and custody have once again yielded a robust, healthy crop and thrive in Mount Independence soil.

PENULTIMATE ADDENDUM

You will note that I have not submitted an expense report. Professor McAleer put Lily and me up for the night and his wife put on a spread of Webster Island chicken flanked by oyster stuffing, glazed carrots, marinated asparagus, and whipped potatoes cut with half and half. Further, since I missed my poker game with Saul, and Saul's been having another one of his hot streaks, I figured the annual inspection saved me at least a few hundred balloons, anyway.

ADDENDUM

I reserve the right to change the above should Saul's streak continue.

CC: Professor John J. McAleer — Via First Class U.S. Mail
Jean Quinn — Via First Class U.S. Mail [*Then editor-in-chief of The Gazette* — MK]
Theodore Horstmann — Via Elevator

ARCHIE AND THE GREAT AMERICAN PASTIME

by Charles E. Burns

We're talkin' baseball!!!

When I mentioned to the Great Werowance [*Ellen Krieger* — MK] that Carleton Fisk, Chicago White Sox catcher and future Hall of Famer, raised orchids as a hobby, she threw me a curveball. She innocently [?] suggested that I consider an article on Archie's interest in the great American game.

Like most curveballs, it looked deceptively easy to hit - until you gave it your best home run swing and, like mighty Casey of yore, you shattered nothing but air. While I was well aware of Archie's interest, I had no realization of the extent to which baseball terminology and events were such an integral part of the *Corpus*. You might consider some of the following as mere "baseball trivia." But that is a definite oxymoron. To the true *aficionado*, nothing about baseball is trivial. And certainly there is nothing trivial in the *Corpus*!

Archie's interest in baseball was undoubtedly influenced by his literary agent.

Once Rex Stout started on a story, he would let absolutely nothing interfere until he was finished. He interrupted this routine only once — when writing "When a Man Murders." The reason? To attend the World Series [See the wonderful biography on Stout by Professor John McAleer].

To aid in orientation, this article is presented in a chronological order, including the year of the events, as established by the Reverend Frederick G. Gotwald in *The Nero Wolfe Handbook*. So, get ready! I am about to step into the batter's box. And here comes the pitch . . .

The Early Years

There are relatively few references to baseball in the early novels and short stories. Still, a couple of Archie's statements indicate an awareness and interest.

The Rubber Band (1935): As this adventure begins, Archie is reading an article in the *Times*, written by S.J. Woolf, and teasing Wolfe. "Why" he asks, "wouldn't it be good for business if this S.J. Woolf did a picture of you and an article in the *Times*? This guy Woolf only hits the high spots . . . there's been Einstein and the prince of Wales and Babe Ruth and three Presidents of the United States and the King of Siam." His teasing may seem irrelevant but the article is about the Marquis of Clivers who, unknown to them at this time, plays a key role in the upcoming story.

Too Many Cooks (1937): Archie muses, "Out in the country something might as well be growing or what would you do with all that space, but I must admit it's a poor place to look for excitement. Compare it, for example, with Times Square or Yankee Stadium."

Some Buried Caesar (1938): When Captain Barrow of the State Police claims that a deputy sheriff overheard Howard Bronson implicating "Goodwin," Archie responds, "Maybe the name was Doodwin or Goldstein or Dimaggio." [Unfortunately, none of these alternatives kept Archie out of jail!]

"Bitter End" (1939): Archie uses baseball terminology to describe Fritz: "Fritz was such a cook that Marko Vukcic of Rusterman's famous restaurant had offered a fantastic sum for his release to the major leagues."

"Instead of Evidence" (1949): Archie says to Martha Poor, "You are trying to go to bat when your side has three outs in the ninth, and that's against he rules."

"Before I Die" (1946): Archie expresses his irritation, "I thought the only reasons Wolfe asked Saul to lunch was to have someone to talk to about something pleasant. I was so firmly convinced that it was a hell of a time for a man to sit and eat that I had to grit my teeth to stay in my chair, and you can neither chew nor talk very well with your teeth gritted. So the conversation was almost exclusively confined to Wolfe and Saul . . . They discussed plant germination, the meat shortage, books about Roosevelt, and the World Series. [Baseball was not in Wolfe's "field of knowledge." This is about the only time he expresses an interest and he might have done it simply to annoy Archie. Of course, he later attends a World Series, but he was conned into that.]

Season Tickets

Too Many Women (1947): Baseball is a major topic in *Too Many Women* as Archie plays along with Mrs. Cecily Pine, who would like to add him to her string of toys. At the same time [with malice aforethought] he manages to upset Wolfe. Mrs. Pine offers to set Archie up in business for himself, then asks, "Do you like symphony concerts?" Archie responds, "Yes, some, when I'm lying down. I mean on the radio." She laughed and continued, "Anyway, it's nearly April. Boating? Golf? Baseball?" Archie replies, "Baseball. I go as often as I can get away." "It's a wonderful game," she says, "Yankees or Giants?" "Both," says Archie. "Either one, whichever's in town." "I'll send you season tickets," she promises.

The saga of the tickets continues, much to Wolfe's annoyance. Mrs. Pine phones Archie to tell him they'll be available the following week. Later, Wolfe reports, "By the way, Mrs. Pine came to see me this morning." Archie asks, "What? Cecily?" [Note, he purposely stresses the first-name basis.] "What did she want?" Wolfe replies, "I haven't the slightest idea. She asked me to tell you that the baseball tickets will reach you Thursday or Friday. Archie, that woman is a wanton maniac. It would be foolhardy to accept baseball tickets . . ." Archie had him!

Later, in Wolfe's office, she arrives and gives Archie the tickets. "I thanked her," he says, "trying to speak like a pet." When he asked her why she came, she explains, "These tickets came today and I wanted to get them to you." The saga of the tickets ended with their return just as Archie knew all along it would. His letter of transmittal is still worth quoting:

Dear Mrs. Pine: [What happened to the first-name basis?!]
   Last night I went to a fortune-teller, which is something I seldom do. What was bothering me was your remark the other day that everybody gets tiresome sooner or later, and I wanted to find out where I stood. She told me that the most I could count on was two months. It seems that I am wonderful as long as I last and then I go tiresome all at once, without warning. I regret to say that under the circumstances it wouldn't be worth it to you, and I am therefore returning herewith the baseball tickets. It is still two weeks before the season starts, so you have plenty of time to dig up another prospect. (After some debate with himself, Archie signed it - with his full name.)

The Pinch Hitter

In the Best Families (1951)): Wolfe has left for parts unknown in his quest to defeat Zeck. Alone in the office, after much soul-searching, Archie sits in Wolfe's chair to greet a visitor, Calvin Leeds. His reasoning: "When a pinch hitter is called on, he stands at the plate to bat, not off to one side . . . So again, this time intentionally, I sat behind Wolfe's desk." Later, recovering his sense of humor, he tells Leeds, "Mr. Wolfe has gone south to train with the Dodgers. He will play shortstop."

The World Series

"This Won't Kill You" (1951): In the seventh and deciding game of the World Series at the Polo Grounds, the Boston Red Sox were leading the Giants 11 to 1 at the end of the sixth inning. The Red Sox had only three hits, the runs being the result of a comedy of errors by the Giants. And Nick Perrone, star player for the Giants, had been murdered.

This is the only story in the *Corpus* where, for obvious reasons, the game and the players are fictional. Perhaps that is why it doesn't ring quite true. From the way the Giants were playing, it would have been obvious that they were drugged. It stands to reason that the umpires or the Commissioner of Baseball would have stopped the game long before it even got to the sixth inning. In fact, one from the stands shouted, "Say it ain't so, Joe!" referring to Shoeless Joe Jackson of the infamous 1919 Chicago White Sox [also known as the abhorrent Black Sox] who "threw" the World Series to Cincinnati. Of course, their efforts were not nearly so obvious. For fascinating insight into the infiltration of gamblers in that 1919 series, I suggest *Eight Men Out*, by Eliot Asinof. Incidentally, none of the eight culprits were convicted in a court of law, but they were all banned from baseball for life. Getting back to the 1951 Series, it was the New York Yankees who beat the Giants that year. [*The next sentence, at the bottom of page 21 of the Fall 1991 Gazette, begins "(The) Reverend Gotwald points out that there were rumors of —" but the rest of it does not appear at the top of page 22, or elsewhere in that issue.* — MK]

The Giants Fan

Before Midnight (1958): As Archie pointed out in "This Won't Kill You," "I love baseball and I love the Giants." That was, of course, the New York Giants — before they moved to San Francisco. As *Before Midnight* begins, Archie asks Wolfe if there were any chores. He explains, "That was insurance. I had notified him that I intended to take Thursday afternoon off for the opening of the baseball season at the Polo Grounds." Later, still following the progress of the Giants, "At six-forty-five I turned the radio on to see how the Giants made out with the Phillies, and got no glow out of that." Later still, "I had turned on the television and got the ball game, Giants and Dodgers, Willie Mays was at bat in the fourth inning with a count of two and one. I saw Mays pop a soft blooper into center field that I could have caught on the tip of my nose."

Might as Well Be Dead (1955): It's only natural that Archie should think of both food and baseball. He combined the two in a strange way. "I was thinking, as I dished out the pork, of the best diet for a ball player. I suppose it depends on the player. Take a guy like Campanella who probably has to regulate his intake . . ." [Roy Campanella was BIG - and an excellent catcher for the Brooklyn Dodgers until a tragic accident, just before the Dodgers moved to Los Angeles in 1958, confined him to a wheelchair, ending a most promising playing career.]

If Death Ever Slept (1957): In investigating a potential client. Archie states, "I had learned through Lon Cohen that he [Otis Jarrell] had a reputation as a tough operator who could smell a chance for a squeeze play in his sleep!" Lon, of course, is a fount of information on a variety of subjects. Archie tells us, "I dropped in [-to *The Gazette*] to ask Lon Cohen if the Giants were going to move to San Francisco." [They made the move in 1958.] Later, in a lull during the case, Susan Jarrell asks Archie, "Shall I leave the TV on for the news?" "Sure, might as well," says Archie, "I haven't heard the baseball scores."

Champagne for One (1958): Inspector Cramer is questioning Archie about the fatal incident at Mrs. Robilotti's party: "You won't discuss the possibility that you're wrong?"

Archie replies, "'That, no. You wouldn't expect me to discuss the possibility that I'm wrong in thinking you're Inspector Cramer, you're Willie Mays?"

The Yankees

Plot It Yourself (1959): While we have seen that Archie is primarily a National League Fan, he was not above taking in a few Yankee games. He is a little upset when the current case interferes with his holiday: "What a hell of a way to spend Memorial Day. I had been invited to accompany a friend to Yankee Stadium that afternoon." Later, reporting verbatim, he quotes Mr. Oshin. "Let me know if you need a bat boy."

"The Rodeo Murder" (1959): The Rev. Gotwald points out that Archie made a minor slip "which was natural for an avid baseball fan, when he referred to the 'World Series' Rodeo at Madison Square Garden instead of the 'World Championship' Rodeo."

The Final Deduction (1961): Archie remembered that, "Noel Tedder had once landed a helicopter on second base at Yankee Stadium in the middle of a game."

"Murder is Corny" (1961): Inspector Cramer is questioning Archie's alibi: "Where had you been?" Archie immediately replies, "Ball game. Yankee Stadium." Cramer continues, "What happened in the ninth inning?" Then, not waiting for an answer, "To hell with it. You know all right, you'd see to that." Later, Archie comments about Susan McLeod: "She's a lousy dancer. And after a prize fight or a ball game, I want an hour or two with a band and a partner."

A Right to Die (1964): Archie says to William Magnus, "You fed me a slider and I just happened to connect." Magnus replies, "Okay, you're on base. Shall I try to pick you off?" In a little one-upsmanship, Archie says, "I might steal on you. Let me toss one."

The Doorbell Rang (1965): Baseball takes over in one of the most dramatic moments in the entire *Corpus*. The scene is set when Archie tells Wolfe, "We'd never get to first base." [Now there's a picture!] Later, he corrects that assessment, "Wolfe had stolen another base. " Then, as Archie, Saul, and the gang wait in the darkened office to confront the two G-men who had illegally broken into the office, Archie begins the action by shouting, "Play ball!" He raised his Marley, flipped the switch, and there was light. As Archie describes the scene, "One of them just gawked, but the one with the flash dropped it and started his hand inside his jacket. But not only did I have my gun out, Orrie was there beside me with his, and Saul's voice came from the door of the front room, 'Strike one!'.'

The New York Giants

Death of a Doxy (1967): Wolfe, annoyed that the radio in the office is on, asks Archie, "Is there an urgency?" Archie flippantly replies, " Yes, sir. Will the Braves play in Milwaukee or Atlanta?" Wolfe, of course ignores the question. [Actually, either answer would have been right. The Boston Braves did move to Milwaukee in 1953. But, seeking even greener pastures, they further moved to Atlanta in 1966.] Later, in Lily's penthouse, Archie tells us, "I was leaning back with my eyes closed, trying to decide which one I would rather have, Willie Mays or Sandy Koufax, on my team." Still undecided, while driving home, he continues, "I told my mind it might as well go right on with Willie Mays and Sandy Koufax. There was absolutely nothing else for it to do. As I turned into the garage, I decided definitely for Willie Mays. Koufax's arm was too much of a gamble."

The Mets

The Father Hunt (1967): After the Giants moved to San Francisco and the Mets had replaced them as an expansion team in 1962, Archie became an avid Mets fan. Early in *The Father Hunt*, he relates, "That Thursday afternoon in August we [Archie and Lily] had been to Shea Stadium to watch the Mets clobber the Giants, which they had done 8 to 3." In Lily's penthouse, "By the time I got to the terrace with the tray, she was there, at a table under the awning, studying the scorecard I had kept. 'Yes, sir,' she said as I put the tray down, `Harrelson, got three hits and batted in two runs. If he were here I'd hug him good.' `Then I'm glad he's not here,'" Archie replied. "I gave her her drink and sat. If you hugged that kid good you'd crack a rib . . . We talked baseball, concentrating on what the Mets had, if anything, besides Tommy Davis and Bud Harrelson and Tom Seaver, and what they might have if we lived long enough." [1967 wasn't the Mets' year. They finished dead last (in tenth place) with a record of 61 wins and 101 losses - 40 1/2 games behind the first-place St. Louis Cardinals! In 1968 they did a little better - moving up to ninth place. (But wait until next year!)]

Later, in a black mood, "I slouched in the taxi and tried to steer my mind back to baseball and the Mets." Later, Archie mentioned an unusual luncheon topic for Wolfe, "the effect of organized sport on American culture." And, finally, in *The Father Hunt*, "I took Lily Rowan and Amy Denovo to a doubleheader at Shea Stadium."

More Baseballese

Death of a Dude (1968): Although far from his beloved New York, Archie's mind was still on baseball. In a memo to Wolfe from the Bar JR Ranch in Lame Horse, Montana, he wrote, "Television here is a bust, and I have to be back in time for the World Series." Baseballese even permeates his description of summer in Montana: ". . . there on the eastern slopes of the Rockies, the summer bats around .900." He describes a luncheon as, "For him (Wade Worthy) we were just fellow guests to discuss things with — like baseball (me) or structural linguistics (Wolfe)." When Sheriff Haight tells Archie, "I guess you can read," Archie "didn't bother to bat that back."

The Miracle Mets

Please Pass the Guilt (1969): With the exception of "This Won't Kill You," *Please Pass the Guilt* includes more baseball than any other account in the *Corpus*. Perhaps that's because 1969 was the year of the Miracle Mets. It begins when Archie learns that a prospective visitor to the office is named Ronald Seaver . . . Archie explains to Wolfe: "One of your ignorance areas, baseball. Ron Swoboda is an outfielder and Tom Seaver is a pitcher [with the Mets]. Ron Seaver is obviously a phony. but it might help to know he's a Mets fan, if a clue is needed." Archie later tells the visitor, "If you had told me on the phone you were Ron Seaver I would have asked you to come and discuss the outlook." The visitor, embarrassed, mumbles, "they're doing better." Later that evening, Archie goes to his room "to catch the last inning or two at Shea Stadium on television." On Saturday afternoon Archie is hoping nothing would interfere with his "weekend pleasure at Shea Stadium." But a call from Mrs. Odell, a prospective client, does interfere. She wants to see him promptly at three o'clock. Even though that would be "about the fourth inning" and his intention was "to get to Shea Stadium a little after one and enjoy a couple of hot dogs and a pint of milk while watching batting practice," he agrees. When he arrives, he is pleasantly surprised to see she is watching the game on TV. "Ralph Kiner was talking." (He still announces Met games on TV.) From the time Archie asks, "What's the score?" and she replies, "Mets two, Pirates four, last of the fourth," they seem more interested in the game than in the business at hand, which is to find out who murdered her husband. Archie, again, "I went to a chair not far from the couch which faced the TV set. Ed Kranepool was at bat. He went to three and two and then grounded out, ending the inning, and a commercial started yapping." When the commercial ended, "a Pirate was coming to bat. She left the sound off but sent her eyes back to the game, so I sent mine, too. 'I work for Nero Wolfe,' I told to the Pirate as he swung and another one had popped up to the infield. Now a third one lofted a major-league blooper out to left-center and both Cleon Jones and Tommy Agee were on the gallop. It would fall in . . . but it didn't. Jones stretched an arm and one-handed it, and kept it. A good inning for Koosman [the Mets pitcher]."

When Archie started to leave, he said, "'Thank you for letting me see Jones make that catch." But she told him to sit down. "I did, and as I sat, Grote lined a double to the right field corner. Bud Harrelson beat out a bunt and Grote moved to third. More action and two Mets crossed the plate. When Ed Charles made the third out, the score was tied." Archie then tells Mrs. Odell to come see Wolfe. "Six o'clock would be a good time, he'll be available then, and the game will be . . ." She refuses and Archie leaves. "I walked to Madison Avenue, turned downtown, and headed for a bar where I knew there was a TV." [Incidentally, the Mets won 7 to 5.]

The next day, after breakfast, Archie "rang Lily Rowan and told her I was stuck for the day and would send the tickets for the ball game by messenger, and I hoped she could find someone who could yell at the umpire as loud as I could." As the case progressed, and Mrs. Odell became irascible, Archie told her, "You tried to steal home and got nailed." Archie later says of Wolfe, "He hadn't really bitten into it. It was still just batting practice." On the following weekend, Archie says, regretfully, "The best spot in the metropolitan area at four o'clock on a Saturday afternoon in June is an upper box at Shea Stadium, but I wasn't there that Saturday." The reason was that he had learned that Sylvia Venner didn't care for baseball, so he took her fishing. This was rather appropriate as Archie was fishing for information. Unfortunately, he didn't catch either — fish or information.

As the case became more difficult, Archie informed us, "The only thing that happened that day worth reporting was that Lily Rowan and I at Shea Stadium watched the Mets take the Cardinals 7 to 3." And finally, Archie asks Mrs. Odell if he could come to see her at five o'clock "because earlier she would probably have the television on and I didn't want to share her attention with Cleon Jones at bat or Seaver on the mound." So, what did Archie do in the meantime? He spent it "looking at the telecast from Montreal, where the Mets were playing the Expos, on the color television in my room."

1969 was a great year for Mets fans. The Miracle Mets came from the depths of past seasons to win the National League pennant, and then went on to to defeat the Baltimore Orioles in the World Series four games to one!

A Whole New Ball Game

A Family Affair (1974): At the turning point in solving this final case, Archie remarks, "It's an entirely new ball game." His words were prophetic - just as Cramer's were when, after spinning the big globe in Wolfe's office, he said, "I may never see this room again." Well, they've all passed into memories. But just as the memories of baseball linger forever in the minds of true fans, so, too, will all of the colorful characters who brought the pages of the *Corpus* alive, linger in the hearts and memories of us all.

A TOAST TO
ARCHIE GOODWIN

Made on December 1988 at the
Black Orchid Banquet

by Tenby Storm

By the shores of Gitchee Gumee —
Also known as the Hudson River —
Stood the brownstone of man Nero
And his henchman, Archie Goodwin.

Brave and brash, this fellow Archie —
Son of tribes out in Ohio —
Though his Indian blood is meager,
Still it gives him "bloodhound" talent.

Big Chief Nero does respect him
Even when they disagree;
Their relationship's notorious
For its shaky harmony.

As unto the bow the cord is
So unto the man is Archie.
Though he mocks him, he obeys him;
Though he prods him, yet he follows —
Useless each without the other.

Let's not dally — let's get on with it —
Recognition's overdue!
Raise your glasses high and toast him —
Archie Goodwin, here's to you.

THE WORLD OF WEST 35th STREET

THE VARIETY of articles in *The Gazette* is amazing and surprising. Amazing because of the intense scholarship applied to the minutiae of the *Corpus*, a characteristic shared by few other literary publications other than those devoted to Sherlock Holmes, Charles Dickens, and William Shakespeare. Surprising because of the unexpected lacunae; writings and speeches about Mr. Wolfe and Archie abound, but in twenty-five years, the pages of *The Gazette* yields very little information about Wolfe's attorney Parker, Inspector Cramer, Purley Stebbins, Orrie Cather, Theodore Horstmann (personally, I've always pictured him sounding and looking like my late friend Brother Theodore), or, perhaps most startlingly, Lily Rowan

Oddly, though, the brownstone itself receives respectable attention, beginning with Tamar Crystal's discussion in the Premier issue of the brownstone's changing address. I don't know if I am unique in The Wolfe Pack, but I am a member of the Steering Committee with an office actually on West 35th Street, much further east, though, than where Mr. Wolfe's establishment had to be situated. And if you have any doubts about that, just read Ellen Krieger's knowledgeable views on the subject that perhaps only a New Yorker (no, only a *West Sider!*) can fully appreciate. As Werowance of The Wolfe Pack for many years, Ellen wrote regular items for *The Gazette;* this one about the location of the brownstone appeared in the Summer 1988 issue, Volume VI # 3, whereas the Special Commemorative Edition in December, 1997, finally reveals the "actual" location (Wolfe might prefer "situs") in Joe Sweeney's report on the plaque placed by The Wolfe Pack.

Also in this section: Patricia Fanning discusses the internal geography of the Neronian establishment as it evolved over the years; her piece derives from Winter 1984 *Gazette,* Volume III # 1.

Veteran Wolfe Pack Steering Committee member Stephen Schwartz, who is a pediatrician and also physician to the chimpanzees at the Bronx Zoo, is uniquely qualified to discuss both the doctors and the animals in the *Corpus*, as he does with great panache in the well-named *More Than a Pair O' Dox* (*The Gazette,* Winter/Spring 1996, Volume XII # 1) and *Not a Wolf in the Pack*

(Spring 1990, Volume VIII # 2). In the latter issue, Joel Levy, late long-time editor of *The Gazette*, also talks about Wolfe's and Archie's invaluable journalistic source/friend Lon Cohen.

Over the years, Wolfe and Archie had their share of happy meals at the four-star restaurant, Rusterman's, the special province of Wolfe's best and oldest friend, Marko Vukcic (one of the few people who called the great detective by his first name). From time to time, The Wolfe Pack attemps to nominate some promising venue as heir to the name; its location, at least, is no longer a mystery, thanks to the excellent sleuthing of Phil Fischer in *The Rusterman Hunt* (*The Gazette*, Fall 2001, Volume XVI # 2.)

From Zeck to Moriary to Wild traces Nero Wolfe's Moriarty-esque antagonist Arnold Zeck back to the historical source of both Conan Doyle's and Rex Stout's villains. Originally a term paper written when I was an undergraduate at Penn State, it was the basis for a speech delivered to The Wolfe Pack in 1981, and subsequently an article that appeared in Volume IV # 4 of *The Gazette* in Autumn of 1986.

The Fall 1991 edition of *The Gazette* (Volume IX # 4) was an especially interesting issue. In addition to Charles E. Burn's study of the influence of baseball in the *Corpus*, which appears in the preceding section of this collection, the same periodical also contains both Jean Quinn's superbly researched *Take a Letter: Secretaries in the* Corpus and Ann Zawistowski's *Fritz's Herb Garden*, which not only discusses the topic with authoritative knowledgeability, but also includes some wonderful recipes patterned after meals served in the brownstone on West 35th Street. It is fitting to conclude the section with Jane O'Brien's toast to Fritz from the Spring 2004 *Gazette* (Volume XVI # 1).

A WORD FROM THE WEROWANCE ABOUT THE BROWNSTONE

by Ellen E. Krieger

SEVERAL YEARS ago, Dilys Winn asked Marjorie Mortenson and me to talk about Nero Wolfe's New York as part of a mystery bus tour of Manhattan. I don't remember much about the tour itself, except having to ad lib for what seemed like hours while we were caught in a traffic jam (something to do with transporting floats for the Puerto Rican Day parade). What I do remember is the frustration of trying to pinpoint the actual site of Mr. Wolfe's elusive residence.

Along with the perfect cast for a Wolfe movie, the location of Wolfe's brownstone is a favorite subject for debate among Wolfeans from Tamar Crystal ("Which Doorbell Rang?," *The Gazette*, Vol. 1, No. 1) to Ken Darby (*The Brownstone House of Nero Wolfe*). Obviously, Archie intentionally obscures the real address in his accounts of Wolfe's cases. No one with his nearly photographic memory could have as much trouble remembering his street address as Archie seems to in the *Corpus*. Wolfean scholar Lawrence Brooks believes that keeping the exact location of the brownstone secret is a condition of Mr. Wolfe's permitting Archie to publish his accounts of Wolfe's cases. It's hard to imagine Mr. Wolfe tolerating this invasion of his privacy (Brook's theory is that Mr. Wolfe's motivation is economic: in allowing Archie to profit from his genius — by earning royalties from the books — Wolfe justifies keeping Archie's salary lower than it might otherwise be); it's inconceivable that he would suffer his inner sanctum's becoming a tourist attraction by having the real address revealed in Archie's accounts. Clearly a working private detective who does not even list his phone number in the Manhattan Yellow Pages does not want his address known to the general public.

If Archie's published accounts do little to help the Wolfean sleuth track down the peripatetic brownstone, a walk along West 35th Street isn't much more productive. I started my investigation at 8th Avenue, even though none of the "Corpulent" references to the brownstone place it any further east than 9th Avenue. It's a shame, really, because there's a modern police station — Midtown South Precinct — on the south side of the block between 8th and 9th Avenues. It's amusing to contemplate Mr. Wolfe's reaction to the construction of a police station next door to his brownstone. He would find it intolerable living cheek to jowl with the NYPD, and Archie certainly wouldn't enjoy having to dodge double parked police cars whenever he took the Heron out on a case. Of course, the absence of any brownstones on the block raises an even more interesting possibility, that the city bought out Wolfe to build the precinct on the site of the brownstone. It's hard to imagine anything giving the Police Commissioner, not to mention Cramer and Rowcliff, greater pleasure.

The block between 9th and 10th Avenues contains the only extant building on West 35th Street that bears any resemblance to a townhouse, but it's easily rejected as Mr. Wolfe's home. In the first place, the house, at 455 West 35th Street, is on the north side of the street; all of the street numbers Archie provides in the *Corpus* are even numbers, firmly placing the brownstone on the south side of the street. Besides, 455 West 35th Street is brick, not brownstone, is single, not double width, has four, not three stories, has eight, not seven steps to the stoop, and has no greenhouse on the roof. Most damaging of all, there's no doorbell for Hoover to ring.

The block most frequently mentioned as the site of Mr. Wolfe's home — between 10th and 11th Avenues — is particularly disappointing to Wolfeans in search of the brownstone. All of the buildings on the south side of the street are old, clearly in existence throughout Wolfe's years as a private detective, and none is residential. In addition, there are no vacant lots large enough to have accommodated the two brownstones, Wolfe's and Dr. Vollmer's (one of them double width), that we know shared the same block.

It's easy to see why many Wolfean scholars have gotten discouraged and reached the conclusion that the brownstone was never on West 35th Street to begin with. Lawrence Brooks favors Chelsea as the actual location of Mr. Wolfe's home, and the theory makes some sense — Chelsea is a mere ten blocks south of West 35th Street, so Archie would have to make only minor adjustments to recounting his peregrinations around the city. Ken Darby's theory, placing the brownstone on Gramercy Park, could be proposed only by a Californian with no more than a passing knowledge of the idiosyncracies of New Yorkers. Gramercy Park is on the East Side, and no East Sider, taking literary license with his neighborhood to maintain anonymity, would transport it across Fifth Avenue. No, East is East and West is West, and Archie's is clearly the voice of a West Sider.

But do we really need to move the brownstone from West 35th Street at all? Some of Archie's landmarks are still there — the garage at 10th and 35th, and a seedy diner at 9th and 35th where it's easy to imagine him downing a corned beef on rye and a pint of milk. I suggest that the brownstone once stood west of 11th Avenue, on the current site of the Jacob Javits Center.

There are several clues that the brownstone was located as far west as possible. Most of the street numbers that Archie uses are in the 900's, far higher numbers than actually exist. (This fact has encouraged some wags to proclaim that Mr. Wolfe really lived in a houseboat on the Hudson River, but of course the concept of him actually living in a moving object is laughable.) Further, Archie frequently describes the brownstone as being "a few steps from the Hudson," which would place it close to 12th Avenue. In *Fer-de-Lance*, when presumably Wolfe's fame was not as great as in later years and Archie may not have been quite so careful about obscuring the location of the brownstone as he is later, he mentions walking two blocks to the garage at 35th and 10th, also suggesting a location at 12th Avenue.

The length of time it took to get the Javits Center built suggests that there was a holdout, a property owner on the block too stubborn and greedy to be bought out easily. Does this sound like anyone we know? But given Mr. Wolfe's aversion to work, it's reasonable to assume that the city eventually made him an offer he couldn't refuse, one that would allow him to retire, at least for several years. This would explain the lack of cases for Archie to record between *A Family Affair* and *Murder in E Minor* [*One of the Nero Wolfe novel pastiches by Robert Goldsborough* — MK].

In my research for the aforementioned bus tour, I called the New York Historical Society to determine if West 35th Street between 11th and 12 Avenues had ever been a residential block. Their records, which go back as far as 1854, show that it never was, but it's easy to imagine Mr. Wolfe making it a condition of the sale of his beloved home that the city records be altered to confuse historians and discourage curiosity seekers. As I listened to a New York Historical Society staff member reel off the list of incarnations the block had seen, I pictured Archie, in a fanciful mood, leaning back in his chair in the office, intoning, "just say it was a lumberyard, and a cattleyard, and then railroad freight-yards, and then hay and feed stores . . . definitely feed stores."

Of course, if we place Mr. Wolfe's home on West 35th Street between 11th and 12th Avenues, we are confronted with the sad reality that it is no longer in existence, and are faced with the question, where are he and Archie now? Ken Darby has Mr. Wolfe living in Egypt and Archie and Lily married and living in Montana. J. G. O'Boyle claims that Wolfe is alive and well in Philadelphia, a theory of which the less said the better. Surely a man who never — well, hardly ever — budged from his home would be loathe to pick up plants and books and staff (and can you imagine Wolfe living without Fritz and Theodore, not to mention Archie?) and move to another city. No, I prefer to believe that Mr. Wolfe and Archie are still in New York, comfortably relocated to another brownstone, probably in the Village or Chelsea, and conducting business as usual. As I wander down quiet brownstone blocks on summer evenings, I find myself searching roofs for greenhouses, peering into basement level kitchens for a glimpse of Fritz at work. Someday I'll find them — I know I will!

WHICH DOORBELL RANG?

by Tamar Crystal

NO WONDER Nero Wolfe never wanted to leave his house. With the location of his old brownstone peripatizing amongst 918, 506, 922, 902 and 914 West 35th Street, he wasn't sure he'd ever find it again where he left it. In 1936, when Llewellyn Frost came seeking Wolfe's help in *The Red Box*, home was at No. 918. Two years later, it had mysteriously shifted four blocks east, to 506 West 35th. At least, that's the address that Archie Goodwin gives John P. Barrett in *Over My Dead Body*. Another shift, westward this time, brings the house briefly to rest at No. 922 in *The Silent Speaker* in 1945, when Archie has this address engraved on his business cards.

The early 1950's witness a most unWolfe-like flurry of activity as he moves, brownstone and all, from No. 902 (*Murder By the Book*, 1951) to No. 914 (*Prisoner's Base*, 1952), and back to 918 ("Easter Parade," 1956). Apparently Wolfe found this location the most congenial: he was still there in 1960 when the corpse of a woman is found in a taxi in front of that address ("Method Three for Murder.")

Which address is the right one? We've no choice but to believe they all are, since the reports come from Archie Goodwin whose memory, we know, is never wrong. (It's interesting to note that the one address Archie never misses on is a certain penthouse between Madison and Park Avenues on 63rd Street.) One can only surmise that geography wasn't a required subject back in Archie's hometown of Canton, Ohio.

We've all heard of names being changed to protect the innocent, but changing addresses so often must have been hard on those delicate plants. Not to mention the strain on all those decorators who must have been constantly employed making a series of brownstones completely identical. Each variation, of course, had to look as if it had been lived in for twenty years by four particular bachelors who just weren't too particular about the exact location of their house. It sounds ludicrous, but so's the only other possible explanation: shifting the whole four-story structure — pool table, herb garden and all — four blocks or forty feet. At the very least it must have kept Archie footsore at the Flamingo finding plots with cunning little secret passageways to 34th Street. As well as finding a moving company which could move intact not only a whole house but Nero Wolfe as well.

Not that shifting the houses either way would have mattered much. It doesn't take a genius of Wolfe's stature to figure out that every address except No. 506 would be right in the middle of the Hudson River. Terribly convenient for fresh fish and for watering 10,000 orchids, but a bit chancey for asking in people and police. In fact, the real reason for the reluctance of most suspects to answer a summons to Wolfe's door only now becomes apparent. Any doubts about their riverbed living are removed by Archie's statement at the beginning of *Fer-de-Lance* that he "went out for ten minutes worth of air, hoofing it around the piers and back again."

I personally believe Archie's a bit more of a mammal than an amphibian and that those too west and too wet numbers were a blind to discourage women visitors and other unwelcome guests. But he goes to such pains otherwise to locate "the old brownstone house on West 35th Street not far from the Hudson River" that it's aggravating when he can't make up his mind which block it's on. No wonder Lt. Cramer is so annoyed every time he rings that doorbell. Each time he comes he has to check out an entire two blocks just to see where the house may have meandered.

In *In the Best Families* (1950), Archie's description places it about a block from the Hudson. "As I left the West Side Highway at 46th Street I had to cross to Ninth Avenue to turn south," he says. "Turning right on 35th Street, I went on across Tenth Avenue on nearly to Eleventh and pulled to the curb in front of Wolfe's brownstone." But in 1954 and 1974 deduction places the house farther from the river, between Ninth and Tenth Avenues. In "The Next Witness" Wolfe says, "To the garage for the car," and Archie reports they headed west to the garage "on Thirty-Sixth Street near Tenth Avenue." And in *A Family Affair*, Parker drops Archie off at Eighth Avenue so he can stretch his legs for a block and a half.

Nor is Archie satisfied with shifting houses and blocks; in 1953 he's also shifting the flow of traffic in Manhattan. As anyone who's ever been to Macy's can tell you, 35th Street is one way west for everyone. But Archie makes an exception for Pete Drossos. Working the wipe racket at Ninth and 35th, Pete is asked for help by the lady with *The Golden Spiders*. "I thought I might catch the car at Eighth Avenue and ran as fast as I could down 35th," he later tells Archie. One wonders just how fast that car must have been backing up to outrun a fleet street-kid. A harder question is how the car managed to escape at all in the traffic-choked streets of the garment center from Seventh to Ninth Avenues and from 40th to 35th Streets.

I suppose we just have to hold the old brownstone firm in our affections. Trying to place it precisely on West 35th Street doesn't seem to figure in the general scheme of things.

RENOVATIONS TO THE OLD BROWNSTONE

by Patricia Fanning

THE IDEAL way to read the Nero Wolfe mysteries is, of course, in chronological order. If you have been introduced to Archie, Wolfe, and their home on West 35th Street in a piecemeal fashion, however, try reading the early novels with a keen eye to the structure of the old brownstone. The habitat, far from being complete at the start, undergoes numerous subtle (and not so subtle) changes before the familiar floor plans are refined to perfection.

In the initial Wolfe story, *Fer-de-Lance*, the occupants' sleeping arrangements are described in detail: "Fritz slept up above, across the hall from the plant rooms; my room was on the second floor, the same floor as Wolfe's . . ." Theodore slept in a small area partitioned off in a corner of the plant rooms, which are apparently located on the third floor, since Archie hears Wolfe walking in the plant rooms directly over his second-floor bedroom. Quarters, however, were cramped, with no room for visitors. It is not long before the household expands.

Perhaps because of Archie's constant harassment, Wolfe's bank account burgeons, making possible the installation of custom-made plant rooms on the roof. In fact, work may have been in progress during Wolfe's investigation of Peter Oliver Barstow's death since the project was completed by the time Andrew Hibbard and the League of Frightened Men sought assistance. Following his reappearance, Hibbard is brought to West 35th Street. Wolfe gives instructions: "Archie, if you would show Mr. Hibbard the south room, the one above mine." To corroborate the theory that the plants have been moved to the roof, Archie discloses that he climbs three flights from the office to the plant rooms. With Theodore and the plants in expanded quarters, there is a bit more breathing room for the tenants.

Between *Fer-de-Lance* and *The Rubber Band*, Fritz moves his belongings from the third floor to his basement hideaway. It is plausible to assume that renovations on Fritz's basement apartment were concluded shortly after work on the plant rooms had been completed. Undoubtedly, Wolfe would not want strangers in his home longer than necessary. It is fairly certain that Fritz Brenner took up residence in the basement at the same time the orchids were relocated to the roof. This maneuver left the south room available for unexpected house guests.

By the time of *The Rubber Band*, the old plant rooms have been sufficiently renovated for Wolfe to comment about them. Once he decides that Clara Fox must stay in the house, Wolfe assures her that "You will find our south room, directly above mine, quite comfortable." Subsequently, Saul Panzer stays here as well. Wolfe instructs that he be placed in "the north room, Archie, above yours." This room concludes the major renovations to the brownstone.

Archie abandons the second floor for the privacy of the third floor, north room, sometime after he meets Wolfe's adopted daughter in *Over My Dead Body*. Perhaps it is Madame Zorka's escape from the south room that prompts Archie to keep a closer watch on guests who might abuse Wolfe's hospitality. At any rate, when Wolfe agrees to unscramble the affairs of the late Noel Hawthorne in *Where There's a Will*, Archie refers to the south bedroom as "the spare on the same floor as mine." Wolfe remains in his original room although there is very little mention of the spare room which Archie's departure must have left on this floor. By the eighth Wolfe novel, the occupants of the brownstone are permanently ensconced on separate levels.

Although the relocation of sleeping quarters and the expansion of the plant rooms are the only major renovations in Wolfe's house, there are a few minor refinements made as well. Perhaps the most important of these is the soundproofing of the front room. In *Fer-de-Lance,* Archie escorts someone from the office on the pretense that Wolfe must retrieve something from his safe:

> I led the dick into the front room, closing the door behind us. I supposed Wolfe would monkey with the safe door so we could hear the noise, but just in case he didn't take the trouble, I made some sort of conversation so O'Grady's ears wouldn't be disappointed.

Apparently the soundproofing of the front room was not needed in Wolfe's previous, unrecorded cases, but it would soon become a necessity. In *Fer-de-Lance* alone, Archie and Wolfe twice lower their voices to prevent visitors overhearing vital conversations. By the time of "Black Orchids," Archie specifically mentions soundproofing: "Cramer took her to the front room and shut the soundproof door behind him."

Another refinement of the brownstone is the one-way glass panel in the front door. Archie first uses it in *The Rubber Band*:

> I was back in the office but not yet on my sitter again, when the doorbell rang. I wasn't taking any chances, since Fred had gone home and Saul was upstairs asleep. I pulled the curtain away from the glass panel to get a view of the stoop, including corners, and when I saw Cramer was there alone I opened up.

He uses the panel several more times during the investigation. Following this case, however, the panel disappears for a while; on more than one occasion in *Over My Dead Body*, Archie is forced to open the door a crack or peek through a window curtain to see who is at the front door.

Archie uses the panel again in "Black Orchids": "Fritz was upstairs at the moment, so I went for it, and through the glass panel saw it was Inspector Cramer, unattended." The panel is Archie's constant tool after this investigation.

With the reinstitution of the glass panel and the successful soundproofing of the front room, the brownstone is complete. The other special effects had already been introduced. Wolfe's alarm system was present from the beginning. Archie describes his bedroom in *Fer-de-Lance* and explains the alarm system:

> There was nothing unusual about the room, it was just a good room to live in, except for the big gong on the wall under the bed, and that was out of sight. It was connected up so that when Wolfe turned on a switch in his room, which he did every night, the gong would sound if anyone stepped in the hall within five feet of his door or if any of his windows was disturbed, and also it was connected with all entrances to the plant rooms.

Finally, Archie utilizes the peephole to spy on Rudolph Farber in *Over My Dead Body*:

> I . . . proceeded three paces towards the kitchen. Where I stopped there was hanging on the left wall, the one that separated the hall from the office, an old brown wood carving, a panel in three sections. The two side sections were hinged to the middle one. I swung the right section around, stooped a little —

for it had been constructed at the level of Wolfe's eyes — and looked through the peephole, camouflaged on the other side by a painting with the two little apertures backed by gauze, into the office.

It took Archie and Wolfe only about three years to complete refinements on their West 35th Street home. Considering the major renovations needed on the roof, third floor, and basement, that was fast work. Thus, by the time of the events recorded in "Black Orchids," the brownstone had attained the proportions it would maintain throughout the *Corpus*.

MORE THAN
A PAIR O' DOX

by Stephen Schwartz, M. D.

[N. B.: These two articles from speeches delivered at Wolfe Pack assemblies, contain a number of "spoilers." If you have not yet read all of the Corpus — and why on earth haven't you?! — you should be warned that several murderers are named below. — MK]

AS I DID the research for this talk, I must admit I was gratified to see that Nero Wolfe, a man for whom I have a high regard, appears to have a similar high regard for the members of the medical profession.

Not counting Doc Vollmer, doctors appear in the Corpus numerous times. Their roles are anything from being incidental characters, providing major clues, or, on several occasions, being the actual murderers.

The first doctor we encounter in the Corpus is not, as we might suppose, Doc Vollmer, but is actually Nathaniel Bradford, doctor and friend to the Barstow family in Fer-de-Lance. As we recall, Barstow had died while playing golf, and Dr. Bradford had certified the cause of death as a heart attack. Although from a medical perspective this is not unusual or suspicious, Archie believes that Dr. Bradford is covering up his own involvement in the case. He is forced to change his mind when he learns that Dr. Bradford was giving a paper at a medical meeting when Carlo Malfi was murdered. He then goes to see Dr. Bradford, meets him, and is convinced of his innocence.

"One look at Dr. Bradford was enough to show me that I had been casting a lot of pleasant suspicions which might have been avoided if I had happened to catch sight of him somewhere. He was tall and grave and correct, the distinguished old gentleman type, and he had whiskers! There may have been a historical period when it was possible for a guy with whiskers to pull a knife and plunge it into somebody's back, but that was a long time ago. Nowadays, it couldn't be done. Bradford's were gray, so was his hair. To tell the truth, as tight as his alibi for June 5th had been made by my trip to Forty-first Street, I had been prepared to try to find a leak in it until I got a look at him."

This description of a doctor as being a distinguished individual is seen in almost all of the medical characters in the *Corpus*. A notable exception was Theodore Gamm, MD, who came to see Wolfe in *Death of a Doxy*. Dr. Gamm appears wearing a brown tweed overcoat and a smooth blue narrow rimmed hat, an outfit that Archie finds ridiculous. Dr. Gamm is described as short and round all over, not your normal image of a distinguished physician. Dr. Gamm lives up to his appearance by berating Wolfe for taking on the investigation.

Several other doctors have appeared in the *Corpus* playing minor roles. These include:

• The doctor who sews up Wolfe's cheek after he is shot in *Too Many Cooks*;

• Dr. Sackett, who examines Clyde Osgood's body in *Some Buried Caesar*;

• Dr. Horton Soffer, who discovers that the soft drink Beebright has been drinking was drugged, and who examines Nick Berrone's body in "his Won't Kill You"

• The coroner who has done the examination of Marko's body in *The Black Mountain*;

• Dr. Frank Milhaus, who examines the body of Sam Peacock in *Death of a Dude*.

I would like to think that evidence for the high regard given physicians in the *Corpus* is found in the fact that in only one story, *The League of Frightened Men*, is a doctor a murder victim, in this case, Dr. Loring A. Burton.

In *The Father Hunt*, James Odell Worthington, M. D., provides the information that Eugene Jarret is sterile, and therefore cannot be the father of the infant left with Lucy Valdon. In the story "Omit Flowers," Wolfe gets Dr. Frederick M. Cutler to tell him about the attack on Mrs. Floyd Whitten that leads Wolfe to Julie Alving. Dr. Michaels dines with Wolfe in *And Be a Villain*, and gives Wolfe the first concrete evidence about the blackmail plot using weekly magazines. In "A Window for Death," Dr. Frederick Buhl tells Wolfe about the pneumonia patient he had who died when a window was left open on a winter's night. He also tells Wolfe that he checked the air conditioner in Bertram Fyfe's room, and that it could not have made the room cold enough to cause Fyfe's death. Dr. Buhl also supports Nurse

Goren's account of having filled the hot water bottles.

Although Wolfe and Archie have a high regard for doctors, they do not automatically eliminate them from suspicion. In *The League of Frightened Men*, Leopold Elkus is suspected of being Paul Chapin's accomplice in the murder of Dreyer.

In "Cordially Invited to Meet Death," Alan Brady is suspected of infecting Beth Huddleston with tetanus, especially after Archie learns that Dr. Brady collected manure supposedly for the purpose of doing studies with the tetanus germs. It might be noted at this time that medical references in the *Corpus* are relatively accurate. The description of tetanus in this story is quite clear and extremely interesting to modern-day readers who have a connection with the medical profession. Tetanus today is a rare disease in the United States because of the widespread use of tetanus toxoid for immunization. If an author writing a murder story in the present day had the murderer infect Beth Huddleston with tetanus, either nothing would have happened, or she might have gotten a localized infection that would be easily treated with antibiotics. I guess this is an example of how modern-day medicine makes a mystery writer's life more difficult. However, in defense of my profession, new medical techniques have opened many doors for mystery writers as well as for writers of other forms of fiction.

Wolfe and Archie are not above revealing the fact that doctors are human, and can even be murderers. In two instances it is indeed the physician who is responsible for the taking of a human life, in both cases using his medical knowledge or position.

In *Gambit*, Dr. Victor Avery is asked by Matthew Blount about what substance he can put in Paul Jerrin's chocolate that will make him ill and unable to continue with the chess match. Avery uses this knowledge of Blount's trick to poison Jerrin with arsenic while treating his illness, leaving the finger of suspicion pointing at Blount.

I will leave my discussion of the second murderer for a while in order to talk about our favorite doctor.

Any discussion of doctors and Nero Wolfe would not be complete without mention of Edwin A. Vollmer, M. D. Although he is a familiar character in the *Corpus*, we actually know very little about him. We know that he lives about 60 yards from Wolfe's house, with a housekeeper, Helen Gillard, to quote Archie, a dark-haired woman with fine frontage (*The Final Deduction*). He is described as a sad-looking little guy with lots of forehead and not much jaw. He has at least one son, Bill, in whose room Archie and Wolfe stay in *The Final Deduction*. At that time Bill is away at college.

Although no one in the brownstone is ever significantly ill, we know that Vollmer takes care of medical problems at the brownstone because of remarks made by Wolfe. When Archie indicates that he did not make a deposit because it was raining, Wolfe asks him to call Doc Vollmer; Archie then tells us that was Wolfe's way of saying Archie must be sick if he would let a little rain deter him.

Even though we never see Vollmer treating Wolfe or Archie, it is apparent that Vollmer is actually Ben Casey, Marcus Welby, Quincy, and Dr. Kildare all rolled into one. We first meet Vollmer in *The League of Frightened Men*, when Archie gets him to sew up the self-inflicted wound on Dora Chapin's neck (Ben Casey). He later comes to tend to Archie as he is recovering from his drugging at the hand of Dora (Marcus Welby). In *The Second Confession*, Wolfe asks Vollmer to play the role of a pathologist when he sends him to White Plains to examine the body of Louis Rony (Quincy). In addition, he is called to the brownstone several times to examine the various victims who have met their demise in or near the premises: Cynthia Brown ("Disguise for Murder"), Borden McNair (*The Red Box*), and Phoebe Gunther (*The Silent Speaker*). Archie calls for him to examine Bertha Aaron in "Eeny Meeny Murder Mo," but for the only time I could find in the entire *Corpus*, Vollmer is out.

Vollmer is also a font of knowledge for Archie and Wolfe. He knows all the doctors in New York and can identify them for Archie, confirms medical statements given by all kinds of medical specialists, knows where to send bogus iodine to be tested and gets results almost immediately, and can even tell Archie where to get information on the medical aspects of dry ice.

Vollmer really knows his stuff playing Dr. Kildare, when asked to help Wolfe, who is feigning a breakdown and persecution complex (*The Silent Speaker*). Archie reminds him that he owes Wolfe a favor since Wolfe helped him with a phony malpractice case. Vollmer points out that he offered to do Wolfe a favor any time Wolfe asked, but he signs the medical certificate, even though Wolfe does not personally ask for help, and then holds the fort against the pressures generated by the police.

One could question the ethics of Doc Vollmer as he is involved in many of Wolfe's adventures, since he is not above failing to report several instances of violent crimes to the police. However, he does show a high regard for legal procedures, when, in "Disguise for Murder," he refuses to leave the room after examining the body, but instead stands in the corner while covering his ears so he can't hear the discussion between Wolfe and Archie.

It is a tribute to Doc Vollmer's character that we all feel we know him very well and would all love to have him for our personal physician, even though we are given so little factual information about this remarkable man.

You may have realized that I have not yet spoken about the second physician murderer found in the *Corpus*. This is because I found this particular crime fascinating, and did considerable research into the situation.

In "The Gun with Wings," Albert Mion is murdered by his physician, Dr. Nicholas Lloyd. Dr. Lloyd had operated on Mion's throat after it was damaged in the fight with Gifford James, and had botched the job. Since this fact would be revealed when Mion planned to get a second opinion from Dr. Abraham Rentner, Dr. Lloyd killed Mion by placing a gun in his mouth while examining his throat thus making the murder look like a suicide. Wolfe and Archie explain that when a doctor examines someone's throat, the patient invariably looks up during the examination, affording the chance to place a foreign object into the unknowing patient's mouth, in this case a gun. As a physician I initially found this scenario hard to believe, since an examination of Mion's throat, after the type of surgery he had, would have required specialized equipment, rather than just a light and a tongue depressor. However, I realized that while this might be evident to a physician, it would not be so to laymen, who would see nothing unusual about the examination.

This method of murder continued to intrigue me, so when I did my research for this talk, I included a scientific study to determine the feasibility of committing a murder in this way. Since I am a pediatrician, I examined twenty pediatric patients to see if their eyes would actually roll up when their throats were examined. The results of this very scientifically controlled study were as follows: 70% of patients looked me straight in the eye. If eyes could speak words, I couldn't repeat them here. 10% threw up, 10% ate the stick, 5% required three people hold them down, and only 5% rolled their eyes up. In evaluating this data I came to the following conclusions: 1. Pediatricians should continue their policy of not wearing their best suits to the office; 2. Pediatric patients would not be good candidates for this type of murder because they don't trust their doctors and therefore won't take their eyes off them.

I conclude that although Mion's behavior at times could only be described as infantile, his trust in his physician was more adult. If, however, my statistics would hold true for the adult population, then Dr. Lloyd was extremely lucky that Mion was one of the few people who roll their eyes up when their throats are being examined.

In summary, I can only happily say that, unlike members of the legal profession, members of the medical profession can share in Wolfe's and Archie's adventures knowing that they are considered friends, allies, and fellow members of the human race by these two superlative detectives. I welcome the rebuttal from members of the legal profession at next year's Assembly.

NOT A WOLF IN THE PACK

It has been of interest to me that Nero Wolfe, that stay-at-home gourmet whose favorite relationship with the animal kingdom is that of eater to eatee, has been involved in several cases in which animals (the living kind) have played a major part. Animals have had a significant part in fourteen of the cases that Archie has reported to us.

A reading of the *Corpus* tells of many things about the relationship between those living in the brownstone on 35th Street and the animal kingdom.

In "Die Like a Dog," Archie tells us that Theodore, besides caring for Wolfe's orchids, has time also to care for at least two parakeets, and Fritz has a turtle that we can assume is kept for a reason other than providing an ingredient for turtle soup.

Archie was born on a farm in Ohio, and Iherefore must have an understanding of the role of the animal kingdom in current society. He is at home with many non-human creatures he encounters during his activities, and is prepared for almost everything. Tripping over an alligator (????), playing tag with a chimpanzee (????), and ducking from two bears (????) who are fleeing from the chimp does strain our hero's abilities to the limit, however. He even considers "chimpicide" when Mister "laughs at him."

Archie's most common interaction with the animal world is with the finned variety of beast. Before *Too Many Cooks*, he was fishing in Maine for his vacation. In *Please Pass the Guilt*, Archie spends a Saturday afternoon on a boat in Long Island Sound fishing with Sylvia Venner. He can show his fishing ability by catching flounder, using salmon eggs for bait. He explains that they had spent several hours trying for stripers and blues without success. Only fairly experienced fisherman go out looking for specific types of fish, and know the different types of bait needed for each.

However, we have earlier evidence of Archie's fishing skill. In "Immune to Murder," Archie decides to spend some time fishing while Wolfe is preparing to cook brook trout for his host and the other guests. Archie has told us that since the age of seven he cannot look at wild water without thinking two things: 1) "There must be fish in it, and 2) they needed to be taught a lesson." After being snubbed by Adria Kelefy and Sally Leeson, Archie begins his fishing adventure by sitting in a lounge chair on the back lawn, and casting his fly into the water. As luck would have it, he gets a strike, but it is only "Junior."

At this time, Archie shows his concern for wildlife and nature. Since Junior is too small to keep, Archie leaves his chair to use a wet hand so that the fish can be released safely back into the stream. Many of us, if trying to make an impression as Archie was trying to do, might not have bothered to show the concern for his fellow creature as he does. It is a short time later that Archie's true sporting spirit shows. While fishing on the stream, Archie hooks Grandpa and begins the fight to land the fish. Coming around a bend in the river, two things occur almost simultaneously. Archie sees the fish and finds a body. Being a true sportsman, Archie makes sure of his catch while simultaneously examining the body and pulling it from the water. Indeed, we are given a lesson in playing a large fish as Archie explains how to give line or hold tension on the line when needed. One question not answered is what happened to the fish? We can presume that the fish must have been taken for evidence since we are told that the police did take the Ambassador's fish.

Archie has had other experience with animals as evidenced by his keen eye when describing Keyes' horse in "Bullet for One," or the several horses in *Too Many Cooks*. One final word about Archie. I have spent several hours wondering about the long story of how Archie's best belt was eaten by a porcupine (????). The possibilities are endless and intriguing.

Nero Wolfe's attitude toward animals is more difficult to understand. Early in the *Corpus,* the only animals in the brownstone besides Theodore's parakeets and Fritz's turtle are Wolfe's aphids and other creepy crawlers that occasionally infest Wolfe's orchids, and we know how Wolfe feels about the latter. In "Immune to Murder," Wolfe shows a knowledge of fish when he refuses to cook the Ambassador's trout, but this represents his knowledge of food rather than live animals.

We are told by Archie in "Home to Roost" that "there has never been a dog in that house" when he chooses to leave Mrs. Rackell's collie in the taxi. However, Wolfe's apparently negative feelings about having dogs in the brownstone are called into question by his attitude in "Die Like a Dog," when Archie brings a Labrador Retriever home, an episode I will discuss in detail a little later.

Although Wolfe lives in NYC, most of the animals in the *Corpus* are not what we would normally consider common domestic house pets. Dogs appear in only three stories, and cats in none unless we include Archie's looking for his "wife's" cat as he flees from Miltan's studio in *Over My Dead Body,* or the code phrase, "A cat may look at a king," used in *The Doorbell Rang.*

Horses appear in the Corpus the most often, six times (twice within NYC). However, most often the animals we hear about are of a more exotic variety (including alligators, chimpanzees, pigeons (????), bears, snakes (????), and bulls (*Some Buried Caesar*).

At this point I would like to discuss some of the cases in which animals play a large part, either in developing the plot or in the actual solution of the case.

In the very first case reported by Archie (*Fer-de-Lance*), Wolfe deduces that Peter Oliver Barstow was killed with a needle that had been coated with snake venom. When Wolfe kills the snake that Manuel Kimball has left in his desk drawer, he identifies the snake as the fer-de-lance, or Bothrops atrox, the most dreaded of the vipers except for the bushmaster. The *Encyclopedia Britannica* tells us that the fer-de-lance, also known as the barba amarilla or yellow chin, is about 4-7 feet long. It has a bite that can be fatal to humans. The Bothrops atrax, however, is not the most deadly snake in South America. It seems unlikely that the venom could be so toxic that the small amount that could be smeared on a needle would be fatal. It is true that there are several different snakes found in South America that are commonly called the fer-de-lance, including the habus, wutu, jumping viper, and jararaca.

The habus does not have a very potent venom, but its bite might cause death. The wutu and jumping viper do not appear to be especially dangerous. On the other hand, the jararaca, a snake found mainly in Brazil, is similar in appearance to the Bothrops atrox. It has a more toxic venom, being responsible for many deaths from its bite. It would appear that the jararaca is a more likely candidate for the snake used by Kimball, than the true fer-de-lance that Wolfe identifies. I leave it to you to decide if Wolfe has gotten careless in his identification of this snake, or if Manuel Kimball had found a method of concentrating the venom of his true fer-de-lance.

In the novel, *In the Best Families*, we recall that when Mrs. Rackham is murdered, her injured dog Nobby comes to Leed's house. When Archie and Leeds find the dog, Nobby bares his teeth and snarls. Wolfe later uses this fact to bolster his deduction that Leeds had murdered Mrs. Rackham. He points out that she was stabbed before the dog, and only someone who knew and could control the dog would have been able to stab her. Wolfe then goes on to say that Nobby did not come to Leed's door because he wanted to be with a friend when he died, but because he wanted "to sink his teeth into [Leeds] just once."

Wolfe's evidence for this is because when Leeds put his hand on the dog, Nobby snarls at him. I find this scenario hard to believe. Those of us who know dogs know that they are wonderful animals, but are not so reasoning as Wolfe would have them be. In fact, when we inadvertently hurt our dogs, they may snarl or snap immediately, but then are forgiving and remorseful as they try to earn our good favor again. It would be more likely that Nobby was snarling at the presence of a stranger, namely Archie, than he was snarling at Leeds. I would like to think that Wolfe was well aware of this, but that he couldn't resist the chance to add to the punishment he was handing out.

The third example of Wolfe's interaction with the animal kingdom I feel is especially fitting for a meeting of The Wolfe Pack. After all, since discussions of the relative merits of beer and wine are no longer permitted [*A reference to a belabored debate between me and Werowance Jonathan Levine.* — MK] , where will the bull come in. Then, of course I am referring to Hickory Caesar Grindon, the national champion AR Guernsey bull (in *Some Buried Caesar*, of course). Wolfe is able to solve the case when he realizes that the bull in the pasture was not Caesar, but his brother, Hickory Buckingham Pell. Wolfe obtains the sketches of the bulls from the National Guernsey League, and uses them to make copies in his notebook. He then uses these copies to make the murderer confess. It may seem unrealistic to think that the identification of a champion bull or cow would be formalized by hand-drawn pictures, but that is the method used even today. However, in place of sketches, tattoos or photographs can be used as an alternative when registering your Guernsey bull or cow. At the time *Some Buried Caesar* occurs, tattoos would only have been used for solid color animals.

The AR or Advanced Register referred to in the book was a method of determining the quantity and quality of the milk produced by a cow. Meeting set requirements enabled the farmer to have a cow placed in the Advanced Register. Records were kept on how many AR cows a bull had produced. This was done in an attempt to improve the quality of the dairy herd. The person who did the testing of the milk was required to remain on the farm overnight, measuring milk samples from the cows being tested. This cumbersome process has been replaced by a more automated series of tests. The name of the listing has also been changed from AR to DHIR or Dairy Herd Improvement Register.

The final episode I would like to examine is the entrance of a new member into the brownstone on 35th Street, namely Jet, Nero, or Bootsy, depending on who is calling him. Jet follows Archie home from a building in which a murder has occurred, and Archie decides to ride Wolfe by bringing the dog into the house. Archie explains that he wants to have a pet, since Fritz has his turtle and Theodore his parakeets. Wolfe, however, surprises Archie by reminiscing about the mongrel he had as a boy in Montenegro. Soon Jet (or Nero as Archie calls him) is settled down in the house. This brings me to the major mystery in the *Corpus*, one I believe has never been answered. In all the *Corpus* there is a continuity of episodes and experiences. When Archie wants a new car after the end of a story, he may get that at the beginning of the next story. Archie is constantly referring to earlier episodes while telling us about Wolfe's current case. After "Die Like a Dog," the dog is apparently a member of the household in good standing since Archie assures us that "he responds to Jet now as if his mother had started calling him that before he had his eyes open." WHAT HAPPENS TO JET? We never hear of him again. It is as if Jet never existed. Knowing Wolfe, can we deduce what has happened to him? It seems that there are only a few possibilities:

1. The dog was claimed by someone from Kampf's family. Possible, but if Wolfe wanted to keep Jet I'm sure he would have found a way.

2. Jet committed an unpardonable sin and was banished from the household. This seems to be a possible solution, but what could the sin have been? Could Jet have stolen the goose, thereby short-circuiting one of Wolfe's relapses? Could Jet have mistaken one of Wolfe's prize orchids for the fire hydrant that must have been near, but outside the house? Since Archie, however, seems to agree with the prohibition of the mention of the dog, Jet must have done something that gravely offended both he and Wolfe. This is more difficult to imagine. Could Jet have eaten the red chair? Could Archie and Wolfe both have missed an obvious clue, and did the population of the brownstone increase dramatically when Jet presented the household with seven puppies?

To paraphrase Archie as he begins telling us the story "Cordially Invited to Meet Death," if you think that the story in "Die Like a Dog" is over when the murderer is caught, all I have to say is you don't know a mystery when you see one.

LON COHEN: ACE JOURNALIST?

by Joel Levy

LON COHEN is a powerful information source for Wolfe. His central position at *The Gazette* puts him at the center of a network of information provided by this major New York daily. For a meal and an occasional scoop, he shares this information with Wolfe and Archie. He appears first in *The Silent Speaker*, which was published in 1946.

This initial appearance is not very auspicious, but we should begin this little discourse by recalling Cohen's role in this, his first appearance on the scene of Wolfe's world. The first reference to Cohen is on page 179 of *The Silent Speaker*. [*The author does not specify which edition.* — MK] Wolfe is in the middle of the Cheney Boone muddle, when Archie notes, "Friends on papers, especially Lon Cohen of *The Gazette*, thought I ought to tell them exactly who would be arrested and when and where." That's it — certainly not meritorious.

Later, when Archie needs to know where Inspector Cramer is (remember he has been deposed in the investigation by the crude Inspector Ash), he naturally gets in touch with Cohen. "Lon Cohen told me he had taken a two weeks' leave of absence, for sulking, and when I dialed the number of Cramer's home he answered the phone himself." Believe it or not, that's it. There is no further sharing of information and, in fact, when the surprise murderer . . . [*Here the author names the murderer.* — MK] is identified, Archie does not rush to the phone to give Cohen the scoop.

In his second appearance in the *Corpus*, however, acknowledgment is made of Cohen's stature at *The Gazette* and as a premier journalist. Here, in *Too Many Women*, according to Archie, Lon "knew more facts than the Police Department and the Public Library combined." His predecessor at *The Gazette*, Harry Foster, also provided Wolfe and Archie with information, but Harry never grew to the stature at the newspaper that Lon achieves. He appears in forty-four stories, more than any character in the saga except Wolfe, Archie, Fred Durkin, Fritz Brenner, and Saul Panzer. He is also a close friend of Archie's, and is a regular at the weekly poker game played at Saul's apartment. In fact, Archie says he is the best player next to Saul. It might be instructive for a moment to check out this poker ritual. Although there does seem to be a minor change in the evenings when the game is played, most of the time it is on Thursday. In the last game played, in *Death On Deadline* [*The 2nd novel of the Nero Wolfe continuations by Robert Goldsborough* — MK], the players are Archie, Lon, Saul Panzer, Fred Durkin, and Bill Gore. The first four of these are certainly the core group, although others, even including Fritz Brenner, have been known to sit in. Saul and Lon are the best players and, apparently, Archie doesn't usually fare too poorly.

Archie says that Lon "had been rank and file, or maybe only rank, when I first met him, but was now second in command at *The Gazette's* city desk" (*The Second Confession*). Later, in *The Golden Spiders*, Archie says:

> I don't know what Lon Cohen is on *The Gazette* and I doubt if he does. City or wire, daily or Sunday, foreign or national or local, he seems to know his way in and around without ever having to work at it. His is the only desk in a room about nine by twelve, and that's just as well because otherwise there would be no place for his feet, which are also about nine by twelve. From the ankles up he is fairly regular.

He is in his mid-forties, placing him somewhat older than Archie, and married. We can be firm about his being married from two references. The first is from *Gambit*, where he and Archie are discussing the attractions of Anna Blount. Lon says, "I've told my wife that she needn't wonder what I'll do if she dies. I'll get Anna Blount. I don't know how, but I'll get her." Later, "As you know, I'm happily married, and my wife is healthy, and I hope she lives forever, but it's nice to know that such a one as Anna Blount is around just in case."

In *Death on Deadline*, Lon and Archie are sharing a cab ride home and discussing the bleak future at *The Gazette* if Ian MacLaren takes over. Lon is threatening to quit and tells Archie, "What the hell, my profit-sharing and pension will take care of my wife and me just fine for the rest of our lives."

In *Too Many Clients* he is described by Archie as follows: "He was very dark — dark skin stretched tight over his neat little face, dark brown eyes, hair almost black, slicked back and up over his sloping dome." He obviously relishes good food, and is easily bribed by Wolfe with a meal from Fritz. Just a good steak, cooked by Fritz, sits well with him. Especially followed by an excellent brandy from Wolfe's superb cellar. On balance, he and Wolfe enjoy a sense of parity, information services for news scoops.

Cohen is obviously Jewish, and with Saul Panzer, serves to acknowledge Stout's knowledge that Jews make up a large percentage of the New York City population. Unfortunately, like Panzer, he is not very Jewish. He eats the continental cuisine served by Fritz Brenner, and never displays any Jewishness. Of course, it is not essential for Stout to endow any characters with unique behavioral factors that would equate them with their heritage. One of his peculiarities, in fact, is that all the characters appear to have sprung from a Midwestern area. All, that is, except Wolfe himself. Even Fritz, with only occasional lapses, does not really appear Swiss. As Stephen Pearl notes in his forthcoming article in *The Gazette*, entitled "Nero Wolfe — Linguist," Wolfe never even takes the opportunity to speak French to Fritz, although the latter can be found occasionally to utter oaths in his native tongue.

With an Italian wife, Fred Durkin never displays any knowledge of Italian — although Stout does have him drink like the Irishman he is. One doesn't often think of the heritage-less creatures who populate the world of Nero Wolfe, but there it is. All the characters are true-blood Americans, with nary a trace of their forebears. But this whole area is best saved for another time — I plan to address it in the future.

Despite the number of times Lon appears in the *Corpus*, we actually know little about him. We don't know how he came to the journalism game, nor do we know the path to success he followed. When we first meet him, he is already there — right up at the top.

[ED. — *This little report was first presented at the Tenth Nero Wolfe Assembly in December, 1988.*]

THE RUSTERMAN HUNT
by Phil Fischer

RUSTERMAN'S Restaurant occupies the first three floors of a building on Lexington Avenue between 49th and 50th Streets. The front door on the first floor is attended by a doorman and just inside the door is a cloakroom to drop off your hat and overcoat and an elevator to carry you to the upper floors. Beyond is the big front room, which must be crossed on the way to the dining room that is used by the dinner crowd. The front room is used by luncheon customers and there is a green rope to control those waiting for a table. It has a bar at the far side and a side door to the outside world. There are tables throughout the room and a banquette at the left wall.

The kitchen lies beyond the dining room at the rear of the first floor along with storage areas for food, linens, table service items and miscellaneous equipment There is also a locker room for the restaurant employees to keep their personal belongings. Outside behind the restaurant there is a receiving platform and a narrow alley, which begins at a side street about fifteen yards away and ends at the wall of a building a few feet beyond the platform. The kitchen windows are painted on the inside to prevent curious children observing kitchen routines.

The second floor is a continuation of the first floor dining room, probably used to handle overflow. There are curtained booths along the left wall providing privacy for the diners who can draw or open the curtains as desired.

The third floor houses the restaurant's office in the front and three rooms for dinner parties in the rear. The smallest of these rooms is soundproof and is used by Wolfe, Archie, and Fritz Brenner on their monthly visits to the restaurant.

There is also an apartment on this floor which was used as living quarters by Marko Vukcic before he relocated to the top floor of a building on East 54th Street. After Vukcic's death, the apartment was occupied by Felix Martin and his family until the children were grown and moved out.

Rusterman's Restaurant was owned and operated by Marko

Vukcic, a boyhood friend of Nero Wolfe. Vukcic came to America from Montenegro in 1929 and is first mentioned in the *Corpus* in the *Some Buried Caesar* case in 1937, when he was master chef at Rusterman's and a member of Les Quinze Maitres (The Fifteen Masters), a group comprising the best chefs in the world. Marko Vukcic had a special chair built that could withstand Wolfe's seventh of a ton. The chair was kept in Vukcic's personal den and moved to the small dining room when Wolfe came to dinner.

When Vukcic died in 1954, he willed one-third interests in the restaurant to waiters Felix, Joe, and Leo. Felix took over management and the position of Maitre d'. Interestingly, Felix is given three names in the *Corpus*. He is Felix Martin in *The Black Mountain* (1954), Felix Courbet in "Poison a la Carte" (1958) and Felix Maurer in *A Family Affair* (1974).

There are more than seventy people employed at Rusterman's Restaurant. Other emnployees mentioned in the *Corpus* included Philip Correla, cook; Pierre Ducos, Wolfe's personal waiter; Ernest, waiter; Noel, waiter and goose-napper; Zoltan, cook; Vincent, doorman, and Bruno, waiter.

There are several clues in the *Corpus* to the location of Rusterman's Restaurant.

In *The Black Mountain* (1954), Wolfe and Archie walked from Marko Vukcic's residence on 54th Street between Lexington and Third Avenue, four blocks up Lexington and through five intersections to Rusterman`s.

In *If Death Ever Slept* (1957), Archie walked thirty blocks from Rusterman's Restaurant to the Jarrel mansion on Fifth Avenue in the seventies.

In "Murder Is Corny" (1961), the farmer's daughter asked Archie to meet her at the 48th Street entrance to the alley at the rear of Rusterman's.

In *Please Pass The Guilt* (1969), Archie and Lon Cohen walked the eleven blocks from Rusterman's to Saul Panzer's residence on 38th Street between Lexington and Third Avenues.

In *A Family Affair* (1973), Archie and Wolfe were seated at a table near a window that looked down on Madison Avenue. Walking north 'up' Lexington Avenue from Marko Vukcic's residence on 54th Street to reach Rusterman's Restaurant would eliminate both the Jarrel mansion and the Saul Panzer residence clues since the Jarrel mansion wouid have to be on Fifth Avenue in the eighties and the Panzer residence more than sixteen blocks from Rusterman's. However, walking four blocks south 'down'

Lexington Avenue from Marko Vukcic's residence on 54th would put Rusterman's Restaurant on the west side of Lexington Avenue between 49th Street and 50th Street. The Jarrel mansion is then thirty blocks away in the seventies on Fifth Avenue and Saul Panzer's residence is eleven blocks from the restaurant and the alley entrance on 48th Street is only one block south of the alley behind the restaurant.

Acceptance of the clue from *A Family Affair* that the table occupied by Archie and Wolfe overlooked Madison Avenue would negate clues in *If Death Ever Slept*, "Murder is Corny" and *Please Pass the Guilt* and is therefore considered errata. In fact, that table must have overlooked Lexington Avenue. Perhaps Archie was sampling too many cocktails at this particular dinner.

TAKE A LETTER: SECRETARIES IN THE CORPUS

by Jean Quinn Manzo

[N. B.: The identity of many murderers in the Nero Wolfe mysteries are revealed in this article. — MK]

A wide variety of professions are found in the *Corpus*, but perhaps no occupation is more strongly represented than that of the secretary. Stout knew secretaries were an excellent device to move the story along. Many secretaries work for wealthy people who find it necessary to engage a famous private detective. Secretaries answer phones, type and send letters and contracts, make appointments, and talk indiscriminately to co-workers. Secretaries generally have an intimate knowledge of their employers' business and personal affairs and can give Wolfe valuable information. And secretaries have been known to become romantically involved with their employers.

Perhaps, too, sexism is involved. As Joel Levy says in "Doctors in the *Corpus*" (*The Gazette*, Winter 1990), Wolfe is a misogynist and Archie sexist, and Stout is their creator. A secretary is a woman in her proper place. Her status as a subordinate makes her submissive and more likely to be victimized, although it is hard to think of some of Stout's secretaries in these terms.

I believe I have a unique perspective of the secretaries in the *Corpus*. I trained as a secretary, then advanced to the point where I had a secretary, and now find I am a secretary again. Of course if I had read Rex Stout in my youth I surely would have chosen a less violent profession.

I have used my expertise in the secretarial arena to prepare brief biographies of the secretaries in the *Corpus* which I hope you will find informative and entertaining. I have listed the secretaries under categories. Sonic secretaries fall under two or more categories; such as Amy Duncan ("Bitter End"), former secretary to a murder victim, employed by a murder suspect, and Wolfe's client. I have taken editorial license in categorising — usually choosing the more sensational category.

I have also included stenographers, as the primary difference between secretaries and stenographers is the salary grade of the dictators and transcribers and not the work involved. Included also are former secretaries by dint of their continuing relationships with former employers and/or associates.

Archie refers to himself as a secretary ("Bitter End," *Too Many Cooks*) when listing his numerous duties. As the *Corpus'* most famous and certainly most gifted secretary, Archie's phenomenal skills and his duties will be addressed in detail at a later date.

Secretaries as Murderers

Sarah Dacos (*The Doorbell Rang*) — Secretary to Mrs. Lloyd (Rachel) Bruner, Sarah is tempestuous enough to murder her lover, and clever enough to throw suspicion on the FBI. She reads Keats.

Jean Estey (*The Golden Spiders*) — Jean described herself as "a sweet innocent small town girl from Nebraska." Comely, greenish brown eyes, and under 30, Miss Estey dresses as a man to kill 12 year old Pete Drossos, and kills Matthew Birch and Mrs. Damon "Laura" Fromm, her employer, to protect her lucrative blackmailing of displaced persons.

Secretaries as Murder Victims

Bertha Aaron ("Eeny, Meeny, Murder, Mo") — Private secretary to senior law partner Lamont Otis. She is strangled with Wolfe's necktie in his office. Bertha was 42 years old, 120 lbs., and wore sensible shoes. She was murdered by Rita (Mrs. Morton) Sorrell.

Delia Brandt (*Might as Well Be Dead*) — She had a mind that soared, which is probably why her boss, Mike Molloy, never discussed business with her. He did buy her dinner and slap her around. Delia drank gin and ginger ale. She was murdered by Patrick Degan.

Elinor Denovo aka Carlotta Vaughn (*The Father Hunt*) — Carlotta Vaughn was Mrs. Jarrett's, then Mr Jarrett's secretary. Following the birth of her child and under the name of Elinor Denovo, she started as stenographer advancing to vice president of Raymond Thorne Productions. Raymond Thorne told Archie, "Of course I had my secretary and she had hers, but she still did shorthand, and dictating to her made it different. It came out better."

James L. Eber (*If Death Ever Slept*) — Jim was accused of leaking information to Otis Jarrell's business rivals and was fired. Single, he played golf and bridge. He was murdered by Jarrell's snake of a daughter-in-law, Susan (Mrs. Wyman) Jarrell.

Phoebe Gunther (*The Silent Speaker*) — Beautiful, blond and 27, Phoebe worshiped her boss, Cheney Boone. Wolfe says, "She had displayed remarkable tenacity, audacity, and even imagination, in using the murder of Mr. Boone for a purpose he would have approved." Phoebe was murdered by Alger Kates.

Naomi Karn (*Where There's a Will*) — Naomi quits secretarial work to become Noel Hawthorne's mistress and, when he is murdered, a major beneficiary in his will. Not bad for a girl who started out in the steno pool and two years later became secretary to a junior partner of Dunwoodie, Prescott & Davis. Naomi was murdered by Glenn Prescott.

Bonny Sommers (Mrs. Martin) Kirk ("Blood Will Tell") — Bonny worked for an architectural firm prior to marriage to an employee at age 25. She was murdered by her landlord, James Neville Vance.

Dinah Utley (*The Final Deduction*) — Secretary of seven years to Mrs. Jimmy (Althea) Vail, she conspires with her employers to cheat on their income tax with a fake kidnapping. Wolfe immediately suspects her of complicity. Her attempt to convince her employer to abandon the plan fails. Mrs. Vail murders Dinah, and subsequently her husband, Jimmy.

Secretaries as Murder Suspects

Joan Snyder (Mrs. Dennis) Ashby ("Kill Now, Pay Later") — A former secretary with financial and alcohol problems was suspected of killing her husband. A big girl with dark eyes, Joan's alibi was that she was shopping.

Viola Duday (*Prisoner's Base*) — Viola was the secretary, then assistant to the president. A rugged individualist, she doesn't wear lipstick. She is suspected of killing Priscilla Eads.

Gwynne Ferris (*Too Many Women*) — A non-spelling stenographer who looked like a Powers model had been dating Hester Livsey's fiancee.

Celia Fleet (*Where There's a Will*) — Celia and Andy Hawthorne find Noel Hawthorne's body. Her alibi was that she was answering her employer's fan mail.

Julia McGee (*Too Many Clients*) -Julia has my vote as "Secretary from Hell." Secretary to the licentious Thomas Yeager, she sleeps with the boss, betrays his confidences, and lends a key to the love nest to the co-worker who kills him. Wolfe calls her a harpy or a lamia, "not judging you, merely classifying you."

Beth Tiger (*A Right to Die*) — A beautiful stenographer, Beth would have been a better choice than Liz Taylor to play Cleopatra. Her drink is gin and tonic and she is in love with murder suspect Dunbar Whipple. Beth has the distinction of being the only black secretary in the *Corpus*.

Anne Tracy ("Black Orchids") — Secretary to the President of the firm, she was the first female in captivity to wear a black orchid. Archie refers to her as his future wife and says her legs "are absolutely artistic." Wolfe disagrees, her legs are too long from the knees down. Her salary is garnisheed each week to repay her father's theft. She was suspected of killing Harry Gould.

Secretaries as Potential Murder Victims

Helen Lugos (*Please Pass the Guilt*) — The bomb in Browning's desk drawer killed Peter Odell, but the investigation is hampered by not knowing who the bomb was intended to kill. Secretary to Amory Browning, Helen wouldn't say whether she checked the bourbon supply in her boss's desk every day. Kenneth Meer knew she did.

ElmaVassos ("Kill Now, Pay Later") -The daughter of Wolfe's bootblack, Elma says "I'm a stenographer. Not anybody's secretary." Wolfe fears an attempt on her life, so Elma moves in with the "greatest man in the world," and Archie, too.

Secretaries to Murder Victims

Charlotte Adams (*Murder by the Book*) — Charlotte refuses to believe her boss, James A. Corrigan, committed murder, betrayed his partner and/or committed suicide. Of course she was fond of him — he had always done quite a bit of his own typing.

Mr. Blaine (*Fer-de-Lance*) — Secretary to E. D. Kimball, Blaine professes "I know more about his business than he does." He has a square jaw.

Lina Darrow (*In the Best Families*) — Archie never saw a finer pair of eyes although she underplayed what was behind them. Lina put those eyes on Barry Rackham, attempting to expose him as the murderer of his wife, her employer, Sarah Rackham.

Selma (Mrs. Michael) Molloy (*Might as Well Be Dead*) — She fully deserved to be called Selma. When she married the boss, Mike Molloy, Delia Brandt got the job.

Maryella Timms ("Cordially Invited to Meet Death") — The anonymous letters to employer Bess Huddleston were typed on Maryella's typewriter. In the course of the investigation, Bess is murdered and Maryella teaches Wolfe to cook corned beef hash with chitlins. A southern belle, her appearance is in no way disappointing. She gets closer to Wolfe than any woman Archie has ever seen, "her hand slipped between his arm and his bulk."

Secretaries as Clients or Potential Clients

Amy Duncan ("Bitter End") — Wolfe is after the person who put quinine in his food and Amy has something better than money — information. Amy, the niece and former stenographer to murder victim Arthur Tingley, finds his dead body. She is employed as secretary to murder suspect Leonard Cliff.

Lucy (Mrs. Barry) Hazen ("Death of a Demon") — Lucy was the secretary to an inventor when she met and married a black-mailer. Wolfe clears her name. Lucy has nice teeth and wears mink.

Nora Kent (*If Death Ever Slept*) — Calling Nora Kent a stenographer "was like calling Willie Mays a bat boy." Her personal net worth was over a million dollars and she wanted her interests protected. Wolfe already had her boss, Otis Jarrell, as a client.

Secretaries to Murderers

Lucille Adams (*Where There's a Will*) — The former secretary to Glenn Prescott, her death from tuberculosis removed an impediment to rewriting Noel Hawthorne's will.

Miss Fromm (*Champagne for One*) — Miss Fromm simplifies introductions by giving Archie the names of those attending the Grantham House Annual Dinner. She is employed by Mrs. Robert Robilotti.

Dorothy Riff ("Invitation to Murder") — "As a spectacle there wasn't a thing wrong with her." However her boss, Theodore Huck, murdered his wife for the housekeeper.

Dorothy did not return to Huck the watch from Tiffany's.

Audrey Rooney aka Annie Rooney ("Bullet for One") — Former secretary to murderer Victor Talbott, Audrey had been unjustly fired for theft.

Secretaries Secretarying

Miss Barish (*The Rubber Band*) — Ramsey Muir's secretary of eleven years is homely and emotional. She doesn't like Clara Fox, but doesn't falsely implicate her in a theft.

Claire Burkhardt (*Murder By the Book*) — Claire is just out of high school, or cheating.

Sue Dondero (*Murder By the Book*) — Archie's idea of a girl to have around. Sue is secretary to law partner Emmett Phelps.

Judith Frey (*Plot It Yourself*) — An attractive young woman with a clear strong voice found evidence for a plagiarism claim in a filing cabinet.

Eleanor Gruber (*Murder By the Book*) — Louis Kustin's secretary, her eyes didn't actually slant.

Charlotte Haber (*Please Pass the Guilt*) — Archie notices her surprise when he begins to touch type. Secretary to Mrs. Peter J. Odell, Charlotte knows where to get LSD.

Hester Livsey (*Too Many Woman*) — Hester must be the strangest secretary in the *Corpus*. She takes the death of her fiance very hard and knows his murderer is the president of Naylor-Kerr. She refuses to cooperate with Wolfe or the police because, "I want to keep my job here." Mr. Rosenbaum must be a great boss.

Nina Penman (*Murder By the Book*) — Tall and straight with big slow-moving eyes, Nina is a stenographer and works with Helen Troy.

Lila Pilelli ("Murder is Corny") — Lila has a secretarial service on 8th Avenue. Wolfe uses her services as a notary public.

Helen Troy (*Murder By the Book*) -A plump stenographer working for the firm of Corrigan, Phelps, Kustin & Briggs.

Secretaries That Shall Remain Nameless

Nat Driscoll's Secretary (*Over My Dead Body*) — Driscoll forgot he gave the box of diamonds to his secretary. The secretary, with big round blue eyes and an icy voice aids Archie in Carla Lovchen's escape from the Maidenstone Building.

Mr. Hewitt's Secretary ("Christmas Party") — Archie doesn't want to go to the Hewitt estate and gives the excuse, "Hewitt's secretary knows orchid terms as well as I do."

Otis Ross aka William A. Donahue's Secretary ("Too Many Detectives") — A future murder victim hires Wolfe to tap his own phone line to "catch a double-dealing secretary." The tap is illegal and the secretary truly fictional.

Jack Sandler's Secretary (*Plot It Yourself*) -The theatrical agent's secretary found evidence to support a plagiarism claim in an old file.

Peter Truett's aka Archie Goodwin's Stenographer (*Too Many Women*) — "Truett" tells an easy-to-look-at female, "I don't want you, just your typewriter." Shocked, she refuses.

Undercover Secretarial Assignments

Sergeant Dorothy Bruce ("Booby Trap") — Posing as a WAC secretary, the sergeant is a spy for the United States. Wolfe says she has streaks of brilliance.

Alan Green aka Archie Goodwin (*If Death Ever Slept*) — Replacing Jim Eber, the boss's wife says, "You don't look like a secretary."

Notable Clericals

Maud Jordan aka Marjorie Ault (*A Right to Die*) — A millionairess masquerading as a switchboard operator wanted to be close to her deceased son's love, Susan Brooke. Maud kills Susan when she becomes engaged to a black man.

Frances Cox ("Kill Now, Pay Later") — A receptionist who functioned as murder victim Dennis Ashby's secretary. Mrs. Ashby had tried to get her fired. Mr. Ashby gave her two raises in pay.

Rosa Bendini aka Mrs. Harold Anthony (*Too Many Women*) — "The Curves" is separated from her husband and doesn't know how to talk to men until they've kissed her.

Archie obliges. Rosa is an assistant chief filer.

Blanche Duke (*Murder By the Book*) — A tri-shade blonde switchboard operator drinks a special recipe at cocktail time.

Clara Fox (*The Rubber Band*) — A cable clerk, she translates and decodes all telegrams and cables. Clara hires Wolfe to help her settle a forty-year-old claim and he investigates a charge of larceny against her. Wolfe tells Clara, "You have unusual beauty."

Marie Willis ("The Next Witness") — A switchboard operator employed by Bagby Answers Inc. is murdered by Clyde Bagby when she endangers his blackmailing scheme.

Temporary Secretaries

When Archie is on vacation or otherwise unavailable, Wolfe has the agency send a man whom he or Fritz, usually doesn't like (*In the Best Families*). Johnny Keems learned shorthand in the hopes of getting Archie's job (*The Rubber Band*).

Saul Panzer types the answers to the Pour Amour contest and mails them to the contestants (*Before Midnight*). Wolfe dictates to Orrie Cather, although Orrie is a poor speller (*If Death Ever Slept*).

There are a total of forty-six secretaries in thirty-two books and short stories. As you know, the *Corpus* contains a total of seventy-two Nero Wolfe books and short stories. Now that you have been reacquainted with them, it is easy to see why secretaries appear with such frequency.

Rex Stout treats the secretaries fairly well. Neither Wolfe nor Archie have a "just a secretary" attitude. Instead Wolfe goes on the basis that a secretary is intelligent unless proven otherwise. Secretaries appear to be exempt from Wolfe's dislike of career women. It is a group of secretaries and other clerical employee who were the first outsiders allowed in the plant rooms without Wolfe present (*Murder By the Book*). Archie has fallen in love, or should I say lust, with several secretaries and he is always willing to challenge a secretary in the old game of "Whose boss picks up the phone first."

The secretaries are colorful characters who seem to gravitate toward trouble. Many are young and very attractive — Rex probably wrote them in on Archie's insistence. Even Wolfe succumbs to their charms, notably Phoebe Gunther and Maryella Timms. I hope you have, too.

FROM ZECK TO MORIARTY TO WILD

by Marvin Kaye

[This article is drawn from a lecture delivered December 5, 1981, at the 3rd Nero Wolfe Assembly in New York City.]

NERONIAN AFICIONADOS often draw parallels between Rex Stout's arch-villain Arnold Zeck of *And Be a Villain, The Second Confession,* and *In the Best Families* and Arthur Conan Doyle's Napoleon of Crime, Professor James Moriarty.

Both evil geniuses have much in common. Both dwell at the hub of a radiating system of lieutenants and sublieutenants who oversee their kingpin's nefarious interests and incidentally protect the commander from incrimination, or even a whisper of crime. Zeck hides behind a veneer of respectability; Moriarty, a brilliant but little-known mathematician, is concealed by a smokescreen of "honest" obscurity.

It is an apt parallel as far as it goes, yet both Zeck and Moriarty derive from a common historical source. It may be news to some Holmesian and Neronian scholars that this pair of criminal geniuses are distantly related to a character in a Henry Fielding novel, as well as Mr. Peachum in the popular Bertolt Brecht musical, *The Threepenny Opera,* and the identically-named personage in John Gay's *The Beggar's Opera.*

All of them share the same ancestor, a man referred to in *The Newgate Calendar* as "The Prince of Robbers." His name was Jonathan Wild. His life inspired Henry Fielding to write a novel celebrating Wild and this, in turn, was the basis for Edwin Justus Mayer's brilliant black comedy, *Children of Darkness,* performed many years ago starring George C. Scott at New York's Circle in the Square theatre.

Conan Doyle freely acknowledged Jonathan Wild as the model for Moriarty. In *The Valley of Fear,* Sherlock Holmes tells Inspector MacDonald that "Wild . . . was a master criminal, and he lived last century — 1750 or thereabouts. . . . Everything comes in circles, even Professor Moriarty. Jonathan Wild was the hidden force of the London criminals, to whom he sold his brains and his organization on a fifteen percent commission. The old wheel turns and the same spoke comes up. It's all been done before and will be done again." (It is unlikely that Holmes was familiar with the then-obscure works of Friedrich Nietzche, yet here he states with amazing similarity that woefully misrepresented philosopher's theory of the Eternal Recurrence.)

From Wild to Moriarty to Zeck. Like his fictional counterparts, Jonathan Wild was affiliated with nearly every robbery and murder in the London of his day. His system of spies enabled him to ruthlessly suppress treason within his organization. He hid behind a cloak of bourgeois respectability.

To comprehend his life and career, one must imagine a great general or a keen financial wizard turning to a life of crime. Invest him with the resourcefulness of Archie Goodwin, the power machine of Arnold Zeck, the ruthlessness of Tsar Ivan, and the hypocrisy of Mr. Pickwick's nemeses, Messers. Dodson and Fogg. Add two drops of the pride of Dryden's pompous hero Almanzor and you have a fair portrait of Jonathan Wild. He was so audacious that when the law was expressly rewritten to put him out of business, he circumvented it so masterfully that his new system not only earned him his livelihood but actually brought him a measure of recognition as a public benefactor because he helped "catch" so many thieves — by turning them over to the police when they displeased him. At the height of his career, he received the approbation of the crown and on occasions of state could be seen carrying a silver wand symbolizing his position as Thief Taker to the King. Had fortune continued to look kindly on him, Wild might have died with honors and received burial in Westminster Abbey.

Jonathan Wild was born circa 1682 in Wolverhampton, Staffordshire, the eldest son of a tradesman who saw to it that his boy was sufficiently educated, then apprenticed at age fifteen to a Birmingham bucklemaker. Wild lived in that town about seven years before returning home to marry his first and only legal wife. She bore him a son, but two years later Wild deserted his family and made for London to "get on."

He got on at first, Fagin-like, by organizing beggarly children to pick pockets. Other youngsters were told to collect dead animals, decayed produce, and manure. This offal was sold to spectators at executions for the purpose of pelting the damned. A small lad who resisted Wild's rule got off mercifully with a thrashing, but an older rebel would be "peached-on" (hence Peachum's name in both the Brecht and Gay operettas) and impeachment to the authorities generally meant death, even for minor infractions.

In spite of his racketeering, Wild soon ended up in debtor's prison, where he remained for some four years. Many years later, while awaiting execution, Wild wrote a pamphlet about himself. Here he stated that in debtor's prison he learned the trade secrets of the professional criminal and made the acquaintance of many of the thieves and murderers whom he later employed.

He met his second "wife" in prison. Mary Milliner, a benevolent whore, helped Jonathan set up his criminal operations after they were released. Jonathan and Mary lived together many years and separated only after they had a tiff, during which Wild cut off one of her ears.

Initially, Wild flourished as a receiver of stolen goods. No law existed to punish "fences," which enabled his business to flourish. Then Parliament held a special session to counteract the problem, and a new ordinance was drafted and put into effect. Wild rose to the occasion. Summoning his chief henchmen, he argued that the new law would drive many timorous souls from the fencing racket. Those few who remained would naturally charge dearly for their services. Wild proposed an ingenious alternative: he would set up shop as a purchaser of stolen goods — no questions asked, except the name of the victim. Wild could then approach the "mark" and say that he'd heard news of the whereabouts of the missing valuables, which he might be able to recover if his informants were paid.

Wild never charged the "mark" for his services, nor would he store stolen goods on his premises. He merely did what he could to assist the helpless public who were at the mercy of evil criminals. If someone benefited from Wild's aid and wished to bestow largesse upon him, he might indeed be gratified, but never did he call it a fee. (Meanwhile he took his percentage from the monies paid to his "informants.")

Not only was Wild not culpable in the eyes of the law, he soon became well known as a fine individual to whom the victim of a robbery could turn to in distress. Respectable citizens began to seek him out on their own. He listened to their plaints carefully and devised a cynical twist to the thieving trade. He instructed his employees to seek out items of sentimental value, goods they might normally pass over in favor of jewels and precious metals. Wild explained that the account books of a business, a souvenir of a departed parent, or an indiscreet love letter might be worth far more than a gold watch or pearl necklace.

Wild's respectability was rooted in "public service," but that did not just entail recovering stolen goods. True, there was some question concerning his uncanny ability to know what so many criminals did with their booty. Jonathan frequently explained that his system of information depended for its effectiveness on his not asking many questions of his intelligencers. Still he soon saw that his reputation as well as his own safety within the organization he created depended upon judicious "peaching." He befriended a corrupt city marshal, Charles Hitchens (the model for Tiger Brown in *The Threepenny Opera*), and turned over for justice any recalcitrant gang member or any thief who did not give up his entire loot to Wild. (Wild jealously checked the victim's tally of missing property with the inventory received of each robbery.) Eventually, Wild's repressive policies fomented internal rebellion. He was stabbed by a ruffian he'd "peached" called Blueskin. Wild survived, but at length another one of the men he sent to the gallows told all and Jonathan Wild was arrested and sentenced to be hanged at Tyburn. On the very morning of his execution, he was still doing illegal business through the bars of his cell. An accomplice smuggled him a narcotic in this manner, but it did not work well and Wild was dragged screaming to the gallows where it was his turn to be pelted with offal. Upon first being taken, Wild objected that "I am a poor honest man who has done all I could do to serve people when they have had the misfortune to lose their goods by the villainy of thieves. I have contributed more than any man living to bringing the most daring and notorious malefactors to justice."

The irony of this statement was no accident. The papers and utterances of Wild contain many touches of grim humor and gloating hypocrisy. It would probably have delighted him to attain immortality of a sort through the writings of Fielding, Gay, Brecht, Mayer, Conan Doyle, and Rex Stout. Perhaps he would admit to the accuracy of Fielding's observation that "a man may go to heaven with half the pains which it costs him to go to hell." But I suspect Jonathan Wild would sooner appropriate as a motto that passage from Fielding which Mayer saw fit to include in his play, *Children of Darkness* - "I had rather stand on the summit of a dung-hill than at the bottom of a hill in Paradise!"

FRITZ'S HERB GARDEN
by Ann Zawistowski

NERO WOLFE was a gourmet, to have the very best in food, he had Fritz Brenner, the very best chef outside of Wolfe himself, prepare his meals. That is not to say that he and Fritz never argued over what to put into various dishes. They did. Archie tells us in *The Mother Hunt*, "He [Wolfe] crossed to the door and in the hall turned left, toward the kitchen. Lunch was to be shad roe in casserole, one of the few dishes on which he and Fritz had a difference of opinion that had never been settled. They were agreed on the larding, the anchovy butter, the chervil, shallot, parsley, bay leaf, pepper, marjoram, and cream, but the argument was the onion. Fritz was for it and Wolfe dead against."

Although they may have disagreed about the onion, which is not exactly an herb, I think they would have agreed with Charlemagne when he said that an herb is "the friend of the physician and the pride of cooks." Fritz knew that the secret of fine cuisine is the use of fresh herbs, and without them food could be made good enough to eat, but not good enough to be food fit for a gourmet such as Wolfe,

To this end, Fritz had a little garden in the back yard of the brownstone, where he grew as many herbs as he could. In *Trouble in Triplicate*, Archie reports, "I left by way of the kitchen and back stairs, emerging into our little private yard where Fritz grows chives and tarragon and other vegetation." Another time in *Gambit*, Archie tells us, "The back door leads to the small yard where Fritz grows herbs, or tries to . . ."

In fact, Fritz seemed to grow his herbs as part of the landscape, such as it was in NYC, As Archie tells us in *Gambit*, "But if you're expected and you knock on the gate it will open, as it did for Lucy Valdon at ten minutes past six that Monday afternoon, and you will he led along a brick walk between rows of herbs, down four steps and on in, and up a stair with twelve steps."

TARRAGON

Archie's favorite herb was tarragon, especially with chicken and mushrooms. Tarragon came to us from Siberia by way of France. It is a perennial, which survives the cold winters in New York, and can be divided and potted up and brought into the house for the winter. The Greeks knew of tarragon as early as 500 B.C. Arabs in the 13th century called it tarkhum, meaning dragon, because it fought against pestilence. It reached Europe in the 16th century and is now native to parts of southern Europe, Asia and the eastern US.

Tarragon goes well with chicken, which Archie liked, and also many other dishes, notably fish, cheese, and egg dishes and almost any vegetable. In some of the recipes in the cookbook [*The Nero Wolfe Cookbook* — MK], where it calls for fresh tarragon, they also say that you can use dry tarragon leaves instead. Not so, as tarragon is best used fresh. It loses its flavor and aroma, which is similar to licorice or anise, very quickly when dried.

BASIL

Another delightful herb which Fritz used in many dishes is basil. This herb is a favorite herb of cooks, especially Italian cooks, and it reigns in the kitchen. Basil is native to India and Asia, and has been cultivated there for over 5,000 years. It is grown as a perennial in warm, tropical climates. In New York, where Fritz had his herb garden, it was killed by the first frost, as it is a very tender plant. I often wonder if Wolfe allowed Fritz to keep some pots of herbs in among his precious orchids. I'd like to think so, for he would then be the beneficiary of having them available all winter.

The very tender leaves of this plant have a sweet, pungent odor when crushed, or if people brush by the plant in the garden. There are several kinds of basil, and the most commonly used is sweet basil. Another basil that is used for balsamic vinegar is opal or purple basil. It gives a ruby color as well as a great flavor to vinegar for salads. It is even a good plant to use in the garden as an annual border — it's fragrant, it has little flowers, and it will be readily available when you decide to cook an Italian meal — lasagna, spaghetti, and pizza, which is heavenly with chopped or just plain basil leaves. One of the best things made with basil is "il pesto." Pesto is quite the rage now; but Wolfe ate and enjoyed it before it became popular in this country in the late 80's. Even Inspector Cramer was able to enjoy pesto when he was given a taste in "The Zero Clue." "When I returned to the office with a supply of provender, Cramer was riding Wolfe, pouring it on, and Wolfe was leaning back in his chair with his eyes shut. I passed around plates of Fritz's il pesto and crackers . . . in four minutes, Cramer inquired, 'What is this stuff?' Wolfe told him, 'il pesto.' 'What is in it?' 'Canestrato cheese, anchovies, pig liver, black walnuts, chives, sweet basil, garlic, and olive oil.' 'Good God.' In another four minutes Cramer addressed me in the tone of one doing a gracious favor. 'I'll take some more of that, Goodwin.'"

SAGE

Sage grows wild in Yugoslavia and Albania and is a favorite seasoning in many native foods. No doubt Wolfe was well acquainted with sage, as it was a plant native to the land where he grew up. Sage is a plant that also has a long tradition of medicinal importance. The word sage itself comes from the Latin word, *salvere*, which means to be salvaged (saved). The plant is supposed to have curing properties. It was a medicinal cure-all, people even thought it would cure baldness. Another belief was that sage helped improve the memory, and made people wise. Our word for wise man, a sage, comes from this belief.

This is one of the plants which Fritz probably had in his herb garden, even though it is not mentioned specifically. Because it is a perennial and is very hardy, Fritz was able to gather fresh leaves well into the winter months for use in his cooking. We think of the stuffing of our Thanksgiving turkey which uses sage in abundance. It does enhance many dishes, especially pork stuffing, cheese, sausages, egg dishes, and cooked vegetables. One of the dishes that Fritz made that Wolfe would not touch without the sage was grilled starlings. In *The Golden Spiders,* we are told, "Each year around the middle of May, by arrangement, a farmer who lives up in New Brewster shoots eighteen or twenty starlings, puts them in a bag, and gets in his car and drives to New York. It is understood that they are to be delivered to our door within two hours after they were winged. Fritz dresses them and sprinkles them with salt, and, at the proper moment, brushes them with melted butter, wraps them in sage leaves, grills them, and arranges them on a platter of hot polenta, which is thick porridge of fine-ground yellow corn meal with butter, grated cheese, and salt and pepper. It is an expensive meal and a happy one, and Wolfe always looks forward to it, but that day he put on an exhibition. When the platter was brought in, steaming, and placed before him, he sniffed, cocked his head, and sniffed again, and straightened to look up at Fritz. 'The sage?' 'No, sir.' 'What do you mean, no sir?' 'I thought you might like it once in a style I have suggested, with saffron and tarragon. Much fresh tarragon, with just a touch of saffron, which is the way. . . ' 'Remove it.' Fritz went rigid and his lips tightened. 'You did not consult me,' Wolfe said coldly. 'To find that without warning one of my favorite dishes has been radically altered is an unpleasant shock. It may possibly be edible, but I am in no humor to risk it. Please dispose of it and bring me four coddled eggs and a piece of toast.'

CHIVES

When you mention chives, people immediately think of sour cream and a baked potato, or probably cream cheese and chives. This is another plant that Fritz had in his garden. Chives are very easy to grow, and are a very hardy perennial. They grow in a clump, and when needed, you just go out and give the plant a haircut. When you need a mild, oniony flavor, chives are just the thing. Fritz used chives in the recipe for Herbed Stuffed Potatoes. Saul knows you can even grow them in a pot in your kitchen, as Archie tells us in *A Family Affair*. "A little after ten I had called the *Gazette* and left word for Lon Cohen that I could be reached at Saul's place until eleven and then at the office. I hadn't called Wolfe. I had told him we were going to decide what to do, and let him think we were spending the night at it. For breakfast Saul and I had had two thick slices of broiled ham, six poached eggs, and about a dozen thin slices of buttered toast sprinkled with chives. Saul grows chives in a sixteen-inch box in his kitchen window."

PARSLEY

Parsley is such a familiar herb, easy to grow, but also readily available in most any produce store. No one knows where it came from originally, but it is believed to be native to the Mediterranean area. It is another herb used widely in Wolfe's second homeland. People think it is put on your dinner plate to look pretty, because it has an attractive leaf, and a bright, green color. It is used as a garnish, but it is Mother Nature's original "breath freshener." It has a peppery flavor, and is just the thing to eat when you have finished a meal that has lots of garlic. Many of the foods that Fritz cooked called for parsley, which was right there in his garden. Two dishes using parsley are Herbed Stuffed Potatoes and Baked Scallops.

THYME

This herb is native to Europe and Asia. It is a perennial evergreen, so Fritz could gather it from his garden all year round. It is highly aromatic, and the Greeks used it as incense. It has been cultivated for centuries, so that now there are over 60 varieties. Thyme is used in cooking and in the garden as a ground cover, and it is a favorite plant in many rock gardens.

Thyme is one of the most valuable kitchen herbs. It goes well with carrots and onions, and is especially good in meat dishes. Add some dried thyme leaf to your barbecue sauce. This herb is excellent with fish, and is a traditional ingredient in clam chowder. Many of the dishes that Fritz prepared, such as Roast Leg of Lamb and Pork Stewed in Beer, call for thyme.

These herbs are just a few of the many that can be used in cooking. Nowadays, with the renewed interest in herbs, they are more available at your local supermarket, especially basil and chives. Here in New York, you might think that it is very hard to grow herbs to use in your kitchen for cooking. It's not as hard as you think. These plants are available at a garden center, or perhaps you know someone who already grows some, who could give you starter plants. If you have sun for about six hours a day in your yard or deck or terrace or even kitchen window, you can grow herbs. You do not need rich soil. In fact, herbs, which were wild plants in places like Albania or Greece, learned to thrive in poor soil. All it takes is a good sized pot, a plant and the sun. Water your plant every few days, and when you're making that special dish that calls for chives, why, just get out your kitchen shears and cut some, and voila! Gourmet cooking! It's that easy.

HERB VINEGAR

Herbs mellow vinegar just as aging mellows wine. You can use herbs that are fresh or dried, but fresh herbs make better vinegars because they contain more oil than dried herbs.

As a general rule, use one cup fresh herb or one-half cup dried herb to flavor one quart of vinegar. Use cider, red wine or white vinegar, depending on your taste.

To avoid the possibility of chemical reaction, use glass bottles or jars with non-metal caps. Stoppered carafes, decanters or recycled wine bottles are pretty.

Pick branches just before flowering, or use just the leaves and tips. You can also use herbs that are fresh, and bought at the produce section of the supermarket. Wash and dry well. Fill bottles loosely with herbs. The proportion of herb-to-vinegar is a matter of taste, but remember that some herbs are stronger than others. This is especially important if you are combining two herbs in one vinegar. Cover with vinegar, cap and label. Store in a warm place for two to four weeks. Check after a few days to see that all of the herb is covered by vinegar. If not, add more. The flavor of the vinegar will strengthen the longer the herbs are in the mixture. If you want a mild-flavored vinegar, strain the herbs out within a few days. If the herb flavor becomes too strong, dilute with additional vinegar. You may also want to use the herbs as needed for salads and cooking. Some favorite herb vinegars are fennel, sage, rosemary, garlic and chives, and especially the opal, or red basil. It makes the vinegar a lovely ruby color.

HERB BUTTER

For that special touch for a special dinner, party, or holiday gathering. try these herb butters. I prefer unsalted butter, but salted is all right. Let butter soften to room temperature. Cream or beat softened butter and stir in the various herbs. Pack into molds, shape with hands into logs, or put into fancy crocks or small dishes. Refrigerate for at least three hours to allow flavors to blend. Use fresh herb butters within a day or two. They will keep several weeks when frozen.

FINES HERBES BUTTER

1 cup sweet butter
2 tablespoons parsley, chopped
2 tablespoons chives, chopped
1 tablespoon tarragon, chopped

Try with fish, meats, poached eggs, vegetables or French bread.

BASIL BUTTER

1 cup sweet butter
1 cup fresh basil leaves, chopped (lightly packed)
4 tablespoons parsley, minced (optional)

Use with vegetables such as zucchini, eggplant, green beans; to season vegetable soups and with sauteed fish. Try frying eggs in basil butter, or use on top of poached eggs.

Try other combinations of herbs with butter. As a general rule, use one tablespoon of fresh herb, one and one-half teaspoons dried or one-half teaspoon seed for each stick or one-quarter pound of butter. If you combine two or more herbs, use less of the strongly flavored ones.

STARLINGS

18 or 20 starlings
1 cup dry sherry
salt
½ pound butter
chervil
18 or 20 sage leaves (or thyme basil)
pieces of aluminum foil

Dress the birds and sprinkle them with salt. Let them stand for about five minutes and then sprinkle them with a pinch each of chervil, basil, and thyme — or whatever other herbs you have fresh, except for tarragon and saffron, which are not advised. Melt the butter and combine with the sherry. Brush each bird with the mixture and wrap individually in sage leaves (or aluminum foil). Seal the edges tightly to keep the juices in. Grill for fifteen to twenty minutes in a hot (400 degree) oven or over coals. Serve them in the wrapping, or arrange on polenta (see recipe below) and pour the juice over each bird before serving.

POLENTA

2 cups yellow corn meal
8 tablespoons butter (1 stick)
4 cups boiling water
½ teaspoon ground sage
1 teaspoon salt

Sprinkle the corn meal slowly into the boiling water. Add the salt. Stir the meal until it thickens. Cover and continue to cook for twenty-five minutes over hot water, stirring occasionally with a wooden spoon. Stir in the butter and sage. Serve hot.

VARIATION: *Instead of serving hot, pour the polenta into a buttered mold and chill thoroughly. Unmold and slice. Sauce the slices in butter until browned on both sides. Serve with warm autumn honey.*

HERBED STUFFED POTATOES

2 large potatoes
2 teaspoons chopped fresh chives
4 tablespoons butter
1 teaspoon chopped fresh tarragon
¼ cup heavy cream
(or ½ teaspoon dried leaves)
½ teaspoon dry mustard
salt and pepper to taste
1 teaspoon fresh chervil
2 teaspoons chopped fresh parsley (or 1/2 teaspoon dried leaves)

Preheat oven to 325 degrees. Rub the potatoes with a little butter and poke with a fork. Bake them for an hour, or until done. Cut in half lengthwise and scoop out the potato into a bowl, taking care not to break the skins. Add the remaining ingredients (reserving one tablespoon of butter) to the potatoes and mix thoroughly. Return the mixture to the potato skills and dot the top of each with a bit of butter. Run the potatoes under the broiler to brown the tops.

LEG OF LAMB

1 leg of lamb, weighing 5 to 6 pounds
1 teaspoon crushed thyme leaves (or 1/2 teaspoon dried leaves)
2 cloves garlic, crushed
1/2 cup Dijon mustard
1/4 teaspoon powdered ginger
1 tablespoon good soy sauce
1 tablespoon olive oil

Preheat oven to 350 degrees. Trim the fat from the leg of lamb, but do not remove the filament covering the meat. Blend the garlic with the mustard, soy sauce, thyme, and ginger. Gradually beat in the olive oil until the sauce is creamy. Rub over the lamb and set it on a rack in a roasting pan. Roast the lamb for one to one and a half hours, depending on your taste for rare or well-done meat. (Serves 6)

CHICKEN WITH MUSHROOMS AND TARRAGON

2 whole chicken breasts, boned and split (from chickens raised on blueberries, if possible)
1 teaspoon chopped tarragon leaves (or 1/2 teaspoon dried)
buttered waxed paper cut to the dimensions of baking casserole
¼ teaspoon salt
¼ teaspoon white pepper
5 tablespoons butter
¼ cup chicken broth
1 tablespoon minced shallots
¼ cup White wine
½ lb. sliced mushrooms
1 cup heavy cream
lemon juice to taste

Preheat the oven to 400 degrees. Sprinkle the chicken breasts with salt and pepper. Heat the butter in a heavy casserole, with a cover, until it foams. Stir in the shallots and sauté one minute.

Add mushrooms and tarragon and sauté two minutes more (do not allow to brown). Add the chicken breasts, rolling them quickly in the butter. Lay the buttered paper over the chicken, cover the casserole, and place it in the oven. Cook seven minutes, or until meat springs back when pressed. Remove the chicken to a platter and keep it warm. Pour the chicken broth and wine into the casserole and boil the liquid on top of the stove over high heat until it is syrupy. Add the cream and boil rapidly, stirring, until the sauce thickens. Taste for seasoning and add more salt and pepper, if needed, and drops of lemon juice to taste. Pour the sauce over the chicken and serve immediately. (Serves 4)

IL PESTO

¼ pound pig liver
½ cup grated Canestrato cheese (see note)
2 tablespoons butter
1 teaspoon salt
2 cups fresh basil leaves
½ teaspoon freshly ground black pepper
2 cloves garlic
¾ cup olive oil
¼ cup black walnuts
1 teaspoon chopped chives

Sauté the sliced pig's liver in the butter; when cool, remove from pan and chop coarsely. In a blender combine the basil, garlic, black walnuts, chives, cheese, salt, pepper, and one quarter cup of the olive oil. Blend at a low speed until a pureé consistency is achieved. Slowly add the remaining olive oil, blending at low speed until the oil is completely incorporated and the consistency is that of whipped cream. Add the liver and blend for another five seconds and no longer; the texture of the liver should be discernible. Serve as a spread with crackers or as a sauce for spaghetti; in which case the amount of oil should be increased to one and a half cups. *Note:* Canestrato cheese is a Sicilian grating cheese, very sharp and white, sometimes containing whole black pepper. If it is not available, substitute Cacciocavallo.

SQUABS MARINATED IN CREAM

6 squabs
¼ teaspoon powdered clove
2 cups light cream
1 teaspoon fresh thyme leaves
½ cup all-purpose flour
(¼ teaspoon dried)
½ teaspoon salt
4 crushed juniper berries
¼ teaspoon freshly ground
¼ cup olive oil
black pepper
6 slices white bread
generous pinch nutmeg
1 cup red-currant jelly

Cut squabs down back, leaving backbone intact. Flatten birds slightly with the palm of your hand and, using a very sharp knife, remove backbone and ribs. Put squabs in a bowl and cover with cream. Set aside for one hour. Combine flour with salt, pepper, nutmeg, clove, thyme, and juniper berries. Remove squabs from cream and roll them in seasoned flour, shaking off excess. Heat olive oil in a large skillet and sauté squabs until browned on both sides and cooked through (about twenty-thirty minutes). While squabs are cooking, make sauce (see below) and toast the bread. Spread toast with jelly and place cooked squabs on top. (Serves 6)

MADEIRA CREAM SAUCE

2 tablespoons all-purpose flour
2 tablespoons Madeira
2 tablespoons butter
salt and pepper to taste
1 cup milk

Melt butter in heavy-bottom saucepan. Add flour. Cook gently for three minutes; gradually add milk. Stir constantly over low flame until sauce thickens. Add Madeira, salt and pepper to taste. Pour hot sauce over squabs. Serve immediately.

NERO WOLFE BROWNSTONE PLAQUE IS DEDICATED

by Joe Sweeney

ON A partly sunny Saturday in June, 1996, some thirty-five members of The Wolfe Pack descended on 454 West 35th Street to forever put to rest the controversy over exactly where Mr. Wolfe drank beer, raised orchids, ate breakfast, lunch, and dinner, and — oh, yes! — occasionally solved a murder.

The following press release was issued the week prior:

> London has Sherlock Holmes of 221b Baker Street
> New York City has Nero Wolfe of West 35th Street

New York City and The Wolfe Pack will honor writer Rex Stout and his fictional eccentric private detective Nero Wolfe with a bronze plaque at 454 West 35th Street on Saturday, June 22.

In Rex Stout's seventy-three Nero Wolfe mysteries, the street address of Wolfe's West 35th Street brownstone wanders as far east as 9th Avenue and as far west as the middle of the Hudson River. The Wolfe Pack — donating a bronze plaque to New York City to honor Stout's work — has identified 454 West 35th Street as the probable site of the fictional brownstone. The actual building now at the location is an apartment building renovated and managed by Clinton Housing Development Company.

Clinton Housing Development Company is a not-for-profit, community-based organization dedicated to preserving and creating affordable housing in Clinton. The apartment building is maintained by the group for mentally ill and elderly people. The nationally recognized group also sponsors the Clinton South Community Center for children and teenagers in the surrounding neighborhood.

With an international roster of more than 400 members, The Wolfe Pack, founded in 1978, is a non-profit organization for aficionados of Rex Stout's Nero Wolfe mystery novels. The group publishes a newsletter called *The Gazette,* and annually awards the "Nero" to an outstanding work of current American detective fiction. In honor of Stout's orchid-loving, corpulent detective, Nero Wolfe, The Wolfe Pack meets regularly for gourmet meals including the annual "Black Orchid Banquet" and "Shad Roe Dinner."

The plaque reads: "On this site stood the elegant brownstone of the corpulent fictional private detective Nero Wolfe. With his able assistant Archie Goodwin, Mr. Wolfe raised orchids and dined well, while solving over seventy cases as recorded by Rex Stout from 1934-1975."

It was donated to the Wolfe Pack by English producer Harry Towers, who is currently developing a television series for Showtime based on the Wolfe mysteries. Prior to the 1:30 p.m. dedication of the plaque, The Wolfe Pack is hosting a party for the community center's children, including lunch and a non-violent interactive mystery game created especially for the event. The Wolfe Pack also is donating a selection of Nero Wolfe books to the community room at 454 West 35th Street, and a collection of children's books to the community center, including reference works and autographed copies of books by New York children's authors Bonnie Bryant and Elizabeth Levy.

Rex Stout's grandson, Reed Maroc, who is also a writer, will attend the event. "I know it would mean a great deal to my grandfather that his Nero Wolfe stories are still read twenty years after his death, and that there are people who so appreciate his work that they want to put up this plaque in his honor. And donating books to children in this neighborhood, encouraging them to read, that would please him tremendously. Aside from the fun he had with life in general, reading was his greatest pleasure."

A TOAST TO FRITZ BRENNER

by Jane O'Brien

ON MR. Wolfe's note of "Have you eaten?" I'd like to make a toast to Fritz Brenner.

Where would Mr. Wolfe and Archie be without Fritz? He is the stable center of the household, ensuring their routine and minimizing distraction.

His resourcefulness with food is evident in his collaborations with Mr. Wolfe. Supportive but never submissive, he defends the use of onion in the shad roe mousse, decapitating anchovies for fritters, and is firm in the number of juniper berries for the venison.

His ability in the kitchen is responsible for the men Mr. Wolfe and Archie are, both in size and temperament.

Fritz is multifaceted — when needed, he helps Archie eject visitors or hold suspects at gunpoint.

Archie calls him "the chef and household jewel." He tells Fritz, "I think you're a genius. Two geniuses in one house and one of them is easy to live with."

Archie also tells us that the only slang Fritz ever used was, "And how!"

Here's to Fritz Brenner. And how!

NERO WOLFE
REDUX

A moderate number of new Nero Wolfe mysteries by other authors than Rex Stout have appeared in The Wolfe Pack *Gazette;* some are reprints from other publications, most are original. Occasionally they are parodistic, but more often were written as closely patterned as possible to Archie Goodwin's breezy writing style and Nero Wolfe's inimitable ratiocinative gifts. The following pages feature four of these pastiches.

A Healthy Way to Die by Maggie Jacobs captures the Stoutean tone so well that it won a Nero Wolfe Short Story contest conducted by The Wolfe Pack and was published in the Spring 1998 issue of *The Gazette,* Volume XII # 3.

The late Henry Enberg was one of the most beloved members of The Wolfe Pack, and one of the very few who could have met Mr. Wolfe as an intellectual equal. He contributed two delightful radio plays to *The Gazette,* both of them performed in New York City: *Too Many Politicians* (coauthored with Andrew Joffe) and *The Daughter Hunt,* whose title echoes two of the *Corpus* novels, *The Mother Hunt* and *The Father Hunt.* The script appeared in two issues of *The Gazette,* Volume VI # 3 and 4.

Once, "Pack" members voted for writers (other than Robert Goldsborough) who they believed the best choices to continue the series. The names advanced were Robert B. Parker, Lawrence Bloch, and (my blushes, Watson!) myself. But the only Neronian mystery I ever wanted to write was the case in which Wolfe and Archie first met; I was intrigued by the tantalizingly brief references to it in the *Corpus.* But there is no need for me or anyone else to attempt it, because in *"Firecrackers",* Charles E. Burns accomplished the task splendidly. His novella was serialized in three issues of *The Gazette,* Volume IX # 1, 2 and 3. It is a flavorful period piece that reveals the "facts" behind how the Great Detective discovered and hired his midwestern "Watson." [*A Pack member grumbled in the Letters section of the Fall 1991 Gazette "that the writer of 'Firecrackers' did not (grow) up in Ohio" and cited several errors, among them the observation that 'butter beans' and 'narcissus' are locally referred to as 'lima beans' and 'daffodils.' The Gazette editor replied, "— my excuse is that I've never even been to Ohio!" I, being a*

Pennsylvanian, appreciate that sentiment. — MK]

Greg Hatcher's *Memo for Murder* was divided into two *Gazettes*, Volume XIII # 1 and 2. To my mind, it not only reads like a genuine Nero Wolfe adventure but also ranks with the best of them, and features a damsel in distress who not only challenges Lily Rowan's hold on Archie, but thoroughly charms the distaff-suspicious Wolfe, as well as Fritz; Theodore is the only man in the house on West 35th Street she doesn't win over!

A HEALTHY WAY TO DIE

by Maggie Jacobs

"NO," Wolfe said, leaning back in the only chair in the world that could fully support his one-seventh of a ton and frowning at me. "It's a farcical idea. I will not be a party to it."

"You could at least see her," I objected.

"I will not. Send her away." He picked up his book.

I regarded him, not fondly. There was plenty of money in the bank just then to pay for the new shipment of orchids that had just arrived, as well as the salaries of Theodore, the orchid nursemaid; Fritz (currently in the kitchen preparing lamb chops and rice cakes with thyme); and myself, Archie Goodwin, chief assistant detective. Under these circumstances, getting Wolfe to take a job is just about as hard as moving mountains, and presents many of the same obstacles. "It means nothing to you that your fellow man is crying out for your help," I said argumentatively. "Of course, in this case your fellow man happens to be your fellow woman, but so what? She needs a few hours of your time, and she's willing to pay for it. It's true the scenario is a bit peculiar, but we've done stranger things in pursuit of truth, justice, and a fatter bank balance."

I waved a hand. "Look at it. This girl, Jean Harper, believes that someone is trying to kill her. Yesterday, in her position as shop clerk at the Healthy Way natural grocery store, she was present when the assistant store manager, Elizabeth Treefall, sampled a container of pesto as part of her normal duties, keeled over, and was dead in two minutes. Last night, someone tried to break into her apartment, and this morning she was almost run down by a hit-and-run driver.

"She's convinced, whether rightly or wrongly, that she saw or heard something yesterday that would point to Elizabeth Treefall's murderer, and that this person is now trying to kill her. She doesn't know what it is that she knows. What does she do? She comes straight to you. She asks you to listen to her story about what happened yesterday and to question her minutely about it. She asks me to type up the transcript of the conversation and let her sign it. She asks you to insert a notice in the paper stating that you have talked with her. She figures the murderer will see it, realize she's told you everything she knows, and decide it's pointless to kill her now."

Wolfe's mouth quirked, but he didn't lift his eyes from his book. I went on. "Sure, it's crazy, but you have to admit it's an ingenious way of avoiding being murdered, and she pays you the compliment of assuming that the mere fact that she's talked to you will scare the murderer off. She is also willing to pay you three thousand dollars."

Wolfe spoke without raising his head. "Archie. I assume you have been bedazzled by this woman. There's no other explanation for your attempts to get me to agree to this preposterous proposal."

"No, sir. She's not a dazzler. She — "

"Then you are entirely without excuse. Get rid of her. She is obviously suffering from delusions."

"Yes, sir. That's just what Rowcliff said."

Wolfe's head jerked up. "She's seen Rowcliff?"

"Uh huh. She spent most of yesterday afternoon with him. It sounded like she wasn't too impressed with him. When she called the police station to report the attempts on her life, she got him again. He told her she was a nut case and not to bother him any more." I stood. "She was sure she'd get a better reception from you. I guess I'll have to go tell her she was wrong." I started for the door to the front room, where she was waiting.

Wolfe's lips tightened. "Wait." I stopped obediently. "Confound it," he growled. "I suppose I'll have to see her, or I'll never hear the end of it. Very well, bring her in."

"Yes, sir." I started for the door again.

When I brought Jean Harper in, Wolfe waited until she was seated, then grunted, "Miss Harper. I'm Nero Wolfe."

"Hello," she said in a small voice. She looked all right in the red leather chair, with her neat black jeans and her green checked shirt. She was slender, with short dark hair and a face that somehow missed being pretty. Glancing at her, I decided that she had calmed down some in the forty minutes or so she had spent in the front room, and that was a good thing because, as I had told her, Wolfe will not deal with a hysterical woman.

"I told Mr. Goodwin that I could pay three thousand dollars," she was saying. "I hope that will be enough? I could probably borrow another 500 dollars, but I would rather not have to."

"Three thousand will be sufficient, if I decide to take the job," Wolfe said brusquely. "You'd better tell me about it."

Of course I had heard it before, and Wolfe and I and a few million other people had read about the murder in the morning paper. She told it well, but then she must have had a lot of practice the day before.

"I'm a clerk at the Healthy Way grocery store. Yesterday morning I got there at 8:00, my normal time. The other people there were Bill Entworth, the store manager; Elizabeth, who was the assistant manager; and three other clerks: Paul Garcia, James Lester, and Maureen Vidrio. We worked for an hour, getting the store ready; we open at 9:00. I was on the cash register between 9:00 and 11:10, and the others were doing the normal stuff, in and out of the back room, stocking dairy products and produce and fresh bread and so on. Bill and Elizabeth have small offices partitioned out of the back room, and they spent some time in there doing paperwork as well.

"I was at the cash register all morning, so I wasn't there when the pesto was delivered, but Bill and Paul were in the back room, and they both say it was about 9:50. They put it away, but they left one container out on the side table for Elizabeth to taste later. We've had quality problems with that brand recently; three customers have returned it in the past two weeks. Quality control is Elizabeth's job, and believe me, nobody else would have tasted that pesto. Elizabeth almost fired Paul last month when she caught him taking a spoonful of hummus.

"I'm pretty sure that everybody except me went into the back room at some time between 9:50 and 11:10. I think Elizabeth was there the whole time. You can see the back room door from the cash register, and I always keep an eye on people so I know who's around to do price checks. I had three price checks that morning. James did one of them and Maureen did the other two. I also had two check approvals. I have to call Bill for those. Both times he came out of the back room. It's normal for him to spend a lot of time back there in his office, paying bills and making phone calls.

"Paul is supposed to relieve me at the cash register at 11:00, so I can go for my break, but yesterday he was ten minutes late. James waited for me —" she flushed a little — "and we went together to the back room. We got a couple of bottles of juice and sat down, and he was starting to tell me about a problem with one of our yogurt suppliers when Elizabeth came out of her office. She had a cup of tea and some crackers on a plate, and she came over to the table and scooped up a bite of the pesto. Then. . ." she trailed off and looked over at me.

She was looking pretty green, and I certainly didn't want her to blow it now, so I spoke up. "That's okay, we read the papers. Mr. Lester called for an ambulance, and you stayed with Miss Treefall and tried to help her, but she died before the ambulance arrived. Symptoms characteristic of cyanide, but they won't know for sure till after the autopsy. Proceed. The police came?"

"Yes. They questioned us all afternoon — at least, they certainly questioned me. They were really angry that I couldn't say who had been in the back room when, or if anybody had been there alone, but I just couldn't. It wouldn't matter, anyway. I know everybody was in and out of it all morning, and it's so big and has so many odd corners that you wouldn't necessarily see anybody else when you were back there."

Wolfe's eyes were closed, a sign that he was concentrating. "You said that you have been attacked."

"That's right, two separate times." Jean swallowed. "After they were done with me at the police station, about 7:30, I went home. I was tired and too upset to eat, so I went straight to bed, but I couldn't sleep. I lay there for what seemed like hours. I suppose it was hours. I heard some noises, and they seemed to be coming from the fire escape — I have a fifth-story flat. After a few minutes I got nervous and got up and looked out the window, and I saw someone on the fire escape just below me. I screamed, and he ran down and got away.

"I couldn't sleep after that. As soon as it got light, I went out. I thought I'd be safer at a friend's place. It was still quite early, and the streets were empty. I was starting to cross a street three blocks from home, and a car came around a corner and almost hit me. I jumped back to the curb, and it took off down the street. I didn't get a look at the driver.

"I sat on the curb for a minute. Then I found a phone and called the police station. I talked to Lieutenant Rowcliff, the same one who questioned me yesterday, and he as good as told me I was crazy." Her voice was quivering again, this time with indignation. "So I went and got a cup of coffee and tried to decide what to do, and I thought of you. I was reading about you last month, how you figured out who stole those diamonds from Parma's by talking to all the people who were there for six hours. When the bank opened at 10:00, I went and got that check, and came straight here."

Wolfe had been leaning back in his chair during her narrative. Now he straightened up and opened his eyes. "Madam. I concede your assumption that it is unlikely that you were the target of two random attacks within the space of a few hours. It seems probable that they are related to the murder of Miss Treefall. Therefore, I am willing to proceed with the job as you described it. You understand that I can give no guarantee of success?"

"Yes." Her dark eyes were on him.

"Very well. I will have many questions. Some will seem irrelevant. You will answer them, anyway. It will be a long process, many hours. Until it is completed, you will remain in this house unless your presence is required at the police station, and you will communicate with no one. Mr. Goodwin will inform Mr. Rowcliff of your whereabouts."

"All right." Jean was staring at him, but apparently felt that it wasn't her place to make any comments. As for me, I had to hand it to him. By leaving it open-ended, he gave himself the option of kicking her out at any time if the presence of a woman under his roof became too great a strain.

Wolfe glanced at the clock. "It is now almost time for my lunch, and I do not discuss business during meals. You will lunch with us, and we will begin afterwards."

"I don't think I can eat anything," Jean said faintly.

"Nonsense. You had no dinner last night, and I presume no breakfast this morning. The brain cannot function without nourishment, and yours will need to be in good working order."

He pressed the buzzer on his desk, and in a minute Fritz was there. "Fritz," Wolfe said gruffly, "my client, Miss Harper, will be joining us for lunch. It is inadvisable for her to leave the house at this point. She has not eaten for — er — some time, so please make sure there is sufficient. I trust there will be no problem?"

Fritz looked almost as stricken as Wolfe. Lamb chops don't stretch easily, and he knows how I love his rice cakes. But the honor of the kitchen was at stake. "Certainly not, sir," he said, and retired to make some last-minute adjustments in the menu.

When we were seated at the table, however, and Fritz had placed a dish of lamb chops in front of each of us, I saw Jean looking at her plate in dismay. "I'm sorry," she said. "I can't eat this. I'm a vegetarian."

The glare Wolfe directed at me would have frozen my lamb

chops, had it been aimed a little lower. Not only had I landed him with a female guest for an unknown duration, but now he had a vegetarian at the table. Worse yet, a starving one. "What will you eat?" he said icily to her.

Jean looked around the table. "I could eat those," she replied timidly, pointing to the rice cakes.

I suppose that eventually Wolfe recovered enough to speak, but I couldn't tell you what topic of conversation he chose for that meal. I was too busy watching Jean Harper eat. Wolfe and I each got a couple of rice cakes, and she polished off the rest of them. Meanwhile, Fritz had whipped up a mixture of fresh vegetables as only he can do them: baby carrots, small new potatoes, fresh green beans, and so on, in a lemon-lime butter sauce. I got a couple of spoonfuls of that, but by the time I was ready for seconds, there weren't any. Fritz brought in a loaf of his home-made bread and some cheese, and by the end of the meal there was none left for him to take back, although I admit Wolfe and I helped out on that some. Then we got to the salad, and she ate most of that. She was slowing down by the time we reached dessert, and only had two pieces of blackberry pie.

As we were finishing our pie, Wolfe asked politely, "Did you have enough?"

"Yes, thank you."

"Good. Then we'll adjourn to the office." Back in the office, Wolfe, if not exactly beaming at her, was at least no longer scowling. He likes people who appreciate good food. "If you're ready," he said, "we'll get started."

Normally, he doesn't like to work right after lunch, but this was a rush situation. Until he had wormed every last fact and impression regarding the Treefall murder out of Jean Harper, she was planted in his house. She would have to stay overnight as it was, because it was too late to get an advertisement in the evening papers now, and she couldn't leave until we had reasonable assurance that the murderer would have seen it.

"I'm ready," Jean said. Maybe it was my imagination, but she seemed to fill out the red leather chair more than before, and her color was better. She had definitely needed a meal.

She answered all of Wolfe's questions fully and without balking, even the most personal ones. Of course, she was paying him a lot of money to ask her questions, and her life depended on his doing a good job, but even so. We learned that Elizabeth Treefall was not universally loved; far from it. Even William Entworth, her supervisor, and the man who had promoted her to her current position, had not been fond of her. She was a constant thorn in his side, nitpicking him about prices and delivery dates. But she was intelligent and a hard worker, so he had kept her on.

Elizabeth had been a floor clerk before her promotion ten months before. She had worked with the clerks who now reported to her. Even then, she had not been popular, but now she was less so. Paul Garcia lived in constant fear of being fired. She had given him two written warnings already, and a third one could have cost him his job. Maureen disliked her, because she felt that she ought to have gotten the assistant manager's job. Wolfe asked Jean her opinion, and she said that Elizabeth was better at keeping the shelves stocked, but Maureen would have been better at managing people. Elizabeth was hard to work for. She expected a lot, and never thanked you for a job well done, though she was always ready to let you know when you had screwed up. Jean had thought about leaving, but she needed the job. She was in school, working towards a degree in business management, and her part-time work was paying the rent.

Although she didn't say so, I got the impression that James Lester, the fourth clerk, was another reason Jean hadn't quit. James and Elizabeth had dated for a period of about six months last year, before she got promoted and became his supervisor. The day she got her promotion was the day they stopped going together. Jean had no idea who had ended the relationship, or how James had felt about Elizabeth afterward. He had treated her quite coolly, never speaking to her except about business matters. For her part, she seemed to regard him from that point on as just another store worker. It was clear that Jean would have been happy to console James for his loss, but apparently he hadn't looked her way.

Wolfe took her through the events of the previous morning, but nothing much emerged. The problem was, of course, that Jean hadn't been in the stock room between 9:00 and 11:10. She hadn't seen the pesto until three minutes before Elizabeth Treefall scooped a bite of it up with her unsalted whole-wheat cracker. She was positive that it hadn't been poisoned during those three minutes, but that left a lot of time unaccounted for. Wolfe concentrated on her memory of people's movements in and out of the stockroom, but that was a dead end, too. She simply couldn't remember whether there had been any time when only one person was in the back room. In any case, the side table on which the pesto had stood was off in a corner and partially screened by a line of shelving. It would have been easy enough for anyone to have slipped in and dropped a couple of spoonfuls of rat poison in the pesto and stirred it up, without being observed by somebody stacking boxes on the other side of the room.

At two minutes to four, Wolfe heaved a sigh and pushed back his chair. "Miss Harper, I must leave you now. I have work to do upstairs. Mr. Goodwin will attend to your needs in my absence."

His work upstairs was, of course, his regular two-hour afternoon session in the plant rooms, but I didn't tell Jean that. I attended to her needs by letting her select a book from the bookshelf and showing her to the front room. Then I called *The Gazette* and got Lon Cohen. He had a couple dozen questions for me, and I told him nobody wanted the answers more than we did, and if he would give me the latest scoop I would reciprocate later on. I didn't get much. The autopsy had shown that it was cyanide, and the cops had found a paper spill in a corner of the stock room with traces of cyanide but no fingerprints. There were two other store clerks who weren't on duty that day but could have come in through the back door; but they both had been somewhere else between 9:45 and 11:15, and could prove it. The other containers of pesto had been tested and were cyanide-free. It was highly unlikely that a customer could have entered the back room without being seen by a store employee, and in any case a customer wouldn't have known who, if anyone, would be sampling the pesto that was on the table. And so on. It all boiled down to a lot of nothing.

After *The Gazette*, I went upstairs and checked that there were sheets on the bed in the spare room. Then I hit the typewriter. It had been agreed that I would make a transcript which Jean would sign and which would be given to the cops in the event that the killer wasn't scared off at the thought of crossing Wolfe's path and hit it lucky on the third try.

At 6:00 on the dot, I heard the sound of Wolfe's elevator descending. I went and got Jean from the front room, and they went at it again. This time he concentrated on the moods of each of the store employees throughout the morning, every word they had said, and every glance or gesture they had made. Jean was trying hard, but they didn't seem to be getting anywhere. At 7:30, when Wolfe rose and headed for the dining room with Jean and me tagging along behind, it looked pretty certain that we were going to have a house guest that night, and for God knew how many nights thereafter.

I don't know what Fritz called the stew he served us for dinner. "Stew" is a pretty unsatisfactory word to describe it, anyway. My plate contained plenty of beef chunks and fresh summer vegetables — the same ones I had gotten a taste of at lunch — covered with golden liquid that smelled of white wine and fresh herbs and was too thick to be soup, but too thin to be a sauce. I glanced at Jean's dish and saw that no beef was visible, but otherwise it looked the same as mine.

So I was taken aback when, as I was reaching for a piece of Fritz's homemade sourdough bread, I heard a choking sound from her end of the table and looked up to see her staring into her bowl as if a cobra had suddenly appeared in it. She had turned white and looked like she was about to keel over, so I got there quick. I was pulling her chair back from the table, with my hands on her shoulders to keep her in it, when Wolfe's voice came. "Miss Harper! Archie, has she had any of that soup?"

I couldn't have answered him, since I hadn't been watching her. I bent over to get a look at her face, and she spoke. "Oh my God!" It was only a whisper. "I know — I've remembered now." She looked across the table at Wolfe. "It was the second check approval."

"Yes?" He was leaning forward.

"It was the eighty-three dollar check. I had to get Bill's approval, so I buzzed him. We have a buzzer up front that sounds in the back room. I thought he was back there, so I gave it two short buzzes. That's our signal for check approval."

"And he came?"

"Yes." Her eyes were open, but she wasn't seeing anything in that room right then. "He came down the aisle, and he was wiping his hands off with a Kleenex. He dropped it in his pocket and picked up the check and looked at it. His hands were still a little greasy, and he left a mark on it, right next to the eight. Then he scribbled his initials in the corner and gave it to me. And when I put it in the cash register, I smelled something." She reached forward and picked up a sprig of greenery that was decorating her stew. "I smelled this. Basil."

She probably didn't understand the look of consternation on Wolfe's face, but I did. "Right at the beginning of dinner," was what he was thinking. Circumstances had forced him to discuss a case during a meal, and now it looked like circumstances were going to prevent him from finishing it. Of course, he could put off calling the cops till after dinner, but the longer he delayed, the more likely it was that Jean Harper would spend the night in the guest room.

It took him about seven seconds. His face cleared, and he said, "Archie, at 8:00 you will phone Mr. Cramer. Tell him that Miss Harper and I have important information for him regarding the murder of Miss Treefall. If he and Mr. Rowcliff wish to visit us, we will speak to them after dinner."

Now that's what I call quick decision-making. He knew that it would take Cramer ten minutes to locate Rowcliff and talk him into coming, and another twenty minutes to get here. And he made a sacrifice, too, cutting half an hour off the end of his dinner time. He turned to Jean. "Miss Harper, I'm afraid you will be asked to make another statement at the police station this evening. You won't mind, since it will remove from you the fear of untimely death."

"Of course not." Her color had returned.

"And you will at least have had a meal first." He picked up his spoon.

There isn't much more to tell. Cramer and Rowcliff were on our doorstep at 8:30, and when they had heard what Jean had to tell them, they lost no time swearing out a warrant. Rowcliff, of course, didn't believe that Jean had only remembered about the check that evening. She told me later that he had given her a rough half hour, but Cramer was there to see fair play, and she got out of it with no bones broken. As a matter of fact, Rowcliff should have been grateful to her, since she told him the name of Healthy Way's bank, and he was able to get someone down there in time to grab the check before it went through the check sorter. It had a nice clear fingerprint on it, all right, and the experts were able to identify not only basil and oil, but also a trace of cyanide still clinging to it. Apparently, Entworth had gotten quite a start when the buzzer sounded right while he was dumping the cyanide in — enough to make him dip his thumb into the pesto.

With evidence like that, they hardly needed a motive, but eventually they found one. It seemed that Entworth had been accepting money under the table for some time from various outfits as a reward for carrying their products. Elizabeth Treefall had gotten suspicious when his buying patterns didn't match the store's selling patterns.

Last week, Entworth was indicted for murder. The day after,

Jean Harper showed up at the front door. With her was a tall young man with a shock of brown hair and a long tan face, carrying a large crate. The size of his grin indicated that if I had offered him two bits to tell me all his troubles, I wouldn't have gotten my money's worth. Jean introduced him as James Lester, and told me that after Entworth's arrest, he had been made acting store manager, and had done such a good job that the management had made it official. She was smiling, too. It made her look almost pretty.

"We thought a token of appreciation would be appropriate," Lester said. "If I could just set this down? It's kind of heavy. The kitchen would be the best place."

I led the way through to the kitchen, then helped Fritz unpack the box. It was filled with fresh vegetables and fruits, along with other items such as jars of honey and a selection of dried herbs. Fritz was speechless with pleasure and embarrassment.

"It's to replace all the food I ate that day," Jean said. "And because, after all — if it hadn't been for that basil . . ." Suddenly she leaned forward, put both hands on his shoulders, and kissed his cheek. Fritz turned as red as the basket of cherry tomatoes he had just put down.

We chatted for a few more minutes. Jean told me that she had been promoted to assistant store manager, and I said I was sure she'd do a good job. When they left, I thought for a moment that she was going to kiss me, too, and so did she, but then she changed her mind. It was just as well, with her future husband standing right there. Not that she told me that, but then she didn't have to. I am a detective, after all.

THE DAUGHTER HUNT

by Henry W. Enberg

Copyright © 1986 by Henry W. Enberg

"The Daughter Hunt" makes use of characters created by Rex Stout with the permission of The Wolfe Pack and the Stout Estate. It was written for the Rex Stout Centenary festivities and first performed during The Wolfe Pack's Black Orchid weekend of December 6th,1986.

CAST
(in order of appearance)

ARCHIE GOODWIN . . . . No description needed

NERO WOLFE. . . . . No description needed

EZRA HENDERSON . . . . 75 or so; widower; sr. partner of Bronson, deGersedorf & Henderson; courtly but stuffy lawyer of the old school

ELSPETH COURT . . . . 50 or so; single; founder and CEO of JCN Computers, Inc.; no-nonsense business type

LON COHEN . . . . No description needed

VIOLET HUNTER . . . . . 30; single; station manager of WMDS, major public TV station; came up through engineering and had none of the rough edges worn off

KITTY WINTER . . . . 30; divorced; founder, president and CEO of advertising firm of Winter, Milverton & Gruner; has sweet voice, but knows her way around

FRITZ BRENNER . . . . No description needed

INSPECTOR CRAMER . . . . No description needed

LILY ROWAN . . . . No description needed

BERYL STAPLETON . . . . 30; single; computer consultant; buttoned-up personality, but capable of depths

MARY MORSTAN. . . . . . . 30; affianced; music reviewer and painter; upper class accent and attitudes

EFFIE MUNRO. . . . . 30; married; cabaret singer and author; well on way to being earth mother

Scene 1

SFX: NOISY WORD PROCESSOR UNDER

AG: It was a relatively balmy Monday for November in New York City, though the weather prediction in *The Gazette* was for cold and rain by Wednesday. Of course, the weather wouldn't affect the 10,000 orchids in the greenhouses on the roof, which was why I was entering their pedigrees on Jason the Third. Excuse me, although Wolfe has accused me of "rampant anthropomorphism," I've named the JCN computer lurking in the basement near Fritz's cookbooks 'Jason' and numbered the terminals. I write these accounts on Jason the First in my room. Jason the Second keeps track of the larder, the wine cellar, and the household accounts from the kitchen. And Jason the Third is built into my desk in the office. I was surprised that Wolfe accepted these "infernal contraptions" (another quotation) into the house. It may have been Nathaniel Parker's argument that important tax benefits would be lost under the new law if we waited until 1987. More likely, Wolfe just wanted to keep me within earshot rather than running off to the bank or delivering my accounts of his cases to my literary agent. Although I seem to recall Wolfe's saying that nothing could interest him less than "electronic tomfoolery," I have caught him looking at a screen more than once, and he did read the instruction manual (after forbidding me to call it documentation). It's a good thing the manual was incomplete; I wouldn't want Wolfs to realize that there's a way I could make the typing almost silent, and I'm sure he would be psychologically deprived if he couldn't complain about my typing.

NW: Archie, must you make so much noise?

AG: (ASIDE) A coincidence, a pure coincidence. (TO WOLFE) I'm just finishing the germination records. Try to bear the burden.

SFX: DOORBELL RINGS

AG: That should be the friendly folks from Bronson, deGersedorf & Henderson. I'll just terminate my accessing . . .

NW: Archie!

AG: . . . finish what I'm doing and get the door.

SFX: COMPUTER SHUTOFF SOUNDS, FOOTSTEPS, OFFICE DOOR, FOOTSTEPS

AG: I may have spoken too soon in calling the party from Bronson, deGersedorf friendly. The leader of the pack, who must be Henderson himself, looked not unlike one of the gloomier pharaohs in a Homburg, a three-piece suit, and one of those briefcases that bulges if you put anything in it that's stapled. Number Two (you tell by the briefcase: hers would hold as many as a dozen letters) was fairly attractive, but somewhere around twenty years over my limit. If they weren't so well dressed, I'd peg the other two for porters: you could live out of their brief-cases for a week if you didn't dress for dinner.

SFX: DOOR OPENS

Hend: You must be Archie Goodwin. Mr. Parker told me you are the keeper of the gate.

AG: Unfortunately, my other two heads are in for new collars. Who must you be?

Hend: Ezra Henderson. This is . . . uh . . . Courtney Elsworth of my firm, and my associates, Austin Williston and Kent Corbin. May we come in?

AG: Of course. Your hats?

SFX: DOOR, MUMBLES, FOOTSTEPS, OFFICE DOOR, FOOTSTEPS

Hend: Good morning, Mr. Wolfe. I believe Mr. Parker told you we would be coming. May I introduce Courtney Elsworth, Austin Williston and Kent Corbin.

NW: Good day, Madam, gentlemen. Is everyone comfort-able? Good. Now Mr. Henderson, why did you make an appoint-ment to see me?

AG: (ASIDE) Parker must have done an even better selling job on this appointment than he did for Jason; I'd seldom seen Wolfe so placid. I pulled out my notebook.

Hend: As you may know, my firm represents the Third Foundation. Do you know its history?

NW: Only what has been in the press. It was founded in 1977 with what your firm called a very large endowment. Every December since 1978, it has awarded grants of $250,000 each to ten to twelve persons "in recognition of high achievement and potential service to the community." I understand that the grants are free of income tax on the recipients. Would you be interested in my characterization of those recipients?

Hend: Very much.

NW: Seven or eight people every year are scientists or scholars. Except for 1982, when you duplicated an award, you might almost be picking MacArthur Foundation rejects. One or two people each year are creative artists. What I find interesting is that they are distinguished mainly by their not being in vogue: I must confess I was somewhat surprised that there were so many representational artists, composers of comprehensible music, poets whose works rhyme and scan, and novelists who have not despaired of telling a story, particularly so many of the quality of your recipients. Finally, every year there are one or two young women who have distinguished themselves in some way in the arts, science, or commerce.

AG: I watched old Henderson while Wolfe spoke. He wouldn't do anything so crude as looking away from Wolfe during the presentation, but there was a definite twitch there. If he'd been in the red chair forty or fifty years ago, I'm sure he would have been starting out of his seat every sentence or two.

Hend: Very interesting. What do you think about it, Miss Elsworth?

Court: I hadn't thought it was so obvious . . . the instructions from the Third Foundation, I mean. Yes, I think I can say that we are instructed to select people from those three categories. I don't know why, of course.

Hend: Of course. Since you have analyzed our program so well, Mr. Wolfe, it is relatively simple for me to explain why we are here. The Third Foundation has reached a milestone; there have been sixty recipients in the first class you mentioned and twelve in each of the other categories.

AG: Twenty-one million tax-free dollars is some milestone. What are you planning, a yacht race?

Hend: Something rather less impressive, Mr. Goodwin. We have invited them . . . scientists and scholars to a convocation out by the California Institute of Technology. The creative artists will be treated to a week in London. It is the young women, whom we have invited to New York for a banquet this Thursday, who brought us here.

AG: Although Mr. Wolfe might not be up to squiring rich young things around New York, I can stand it if they can.

NW: Mr. Goodwin occasionally misses the point. How many of them have been murdered?

AG: (ASIDE) I should have seen it coming. (ALOUD) I apologize. Which database has the Third Foundation in the same paragraph as some form of the word murder?

Court: There's no need to apologize, Mr. Goodwin, your memory is not at fault. As far as we know, the Foundation was mentioned in connection with only one death, and none of them was called murder. In fact, three of the deaths weren't reported in New York at all. (BEAT) In answer to your question, Mr. Wolfe, of the twelve grantees, four have died what were called accidental deaths within the past three months.

NW: And the others?

Court: Two died some years ago. We expect the remaining six to be at the dinner Thursday.

Hend: The Third Foundation is Miss Elsworth's client. That is why we are here, Mr. Wolfe. We do not believe those four deaths were accidental, and we wish to see all six women three days from now.

NW: I am not the Secret Service, Mr. Henderson. And even that body with its vast resources has a rather poor record.

Hend: We recognize that. The only way to protect the six women with any assurance, assuming, as we must, that they are in danger, is to identify and quarantine the person who threatens them. Will you help us, Mr. Wolfe?

NW: Miss (SLIGHT HESITATION) Elsworth implied that the deaths were out of state; obtaining information on them might be difficult.

AG: (ASIDE) That was the old Wolfe. If he could find a reason not to take the case, he could enjoy his lunch, which was ten minutes away, in comfort and then return to his latest book, *Novus Ordo Seclorum: Intellectual Origins of the Constitution.*

Hend: Bronson, deGersedorf & Henderson is not without its resources. Mr. Williston, I believe you have the files on the deaths.

SFX: PAPER RUSTLING

AG: (ASIDE) That explained one of the cowhide overnight bags.

Hend: And Mr. Corbin has the files on the survivors.

SFX: PAPER RUSTLING

Court: I see you have a terminal for a JCN Model VS56 computer.

AG: (ASIDE) That was interesting; I didn't remember introducing Jason the Third to her.

Court: If we come across any more data, may we send them to you?

AG: (ASIDE) She pronounced data the way Wolfe does and treated it as the plural it is; I half-expected a purr. (ALOUD) I'll give you my access code. (ASIDE) Wolfe winced.

Court: Does that mean we can rifle your files?

AG: I suppose you could, if you had a large enough computer and enough time to break through the barrier between receiving documents and record-keeping, but unless you're a wine merchant or a poulterer, it would be rather pointless. Nothing we wish to keep confidential is in Jason's memory. (ASIDE) I had expected Wolfe to wince, which he obligingly did, but not Miss Elsworth — and why was she carrying the conversation, anyway? (ALOUD) Could I rifle Bronson, deGersedorf & Henderson's files?

Court: Let's see . . . a good hacker with a large machine might get into our records, and an inspired guess or two might get the intruder into one of the secure areas, but then the intruder would have 30 seconds to log on by the individual file name or our security program would cancel the inquiry, trace the intruder, and, if the intruder stayed around too long, begin cannibalizing the intruder's memory. The security program is also triggered by multiple inquiries after a single file.

Hend: My dear, I'm sure Mr. Wolfe is not interested in our security system. Mr. Wolfe, will you take our case?

NW: (SIGHING) I suppose it would be vain to mention my high fees?

Hend: Supererogatory.

NW: All right. I consider most foundations vehicles of irony: transferring wealth from relatively innocent acquisitors by way of guilt-ridden administrators to equally guilt-ridden bureaucrats, with only the crumbs sifting down to the needy, but there are points of interest about the Third Foundation. I shall take the case.

AG: (ASIDE) I'll spare you, dear reader, the crass commercial details. Suffice it to say that Wolfe will not have to work for several months after this case, however it turns out. The legal eagles, and Miss Courtney Elsworth, whatever her real name and occupation, flew away. And so to lunch.

SFX: MUSICAL. BRIDGE

Scene 2

AG: After lunch, Wolfe looked at the piles of papers, grunted, told me to have Saul find out about the deceased women, and asked me if Lon Cohen owed us a favor, which is why I was walking a familiar corridor at *The Gazette*.

SFX: FOOTSTEPS, OFFICE NOISES, KNOCK ON DOOR, MUFFLED GRUNT, DOOR OPENS AND CLOSES, OFFICE NOISES STOP, FOOTSTEPS

AG: I have seen the future, and it runs on microchips. Where's the terminal you had in here the last time I visited?

Lon: It's still here; I finally talked the office manager into hiding it and turning down the sound. I haven't seen anything in the news lately that would justify your coming down here. Is Lily about to make an honest man of you? I know the sports editor personally, and I bet I could get an announcement in under upcoming fights.

AG: First, Lily prefers me as a cad and bounder; second, if I remember correctly, your last bet was Boston in six.

Lon: So why are you here?

AG: Tell me about the Third Foundation.

Lon: Are you interested for a specific reason? Has Wolfe been named to get a quarter million? Now that would be a story. Of course, he'd complain it wasn't a Nobel, but it still might be worth a paragraph in the section.

AG: Wolfe hasn't been named, or at least I don't think so. It's just my insatiable curiosity. Wolfe was saying just the other day that you owed us some information, and I thought . . . I can always go to the *Times*, I guess.

Lon: You wound me. (AS IF TO AN IDIOT CHILD) The Third Foundation was founded in 1977 . . .

AG: I know what's been published; what's the dirt?

Lon: All right. Then you know that tracing the Third Foundation is no picnic. All trails lead to Bronson, deGersedorf and stop short. We looked into it once and we have some opinions, but nothing we could print.

AG: That's the idea.

Lon: We think the Third Foundation is funded by a Cayman Islands trust.

AG: For how much money?

Lon: I'm getting there. The trust has just enough in it most of the year to pay operating expenses. Every November, it receives enough to pay that year's grants.

AG: You're enjoying this.

Lon: Perhaps. We believe that money comes, and this is the interesting part, from a Netherlands Antilles holding company. And what the holding company holds is $400 to $500 million worth of stock in JCN Computers, Inc. That's how the money comes in. We also found out a bit about how it goes out. Bronson, deGersedorf has a short list of people who pick the grantees. How they pick them and how the law firm made up its list I don't know.

AG: Tell me about JCN Computers.

Lon: The initials stand for Ralph Johnson, Elspeth Court, and Al Nathanson. They handle marketing, design, and financial matters, respectively. The latest Forbes list of the richest people in America has each of them somewhere over $500 million; of course that was before JCN stock took a beating.

AG: (ASIDE) I learned a lot more about JCN — apparently, it's the next IBM or at least Hewlett-Packard — but unless you're a computer hacker or a stock picker, you wouldn't be interested. If I seem to know too much about the company later in this account, blame it on Lon Cohen.

MUSICAL BRIDGE

Scene 3

AG: I got home to find Wolfe in a screaming rage, jumping up and down on the desk. Actually, it was his equivalent; he had taken some books about the founding of the United States written by someone named Wills off the shelf, dog-eared them and was in the process of cracking the spine of one of them when I came in. We exchanged some badinage about the decline of historical scholarship and he surprised me again.

NW: Archie, I have read portions of the reports Mr. Henderson left with us on the surviving young women. Five of them live in New York City and one was scheduled to check into the Churchill forty-five minutes ago. After we have dinner, I would like you to arrange to see them as soon as possible. I do not think it will be necessary to bring them here for me to interview, but if your intelligence guided by experience suggests that, Wednesday at 9:00 would be the best time.

AG: Is there any specific information you want me to find out?

NW: No ... Yes ... Mr. Henderson did not state that his misgivings about the deaths of the four young women were confidential; perhaps your inquiring about them will lead to some further information on motive. We have a few minutes before dinner; what did Mr. Cohen have to say?

AG: (ASIDE) I reported in full, and Wolfe took it all in as he usually does. He had only one comment:

NW: I suspect it is a practice the firm developed to avoid liability in other contexts, but Bronson, deGersedorf & Henderson left out one piece of information. I hope you can confirm that the young women are thirty years of age.

AG: I saw their pictures in the Gazette; thev are all pretty clearly in their thirties.

NW: No, not "in their thirties," thirty. They all should have been born in the calendar year 1956. I suspect that they were born in the first eleven months of the year, but the probability of that is slightly lower.

AG: (ASIDE) Whether Wolfe was correct or not, this looked to be one of the more pleasant assignments I had had in recent years. Talk of business was forbidden at the dinner table, but even Wolfe couldn't keep me from wondering whether bright, rich, young women still danced.

SFX: MUSICAL BRIDGE

Scene 4

AG: Bronson deGersedorf smoothed the way. I was to see Violet Hunter this afternoon and Kitty Winter tonight; Martha Adler, the one from out of town, the first thing tomorrow; and Beryl Stapleton, Mary Morstan, and Effie Munro after lunch. I would have scheduled lunch with one of them (presumably charged to Bronson deGersedorf) if Lily hadn't insisted. Since she was one of the people on Bronson deGersedorf's list of pickers, that was even more of a pleasure than it would have been normally.

SFX: OFFICE, NOISES UNDER

Violet: All right, Mr. Goodwin, you've established that you're street smart, hetero, and either watch WMDS occasionally or subscribe to our monthly guide. I've got a station to manage, could you come to the point?

AG: You received a Third Foundation grant in 1982.

Violet: Yes, and that's why I'm here; whatever you've heard about the salaries in public television, you've got to have a nest egg to work here. I didn't think Bronson deGersedorf insisted I talk with you for a history quiz, but if they did, you have two more questions and it's out the door.

AG: And are you going to the reunion banquet Thursday?

Violet: Yes, the Good Lord willin' and the creeks don't rise. One question.

AG: (UNDERSTATED, OF COURSE) Do you expect the killer to get you tonight, Tuesday, Wednesday, or Thursday?

Violet: (BEAT) If we were on the air, I'd expect an organ sting and a tight close-up of my startled expression. Why a killer? Why me? Why now?

AG: Twelve young women won Third Foundation grants. Two died naturally, six are scheduled for the dinner Thursday, and four very recently died under mysterious circumstances. Mr. Wolfe believes those deaths are related to the dinner.

Violet: Holy sh—! Let me see.

SFX: COMPUTER NOISES

AG: You have a file on the people coming to the dinner?

Violet: I like to know who's likely to steal my breadsticks.

SFX: OFFICE NOISES FADE

AG: (ASIDE) We discussed the possibilities, but the only thing I learned was that Violet Hunter was born June 27, 1956.

SFX: MUSICAL BRIDGE

Scene 5

AG: Over the fricandeau at dinner, Wolfe was slightly below his usual standard. Since the unfortunate events of 1974, he had added politics to his list of dinner table no-nos, and Iranian miniatures of the thirteenth century were a poor substitute for what I suspected he wanted to discuss. During breaks in his longer disquisitions, I reflected that 8.3 percent of the grant winners (heck, 16.67 percent of the living winners) danced. I was to meet Kitty Winter at the Flamingo Club.

SFX: MUSICAL. BRIDGE: FADING INTO BACKGROUND MUSIC: CROWD UNDER

Kitty: (SLIGHTLY OUT OF BREATH) Archie, I didn't know anyone over the age of twenty-one still danced.

AG: A few of us. But you can't have had much time to come to that decision.

Kitty: If I used a line like that in one of my commercials, the FTC would be down on me the next morning. I was born August 15, 1956, and I'm proud of it. Anyway, I'm getting a touch tired of being the infant genius of Madison Avenue, If it hadn't been for the Third Foundation grant, I'd still be working away at some big agency, saving up for my own firm.

AG: Instead, you're founder and chief executive officer of Winter, Milverton & Gruner.

Kitty: Worse yet, I'm sole owner. When I divorced Barry Gruner, I got his shares — and Chuck Milverton sold out to me to start a talent agency.

AG: Looks, wealth, fame . . .

Kitty: Sixteen-hour days, incipient ulcers, nasty innuendos in Ad Age.

AG: And a natural sense of rhythm on the dance floor. If you don't have it made, as they say, you're pretty close.

Kitty: There is one thing, though.

AG: What?

Kitty: If Vi reported your conversation this afternoon accurately, I'm about to be killed.

AG: It's not certain. Mr. Wolfe has been wrong — not often enough to be statistically significant, but occasionally.

Kitty: Tell me about statistical significance! I started out working a computer in market research. What should I do?

AG: First, now that you've caught your breath, join me on the floor.

SFX: MUSIC AND CROWD FADES TO MUSICAL BRIDGE

Scene 6

AG: Morning came late to West Thirty-Fifth Street, along with a twinge of regret that I was punching my own alarm. Wolfe was up in his room having breakfast and hadn't had any messages for me, so I was enjoying my breakfast in some degree of comfort.

Fritz: Archie, I am surprised at you. I had difficulty sleeping last night, and I saw you come in at . . . I saw you come in late. That was not Mr. Wolfe's client. Did the meeting yesterday not result in employment for Mr. Wolfe?

AG: It resulted in employment, Fritz. Even if Wolfe does nothing, our salaries are well secured . . . and you should be able to stock the larder at least until the shad are running. The young lady with me last night was a client, in a way, and my assignment is to guard that body until at least Thursday. That and five other bodies.

Fritz: You do not seem overly upset.

AG: Actually, I have decided to reconsider my career, as of next Friday. If we get these six women through a dinner, Thursday, Wolfe won't need me for at least six months, and a half-dozen rich, young, bright . . . well, at least four or five successful women will think they owe me their lives. I think I'll keep my room here, and of course I'll be here for meals, but most nights it'll be a round of the clubs . . . and weekends I'll fly away. You know, the word gigolo has a second meaning in the dictionary — I looked it up — it means dancing partner.

Fritz: Of course, it is a back-formation from *gigolette,* a girl who frequents public dancing halls. I always thought you might consider that profession. But what will Miss Lily think?

AG: I'll ask her at lunch today. We might be able to set up a bidding war. . . for dancing partners, that is.

SFX: DOORBELL RINGS

AG: I'm finished. I'll get that.

SFX: CHAIR, FOOTSTEPS

AG: (ASIDE) Even Inspector Cramer couldn't spoil my mood. He knows Wolfe's schedule almost as well as I do, so he must be here to see me. Even if it was about the Third Foundation case, those deaths weren't in his jurisdiction, so this might even be fairly pleasant.

SFX: DOOR, GRUNT, FOOTSTEPS UNDER

AG: Come in, Inspector. It's a lovely day for November, but I understand it may rain. May I take your hat?

Cramer: You won't feel the rain on Riker's Island, and I can hang it up myself.

SFX: DOOR OPEN AND CLOSE, STEPS, GRUNT

Cramer: I know Wolfe has his food delivered, but this is the first time I've heard him arranging to have the murder victims brought to him. Were they going to wrap her and put on a bow or just dump her on the doorstep?

AG: Slow down. Who's been murdered? What are you talking about?

Cramer: Can the injured innocence. (BEAT) Maybe you are innocent, for once. Who were you going to meet here in . . . uh . . . twenty minutes?

AG: It's none of your business until you connect it to some

legitimate topic of inquiry.

Cramer: I though it was too unlikely to be true — your innocence, I mean. Were you going to meet Martha Adler?

AG: Without prejudice to my rights — and I still don't see what you have to do with it — yes, I was going to meet Martha Adler.

Cramer: And who else?

AG: I can keep repeating my qualifications, but since you haven't read me my rights yet, I don't think I'll call Nathaniel Parker. I wasn't planning on meeting anyone else. Now, what is this all about?

Cramer: Twenty minutes ago, two young women got into a limousine sent by the law firm of Bronson, deGersedorf & Henderson at the Churchill. One of them gave the driver Wolfe's address. At Forty-Second Street and Seventh Avenue, while he was stalled in traffic, the driver heard one person get out. When he looked in the back, he saw a corpse. It was Martha Adler. She'd been strangled. The driver called the law firm and spoke with an old bird named Henderson. Then he called the police. All he'd say was "Nero Wolfe, Nero Wolfe." That's why I'm here. Let's go back to my first question: since when has Wolfe subscribed to the corpse of the month club?

AG: (ASIDE) There was no reason to bother Wolfe; he had tumbled to the murders yesterday morning, after all. I gave Cramer the works. He finally had to admit that there was nothing he could hold me on, not even as a material witness — and I suspect he didn't want to see Wolfe — so he left a little before 11:00. 1 reported to Wolfe when he came down from the plant rooms. He pfui-ed and said he presumed Bronson deGersedorf would warn the others. Since there was nothing better to do, I went back to the germination records and Wolfe read. At noon, I left for Lily's penthouse and a less pleasant lunch than I had expected.

SFX: MUSICAL BRIDGE

Scene 7

Lily: I remember picking Martha. She was the only pure scholar in the bunch, a mathematician, I believe. This is all confidential, of course.

AG: Of course. I realize you're only telling me about the work you did for the Third Foundation because you can't resist my aggressive masculine charms.

Lily: And because you don't talk in your sleep. Seriously, Archie, I think the Third Foundation does a lot of good, and I gave my word that I wouldn't tell anyone. If you and Wolfe didn't think there was a murderer . . .

AG: It's more than a theory . . .

Lily: (SHIVERING) Let's catch him — I guess it must be her — and end this nightmare.

AG: What else do you know about the Third Foundation?

Lily: Every October, the law firm sends me a bunch of lists — you know, the scholars, the creative people, and the young women. I'm supposed to rank everyone on the list in each category. I send them back and they send me a check. I usually send the check to the Heart Association. In November, they send me the final choices and ask if there's any one of them I absolutely abhor. There hasn't been, but someone else must have a veto, because one or two people are dropped every so often by the time the grants come out. I suppose that's why they're so secretive about the whole thing; it would be dreadful to make the November list and not get the money. That mainly happens to the creative people, come to think of it. At least six times, there was someone on the list who was a bit avante garde; not one got a grant.

AG: That's interesting, but my main concern is the young women. What standards were you given?

Lily: Nothing cut and dried. Potential. Possibilities. Likely to set the world afire. There weren't any politicians on the lists, but if there had been, they would have had to be odds-on to make President.

AG: Let's go at it another way: Hunter, Winter, Stapleton, Morstan and Munro are still alive. What do you remember about them?

Lily: My memory's nothing like yours, but I can do better than rack it. I saved the information we were sent about them — in complete disregard of Foundation rules, by the way.

AG: That's my little scofflaw!

Lily: Condescension will get you nowhere. I don't know who the other judges are, but I find it hard to believe they could pick someone to set the world afire and not follow up the fire marshals' reports. Why haven't you said the obvious?

AG: I expected you to volunteer it. One of these five killed five people, and may kill four more. Do you have any idea who?

Lily: No, but I think I know why.

AG: And you'll keep that secret to their graves.

Lily: Escamillo, I know you crack wise so you can live with violence and murder, and you know it, but sometimes you go too . . . (BEAT) The lists this year were different. Last month, they sent us biographies of all the past winners for us to rank them. And there hasn't been any veto list, though the check came as soon as I sent my list in — and there was a bonus for the Heart Association.

AG: So the early awards were semifinals.

Lily: That's what I think.

AG: Is it some sort of tontine, where the survivors cut up some big pie?

Lily: If it were, why would they have us rank the final people?

No, I think this is some sort of winner-take-all deal.

AG: The scholars and artists seem unaffected; at least Bronson deGersedorf doesn't seem concerned about them.

Lily: I wondered about that when you were describing the meeting with Wolfe. Maybe they don't know about it.

AG: And the women do? 'Tis a puzzlement. (ASIDE) We discussed the grantees I'd met and I read the dossiers. For the record, Martha Hudson was born November 15, 1956. 1 don't know if that disproved Wolfe's theory, but it was interesting.

SFX: MUSICAL BRIDGE

Scene 8

SFX: WHIRRING UNDER

Beryl: Could you keep this short? I'm supposed to help Antioch Steel get the bugs out of their new computer network, and I want to earn my fee before they go under.

AG: Well, Miss Stapleton, I'm glad you could see me at all.

Beryl: If Mr Henderson hadn't asked me . . . go ahead, you have five minutes.

AG: You're attending the banquet Thursday?

Beryl: Yes.

AG: (BEAT) And you're not worried?

Beryl: No.

AG: (BEAT) Did Mr. Henderson tell you your life was in danger?

Beryl: Yes. (BEAT) But his telling me doesn't make it so. I think you and your Mr. Wolfe have ballooned some coincidental accidents into this whole thing just to earn a fee. I'll play along for . . . umh . . . another three minutes, but that's it.

AG: It isn't only accidents now. There hasn't been time for it to make the papers, but you may have heard it on the radio: Martha Adler was strangled this morning.

Beryl: Who?

AG: Martha Adler.

Beryl: That name means nothing to me. Was she one of the grantees?

AG: Yes.

Beryl: (BEAT) All right, maybe there is something to your ideas, but why should anyone kill for a dinner — except maybe your employer?

AG: You don't think there is anything more than a dinner involved?

Beryl: No, of course not.

AG: I have only two more questions: how do you know Mr. Henderson?

Beryl: He handed me my check — I think people tend to get to know people who give them a quarter million dollars.

AG: Nothing more?

Beryl: I suppose it's on record: I helped his firm with their computer.

AG: Yes, you *are* a computer consultant.

Beryl: The best. I set up their security system.

AG: Then you could break into it.

Beryl: You *are* ignorant about computers, aren't you? When I finished that security system, no one could break in, least of all me. You'd have to get by two access interfaces . . .

AG: And calculate an access code within thirty seconds on the first try.

Beryl: How did you . . .

AG: I'm an idiot savant. But if you set up the system, you'd know the codes.

Beryl: Bad guess — and I think you should pronounce the T. I know you get into the system on the phone with BDH666 and that the interior codes are combinations of six letters or digits. I forget what 36 to the sixth power is, but you won't get there counting on your fingers and toes, even if you've got a couple of spares — that's how I know Mr. Henderson. Your second question?

AG: When were you born?

Beryl: January 6, 1956. Good day, Mr. Goodwin -

SFX: WHIRRING FADES, MUSICAL BRIDGE

Scene 9

AG: I hadn't mentioned it to Fritz at breakfast. but Beryl Stapleton exhausted the available potential employers if I decided to go the dancing partner route. Mary Morstan was affianced, as they used to say, and Effie Munro had gone all the way to the altar. Of course, things change, but I don't like having people cut in on me on the dance floor, and I figure other men are the same. Miss Morstan, soon to be Doctor, Mrs. Doctor Jamison (her doctorate was in musical theory, his in medicine), lived on Arbor Street in the Village, and worked out of her home. I guess you can say worked out of there because that's where she wrote her music reviews and painted her pictures, but the easiest place to find her was concert lobbies and gallery openings and her publisher's office. This time it was a gallery opening.

SIX: CHATTER UNDER

Mary: . . . representational art. It is, however, common outside the arts to use the term abstract, but I do not think I am alone in wincing when one does so. You know, you almost did not find me here. I would have rung you with my regrets, of course.

AG: Is the show that bad?

Mary: Well, yes, but . . . let me be frank. I did not know Miss Adler, but Mr. Henderson's telephone call was most distressing.

AG: Did you know the other young ladies?

Mary: Only by name. I was looking forward to meeting them Thursday. Now, I don't know . . .

AG: If you need any protection . . .

Mary: Mr. Henderson has arranged for some sort of body-guard. I believe she's the person with the untasted container of wine over by the puce canvas. I do wish just one gallery would come up with the idea of real glasses and potable wine. I think they could sell anything they hung on the wall just because the purchasers were so happy at what they served. They might have to heat the brie, though, which is beyond most gallery-owners' motor skills.

AG: Did Mr. Henderson also tell you that the the best way to protect the five of you is for Mr. Wolfe to catch the murderer?

Mary: Yes, he did.

AG: Good. Then if you could answer a few questions?

Mary: Certainly.

AG: When were you born?

Mary: Are you sure you know what you're doing? Oh, well, it was August 17, 1956. My sign is . . .

AG: I have never asked a woman her sign: I never will ask a

woman her sign. There's a reason for my question, but I don't know what it is. If Mr. Wolfe cares to tell you — and I suspect he will be speaking with you and the other endangered women — perhaps he can give you the reason. Do you know anything about computers?

Mary: You're sure you're not working off a script from a singles bar? Before my grant from the Third Foundation, I was an editorial intern at a major publisher. They were just adopting a computer system, and I was pretty thoroughly trained — since then, I haven't done much with my training (I really prefer writing on a typewriter and calculating on paper), but I suppose I could be considered knowledgeable.

AG: What do you think is going to happen Thursday?

Mary: Good food, bad speeches, and a paragraph the next day in *The Gazette* or the *Times*.

AG: Nothing more?

Mary: I haven't really given it any thought. I always thought of my grant as seed money, something that would let me follow my career where it led. It's done that. I don't need any more money, and John is a wonderful man.

SFX: CHATTER FADES

AG: (ASIDE) I never learned if Miss Morstan danced, but I did learn more than I cared to know about art, music, and John H. Jamison, M.D. I made it home in time for dinner, with my appetite unimpaired by too-warm wine and too-cold cheese.

SFX: MUSICAL BRIDGE

Scene 10

AG: Dinner was delicious, but Wolfe was getting pitiful. This time it was the economic consequences to King John of the ransom paid for Richard the Lion Hearted. If he started in on Basil Zaharoff and other "Merchants of Death," I would have to take strong action.

Effie Munro wrote and sang, which is about as accurate as saying that Duke Ellington composed and played a little piano. Effie — I don't think she would answer to Miss Munro — was the only singer of her generation — and I wouldn't have to ask this time: it was June 7, 1956 — the only singer worth mentioning with Ella and Billie, and the only writer in a class with Faulkner and Fitzgerald. I met her in the dressing room at Jacqueline's, a club in Chelsea.

SFX: BACKSTAGE SOUNDS UNDER

Effie: Thank you, but I must confess I hate comparisons. They sang their way and I sing my way (GIGGLE) well, I sing anything ever written except "My Way." And they write their books and I write mine. By the way, if we must have comparisons, thank you for not hunting up some black writer: just because I come from Harlem doesn't have anything to do with my writing.

AG: You're welcome. I'd like to ask you a few questions, if I might.

Effie: Yes, I talked to Vi. Let's see, I was born June 7, 1956.

AG: I knew that.

Effie: And I am scared about Thursday, but Leonard . . .

AG: Your husband?

Effie: Yes. Leonard and the person the law firm sent over should keep me safe. If you'd ever worked some of the clubs I've worked, you wouldn't worry about a measly little killer. In fact, I called . . . well, his name is unimportant . . . I called someone who's connected, and anyone who tries to get me is likely to find himself part of a bridge abutment in Paterson.

AG: *Him*self?

Effie: What? (BEAT) You and Leonard! All right, himself or herself. I've met Vi and Beryl and Mary, and they wouldn't kill a soul. And I've got no reason to think Kitty's any different. Oh, sure, they're tough. We're all tough. But kill someone? No way! I guess that answers your other question: no, I don't suspect anyone.

AG: Miss Hunter was pretty thorough, but I did have one more question. I didn't ask her because she answered it before I could. What do you know about computers?

Effie: Computers? (BEAT) I never thought about that . . . Vi and Beryl and . . .

AG: Kitty and Mary and, I suppose, Miss Adler. What about you?

Effie: I suppose I'd be home free if I admitted I hadn't the fog-giest. "We black folk don't know nothin' 'bout programmin' no computers." Sorry. That was my major at Yale. The music fellowships and creative writing scholarships both gave you a leg up if you were black and a woman, and the computer science scholarship didn't. I made it this far on what's inside me, and I didn't want then, and I don't want now, to get things because of how I look . . . except Leonard, of course, but that's not the same.

AG: That takes care of my official questions. By the way, does Leonard dance?

Effie: Huh? No, no sense of rhythm at all. It's strange.

SFX: BACKSTAGE SOUNDS FADE, MUSICAL BRIDGE

Scene 11

AG: I reported to Wolfe and he told me Saul had summarized the records of the murdered women. He is always careful with his adjectives, so I assume there was no doubt left in his mind about the fact that I had talked, or even danced, with a murderer within the past thirty-six hours. It was no surprise, therefore, when he said he had asked Mr. Henderson to arrange a charade at 9:00 on Wednesday for the five women and himself. I even had a fairly good idea why he asked Mr. Henderson to bring — and I quote — "the woman who was in this office Monday morning." The surprise was that he asked me to have Lily Rowan present. I had told him about the oaths of secrecy, but he insisted that she not only appear, but bring the selection records for the five women. When he told me that I could probably best spend Wednesday typing germination records and "if you really desire it," reading Saul's summaries, I had had it. If he wanted to discuss Basil Zaharoff I'd let him. I might even bring up the Rosenbergs and Richard III and let him wallow in self-pity about misinterpreting history. In any event, I was going to bed . . . and he could push his lips in and out as much as he liked without me.

SFX: MUSICAL BRIDGE

Scene 12

AG: The scene was set. The mystery woman was in the red chair over Mr. Henderson's brief objections — he stuck in a "Miss Elsworth" or two, and even a "Courtney," but his heart wasn't in it. The young women were in the yellow chairs. I had considered putting Violet or Kitty (if I was to be their dancing partner, I should be on a first-name basis) in the chair nearest me, but I let aesthetics win out, despite Leonard, and stuck with Effie. Lily was on the sofa along with Henderson and Inspector Cramer, who had explained as he usually did the unofficial nature of the proceedings and that he would caution anyone of her rights if the occasion demanded and that Mr. Henderson was willing to act as their attorney, individually or collectively, and so on. Fritz had brought refreshments. The clock turned 9:00.

SFX: DOOR, FOOTSTEPS; SHUFFLING

NW: Good evening. I hope you have introduced yourselves. I believe I could recognize you from Mr. Goodwin's descriptions, but, if you please.

Kitty: Kitty Winter.

Violet: Violet Hunter.

Beryl: Beryl Stapleton.

Mary: Mary Morstan. And what is this . . . ?

NW: If you please, Miss Morstan.

Effie: Effie Munro. And Mary's right, what is this all about?

NW: I shall explain in a moment. You all know Mr. Henderson and Miss Rowan has introduced herself, as has Inspector Cramer. That leaves you, Miss Court.

Court: Mr. Wolfe!

Hend: (LOUDLY) Mr. Wolfe, I must protest!

NW: Do what you wish, but this pretence has gone farther than is reasonably necessary. Do you deny, Madam, that you are Elspeth Court, founder and chief executive officer of JCN Computers, Inc.?

Court: I told you this would be silly, Ezra.

NW: The word I would have chosen is flummery.

Court: No. I do not deny that I am Elspeth Court. How did you guess? Was it that ridiculous name Ezra picked?

NW: I gave Mr. Henderson at least that much credit. I assume he chose the name precisely because he was thinking two moves ahead. I was supposed to think that you were misleading me, was I not?

Hend: Yes. I thought a transparent substitute for Elspeth Court would lead you to think that I wanted you to believe the lady was Miss Court and therefore, that she was someone else. I see you went the further step.

AG: (ASIDE) If that was clearing away the underbrush to get at the real problem, this was going to be a long evening.

NW: Actually, the name was only confirmation. I mentioned my interest in the Third Foundation. Although there have been no press reports about its connection to JCN Computers — and I think you would agree that you are JCN Computers — the absence of computers scientists among your scientists and scholars and your areas of interest here Monday made your identity (and that connection) quite clear.

AG: (ASIDE) That crack about computer scientists was pure showboating. I presume he remembered the specializations of all the winners — that's a five-finger exercise for the old fraud — but there are any number of occupations they didn't have in common. I wouldn't accuse him of having seen a photograph of the lady (as far as Lon Cohen knew, there weren't any), but the conversation Monday was enough for me.

NW: For whatever reasons, by Monday afternoon I was convinced that you were Elspeth Court.

Court: And that there had been murder done?

NW: And that there had been murder done. I do not wish to interfere with your right of free speech, Miss Court, but in order to speed this evening's course — and, I suspect, to save you some embarrassment — I would prefer it if you let me state my facts and conclusions and ask you for confirmation or denial.

Court: All right.

NW: And the rest of you?

SFX: MUMBLED AGREEMENT

NW: Thank you. But first, may I ask you a few questions, Miss Court?

Court: Certainly.

NW: Are you in ill health?

Court: No.

NW: Are you unhappy with life?

Court: I think I see where you are going. I am extremely happy with my life, which I fully expect will extend many decades more — my grandparents were quite longlived, and if my parents had not died in an automobile accident, I am sure they, too, would have lived into their nineties.

NW: You have no siblings?

Court: Nor, if you wish to be formal, any collaterals.

NW: I might remark your choice of terms.

Court: Remark what you wish. I am not even the slightest bit in love with easeful death. I do, however, wish to retire and enjoy the portion of the good things of life to which the past thirty-five years of effort have entitled me.

NW: Certainly not the full portion. Reading again between the lines of the published reports, and remembering Andrew Carnegie's remark that the person who dies rich dies disgraced, you would have to spend money on a scale unequaled since the Moghul emperors (I do not mention the emperors of Rome) to die in peace, however long you live.

Court: I wish I had met you some years ago.

NW: Nine years ago . . . or thirty?

Court: (STIFLED GASP)

NW: That was over-reaching. I apologize.

Court: Accepted.

NW: Enough questions. Nine years ago, in 1977, you founded the Foundation for three purposes. First, to spend more of the money that your efforts entitled you to. It is quite possible that you thought the amounts you gave would reduce your wealth to a manageable amount. And when you saw they would not, it was unfair to increase them. Is that substantially correct?

Court: As far as it goes, yes. I was also concerned that larger amounts would corrupt the beneficiaries and more beneficiaries would dilute the quality . . .

NW: The quality, yes, that was the second purpose: broadly speaking, to make a better world. To encourage the arts and sciences, and redirect some unfortunate trends in taste.

Court: I'll confirm that gladly. I must take issue with one remark you made Monday, about which I couldn't comment at the time. My scientists were not MacArthur Foundation rejects, they were the people to whom MacArthur should have given its money. In a hundred years, a thousand, 50,000, my grantees will have changed the world. The ideas of the MacArthur Foundation beneficiaries are mules, they will have no progeny.

NW: I thank you for confirming another near certainty of mine, but we shall reach that issue later.

AG: (ASIDE) Something did not fit. What was there in Miss Court's hyperbole and imagery that deserved thanks beyond her explicit confirmation?

NW: What I believe was the third purpose of the Third Foundation was to conduct what I would call a daughter hunt.

SFX: INTAKE OF BREATH BY ALL

NW: You may stop me if any of this is painful to you, Miss Court.

Court: It is all painful, but I realize you must do it. Go ahead.

NW: In 1956, were you married?

Court: If I may minimize the pain, Mr. Wolfe. In 1956, 1 was neither married nor in love. I was, however, pregnant. I do not think it is important how the pregnancy began or how it terminated. It was terminated, and the best doctors in the world have told me that it was the only pregnancy I would ever have. I mourn that potential life, and the one part of my life I would willingly — no, gladly, relive is the time in 1957 when I rejoiced that there was no complication to impede my career.

NW: And the potential life would have been female?

Court: I don't know. All fetuses start out female. I have always felt it would have been a girl. But I do not know.

NW: This will not take much longer, Miss Court. You may

simply nod if I am correct in what follows. You decided when the child would have been twenty-one to find the daughter you never had.

Court: Yes. I think I should speak rather than passively nodding, Mr. Wolfe.

NW: As you wish. And you established the Third Foundation to achieve that purpose.

Court: And the other purposes, too.

NW: Of course. This Thursday, tomorrow, was to be the coronation. It is immaterial, but what was the crown worth?

Court: According to my broker, about seven hundred fifty million dollars. I would still have some tens of millions for my retirement.

AG: (ASIDE) Lon had thought Johnson and Nathanson were junior partners; apparently, they were very junior.

NW: That means you would give ironclad control of the corporation you created to a stranger?

Court: A stranger who was one of ten million in ability, and who had proved she could use a large sum of money wisely.

NW: And had you selected your daughter?

Court: No. I told Mr. Henderson I would make the final choice at the dinner. Perhaps I am a mystic, but I believed that at the moment of decision, I would know, really know. I had Mr. Henderson draw up the papers in a false name; all he would have to do to render them valid was hit a few keys on the computer.

NW: Was that false name Susan Calvin?

Court: How could you possibly know that?

NW: It is of a piece with your thinking. I am sorry this has gone on so long, but we are now ready to consider murder. I can understand why you did not fear that the young women you had chosen would kill for that large a sum of money. I referred in this room to innocent acquisitors. Many of the great fortunes of yesterday and today were almost accidental additions to the creation of great corporations or the invention of beneficial products or services. Also, I suspect you did not believe any of the young women would be aware of the magnitude of the prize, or they would think it would be divided in such a way that murder would make only a marginal increase in their wealth.

Court: I understood that Mr. Henderson would guard the secret with every possible protection.

Hend: And I did. Your Mr. Goodwin asked about breaking into our computers. Even if that were possible, and it is not, there are no memoranda, no files, nothing that would indicate Miss Court's intention.

NW: Miss Court already stated that that is not so, but I appreciate your feelings. I am sure that you do not believe, either, that your secrets may be learned or that those secrets exist outside your mind. We shall return to those questions. If I may, Miss Court, I would like to turn now to the five young ladies. Mr. Goodwin has met them all . . . I would like you to hear his opinions.

AG: (ASIDE) I was on. Not for the first time, I wished Wolfe put less trust in my analysis of women's character. That must be what he was after. He'd decided their birthdates before I met the first one. (ALOUD) I've been told by three of you that the computer at Bronson, deGersedorf & Henderson is impregnable. I don't know about those things, but if there is a room anywhere with six people in it that could breach that wall, this is it. I include you, Miss Court, although I realize you were already within the wall.

NW: Please proceed.

AG: All right. In any event. You are all "tough," as one of you said. I suppose the question comes down to motive. And there are two substantial parts to that question. Which of you would have the motive to find out what the dinner tomorrow was all about? Once you found out, which of you would take action to improve the odds? Look at your careers. The manager of the flagship public television station, the president of a major advertising agency, the high and most-respected consultant in a major industry, the insider's insider in the arts, and the next superstar in the world of entertainment. Which of you would be motivated to look a gift horse in the mouth? Public television has no money and the commercial networks make their gifts in the glare of publicity. Violet Hunter's career would not lead her to look behind the Third Foundation's public front. That is even more true for Kitty Winter. In addition, Miss Winter had good reason to expect to be in a position to dispose of millions herself before many years have passed. Multimillion-dollar foundations out of nowhere are not the characteristics of the fine arts or show business. Mary Morstan and Effie Munro would have no reason to investigate their gifts.

That leaves you, Beryl Stapleton. As an average newspaper reader, I can think of three or four of the richest people in America who made their money from computers — and not as consultants. You were most likely to try to learn if there was more money behind the quarter-million. And then there was the way you five approached your careers. Mr. Wolfe spoke of creation as the motivation of certain types of people. Miss Hunter, you took a cut in pay to work in public television. Miss Winter, you talked about your agency as if it were a jealous lover, but the point is that it was a lover. Even in today's market, Miss Morstan, there is little money in the arts, and your Doctor Jamison seems to supply the rest of your needs. And Miss Munro, even if you hadn't shown your values when you went to Yale, I've heard you speak of your husband and sing of your needs. Again, Miss Stapleton, you are the odd woman out.

NW: Satisfactory, Mr. Goodwin. Only Miss Stapleton had the motivation to investigate the Third Foundation and only she would strike for the main chance.

AG: (ASIDE) I don't know why he bothered; Inspector Cramer knew the words he must use to caution a suspect, but he had pulled out the little N.Y.P.D.-issue card and was studying the back of Beryl Stapleton's head.

NW: You are wise to sit mute, Miss Stapleton. Feigned outrage would only prolong what must be an unpleasant experience. I have only two more points to make. First, there is the computer at Bronson, deGersedorf & Henderson. You did not think there was anything secret in it, Mr. Henderson?

Hend: That is correct.

NW: Where, then, are the forms to which Miss Court referred, the forms that will transfer JCN Computers to one of these five young women?

Hend: Well, they are on the computer, of course, but they're protected. And besides, a lay person wouldn't understand them.

NW: Ah, the arrogance of lawyers: Miss Hunter, Miss Winter, and, of course Miss Stapleton could probably read those contracts as easily as they would read a menu — more easily, perhaps. And your computer system! Did you ever wonder why Miss Court called her fund the Third Foundation?

Hend: You said it earlier. Because it was the third purpose that she cared about. That's what you said, Elspeth.

Court: I'm sorry I had to mislead you, Ezra, but there was another reason, as Mr. Wolfe obviously knows.

NW: I apologize for having to finish this point, Mr. Henderson, but why did you think Miss Court chose the name of Susan Calvin?

Hend: The Protestant work ethic . . . I don't know.

NW: And finally, is the name on this card your six-letter code for the files on the Third Foundation?

Hend: Yes.

SFX: TELEPHONE RING, UNINTELLIGIBLE FILTERED VOICE

NW: (INTO PHONE) Satisfactory, Saul. (TO THE GROUP)

That was Saul Panzer, an operative of mine. He accompanied a detachment of the New York Police Department that just accomplished a search pursuant to a valid warrant of Miss Stapleton's apartment, including the memory of her personal computer. I believe the district attorney will be requesting an indictment. Mr. Cramer, I believe you can read Miss Stapleton her rights and take her away. Miss Court, I believe I have accomplished the task for which I was engaged.

AG: (ASIDE) And that, as far as Wolfe was concerned, was that.

SFX: MUSICAL BRIDGE

Scene 13

SFX: NOISY WORD PROCESSOR UNDER

AG: You may be surprised that I still have Jason. Wolfe said something about 80 percent not being corrupted, but I think it was the time he spent with Elspeth Court after they took Beryl Stapleton away and Lily and I ushered the rest out into the November night, and went dancing ourselves. She's always been my best partner.

I didn't learn until the next morning what was on that card and why Lily had been invited and, in fact, what happened after Beryl Stapleton waived her rights and confessed. The six letter word was ASIMOV; that's right, the good doctor. He wrote some books, I think it's up to five now, about something called the First and Second Foundations. Apparently, 50,000 years and the fact that mules can't have progeny mean something in those books — I must read them sometime. And Susan Calvin is a computer expert in some other books of his; single, brilliant, a lot like Miss Court, except not so wealthy. Why was Lily present? I think I told you Wolfe only bats something like .950 (good enough to take a title, but not 1.000). He wanted to be ready in case Miss Stapleton had no records and Bronson, deGersedorf had some. He was convinced she could not forgo sprucing up her dossier and downgrading her competitors' and he was all ready to have the law firm's files sent to our printer for comparison with the originals in Lily's possession.

And why haven't you heard anything about a new centi-millionaire, to use a neologism Wolfe despises? Simple, there isn't any. Miss Court gave each of the women — even Beryl, which I'll never understand — five million and put the other seven hundred million or so into a trust to continue the grants to scientists, scholars, and creative artists. I think she asked Dr. Asimov's permission and called them the first and second foundations.

So I'm back on the germination records and Wolfe's back with his books, and the only change is that Wolfe has come to terms with himself about whatever it was that had him riled up at mealtimes. At least, I can get under his skin with the keyboard even if he doesn't have to work for a while.

NW: Archie!

AG: Yes, sir.

NW: Miss Court tells me there is something on the special menus for that machine that will stop its infernal beeping. Would you see to it, please?

AG: Coincidence, pure coincidence.

"FIRECRACKERS"

by Archie Goodwin

Edited by Charles E. Burns

FOREWORD

I HAVE often been asked how I first became acquainted with Nero Wolfe, that gargantuan, egocentric, orchid-growing, beer-drinking, self proclaimed genius, undoubtedly the world's greatest detective. Admittedly, my answers have been a little vague, partly in deference to the privacy of people involved but, more important, to safeguard the well-being of one, Archie Goodwin.

You may recall a couple of early references:

"Born in Ohio. Public high school, pretty good at geometry and football, graduated with honor but no honors. Went to college two weeks, decided it was childish, came to New York and got a job guarding a pier, shot and killed two men and was fired, was recommended to Nero Wolfe for a chore he wanted done, did it, was offered a full-time job by Mr. Wolfe, took it."

On another occasion:

"The only girl I had ever been really soft on had found another bargain she liked better. That was how I happened to meet Wolfe — but that story isn't for me to tell, at least not yet. There are one or two little points that would need clearing up some day."

Perhaps that day has finally arrived. Both of the above statements are true, as far as they go. Oh, I know I have a reputation for dissembling, as Inspector Cramer of the NYPD would be glad to attest. Sometimes, bending the truth a little is for a serious purpose. But mostly, it's pure flippancy on my part, merely to satisfy a whim, a mood, or to just plain rebel against conformity, never intended to be taken literally. In fact, about the only person I've never been able to bamboozle at all is the second (and last) girl I've really been soft on, Lily Rowan. When I first met her, I fed her a perfectly plausible line. She simply looked at me, through the most beautiful azure eyes ever created, and asked softly, "Is any of it straight?" In my most sincere manner, I hastened to assure her it was all true but the words which came out, solely of their own volition, were, "No, it's firecrackers."

The events leading up to my initial meeting with Wolfe involved a lot more than firecrackers. You might even call them a whole Fourth of July explosion.

Except that they happened in December. In 1926. When, as an adventurous and (I hate to admit it but you'll find out, anyway) naive youth of eighteen, fresh out of Chillicothe, Ohio, I was ready to take on the Big City of New York.

I

They materialized out of the mist, two dark shadows silhouetted against the dim light from the warehouse office window. A foghorn wailed mournfully in the distance. Somewhere down river, a ship's bell clanged as if in answer.

Silently, the two men advanced towards the window. Peering in, they saw exactly what they expected, a uniformed figure, presumably that dumb kid security guard, back to the window, hunched over his desk, probably half asleep. They never hesitated, raised their Tommy guns and shattered the office window with a series of staccato blasts. Enough bullets to kill a dozen men ripped into the back of the slumping figure at the desk. Another blast from the guns blew away the door lock and sent the door flying open. Without a word, the two gunmen marched through the door to view their handiwork . . .

You want to know how I ever got into that fool predicament? Or, more to the point, how I got out? Then we'll have to go back a way. But relax. I'm far too short of a Wolfean ego to write an autobiography. However, you'll have to forgive a touch of nostalgia.

To begin with, I was born in Chillicothe, Ohio. You thought it was Canton? Or maybe Zanesville? Either would have been quite a trick inasmuch as my mother was in Chillicothe at the time. And I did attend the State University in Columbus for a couple of weeks, mainly to please my mother. Oh, I know that long ago, I implied that my mother and father were both dead. That was half firecrackers. At that particular time, it simply suited my mood to be an orphan. I'm happy to say that my mother is still very much alive, occasionally visits New York, and enjoys dining with Wolfe and me.

But back to college. Although the Jazz Age hadn't quite caught up with Chillicothe, it was running wild on the Ohio State campus. The students, if I may resort to hyperbole, prided themselves on non-conformity. Yet they were all mirror-images of each other in their oversized sweaters, baggy pants and saddle shoes, patent-leather hair combed back, stiffened with slickum, and parted in the middle, appropriate shells for the embryonic brains below. They majored in hip flasks, ukuleles and Greek fraternities with names I couldn't even pronounce, If William Jennings Bryan could have put those morons on the witness stand during the recent Scopes trial, he'd have had no trouble at all proving that man couldn't have descended from monkeys. Descended? The monkeys would have sued for libel.

The few classes I attended were dreary lessons by disinterested professors from dull books written by dead people (i.e., dead now, questionable then.) The only live ones we studied were Albert Einstein and Sigmund Freud. I couldn't understand the one (I doubt the profs did, either) and the answer to any question about the other was "sex." Even the so-called students would have got that right. I would have had A+! Perhaps if the college were co-ed I could have persevered . . .

Mainly, however, I couldn't stand sitting (is that an oxymoron?) in class all day. Even now, when Wolfe and I are between cases or when he pig-headedly refuses to work on a current case, I have to get out of the office and walk through the streets of New York.

My mother wasn't too happy when I returned to the farm and told her I wanted to head for New York. Being the wonderful lady she is, she finally agreed and even staked me with part of the tuition money she'd set aside for college.

When I say "farm," that may be a small firecracker. But you'll have to visualize it to understand the exciting contrast of leaving it for Times Square. It wasn't much of a farm by Midwestern standards, only about three acres. In the garden behind the house were rows of leaf lettuce, radishes, butter beans, carrots, cabbages, potatoes and those two most succulent Ohio crops, lush tomatoes and sweet corn. Around the front of the house were violets, tulips, narcissus, peonies and iris. I can still smell the sweet scent of the honeysuckle that climbed our porch railing.

In the spring, fruit trees blossomed in bursts of pink and white to yield seasonal and fall crops of cherries, plums and apples. In back were clumps of berry bushes, rhubarb, asparagus and an arbor of Concord grapes. What our major domo and chef, Fritz Brenner, couldn't have done with these! If Wolfe had ever known about them, he'd probably have had me commuting to Ohio every week for fresh fruit and vegetables!

Rhode Island Reds pecked away in the yard by the chicken house near the barn. Farther back, in fact a lot farther, a pair of China Poland porkers rooted and grunted in the mud and slurped from the overflowing trough. In the pasture were too few cows to be called a herd but quite enough to supply my favorite beverage. And beyond, the pasture was bordered by dark woods which, when I was a youngster, seemed like the end of the world.

Describing the scenes of my lost youth, I'm tempted to wax sentimental. But at heart, I was never really a country boy. If anything, I always was and still like to think of myself as a man of action. And, to me, the Big City has always been where the action is. After the Thanksgiving Holidays, while I was packing to leave, my mother handed me an old Colt .45-Army automatic which had belonged to my father. She'd heard a lot about crime in New York and figured I should have some protection. To humor her, I tucked it in my suitcase and forgot about it. All it did later was save my life.

As I was leaving, my sister Meg, from childhood the object of bickering and rough-housing that masked a deep underlying mutual affection, handed me a package containing sandwiches and a cake she'd baked especially for me (she who hated to cook). I was startled to see tears in her eyes, gave her a quick peck on the cheek, and had to leave quickly to avoid choking up myself.

I walked to the nearby highway and caught a bus bound for Cleveland where I would board the 20th Century Limited out of Chicago to New York. I'd argued with my mother that it would be a lot cheaper to take the cross-country bus all the way but she insisted I go first class. During the nearly 200 mile trip to Cleveland, I amused myself by watching the billboards as they flashed by. "I'd Walk A Mile For A Camel." I was in good shape — I could do that. "Ivory Soap — 99.44/100% Pure." In this far from perfect world, that seemed close enough. But that slogan will never last. And finally, a series that read, "THE 50 CENT JAR/SO LARGE/BY HECK/EVEN THE SCOTCH/NOW SHAVE THE NECK/BURMA SHAVE." By the time I got to Cleveland, I'd decided to smoke Camels, wash with Ivory and shave with

Burma Shave every day whether I needed it or not. Look out Broadway, here I come!

II

If you're not a native New Yorker (is anyone?) you're bound to remember your first impression of that great metropolis. It was Saturday, a clear, crisp December morning, when my train pulled into Grand Central Station. The porters actually rolled out a red carpet across the platform and into the station. Talk about First Class. Thanks, Mom! Carrying my one bulging suitcase, I walked out onto 42nd Street in a state of exhilaration and excitement right smack into the clamor of Manhattan. More cars, buses and taxis than I'd seen in a lifetime raced each other through the streets. The crowded sidewalks teemed with frantic people rushing in every direction, all with the air of reaching some important goal known only to themselves. The pace was faster, the buildings taller, the girls prettier, the skirts shorter . . .

I turned west on 42nd Street towards Broadway and Times Square, gawking like any tourist at the people, the store windows already dressed in their Christmas finery, and searching for the Woolworth Building, tallest in the world, towering high above the other skyscrapers. As the crowd thinned a little, my eyes were drawn as if by a magnet towards a young woman walking in my direction. Somehow, she stood out from all the others, a tall, lithe, shapely figure striding confidently ahead with exceptional grace and poise. As I watched in ill-concealed admiration, something to which she was undoubtedly accustomed, I noticed a seedy-looking guy dressed in a bulky sweater and stocking cap moving purposefully toward her. Suddenly, he snatched her purse and darted in my direction, dodging pedestrians, none of whom paid the slightest attention. As he came near, I dropped my suitcase and threw myself, all 190 pounds, in a body block that would have made my high school football coach proud. The would-be thief sprawled in one direction, the stolen purse flying from his grasp in another. No longer concerned with him, I hurried to rescue the purse while he raced off and disappeared into the crowd. Still, no passers-by paid any attention, just nonchalantly kept walking by as though this were an everyday occasion. Maybe it was, at that.

Now you might say I acted foolishly without thinking. In retrospect, I like to think I reacted with intelligence and courage.

These are qualities which have always been my guide. In any event, it was a terrific way to meet the most beautiful girl in the world. She was a knockout, a real doll! When I returned her purse, her dark green eyes flashed from shock and anger to relief. High cheekbones accented a tiny nose and perfectly shaped mouth. Auburn hair peeked out from under a perky cloche hat. Her coat matched her eyes and set off her features perfectly.

As she thanked me, one of New York's finest (where are they when you need them?) approached and asked if either of us was hurt. My clothing was a little the worse for wear but otherwise we were both in good shape, especially hers. As the cop was leaving he took me aside and said, "That was a damn fool thing you did. If that mugger had a knife or a gun, you could be dead now. Better leave police work in the hands of the law." I glared at his departing back and don't know if he heard my reply, "Yeah, leave police work in the hands of the law and leave the lady's purse in the hands of the crook." In the years to come, that type of conflict was destined to be played over and over again.

When I turned back I could see the young lady was shivering slightly as the reaction set in. Over her mild protest, I offered to take her home, hailed a taxi, and she gave me an address on 38th Street. During the short ride, she relaxed enough to tell me her name was Dolores Day, that she was a hoofer, a professional dancer, but she was presently "at liberty." She smiled and said, "That's a fancy way of saying I'm currently out of work. Meanwhile, I'm working part time as a stenographer in a waterfront warehouse office."

We reached her apartment all too soon. I dismissed the taxi and escorted her to the door. On impulse I said "If you're `at liberty' and like to dance, I'm 'at liberty,' too. Why don't we try it together tonight? I'm probably not in your class as a dancer, but I promise not to step all over your toes. And we'll go somewhere special for dinner. After all, this is my first day in New York, so help me make it a real occasion!" She hesitated for a moment but to my relief, and frankly surprise, she agreed that I could pick her up at eight. I almost danced all the way back to Grand Central where I bought a road map of Manhattan and a copy of the *Daily News*. Perusing the Classified Section, an ad (I better say advertisement) for a rooming house in Greenwich Village caught my eye. I knew the Village wasn't the swellest neighborhood in New York but somehow it intrigued me. And the advertisement promised clean, cheap, furnished rooms. I grabbed a cab to the corner of 6th Avenue and 9th Street, located the boarding house, examined the available room, liked it, rented it. Finally, I was ready for the Big Adventure.

III

My first week in New York was noteworthy primarily for a whirlwind romance and the prospects of a new job. You don't need details about the former, but a few highlights might be of interest. After settling in my second-floor room, I went out and bought a couple of late afternoon newspapers. *The Evening Graphic*, a tabloid, featured lurid articles such as "Love Nest on Park Avenue," a photo of the esteemed mayor of New York, "Gentleman" Jimmy Walker, in the area of a scantily-clad chorus girl, and a follow-up story on the nationally beloved evangelist, Aimee Semple McPherson. She had failed to return from an excursion last spring. After 37 days, while her whereabouts remained a well-publicized mystery, she staggered out of a desert in Arizona, claiming she'd just escaped from kidnappers. According to the article, there was ample evidence that she'd been off on a month-long fling with her boyfriend. I decided that paper should have been called the *"Porno Graphic."*

The Gazette was a lot different and it became my favorite New York paper. It included a great Amusement Section, filled with movie, restaurant, and night-club advertisements. A restaurant called Rusterman's sounded expensive but probably worth it. My eye was also caught by one for the Flamingo which read as follows: "Sophisticates . . ." (That's me!) . . . "attune your souls to happiness and synchronize your toes with tempo by Paul Whiteman and His Orchestra." I was more than ready for a little soul attunement and toe synchronization!

The landlady charged me a nickel a call on the telephone in the downstairs hall, and stood nearby to make sure the calls were local as I made reservations for both places. That ought to impress Dolores! I shaved with Burma Shave, including my neck, took a bath with Ivory Soap, and dressed with special care in my gray suit with pinstripes, a light blue shirt, fresh collar, and dark blue tie. I was at Dolores's apartment on the dot of eight. She kept me waiting only ten minutes. She was breathtaking in a flowered party dress that came just about to her knees. Her shapely legs were encased in silk stockings, rolled just below the knees, evidently in the latest style. Her gleaming auburn hair was "bobbed" in the most modern fashion. A single strand of pearls adorned her gorgeous neck.

From the beginning, we were completely at ease with each other. The dinner at Rusterman's was the best I'd ever had (Sorry, Mom) but I blanched a little when the check came. At The Flamingo, we blended perfectly and Dolores taught me the latest dance craze, the Charleston. I admit I never did quite get the hang of crossing my hands on my knees, mostly because I thought it was pretty silly.

I was also surprised when, back at the table, she took out her compact and powdered — her knees! But they were cute knees. And she certainly was my idea of a Broadway glamour girl.

During the week, we held hands through the new movie, "Don Juan," starring John Barrymore, Mary Astor and Warner Oland at the brand new Warner Theatre.

It was easy to see why such theatres were called "palaces." The center of the mezzanine was big enough for an eight-day bicycle race. It featured marble figures in a flowing fountain. The walls displayed ancient statuary in gilded niches. The theatre itself seated 5,300 people but they might as well all have been statues for Dolores and I couldn't have been more alone in a crowd.

The movie featured something billed as "REVOLUTION-ARY." It was called Vitaphone Synchronization. During the film, you could actually recognize sounds — like the clashing of swords and the pealing of bells. The movie was preceded by Vitaphone Shorts in which you could both see and hear the Philharmonic Orchestra playing Wagner's overture to *Tannhauser*, plus selections from *Rigoletto* and *Pagliacci*. (Years later, Lily taught me to enjoy that kind of music.) A message at the end announced that someday soon movies would actually talk. I figured this might be a boon to the illiterate movie fan, but on the whole it was probably just another short-lived Hollywood fad.

Dolores also introduced me to my first speakeasy and that newly invented drink, the cocktail. Frankly, I could get along fine without either, especially the latter. She told me there were over 100,000 speakeasies in New York and that you could get a glass of liquor in any building on 52nd Street between 5th and 6th Avenues. Obviously, the constabulary looked the other way. At the Club Gallant, which was in Washington Square not far from my rooming house, I was embarrassed when the doorman asked for my membership card. I needn't have worried. The exchange of a single simoleon brought me an elaborate wallet-sized card, good forever. That was only the beginning, though. Before we got out of there, it cost us nearly a sawbuck.

As we entered, the doorman called my attention to a plaque on the wall, headlined "Rules for Nightclub Goers. I still remember every one.

You might find a few amusing:

"Do not ask to play the drums. The drum heads are not as tough as some other heads. Besides, it has a tendency to disturb the rhythm."

"Examine your bill when the waiter presents it. Remember, even they are human beings and are liable to err — intentionally or otherwise.

"Please do not offer to escort the cloakroom girl home. Her husband, who is an ex-prizefighter, is there for that purpose."

You can see we were having a ball. But don't think it was all fun and games. I was attempting to find gainful employment and always seemed to strike out whenever it came to "experience." One night at the end of our first week, Dolores told me that the manager of the warehouse where she worked part time was looking for a security guard. She said it wasn't much of a job but might tide me over until I found something better. I wasn't too enthusiastic because it meant night work. But she said we could still see each other on occasional afternoons, play that Chinese game, Mah Jongg, which was sweeping the country, go to a movie, or just take a walk in Central Park. Sounded fine. She phoned the manager, a man named Mike Jablonski, and set up an appointment for the next day.

IV

Saturday morning was cold, gray and overcast. My rooming house wasn't too far from the Hudson River. I dressed warmly in a heavy sweater and cap, which I thought appropriate for the waterfront, walked north on 6th Avenue to 23rd Street, then west directly on to Pier 64. The pier was about a furlong removed from the main waterfront buildings. A lone warehouse, seemingly standing aloof from its neighbors, looked out on the Hudson. On close inspection, there was no good reason for this particular warehouse to be putting on airs. Its red brick exterior showed definite signs of aging. Yet it appeared solid enough to withstand any ocean storms.

Everything was quiet on Pier 64, in direct contrast to the rest of the waterfront, which was teeming with activity. Several large ships were docked, with huge cranes engaged in loading and off-loading. Longshoremen were wheeling heavily burdened hand trucks in and out of various buildings.

I wasn't too thrilled with my first view of the mighty Hudson with its odor of dead fish and with filthy flotsam and jetsam bobbing up and down against the dock. Across the river, on the Jersey side, was a large sprawling city which I learned later was Hoboken. Off in the distance to the far left, where the Hudson joined the Upper Bay that led to the Atlantic, I could see the silhouette of the Statue of Liberty. I don't mind saying that my heart beat a little faster at my first sight of this proud Lady.

Like the others, the warehouse loading dock faced the waterfront, where it was handy to ships' cargoes. A narrow alley to the right provided access to non-seagoing vehicles. A solid looking door next to the loading dock evidently led to the manager's office. A man seated with his back to the window was partly visible. I knocked and walked in. "Mr. Jablonski?" I asked.

He swiveled around and glared at me through bloodshot eyes that must have been having a hard time recovering from the night before. Bristly black hair and a bristly black mustache framed a dark-complexioned face with high cheekbones.

An almost invisible scar, running from his right eye to the corner of his mouth, actually emphasized his rugged good looks. His features were quite handsome in a coarse, rough and ready kind of way. His body was big and powerful looking, just slightly showing signs of running to fat. Across the grapefruit sized biceps of his left arm, visible under his rolled up shirtsleeve, was a heart-shaped tattoo with the word, "MOTHER," emblazoned across it. Hey, I figured, if he loves his mother, he can't be all bad. But I still didn't like the look in his eyes.

There was an empty chair next to his desk but he didn't offer it. He didn't offer to shake hands, either. He grunted through half-clenched teeth as though he hated to make the effort to talk.

"You're Goodwin?"

I admitted it.

He waved me to the empty chair.

"Miss Day recommended you," he began, "and her judgment is usually sound, especially where men are concerned. But hell, you're just a kid. I hope she didn't go all female because you happen to be good-looking in a college-boy type of way."

I was beginning to dislike him. Without conscious effort, the remainder of that interview could have become a part of the curriculum of the Harvard Business School as a classic example of How Not To Get A Job.

"Come to think of it," I replied, "she did say I had a profile like John Barrymore." I slowly and deliberately turned my head to the side. "What do you think? A little too much nose?" Then I continued, "But she must have thought I had other assets."

He smiled but there was no warmth in it. "Tell me about 'em, kid." (How I hated that!) "You think you got guts enough to take care of this pier and warehouse?"

That did it. I now decided I didn't want his damn job. So I played the country bumpkin to the hilt.

"Dern tootin'," I drawled, "back home I did a pretty good job guarding our henhouse and barn. There's a lot of dead foxes, weasels, raccoons and dirty rats who could prove it, to say nothin' of some would-be chicken thieves with their rear ends full of buckshot."

He didn't know whether I was putting him on or not. After a moment, he decided to play it straight. "You know how to shoot a gun?" he asked.

"Yep," I said proudly, "I'm a regular Davy Crockett, Dan'l Boone and Buffalo Bill all rolled into one. I kin shoot a squirrel's eye out at ninety feet!"

By this time, he should have booted me out on my rear end, or at least tried. Instead, he put on the hail fellow well met.- "OK, Goodwin," he said, "I like your spunk. You won't have to worry about guns, though. This warehouse is full of precision machine parts. They're valuable enough but they wouldn't be worth anything to a thief. He'd never be able to get rid of 'em. There's never been a robbery attempt here and I certainly don't expect any.

"This is a full-time job, though," he continued, "seven days a week from 7 in the evening to 7 the next morning. These are tough hours, but the pay is good. Also, about once a month, when a big shipment comes in, we have to put on a night shift for a week. We don't need a guard then so you get a week off with pay." He mentioned a salary that was a lot higher than I'd expected. "Come along, and I'll show you around."

I still hadn't decided to take the job, but I went along, anyway. There wasn't much to see, just aisle after aisle stacked to the ceiling with cardboard containers. Several workmen were moving the cartons around in hand trucks. With the boss nearby, they were trying hard to look busy.

Back in the office, Jablonski opened a door to a small closet and brought out a security guard uniform and handed it to me. "I think this will fit you all right," he said. Then, he reached into his desk drawer, took out a revolver, and gave it to me. It was a .38 special, a brand I wasn't familiar with. "You won't need this," he said, "but it's loaded, just in case. Be careful with it. I'll be here Monday night when you check in."

On that note, we shook hands and I left with a good deal to think about.

V

Sunday, I tried to sort out my feelings about that interview with Jablonski. It simply didn't make sense. First, why did he overlook my obviously flippant responses to his questions? That certainly wasn't his style. Second, why offer a salary that was way out of line with the requirements of the job? Third, why hire me at all, considering his expressed contempt for my so-called youth and inexperience? None of it added up.

I examined the revolver he had given me. It looked as though it hadn't been used for years. I broke open the cylinder. Except for the chamber under the hammer, it was fully loaded. I ejected the cartridges and decided to take the gun apart. It was badly in need of cleaning. The firing pin didn't look quite right. On closer scrutiny, I could see that the end was filed down. That gun would misfire. It was useless.

I reassembled it and tucked it away in my bottom drawer. I took out the old Army Colt automatic, cleaned it thoroughly, and made sure the magazine was fully loaded. Then it was time to decide on my future course of action. It was obvious that I was being set up. But for what? Of course the sensible thing would be to bow out and chalk it up to experience. But I was just curious enough, stubborn enough, and, I admit, with enough youthful pride to resent being played for a sucker. I decided to see it through. There was no doubt about Jablonski's role.

Reluctantly, I began to wonder about Dolores. It bothered me so much that it must have taken all of thirty seconds for me to get to sleep that night.

With less than two weeks 'til Christmas, I spent most of Monday morning inMacy's, selecting presents for my mother and sister, and getting the wrappedpackages off in the mail. In the afternoon, for the the first time since I was in the cradle, I took a nap in preparation for my night's work. After a so-so meal in a nearby diner, I dressed for action. The uniform coat was a little large so I wore a heavy sweater underneath. It would probably be cold in that warehouse, even with a Franklin Stove in the office. My Colt .45 didn't make much of a bulge in the pocket. I met Jablonski at the warehouse, determined to show no sign of suspicion. He offered some last-minute instructions which were pretty routine, gave me a key to the office, and his home phone number to call in case of emergency, which he assured me would be unnecessary.

As soon as he was gone, I locked the office door and made sure the overhead doors at the loading dock were securely fastened. I went through the warehouse, aisle by aisle, corner by corner, to make sure I was alone. Then, it was time to find out exactly what kind of precision tools the cartons contained. I very carefully opened several cartons at random, examined the contents, and resealed the cartons. Just as I suspected, the precision tools were all liquid, Scotch, Bourbon, Gin, Rum and Rye. Back in the office, I stayed in the shadows and kept my eye on the door while I pondered this new information. About 2:30 a.m. my reverie was interrupted by a discreet knock on the door. It was another uniformed figure, this time in the uniform of the NYPD. With my hand gripping the automatic in my pocket, I cautiously let him in. In a brogue as thick as the fog rolling off the river, he proudly introduced himself as Officer Francis Xavier Mulrooney. "Sure, 'tis a pleasure to meet you, me boyo," he began. "Me beat's right along Twelfth Avenue and I've got in the habit of droppin' in here each night for a few minutes to warm me old bones. 'Tis not surprised I am though to find another new security guard. Nobody can put up with Jablonski very long. You wouldn't be havin' a wee drop, now would you, to help ward off the chill?"

I told him I thought we could spare a wee drop, went into the back, opened a carton, brought out a bottle of rye, and poured him a generous wee drop. He downed it in one gulp. "Sure an' that hits the spot," he said, so I poured him another. "You know, me boy," he went on, "half the warehouses on the waterfront are filled with bootleg booze. But 'tis no concern of mine. The gangs and unions here take care of their own troubles. As for me, I've got enough troubles o' me own what with the speaks, the street-walkers, the pawnshops and family squabbles on me own beat.

'Tis a rare night indeed when I'm not callin' the paddy wagon to cart someone off to jail."

As he left, he turned to me and said, "You seem like a fine lad, Goodwin, me boy. Take a word o' warnin' from an old cop. Keep a sharp eye on that Polack, Jablonski. He's no good atall atall." It was a warning I didn't need but I thanked him just the same.

The next few nights were pretty much repeats. Mulrooney dropped in for his nightly libation. I suspected he had a few other watering holes as well.

Nevertheless, I began to look forward to his visits. I learned a lot from him about the waterfront and the neighborhood. Although he might prove to be a welcome ally, I kept my suspicions about Jablonski to myself.

Everything exploded into action on Saturday. It began a little after noon when I heard the phone ring in the downstairs hall. In a moment, the landlady knocked on my door. "Mr. Goodwin! You're wanted on the phone. It's a woman!" The way she spit it out made it appear that it must be the Whore of Babylon calling, or at least a "fallen woman."

It was Dolores. She sounded breathless. "Oh, Archie, I'm so glad I caught you. Something terrible has happened and I'm getting ready to leave New York, but I had to see you first." Her voice broke. She was obviously in a state of excitement, bordering on hysteria. I tried to calm her. "Relax! Slow down! Are you at home?" She said she was and I said I'd be there as fast as I could, and broke all records getting to her apartment. She let me in and immediately closed the door, fastened the chain, and broke into tears. I held her and did my best to soothe her. The apartment was in a state of disarray, clothes and personal articles strewn on the floor, open suitcases partly packed.

When her emotions were under control, she brushed away the tears, took out her compact, and repaired the damage to her beautiful features as best she could. I was glad to see that she powdered her nose and not her knees. I took this as a good sign, cleared a place on the divan, sat beside her and listened while she explained, haltingly at first, then with growing confidence.

"I'm so frightened," she began. "I have to tell you that for a long time, Mike Jablonski and I were," she hesitated, then added, "close. Oh, I knew he was a small-time gangster and that the warehouse was full of bootleg booze. Somehow, that just seemed intriguing and made him more interesting. I'd never met anyone like him and, for a time, I was hopelessly in love."

Here, she paused as if groping for the right words. "Gradually, I came to see another side of him, a rough side, a cruel side. I began to be afraid of him, scared even to leave my job. And even though it's been over, on my part, for a long time, I still had to hide the fact that you and I were seeing each other. I'm afraid, though, that he began to suspect. Yet, in my ignorance, when I recommended you for the security guard position, I really thought I was doing you a favor." She shuddered. "Instead, I might have been sending you to your death." A tear rolled down her cheek, but she brushed it away and continued.

"This morning, when I was working at the office, I overheard Mike on the phone. I was typing a bill of lading so, at first, I paid no attention. Mike was mostly just listening, anyway, until suddenly I caught the words `hijack' and `security guard'. I continued typing but tried to listen more carefully. I didn't get it all but heard enough to realize that Mike was planning to have his own warehouse robbed. And it's supposed to take place tonight! The last thing I heard him say was, `You won't have any trouble with the country bumpkin'.

"When he hung up, he looked at me kind of funny and asked if I'd heard any of his conversation. I assured him I hadn't but I don't think he believed me.

"If he decides I heard too much, I know he wouldn't hesitate to kill me. That's when I realized that I don't belong here and why I'm packing to catch the afternoon train back home to Kansas. But I couldn't leave without seeing you for one last time and warning you not to go near that warehouse tonight!

"You know, Archie, I like you, I really do. But I've been kidding myself all along trying to be a Big City girl. It took all this to make me see that at heart I'm really just another kid from the country. You're different. I know you'll make it big in New York. The only thing I'm sorry about is leaving you, that we couldn't get to know one another better. Maybe if we'd met under different circumstances . . ."

Here she stopped, and I was afraid the waterworks would start again. I tried to persuade her to stay, that I'd take care of Jablonski, but it was no use. Finally, I patted her hand, looked into those gorgeous emerald eyes for the last time and said, "If it makes you feel any better, you're more than enough of a Big City girl for me. You swept me right off my feet, which are usually planted solidly on good old terra firma. C'mon, I'll help you pack and see that you get to the station and on that train for home."

Which I did. We kissed good bye, each with our own mixed feelings of relief and regret. Just before she boarded the train, she said, "You know, Archie, even my name is phony. It isn't really Dolores Day. That was just a stage name." She paused and added wistfully, "I guess now it will never get up in lights on Broadway." She didn't offer her real name and I didn't ask. I watched as the train pulled out of the station, leaving clouds of white smoke in its wake, and carrying her off into eternity, leaving only the bittersweet memory of my first love. I'll never forget her. But I won't tell Lily.

So much for sentiment. Now, I had more practical problems to ponder.

VI

It was late afternoon when I returned to my room. There wasn't much time to get ready for the evening's entertainment. I made a few preparations and, making sure my landlady was otherwise occupied, I sneaked out with a couple of pillows under my coat.

At the warehouse, I made the usual survey to be certain I was alone. Then, I got to work, fashioning a man-sized dummy from the pillows and packing straw from the warehouse. Dressed in my uniform coat and hat, hunched over the desk, back to the window, the dummy looked pretty life-like. I stepped outside to make sure. It wouldn't fool anyone on close inspection but, through the window, in the dim light of the office lamp, it should serve its purpose.

Satisfied, I positioned myself in the shadows of the warehouse where I could watch the office without being seen. I was pretty much on edge, not really nervous or afraid, just keyed up from anticipation and from trying to maintain a patience that didn't come to me naturally.

So now we're up to date. You have a good idea of just how I got into the situation described in the opening paragraph of this narrative. Next, you'll see just how I got out of it. Sort of.

Although all my senses were keenly alert, I didn't hear the truck pull into the alley. My watch said 2:03 when the two gunmen arrived, tattooed the window, door and dummy with rapid blasts from their Tommy guns, as I previously explained, and marched through the door to view their handiwork. That's when I stepped from the shadows of the warehouse interior, my

Colt .45 leveled unwaveringly at the two men. For a moment, they stood utterly still, frozen in time, all the world like two statues in a Greek tableau. Alert for the slightest movement, in a voice I was proud came out without a tremor, I quietly told them to drop their weapons, which were now dangling from their arms pointed towards the floor. They reacted exactly as I had anticipated. Recovering quickly from the shock of my sudden appearance, they each started to raise their guns in my direction. My first shot caught the nearest gunman dead-center in the chest. My next didn't vary a millimeter as it downed the second. As they fell, I kicked away their weapons and knelt to make sure they were out of commission. They were. Permanently.

Shaken as I was, I couldn't resist one parting remark, quite possibly a fitting epitaph. "Sorry, gentlemen, but the dummy you shot wasn't me." Then, it was my turn to go into shock, but I didn't have time to give in to it.

The sound of running feet outside brought me back to action. I turned, gun still leveled steadily, and was relieved to see my friend, Officer Mulrooney, come puffing into the office.

"Glory be!" he exclaimed, looking at the two bodies on the floor. "Are they dead? Are you all right?"

I assured him that they were and I was and filled him in briefly.

"Sure an' I try to keep out of any trouble on the docks," he said, "but when I heard the gunfire, I thought you might be needin' help. And, indeed, me boy, it seems that you do. The Homicide Bureau doesn't take kindly to killings anywhere, even on the waterfront. And, in spite of evidence to the contrary, which they sometimes conveniently overlook, they're often quick to assume the one doin' the killin' is the guilty party."

He thought for a moment. The racket from the gunfire was evidently no cause for concern along the rest of the waterfront which, I had come to learn, kept strictly to its own business. Finally, Mulrooney, almost as if thinking aloud, offered a suggestion. "Tell you what, me friend, you could be in a heap o' trouble. Now there's a friend o' mine in Homicide who used to patrol this same beat as mine. Many a night, we were partners together. He's tough, but a square shooter. Is that phone still working?"

He picked it up, jiggled the hook, finally got the operator and put through a call to Homicide West. He talked with a Sergeant Cramer, quickly filled him in on the situation here, listened a moment and hung up. He told me Cramer was on his way and warned me to play it absolutely straight with him.

In exactly twelve minutes a police car pulled up on the dock, stopped in front of the office, and two men got out. The first, who gruffly introduced himself as Sergeant Cramer, was a big man with a sizeable bottom and heavy, broad shoulders underneath a thick, muscular neck. His round face was beet-red, probably from the cold. Sharp blue-gray eyes under bushy gray eyebrows looked as though they didn't miss much. He wore an old felt hat. His open overcoat revealed a three-piece suit. The other dick, a Sergeant Purley Stebbins, was also big and broad. His bony face sprouted oversized ears and pig-bristle eyebrows above a firm square jaw. There was a no-nonsense quality to both men.

Cramer took out a big cigar, lit it, and asked Mulrooney a couple of quick questions before turning to me. "All right, Goodwin," he growled, "how did you know these two goons were going to hit this morning?" I expected that question and had a ready answer. "I got a phone call yesterday morning, tipping me off."

Of course, he wanted to know who made the call but I had already decided to make no mention of Dolores. As for Jablonski, I wasn't exactly sure how to deal with him, but I wanted him for myself. So I merely said, "It was Mr. Anonymous."

Cramer didn't believe me, but he gave up for the moment. He told Mulrooney to stay until he could send a lab and forensic crew to take care of the bodies.

Then he gruffly ordered me into the car and Stebbins drove us to Homicide West on 20th Street.

VII

At Police Headquarters, I was immediately hustled into an interview room where both Cramer and Stebbins hammered away at me as though I were the criminal rather than the Knight in Shining Armor. With growing skepticism, they kept asking the same questions in a hundred different ways:

"Who tipped you off, and why?"

"I don't know."

"Who were the hijackers?"

"I don't know."

"Who owns the warehouse?"

"I don't know — a guy named Jablonski manages it."

Cramer turned to Stebbins and told him to get hold of

Jablonski and find out if he knew anything. I could have told him that would be an exercise in futility. Then he resumed with the questions.

"What's stored in the warehouse?" (They hadn't bothered to check.)

"Precision Machine Parts."

The only question they didn't really care about was that last one. By this time, I'd come to realize that the NYPD had no inclination to help the Feds enforce the 18th Amendment.

Finally, I had to remind them, "Hey, I'm the good guy, remember? The guy who was doing the job he was hired for? The guy who took on a couple of hoods? I'm not looking for any medal, but I don't need this. How about knocking it off?"

By the time they gave up, I was thoroughly annoyed. That's when they turned me over to a Lieutenant Rowcliff, a nattily dressed individual who some people might even consider handsome. To me that illusion was spoiled by his fishy pop eyes and a voice that came out in snarls. It was hate at first sight, on both our parts, and the years have only strengthened it. I soon discovered one weakness and was quick to exploit it.

He began with a little different tack which he'd never have taken if he had any idea how I reacted to threats. "Goodwin, is it?" he snarled. He waved my Colt .45 under my nose. "You got a license for this gun?"

I told him the gun had belonged to my father, who left it to me when he died. "It served in the war and it's been in the family for two generations," I said, "I guess that's license enough."

He grinned and rubbed his hands together. "On the contrary," he said. "Under the Sullivan Law, I can put you in jail for twelve months. Keep that in mind while you give me some straight answers!"

The questions were the same I'd been hearing for the last couple of hours. So were the answers. That was when I noticed that Rowcliff had a tendency to stutter. I started to s-s-stammer m-m-my answers. In five minutes, I had him stuttering completely out of control. Kind of mean, maybe, but he gave me plenty of provocation.

It's anybody's guess what might have happened if it weren't for the entrance of still another law official. He was well-dressed, well-groomed and well-spoken. Still, inwardly, I groaned, "Here we go again."

He dismissed Rowcliff, introduced himself as District

Attorney Dick Morley, and offered me a cigarette which I accepted. What next, I wondered, the blindfold and the firing squad? Fortunately, he had other ideas. He explained that he had talked with Cramer and Stebbins, whom he described as thoroughly competent detectives. Nevertheless, he wanted to hear my story first-hand. I gave him the laundered version. When I finished, he surprised me by saying he had no reason to doubt my account of what happened. He added, "I have an idea there are a few details you've chosen to leave out. You evidently have your own reasons and I doubt that these omissions are pertinent."

Then he continued, "That was a profoundly stupid thing you did, taking on two armed gunmen all by yourself. It's a miracle you weren't killed." He paused. "On the other hand, I wish more of our citizens would act with that same courage and resourcefulness. Goodwin, I'd like to shake your hand." We shook. He asked me to drop in at his office on Leonard Street on Monday to dictate a complete report to a steno. He said they'd have to keep my gun as material evidence but that it would be returned when I got a license for it. He offered to get me a ride home, but I decided I needed a walk in the brisk December air to clear out the cobwebs. It was 6:05 am when I walked out of the station. I'd evidently been tried and convicted of being a concerned citizen and released on good behavior. Finally, my day was over. Or so I thought.

VIII

It was still dark when I walked out of the police station. 20th Street was deserted except for a lone figure who seemed to be waiting for someone. He was. For me. He stepped up and introduced himself as Harry Foster, a reporter for *The Gazette*, working the police beat. He'd heard about the shooting on Pier 64. The homicide dicks had refused to give him any details. He wanted to ask me some questions.

As a high school football player back in Ohio, I'd learned that it could be beneficial to cooperate with the news media. Do them a favor and later you could call in your marker. And who knew when I might need a favor? "Harry," I said, "I've just finished answering the same questions 196 times by actual count. Maybe one more time and I can get it right. But at this moment, my nether region, which is usually pretty complacent, is sending up complaints about being empty. See that restaurant across the street?" I asked, pointing. "It's probably a cop hangout, but I'm going over there and order enough ham and eggs to keep two pigs and a flock of hens busy and enough milk to drain a herd of cows. If you want to join me, come ahead."

He was an eager young man and proceeded to ask the right questions. It was a relief not to be treated like a murderous psychopath. I gave him the same story I'd given the cops. He got a real kick out of the dummy, said it made a swell story, and showed his gratitude by actually picking up the check.

With my stomach now mildly complaining about being too full instead of too empty, I felt fortified enough to walk briskly back to my rooming house. I needed a good eight hours sleep. I didn't get it. Before I could turn into the house, I felt a gun jammed none too gently into my back. Two gorillas escorted, if that's the right word, me into a long, black limousine. They frisked me expertly. One drove. The other kept me covered, warned me to keep quiet, and added that The Angel wanted to see me. Fortunately, he was not referring to St. Peter! Just about everyone had heard about The Angel, and I was no exception. I reached into the filing chamber of my mind and came up with a name, Giuseppe DeAngelo. He controlled the bootleg racket in Manhattan. His friends called him "The Angel." He had a reputation for being ruthless to his enemies, unbelievably generous to his friends. I wondered in which category I belonged.

It didn't take long to find out. The limo pulled into a reserved parking space right in front of the Plaza Hotel. With Tweedledee and Tweedledum on either side of me, half carrying me across the elegant lobby, we took the elevator to the top floor and into what was probably the most luxurious suite in the hotel.

The Angel was seated at a table by himself, working on a steak and egg breakfast. I expected to see Neanderthal Man disguised in a pinstripe suit, black shirt and white tie, smoking a cigar and talking out of the corner of his mouth. Instead, the most notorious gangster in New York could have posed for the Chairman of the Board of General Motors. Probably in his late fifties, he was impeccably groomed, with jet black hair slightly grayed at the temples. He was tastefully dressed in a maroon smoking jacket, light blue shirt, open at the neck, Ascot tie, and grey slacks.

One of the gorillas told him I was "clean." He indicated a chair, dismissed the two goons and politely asked if I'd had breakfast. This seemed like such a good sign that I almost ordered a second breakfast but compromised on a cup of coffee. He carefully poured and handed me a steaming cup. I was beginning to feel like Alice at the Mad Hatter's Tea Party.

"I understand," he began in a low, cultured voice, "that you killed two men who were trying to hijack my warehouse."

"Your warehouse?" I asked. "I never did know who owned it."

"My name doesn't appear on the deed," he explained, "but in order to control all the liquor in Manhattan, I own warehouses all over the city. Now, I want to know exactly what happened at Pier 64."

"You, the cops and the great unwashed public," I exclaimed. Then, I recounted exactly what had happened from the beginning. I explained that I hadn't mentioned Jablonski to the cops because I had a score to settle with him myself.

"Don't worry about Jablonski," he said. "I've known for some time that he was skimming off a case or two every now and then, just enough so he figured it wouldn't be noticed. I noticed, all right, but I could overlook minor transgressions. Evidently, he got greedy. I won't overlook that.

"Goodwin," he continued, "you did a damn fine job, trying to keep that warehouse from being sacked. I doubt if the cops will bother to inform the Feds about the warehouse contents. Even if they were notified, I pay them enough to look the other way. Still, you may well have saved me several hundred cases. And I like the way you did it. I could use a man like you. How about coming to work for me?"

"Thanks, but no thanks," I replied. "I appreciate the offer but somehow I seem to have a keen desire to live out my allotted three score and ten. Meaning no offense, the life expectancy in your business seems considerably less than that."

For the first time, he smiled and I swear he was putting me on when he added, "OK, Goodwin. But I could let you have Jablonski's job."

"No, thanks," I responded. "I'm not cut out for warehouse work." Then I added, "Not enough excitement."

This time he laughed out loud. "By the way," he asked, "did you ever get paid for your week's work?"

"Come to think of it," I answered. "I never did."

He opened his wallet, extracted a bill, folded it and tucked it in my pocket. "That ought to cover it." he said. Then, he added in a completely serious tone, "But I still owe you." He tore off a sheet from a notebook, jotted down a telephone number, and handed it to me. "I move around a lot," he said, "but you can always reach me through this number."

I examined it carefully, then tore it into small pieces. His eyes narrowed and his voice was ice cold when he asked, "You don't need a friend?"

I assured him that after all I'd been through, nobody needed a friend more than I. "However," I explained, "I seem to have a magnetic attraction for various officials of the law. I wouldn't want this number to fall into their hands. And I don't think you would, either." I tapped my forehead. "That number is locked in here — permanently. I may never need to use it, but if I do, I can call it out next week, next year or any time in the future. You really don't owe me, anyway, but I sincerely appreciate your offer."

He rose from the table, shook hands and yelled for his two goons. "This man is OK," he told them. "Treat him right. Now take him home or anywhere he wants to go."

Home was fine. When I walked in the door, there was one more obstacle to overcome in the form of the wicked witch, otherwise known as my landlady, who stood with folded arms blocking my way to the stairs. Before she could utter a word, I said, "I know, I know, I owe you for two pillows. And, for the inconvenience, I'll double whatever they're worth."

I reached in my pocket and pulled out the bill The Angel had given me. My eyes bulged. Ben Franklin was staring at me. It was a C-Note — a cool hundred simoleons! I'd never seen one before. Pretty good for a week's work. I hastily put it back, took out my wallet and paid her, suggesting that she could buy two pillows and still have enough left over for a broomstick. With that, on this memorable Sunday morning, I went up, flopped in my bed, and slept until late Monday morning. I didn't miss the pillows at all.

IX

It was early afternoon when I arrived at the District Attorney's office. A shapely receptionist with pert, heart-shaped features set off by long blonde hair, counter to the current style but far more attractive to my eye, ushered me into an empty room. I was immediately joined by a steno whose tailored suit and no-nonsense attitude discouraged anything but the business at hand. She competently typed my report as quickly as I could dictate it, handed me the finished copy, had me sign it, and witnessed it herself.

As I started to leave, and was wondering how to get the receptionist's telephone number (I had recovered quickly from a broken heart!) she informed me that the DA wanted to see me. He was seated behind a large desk, covered with papers and forms. I waited while he glanced at my report, then added it to one of the piles.

"Goodwin," he said, "I thought you should know that Michael Jablonski has dropped out of sight. We wanted to question him. Any idea of where he might be?"

My guess would have been at the bottom of the Hudson River, weighted down with cement blocks. But I didn't say so. "All I had was a telephone number," I replied. "I never even knew his address."

"He lived in a run-down rooming house in the Bronx," explained the DA, "but he's flown the coop. It probably isn't important, anyway. We'll pick him up sooner or later."

Maybe his body, I thought. As far as I was concerned, it was justice well-deserved. After all, Jablonski had forced my girl out of New York and done his best to kill me. Of course, I didn't express these thoughts.

The DA then looked at me carefully as though appraising me for the first time. He said he assumed I was looking for another job. I assured him I was. He explained that an acquaintance of his, who had recently started in business as a private detective, was looking for someone to carry out a special chore. "It might be just a one-time job," he explained, "but who knows? It could possibly lead to something more permanent."

He picked up the phone, gave the operator a number, and spoke into the mouthpiece, "Good afternoon. Dick Morley here. I have a young man with me, Archie Goodwin, who I thought displayed unusual resourcefulness in preventing a hijacking the other night. You may have read about it. If you're still looking for a man of action, he might just be the man." He listened for a moment, hung up, made a notation on a slip of paper, and handed it to me. "He'll see you at 8:30 this evening." He rose from his desk as if ending the interview, then, almost as an afterthought, added, "He's a little, er, eccentric. Don't let that deceive you. He is unquestionably the most brilliant man I've ever met."

I thanked him. On the way out, I stopped at the receptionist's desk and said, "I seem to have misplaced your telephone number." She smiled sweetly and replied, "What a coincidence. So have I." She turned and went back to her work. Oh well, you can't win 'em all. As I went out, I looked at the slip of paper the DA had given me. It simply read: "NERO WOLFE, 918 WEST 35TH STREET."

X

On the way back to the rooming house, I picked up the early afternoon edition of *The Gazette*. The hijacking didn't rate a front page article, but in the first section Foster had done a creditable job of reporting. The use of the dummy was featured prominently.

After an uneventful dinner, I dressed carefully in my best blue suit, blue shirt, clean collar and striped tie, put a shine on my shoes, and brushed off my overcoat and felt hat. I then walked to 918 West 35th Street between 10th and 11th Avenues. No. 918 was a four-story brown house with similar buildings adjacent to either side. Incidentally, if you're ever looking for No. 918 you'll find it approximately in the middle of the Hudson River. For reasons which I'm sure are obvious, the exact location of Nero Wolfe's office must forever remain in the realm of "firecrackers."

It was exactly 8:25 when I mounted the steps of the old brownstone, rang the bell, and was admitted by a pleasant-appearing man of middle age who asked my name and introduced himself as Fritz Brenner. He was casually but neatly dressed in slacks and a sport jacket, the only incongruous article being a pair of worn slippers. He asked for my coat and hat. I assured him I was perfectly capable of hanging them up myself, and did so. Somehow, I've always found it slightly demeaning to be waited on. He led me into a large room, said that Mr. Wolfe would be with me shortly, and left. I'd never been in a room anything like this one. Spacious and high-ceilinged, the walls lined with shelves, it appeared to be a combination office and living room. The floor was covered with the largest, most colorful oriental rug I'd ever seen. A bright yellow couch adorned one end of the room. At least a half dozen yellow chairs were scattered throughout. Yellow drapes were drawn over the windows. To my right was a globe that wasn't much smaller than the world it represented. It must have measured at least three feet in diameter. A huge, old-fashioned safe was in one corner. The shelves held more books than the entire Chillicothe Public Library.

By far the most dominant feature was an enormous desk in the far corner. Its reddish-dark wood literally glowed in the lamplight. Behind the desk was a beautiful leather-covered chair that must have been custom-built for a giant. On the desk was a vase containing a spray of exotic tropical flowers of a kind that never grew in my mother's garden. The Sunday edition of *The New York Times* was open at a half finished crossword puzzle, a fad which had recently become fashionable, presumably among intellectuals. The only other item on the desk was a book with a foreign title I couldn't begin to pronounce, *Mein Kampf*, by somebody named Adolph Hitler. In about the middle of the book was a dog-eared page, evidently marking the reader's progress. On the wall behind the desk was a nondescript picture of the Washington Monument, seemingly completely out of character as part of this tasteful, luxurious decor. Beside a small table in front of the desk was another yellow chair in which I was seated. It's actually taken me a lot longer to describe these unique surroundings than to experience the deep impression they made.! felt comfortable in this room. Somehow, it seemed that I belonged here, and I was fully relaxed when the giant entered.

As impressive as the room was, the mere presence of this man dwarfed everything else. If Paul Whiteman was known as The Prince of Whales, this man must be at least The King of Elephants. Yet, for all his bulk, his movements were smooth, efficient, even graceful, as he walked into the room and lowered his corpulence into his chair. Even seated, he was a most dominating figure, a massive, well-proportioned body, big oblong face which could justifiably be called handsome, gleaming white teeth and dark brown hair neatly trimmed and brushed. He was conservatively dressed in a brown suit with vest. Why wasn't I surprised that his immaculate shirt was bright yellow?

I rose to greet him as he acknowledged my presence with a nod that must have moved his head a whole eighth of an inch. In a low, cultured voice, he said, "Please be seated. I like eyes at a level."

When I complied, he continued, "You are Archibald Goodwin?"

"No, Sir," I replied, "It's Archie. That's the way I was christened and that's the way it is."

"Good," he responded, "I appreciate exactitude. Tell me,

Archie, how many steps lead to my front stoop?"

Of all the questions I might have been asked, this one would never have entered my fertile imagination. Yet, I didn't have to hesitate for a moment. "Seven," I replied firmly.

The folds of his cheeks pulled away slightly from the corners of his mouth. I took this to be a smile. "Excellent." he said, "I could ask that same question of a hundred first-time visitors without getting the correct answer. Nevertheless, I expected it from you. Having read *The Gazette*'s account of your experience at Pier 64, and your ingenious deception with the dummy, it didn't take a genius to infer that you are a devotee of Sir Arthur Conan Doyle. You evidently read books."

"Yes, Sir. When I was a young boy, the Sherlock Holmes stories were my favorites. I was somehow impressed with Holmes chiding Watson for not knowing the number of steps leading from the downstairs hall to their rooms on the floor above. You undoubtedly recall that Holmes told Watson, `You see, but you do not observe.' Ever since then, I've trained myself to observe most carefully, even in seemingly trivial matters such as the number of stairs."

"I am delighted to see that you not only read, you also learn," he said, "And I applaud your choice. I have a boundless admiration for Sir Arthur Conan Doyle, or for Dr. John H. Watson, if you prefer. What other books do you read?"

"Certainly not the kind you do, Sir," I said, "if that book on your desk is any example."

His face darkened and his mouth grew grim. "It is indeed a pity," he growled, "that few people will ever read *Mein Kampf*, fewer will understand it, and even fewer will take it seriously. It is nothing less than a blueprint for the next World War, written by a madman. I know the Germans. I have fought them and killed many. But if we continue with this subject, it will only infuriate me, and I am furious enough already, being shamefully deprived of a decent glass of beer, incidentally the only worthwhile product ever imported from Germany. I have carefully sampled every available substitute, even including Pabst Dopple Beer, near beer. Pfui! I have also tried bootleg beer, so watered down that you might just as well take a bath in it. Prohibition! Bah! The very word is un-American!"

Well, the DA said he was eccentric.

He took in about a bushel of air and exhaled slowly. "I have read the brief newspaper article about the hijacking attempt.

Now, in your own words, I want a complete report."

"Yes, Sir. You want every detail?"

"If your memory is up to it."

"There's nothing wrong with my memory, Sir." Then I proceeded to prove it by giving him every detail, including verbatim conversations from the warning I received from Dolores right through my meeting with the District Attorney. I omitted nothing except my session with The Angel. This did not seem pertinent. As I talked, he sat back in his chair, fingers interlaced over his ample middle, eyes half-closed. For a moment, I thought I was putting him to sleep but some sixth-sense told me he wasn't missing a single word. When I finished, he opened his eyes and asked: "Was it necessary to kill those two gunmen?"

"Necessary?" I asked. "Certainly not. I had two definite options. Either kill them or stand there and be killed. Somehow, although I am far from bloodthirsty, I preferred the former option."

"Understandable," he agreed. "Still, I am a little puzzled that, having been duly warned, you nevertheless chose to return to the warehouse and face a possibly fatal danger."

"Mr. Wolfe," I asked, "has anyone ever tried to make a fool of you?"

"Frequently."

"And you let them get away with it?"

A corner of his mouth twitched. I later came to realize this was about as close as he ever came to a smile.

"Archie," he conceded, "you have made your point." Then he continued, "District Attorney Morley, whose opinion I respect, assured me that you were resourceful and not without valor. From meeting you, I also conclude that you are inquisitive, observant, alert and impetuous. In short, you are a man of adequate intelligence and action. With a little restraint on impetuosity, I find these to be admirable qualities. Now, I shall outline my problem in the event that you are willing to perform a task which may require all of these qualities and may possibly be of some danger."

"I shall try," I replied.

"What did you say?" he cried.

"I said I shall try!" I replied.

"Great Hounds and Cerberus!" he exclaimed. "A man of quality who also occasionally uses the English language with precision!"

With that, he proceeded to outline the task he wanted performed.

XI

Wolfe began his explanation. "There is a restaurant called Rusterman's . . ."

"One of the best," I interrupted. "Their Tournedos Beauharnais are superb. I still have trouble pronouncing it but had no difficulty at all consuming a kingsized portion."

"Archie, you amaze me," he replied. But he seemed more amused than amazed. "Their restaurant serves the finest meals in New York, with one exception, those prepared and served here by Fritz Brenner who admitted you this evening. The restaurant is owned by Herman Rusterman, a fine gentleman of the old school. Now in his eighties, his body is still active, his mind still sharp. He puts in a full day every day at the restaurant, supervising the menu and chatting with longtime customers. He leaves the actual management of the restaurant to a man named Marko Vukcic, whom I have known since we were boys together in Montenegro and whom I value as my oldest and dearest friend. A monthly dinner at Rusterman's is among the few occasions when I venture forth from this house.

"On my last visit, a few days ago, it was evident that Marko was deeply troubled. Yet, being a man of fierce independence, he refused to confide in me. I am worried about him. In the field of haute cuisine, Marko has no peers. Unfortunately, in other areas, he is inclined to be headstrong, gullible, over-sanguine, volatile and naive. It would be no surprise if he were experiencing problems with some woman. But with him, this is constant. It would not upset him to the extent of his present agitation. I believe the problem concerns the restaurant in some way. To investigate and attempt to determine the exact nature of the problem requires a continuing surveillance of the operation at Rusterman's.

"You are indeed observant enough to realize that my anatomical structure militates against the degree of mobility necessary for my continuing presence at Rusterman's. That is why I need a man of intelligence with a potential for action, someone in whom I have complete confidence. On occasion, I employ experienced independent operatives when I require outside assistance. But they are all known to Marko. And I don't want him to have any indication that I am spying on him. Archie, do you have any talent for dissembling?"

"You mean acting? Playing a part? Well, Hollywood never came knocking at my door as a result of my performance in a few Shakespearean plays in our High School Dramatic Society. But I don't think my acting had old Will spinning in his grave. Come to think of it, though, he might have been shaking with laughter. Anyway, I do go along with his premise that `all the world's a stage' and I do not wear my heart on my sleeve."

"You will not need the thespian talent required at Stratford-on-Avon. Do you own a tuxedo?"

"A monkey suit? No, and I'm afraid I left my Rolls Royce at home." He ignored this.

"Rent one. A good one." I assumed he meant a tuxedo, not a Rolls. "Then report to Rusterman's tomorrow at noon. In the meantime, I shall inform Marko that you have been recommended to me by a friend as someone who is planning to open a high-class restaurant in, say, Chillicothe. I shall explain that you would benefit greatly from observing the operation at Ruster-man's in all phases, with special emphasis on the business end. That will give you access to the offices above the restaurant where Marko spends most of his time. You will put in long hours, from the time the restaurant opens at noon until it closes long after serving late-night meals to the Broadway theatre-going crowd. You can pretend to be helping the Maitre D. Keep an eye on the patrons. Wander in and out of the kitchen. Spend time in the business offices. You will see. You will observe. You will report. And while I have no logical reason to fear for Marko's safety except for a certain instinct I have learned to trust, you will look out for Marko as best you can without his realizing it. Can you do all that?"

"If I can navigate through the maze of your multisyllabic vocabulary, I infer that you want me to be a combination actor, diplomat, detective and bodyguard. Yes, I can do that."

"Congratulations, Archie. The number of people who use the word `infer' correctly can be numbered among those who observe such details as the number of stairs. If your dramatic teacher is as competent as your English teacher, you will have no difficulty in performing the task, which is basically as I implied and you inferred."

He reached into his desk drawer and brought forth a .38 automatic. "I doubt very much that you will need this," he said. "Nevertheless, I assure you it is in good working order. I shall make arrangements with Marko for you to be at the restaurant tomorrow noon. I am not sure how long your surveillance will be necessary. Your pay will be commensurate with the job. Report to me by phone at 11 o'clock each morning. Of course, if there is any emergency, report at once."

He rose and offered his hand. At the time, I had no realization of the full significance of that magnanimous gesture. I shook his hand warmly, rescued my hat and coat, and left.

XII

All dolled up in my rented monkey suit, white shirt, black tie and spats, I could have been ready for the junior Prom! But I sure didn't have a ball as I danced through the tragic events of my first day as a restaurateur.

Before that first day was through, I felt like the schoolboy who told his teacher he learned more about whales from reading *Moby Dick* than he cared to know. My lessons in the food business convinced me that all I ever wanted from a restaurant was a good table, competent service and a gourmet menu. At that, I was given the specialty of the house not only in dining but also in education into the mysteries of haute cuisine. You don't need the details but in view of what took place later, you ought to be familiar with the stage and the cast of characters.

Rusterman's was a relatively small restaurant located on East 54th Street, occupying the first two floors of an attractive brown house. You enter past a small cloak room into a large, comfortable lounge with a gleaming mahogany bar at one end. The shelves behind the bar were empty because Rusterman's was one of the few eating establishments in New York that did not serve bootleg booze. I was given to understand that both Mr. Rusterman and Mr. Vukcic, as proud naturalized American citizens, felt a genuine debt to their adopted country, including responsibility for strict obedience to the laws of the land, even those like Prohibition, which they felt made no sense.

The lounge led into the main dining room, elegant, spacious, luxurious in décor. The kitchen was off to one side. The floor above included private offices in front for Rusterman and Vukcic, a business office for general bookkeeping and accounting, and three small private dining rooms in the rear. Vukcic occupied the apartment above the restaurant.

So much for the stage. The main cast of characters included

Herman Rusterman, tall and lean, whose white hair and unlined features belied his eighty-plus years. He was every inch a gracious gentleman, with the courtesy and cordiality of old world charm. In contrast, Marko Vukcic was huge, not fat. His swarthy features were framed by a dense tangle of dark hair, reminiscent of a lion's mane. Impressive and competent, he was one of the world's greatest chefs.

The rest of the staff whom I met that day included Felix Martin, Maitre D, Pierre Ducos, head waiter, Vincent, the burly doorman, Joe, Leo and Antonio, waiters, and Suzanne, fair and buxom bookkeeper.

It was almost 2 AM before things had quieted down enough for me to consider packing it in. A couple of waiters were still cleaning up downstairs. I was in the office with Vukcic when he said, "Archie, aside from the obvious talent of the chef and the service of a competent staff, the key to any restaurant's success is in the quality of food it serves. I take pride that we at Rusterman's pay closer attention to this principle than any restaurant in New York. For example, in the next hour or so, the few hardy deep-sea fishermen who still brave the seas in winter will begin bringing in their catch to the Fish Pier. Many's the cold night I've spent waiting for them to come in so I could select the best and freshest fish. Now I leave that important chore to Felix. He'll be leaving soon. This is a part of your education you must experience personally. So here's your chance to accompany Felix this morning."

His manner was disarmingly pleasant. Suspiciously so. Could this be his sadistic idea of getting back at Wolfe for saddling him with me as a neophyte? Standing at the Fish Pier at 3 am on a cold, wintry night in December was the last experience I wanted. So, naturally, I reached into the depths of my dramatic talent (was Hamlet ever thus harassed?), smiled sweetly and lied, "I'd like nothing better."

As I passed Mr. Rusterman's office on my way to the back stairs, I could see he was still working. Vukcic, evidently headed for his upstairs apartment, whispered to me that Rusterman liked to review the day's activities and make notes of any suggestions for the next day before leaving for home.

The rear entrance led into an alley where Felix was loading the back of a truck with two huge copper tubs filled with cracked ice. I helped him and explained that Mr. Vukcic wanted me to go with him. He seemed glad of the company. On the way, I used whatever tact I had left over at this hour of the morning to pump him about whatever might be troubling Vukcic. He told me it all started a couple of days ago when he heard the sounds of a loud argument coming from Mr. Rusterman's office. He said that Rusterman and Vukcic were behind closed doors with a third man, evidently a stranger, whom he did not see come in. Ever since then, he said, Mr. Vukcic had seemed very much on edge.

After selecting and packing our catch of the day, I could sympathize more with the schoolboy and the whales. Felix offered to drop me off at my room on the way back. I could see that he hoped I'd stay with him to help him unload. Inasmuch as the whole night was shot, anyway, I figured I might as well buy a little good will.

When we drove up to the restaurant, I was appalled to see flashing lights and a couple of police cars parked in front. Even at that late hour, a small crowd had materialized. They always seem to emerge full-blown at a crime scene. And I was afraid to think what this crime scene might be.

We parked the truck in back of the police cars. A uniformed cop tried to stop us from entering, but let us in when we convinced him we were employees. The lights were on both downstairs and upstairs. We rushed up to Mr. Rusterman's office where we were stopped by a burly plainclothes detective. I recognized Sergeant Purley Stebbins, but before I could speak, he snarled, "Hold it! I know you. You're Goodwin! What in hell are you doing here?"

I looked past him into the office. The stark scene is etched into my mind, as clear today as it was then. The body of Herman Rusterman was lying in front of his desk, crumpled in the unmistakable posture of death. A small trickle of blood had stained the carpet beside him. Vukcic was seated, his body slumped, head bowed, hands shackled. Sergeant Cramer was standing beside him. Antonio, the waiter, stood aloof in the corner.

"I work here," I replied to Stebbins, the simplest explanation being the best explanation. "What happened?"

Cramer motioned for me and Felix to enter. In answer to his question, we explained how we had just returned from the Fish Pier. Again, I asked, "What happened?"

Vukcic looked up. "Mr. Goodwin! Archie! You will tell Nero?" Cramer growled, "Who's Nero?"

"A friend of Mr. Vukcic," I replied. For the third time, I asked, "What happened?"

It was Vukcic who replied. Intuitively, I felt it might be best if he kept quiet, but I had to know the facts. Cramer was content to let him talk. The slight accent I'd noticed before became more pronounced.

"Those Cossacks!" he cried. "They do not believe me. I tell them the truth. When you and Felix leave, I remember I have not made out tomorrow's menu. I come back from upstairs and go to my office. In a few minutes, I hear a shot from Mr. Rusterman's office. I rush in and grapple with the hoodlum who shot him. But that slippery devil breaks loose. I pick up his gun, which he drops in the struggle, and chase him down the back stairs into the alley toward the street. I do not dare shoot for fear I would hit some innocent passer-by. I fire in the air to scare him but he gets away. When I come back, Mr. Rusterman is dead." His voice broke but he continued. "That's when that fool, Antonio, comes in. I tell him to call the police. Then we wait. I do not know he is a Brutus! When the police come, Antonio, that liar, tells them he sees me shoot Mr. Rusterman." He paused and looked up at me, tears streaming from his eyes. "You will tell Nero? He will help!"

"Did you recognize the one who did shoot him?" I asked.

"Recognize him? Of course! You think I forget that slimy bastard? I tell these policemen. He was bootlegger who come last week and want to sell booze for the restaurant. I tell him no, no, no! He say he not only sell booze, he sell protection. I say we need no protection. He say I may change my mind and he will come back. I throw him out! You see what he did. You tell Nero?"

Here Cramer interrupted. "This Nero better be good. First, Vukcic here tells a cock 'n' bull story about the little man who wasn't here. No one saw him. And he gives us a description that would fit most of the male population of New York. Then, we find the murder weapon. It will undoubtedly have Vukcic's prints all over it. A paraffin test will show he fired the gun. But he invents another story about shooting in the air. Balls! Finally, we have an eye witness who saw him shoot Rusterman. And Antonio tells us it's common knowledge that Vukcic inherits the restaurant on Rusterman's death. It's an open and shut case. Motive, opportunity, murder! That's more than enough to book Mr. Vukcic and send him to the hot seat. Tell his friend Nero that!"

I said I would and left. Felix came downstairs with me. "That liar, Antonio," he said, "he's no good. I should have fired him long ago!"

That seemed to call for further questioning. I made a mental note to follow up. Right then, I was anxious to get my thoughts together before reporting to Wolfe. When I walked out the door, the dawn of a gray December day was just beginning to break.

XIII

The small crowd outside had begun to break up. Only a few stragglers remained. As I walked past them, a voice called out, "Hey, Goodwin! You shoot somebody else?"

The speaker stepped forth. It was Harry Foster of *The Gazette*. "This is getting to be a habit," he said, "finding you at the scene of the crime. Can you fill me in on what happened?"

"You better put me on the payroll," I replied. "Better yet, I'll tell you what happened in exchange for a little information. Deal?"

"If I can," he answered. "Let's do it over breakfast."

An all-night diner was open about a block down Madison Avenue. While I dug into sausage and pancakes, I pondered just how much to tell Foster. I decided to make no mention of Wolfe, and to stick with my story of getting a job with Rusterman's. Otherwise, I gave him the bare facts as I knew them. Then I added, "I've only known Mr. Vukcic for a short time, but I'm a pretty darn good judge of character. Also, he was decent enough to give me a job when I most needed it. So I feel I owe him. There's no way he could have killed Mr. Rusterman. I'm convinced of his innocence.

"Now, you know and I know the bootleg business in this area is controlled by The Angel. But this doesn't sound like his type of operation. First of all, Rusterman's is too small for him to bother with. In addition, he's too smart to call attention to himself by having a prominent restaurant owner killed. So what's the answer? Someone's trying to muscle in on his racket. I want to know who. You cover the police beat. You must have some idea of who's trying to break in."

He thought for a minute. "Archie," he said, "there's been some activity of this kind among a few of the smaller establishments around here. But I honestly don't know who's behind it. It didn't seem important, at least not until this killing." He paused, then added, "There's one guy on our paper who knows more about what's going on in this city than the cops, the feds and the pols all put together. His name is Lon Cohen. He's an awful busy guy, but I'll try and get you an appointment to see him. Where can I reach you?"

I thanked him and told him I'd call him at *The Gazette* later in the morning. Then I figured it was time to get in touch with Mr. Wolfe. I wasn't looking forward to it. My watch said 8:15 when I stepped into a phone booth, parted with a nickel in the slot, and gave the operator Wolfe's number. Fritz Brenner answered. He told me emphatically that Mr. Wolfe was having breakfast and couldn't be disturbed. I finally convinced him that this was an emergency and he reluctantly put me through. Wolfe answered with one word, "Yes?" It sounded like a bear growling. I quickly outlined what had happened. His response was even more like a bear, "Grrrhhh!" Then, finally, one more word, "Come."

I beat a little old lady to a cab and headed for West 35th Street. Fritz admitted me and led me immediately into the office. The bear was there waiting. Knowing his deep affection for Mr. Vukcic, I was apprehensive about what kind of reception I'd get. His first words both surprised and encouraged me. "Archie, have you had breakfast?" When I assured him I'd eaten, he simply uttered one word, "Report."

He leaned back, eyes closed to mere slits, as I'd seen him once before. The index finger of his right hand was slowly making circles on the arm of his chair, the only indication that he was awake. I reported my activities, including word-for-word conversations from the time I'd entered Rusterman's right through my conversation with Foster. Although my report lasted over an hour, he listened patiently without interruption. When I finished, I awaited his reaction with some trepidation. He took a deep breath, relieving the office of about a bushel of air, exhaled slowly and finally spoke.

"Archie, I can find no fault with your performance. Also, I express my gratitude for your obvious belief in Marko's innocence and in your desire to help. We must begin by accepting the accuracy of his account." My relief at his use of that plural pronoun knew no bounds! Then he continued, "With the damning evidence against him, the only way to exonerate him is to identify the actual culprit and provide evidence of his guilt. Confound it! The police, with all their facilities, could locate him much more easily than we can. But it is so much simpler for them to make a quick arrest and consider the case closed. We can assume they will make no effort in that direction. Bah!

"My first step will be to engage Henry Barber, the best legal counsel available, for Marko's defense. We must get a better description of the assailant. And perhaps Mr. Barber can persuade the police to begin a search for the real murderer, although that is a faint hope.

"I commend your action in seeking information from the news media. Follow up on that as soon as possible and report back to me. For the time being, you can use that empty desk and the phone. We should have no problem in proving that Antonio is lying. I shall have to see him. But that can wait."

I immediately went to the desk and phoned Harry Foster. He said that Lon Cohen had agreed to see me late that afternoon, after the paper had been put to bed. When I relayed this information to Wolfe, he suggested that I get some sleep while I could. "There is a guest room on the floor above," he said. "You might as well use it." He rang for Fritz and told him to make sure the room was in readiness. Then, he turned to me and added, "Archie, after being up all night, I realize you must be exhausted. However, it will be worth your while to take a few minutes to relax first. Come."

We walked into the hall and stepped into a small elevator that was never intended for two, especially when Wolfe was one of the two. I managed to squeeze in and we rose slowly to the floor above. It would be a gross understatement to say I was unprepared for the panorama of color and shapes which surrounded me as we entered the plant rooms. The initial impact was that I had stepped into a tropical forest. I recalled an article I'd read about it long ago, entitled, "The Book of Life," a title Dr. Watson thought was over-ambitious, in which Sherlock Holmes claimed, "From a single drop of water, a logician could infer the possibility of an Atlantic or a Niagara without ever having seen or heard of one or the other." Maybe. But if you've seen one orchid, or even a raceme of blossoms, it would be impossible to visualize the effect of hundreds of these exotic plants in full bloom. We moved slowly from the tropical room through a second room where the temperature was moderate into a cool room, each with hundreds of blossoms. I was not conscious of individual shapes or colors, only of a beauty I had never before experienced. And as often as I have visited those plant rooms (which were soon moved to the rooftop gardens above), they never fail to create an emotion that's as indescribable as their beauty.

Wolfe introduced me to Theodore Horstmann, a dour individual who cared for the plants, even to the extent of sleeping in a small room in the corner of the plant rooms. Fritz, whose room was opposite the plant rooms (before he took over the basement) approached and said my room was ready. Wolfe instructed him to wake me at 4 o'clock.

Wolfe later told me that you don't look at color, you feel it. All I know is that I was thoroughly relaxed and at peace with the world. I walked to the floor below, undressed quickly, and never got to sleep faster or slept more soundly.

XIV

FRITZ AWAKENED ME AT 4 PM. Although I like my full eight hours, I felt remarkably refreshed. My rented tuxedo was a little the worse for wear, but it was all I had, so I climbed into it. I left off the spats. Fritz met me downstairs and politely asked if I'd like something to eat. I told him I'd settle for a glass of milk and followed him into the kitchen. I didn't object when he added a plate of sandwiches, thin slivers of ham topped with pineapple rings on thin toast, warm from the broiler. After putting away two of them, I figured I could easily get used to Fritz's larder. Thus fortified, I decided to walk to *The Gazette* building at the address Foster had given me in the upper Forties near First Avenue. I walked through huge revolving doors into a spacious lobby, lavishly decorated with Christmas trees and greenery, dominated by an enormous *Gazette* sign high up on the marble wall. As I'd been instructed, I took the express elevator to the 20th floor and walked through the open office door that was simply labeled Lon Cohen. If he ever had a title, I don't know to this day what it could be. Yet I was soon to learn that this office, just two doors down from the publisher, is the unquestionable command center of *The Gazette*. You'd never know it from the tiny 9 x 12 area with its cluttered desk. And you'd never take Lon Cohen for the top executive he is, judging from his dark complexion, black hair slicked back on his head, neat appearance and quiet manner. He was talking on one of three phones on his desk, but waved me to a vacant chair. I swept some newspapers on the floor, hung up my hat and coat, and sat down.

"I take it you're Mr. Goodwin," he greeted me as he cradled the phone. "My, aren't we fancy? Do you always make your calls in formal clothes?"

I replied in kind. "Not always," I said. "But I was given to understand that you were a real big shot around here, so I decided to arrive in style instead of in my usual crummy old work clothes."

He smiled. "Mr. Goodwin," he began, but I interrupted him. "I wish you'd call me Archie," I said. "Even in my expensive rented tuxedo, I still think of Mr. Goodwin as my father."

"OK, Archie," he continued. "You seem to have a penchant for turning up at the scene of the crime. First, at Pier 64, now at Rusterman's." So he was well informed.

I decided to level with him. "I never planned to be at the scene of a crime when I took a job at Pier 64. But being at Rusterman's was no coincidence. Nero Wolfe, a private detective and friend of Mr. Vukcic, had an inkling that trouble was brewing at the restaurant. He hired me to help him investigate. Unfortunately, I was unable to prevent Mr. Rusterman's death. Now, Mr. Wolfe and I intend to prove Mr. Vukcic's innocence."

Cohen's eyebrows lifted in obvious surprise. "Archie, I appreciate your candor. It's not often I experience that quality. Seems to me I've heard of Nero Wolfe. Doesn't Saul Panzer do some work for him?"

"Never heard of him," I replied.

"Now I remember," continued Cohen. "Isn't Wolfe supposed to be some kind of genius?"

"He must be," I answered. "He sits at home playing with his orchids and eating gourmet meals while I do all the work."

"OK," said Cohen, "How can I help?"

"We figure that someone tried to shake down Rusterman, lost his head, and ended up killing him. I'm sure you're aware that The Angel controls the bootleg business in this area, but this doesn't sound like his racket. It's probably some small-time hood trying to muscle in. Harry Foster thought you might have some idea of what's going on."

Cohen thought for a moment. "For the last few weeks, we've been aware that someone was playing the protection racket with some of the small businesses in midtown Manhattan. Frankly, it didn't interest us as any great scoop. More lurid crimes are committed here every day. And they're the kind that sell newspapers. However, perhaps I can give you one lead. I happen to know that Dopplemeyer's Delicatessen was recently scared into paying protection money. Jacob Dopplemeter, whom I've patronized for years, told me about it in confidence. I suggested he go to the police but like so many immigrants, he doesn't trust them. I don't have the time, the staff or the inclination to look into such a small-time story, but I do feel sorry for Dopplemeyer. Maybe he might give you some helpful information." He picked up one of the phones, instructed someone to get Dopplemeyer, then held a brief conversation. He wrote down an address and handed it to me. "He's still scared to death, but agreed to see you. Try not to frighten him more." Then, he added, "I'd appreciate getting the inside dope, if it's at all newsworthy."

I picked up my hat and coat. "You'll be the second to know — after Mr. Wolfe."

As I headed out the door, he seemed to have an afterthought. There was a twinkle in his eye as he remarked with studied casualness, "By the way, Archie, as I said, I like a man with candor. Especially in a card game. Do you by any chance ever indulge in the lucrative game of poker?"

With a straight face, I replied, "You never heard of Riverboat Goodwin, the scourge of the Mississippi? Let me say that while I am indeed a man of candor, don't count on that to give you the slightest hint as to whether my hand's full of aces or an absolute bust. In addition to candor, I also have some expertise in dissembling. I just learned that word from Mr. Wolfe, but I learned to dissemble long ago. Sure, I play poker, as long as the stakes aren't too high."

He grinned. "We always leave the suckers enough for carfare," he said. "Call me after Christmas and we'll arrange for a game. But, in the meantime, get rid of that damn' tux. It ain't your style."

"My monkey suit?" I said. "That's my gamblin' outfit. The cut of the coat is just right to hide a few aces up the sleeves."

He waved me away. "So long, sucker," he said. I saluted and left.

XV

It was just after 6 o'clock when I left *The Gazette*. I debated whether to call Wolfe. I'd learned enough about his habits to know he'd be down from the plant rooms but not yet at the dinner table. Still, the next step seemed obvious. I looked at the slip Lon had given me. It showed an address on 39th Street near Lexington. As it wasn't much out of my way, I decided to see what I could learn from Dopplemeyer before making my report.

The aroma as I entered the delicatessen, a blend of all those wonderful deli spices, made me forget I'd eaten just a few hours before. It seemed that all of New York was rushing in and out, departing with last-minute supper selections of fresh bread, cheese, meats, pickles, dumplings, lox and bagels. They were keeping the two counter people busy, a short, roly-poly character, with Dutch Boy blonde hair and a bushy blonde mustache, whom I took to be Dopplemeyer, and a pretty blonde fraülein who was also on the roly-poly side, but with all the rolies and polies in all the right places.

A couple of small tables in the rear, presently unoccupied, were evidently for customers who couldn't wait to get home with their purchases. I decided I was one of them. When I had a chance, I introduced myself to Dopplemeyer, told him I'd wait 'til he had a few minutes, and ordered a glass of milk and a pastrami on rye. He suggested I take a seat and in a few minutes the fraülein brought my milk and sandwich to the table. I was glad to see that the lower portion of her anatomy, which had been hidden behind the counter, was every bit as shapely as the upper region. The sandwich, served with a huge salt water pickle right out of the barrel, was every bit as delicious as I'd anticipated.

After about ten minutes, when the last customer had finally left, Dopplemeyer closed and locked the door and sat down at the table. I was surprised and not at all displeased that he brought the fraülein with him and introduced her as his daughter, Frieda. On closer inspection, she was even more shapely than I thought.

She gave me a big dimpled smile, which I returned, but Dopplemeyer was all business. He was nervous and fidgety, frequently darting glances around as if he were fearful of finding a spy in every corner. I tried to calm him by assuring him I intended to find out who was extorting money from him and put a stop to it. I told him not to worry. He said he wasn't afraid for himself, only for his daughter. I asked him to describe how he got into this fix, starting from the beginning.

It was pretty much the same story as with Vukcic. He was a little vague at first, but with a little encouragement from me, and Roly-Poly chiming in now and then, I was able to extract a few details. Last week, just as he and Frieda were closing, a shabbily dressed man with a stocking cap obscuring half his face barged in and offered to supply bottled booze for him to sell to his customers. Dopplemeyer wanted no part of it. Then the intruder offered protection. When Dopplemeyer protested that he didn't need protection, the bootlegger made it clear that unless he went along with it, bad things could happen to Frieda. He would have resisted, but Frieda was the light of his life and he'd do anything to keep her safe.

The booze was delivered by arrangement late the next night by a couple of nondescript workmen. Word quickly got around among the customers. His business actually picked up. However, Dopplemeyer was scared out of his wits. He didn't know whether he was more frightened of the gangster or the cops. In Berlin, where he came from, the German police weren't exactly friends of the little man.

So far so good. But I didn't get what I wanted most, a good description of the mobster. Dopplemeyer and his daughter had seen him only that one time in a darkened delicatessen. I kept probing, but the most I learned was that the man was big. Dark. Rough. Tough. Wore a stocking cap. Had a mustache. Needed a shave. Smelled bad. That about narrowed it down to half the population of Manhattan.

Finally, I asked if he knew when the first payment was due. His angry response was interspersed with a few choice Teutonic curses I'd never heard but were clearly not meant for polite conversation. Even if I could, I wouldn't translate. After all, this is a family narrative. Anyway, you get the idea.

"*Ja!*" he sputtered. "Dot scum! What time do I close Christmas Eve, he asks. Like a dumkopf I tell him vier — four o'clock. He orders me to wait after closing time 'til he comes to collect. Then, he laughs in my face and says, 'Be sure to have my Christmas present ready!' He was still laughing when he left."

All kinds of possibilities were running through my mind; I thought it best to check them out with the genius. I told Dopplemeyer that he'd hear from me the next day. I wasn't quite as confident as I made out. As I was leaving, Frieda wished me Auf Wiedersehen and insisted on giving me a piece of her very own apple strudel. I chewed on it as I walked toward 35th Street. I also chewed on the information I'd gathered. The information wasn't entirely digestible. The strudel was delicious. About the only thing I decided was that I'd like to have another piece of Frieda's strudel.

XVI

Wolfe was in his office reading one of three books on his desk.

I noticed the title, *The Sun Also Rises*, by Ernest Hemingway. I hoped it would rise and shed a little light on our problem. Wolfe looked up and asked if I'd had dinner. I told him I'd had deli delicacies topped off with roly-poly strudel. He frowned, placed a bookmark carefully between the pages, laid down the book and asked, "Well?"

"Not too well," I replied, "but at least a start." I then gave him a full report. As before, he sat back, eyes closed to narrow slits, sat up and uttered one word, "Satisfactory." I didn't realize then that this was about the highest praise he ever offered.

As I was about to make a suggestion, the doorbell rang. Fritz answered it and ushered in a dignified looking gentleman, well-groomed, nattily dressed in a blue pinstripe suit. Wolfe shook hands with him and introduced him as Henry Barber, the lawyer he'd engaged for Vukcic. Barber told us that Vukcic was being held without bail. Barber had to pull a few strings, but was finally allowed to see Vukcic as long as Rowcliff and Cramer were present. Wolfe asked for a full report. I must admit that I was secretly pleased as, unlike my report, Wolfe had to keep interrupting and asking questions to keep him on track and get the information he wanted.

Barber won my approval by declaring that Rowcliff was an idiot and that Cramer was not nearly as convinced as he pretended regarding Vukcic's guilt. Vukcic had evidently calmed down since I last saw him, and gave Barber a fairly lucid account of what had happened, along with a few details I hadn't extracted.

My attention perked up when he began to relay Vukcic's description of his assailant. It sounded very much like a description I'd heard just a couple of hours before — large man, dark complexion, mustache, stocking cap, dirty, smelly. I really became excited when he mentioned a slight facial scar.

Without saying a word, I got up abruptly, walked over to the empty desk, looked up a telephone number from a book in the drawer and gave it to the operator. When it was answered, I asked one question, listened a moment, and hung up. Wolfe, evidently furious at my seeming impertinence, was glaring at me without a word. Even that couldn't spoil my moment of triumph.

"Mr. Wolfe," I cried, "I believe I know who killed Mr. Rusterman!"

Both Wolfe and Barber looked at me as though I'd lost what

few marbles I might have possessed. I hastened to explain. "That description which Mr. Barber elicited from Mr. Vukcic fits the description of a man I know all too well, one Mike Jablonski! When he turned up missing after that warehouse fiasco, I assumed that The Angel had sent him to a watery grave. But . . . "

If I thought Wolfe would be pleased with this information, I couldn't have been more mistaken. He interrupted in a tone that cut like a knife. "Who," he asked icily, "or what is The Angel?"

For an expert engaged in criminal investigation, there were astonishing gaps in Wolfe's knowledge of the criminal element in Manhattan. I quickly explained about my meeting with Giuseppe DeAngelo and how he had told me he'd take care of Jablonski. "Why," Wolfe asked in a voice that dripped venom, "was I not told about your meeting with this so-called Angel?" I stammered that I didn't think it had anything to do with my assignment.

"Mr. Goodwin," he retorted, "you are not paid to think. Confound it, you are paid to provide information — in its entirety! I shall decide what is and isn't relevant. Bah! With the facts you have just disclosed, this investigation might well have taken an entirely different tack. Now, please continue."

Thoroughly chastened, I went on. "Mr. Vukcic's description of his assailant pretty closely matches the description of the hoodlum who pulled the protection racket on poor Dopplemeyer. I just phoned him and asked if the man who shook him down had a facial scar. That evidently jogged his memory. His answer was, `Ach der lieber! Ja!' I took this for an affirmative. Now all we have to do is catch him. And I think . . ."

I never got to tell him what I thought. Maybe it was because he'd just told me I wasn't paid to think. In any event, he was no longer with me. Slumped in his chair, with his eyes completely closed, his lips began to move slowly in and out. For a moment, I thought he might be having a stroke. I started to rise from my chair. Barber, who knew him well, stopped me. He put his finger to his lips, leaned close to me and whispered, "Shhh. You are witnessing genius at work. Wait."

We waited about twenty minutes. Wolfe slowly opened his eyes, and said simply, "Instructions." He then talked for another twenty minutes while I made a few notes on a piece of scrap paper from the desk. When he had finished, he picked up a book, not the one he'd been reading. Does the man read three books at once? I have trouble enough with one. Maybe he is a genius, after all.

As I was leaving, he called, "Archie!" I was relieved to be on a first-name basis again. He continued, "I usually do not offer free advice but I shall make an exception that might just save you a little of your hard-earned wages. I doubt very much that you would make a good poker player."

While I pondered this, he added, "And, Archie, get rid of that fool . . . monkey suit."

XVII

Early Thursday morning, I was at the delicatessen when it opened. Dopplemeyer greeted me with a hearty "Guten Morgen." I explained the program of the day to him and Frieda. We agreed that I would sit at one of the back tables, with a cup of coffee and a newspaper as props, where l could keep my eye on anything that went on.

With one exception, it was an uneventful day. Frieda kept me well supplied with hot coffee, freshly ground at the counter, and later with a continuing parade of knockwurst and sauerbraten and liverwurst and sauerkraut and, of course, strudel. From time to time I got up and walked around, taking inventory inside and outside.

Early in the morning I noticed a car parked across the street a little way down from the deli. I couldn't get a good look at the driver who was slumped down behind the wheel. An hour later, he was still there. I checked again just before noon and he still hadn't moved, It looked like time to investigate.

I put on my hat and coat, walked slowly across the street, and strolled casually past the parked car. As far as I could see, it was occupied by a nose, attached to a little man in a shabby brown suit, no overcoat in spite of the below freezing weather, and an old brown cap on his head. He was smoking a cigarette. The smoke, drifting through a partially opened window, brought an aroma that reminded me of the stuff we used to put in the fields back home to help the crops grow.

I knocked on the window and he rolled it down without hesitation. My right hand had a firm grip on the automatic in my coat pocket. In my most polite voice, I asked, "Would you mind explaining why you're parked here with your eye on the delicatessen?"

He wasn't the least perturbed. "Please don't misunderstand

this next motion, Mr. Goodwin," he said. So he knew who I was. My hand tightened on the automatic. "I am going to reach slowly into my breast pocket for identification."

I followed his movement closely, ready to act at the first wrong move. But he simply pulled out a leather wallet and handed it to me. I opened it and observed a private investigator's license in the name of Saul Panzer. The name seemed to ring a bell. Then I remembered it was mentioned by Lon Cohen. I handed it back and asked again what he was doing here.

"Mr. Wolfe explained your assignment to me," he replied, "and asked me to provide backup, in case you needed it."

"Why the hell should I need it?" I asked irritably. "I'm only after one man, not an army! And why in hell didn't Wolfe tell me?"

"You'll have to ask him," replied Panzer. "But I can tell you this. I've done work for him before and he frequently operates on the theory that the less anyone knows, the better he'll perform. I don't necessarily subscribe to that theory, but it's hard to quarrel with the success Mr. Wolfe always has. My guess would be that he believed you would be more efficient if you felt the entire responsibility was on your shoulders."

I was still mad, so I took it out on him. "Well, you're one hell of a detective!" I exclaimed. "A baby could have spotted you casing the joint."

"Archie," he said quietly. "Neither you nor anyone else would have noticed me unless I wanted to be noticed. In spite of Mr. Wolfe's theories, I thought it best if you knew you could count on help if you needed it. This way we have both inside and outside surveillance. Otherwise," he assured me, "I wouldn't be out here freezing my butt off and starving to death."

I couldn't stay mad at the little guy. "Stay here," I said, "and I'll get you some of the best knockwurst and sauerkraut you've ever tasted. And maybe you can get the fräulein to warm you up." We shook hands. I returned to the deli and asked Frieda to bring him a hearty meal.

Dopplemeyer closed up shop about 6 pm . I waved goodbye to Panzer and walked to West 35th to make my report. I arrived just at dinner time and was pleased when Wolfe asked me to join him. We sat down in the dining room. As I dug into a heaping plate of savory pork fillets braised in spiced wine, and salad with a delectable dressing that Fritz called "Devil's Rain," I began to report.

He stopped me with, "Archie, there is little enough leisure time to relax and enjoy the bounty of this great land, enhanced by the culinary skills of a master chef. Let us not spoil it by talking business."

He then asked if I'd seen an item in the paper about a Dr. Robert H. Goddard who had fired the first liquid fuel propelled rocket in some obscure little town in Massachusetts. "It rated just one small paragraph in *The Times*," he said. "They have no realization of its tremendous significance. Within our lifetime, the invention of this rocket will enable us to place a man on the moon and to learn more about this universe than we have learned in the entire history of time." He then discoursed for an hour on the exploration of interplanetary space. I thought again about the logician who could infer an entire Atlantic from a single drop of water. But a man on the moon because of a dinky Fourth of July skyrocket? Horse Apples! But I had the good sense not to say anything.

After dinner, we retired to the office. I gravitated to the empty desk as if I belonged there. Over coffee, I gave Wolfe a brief report on the day's surveillance, including my meeting with Panzer. I was careful not to express my initial feelings about having backup. Anyway, by this time, I kind of liked the little guy with the big nose, and agreed to myself that he might be helpful.

Wolfe had no comment except to say that Saul must have felt it would be beneficial for us to work together. This merely confirmed the fact that I hadn't spotted him due to any carelessness on his part.

Wolfe repeated his instructions for the next day, then added, "I have no intention of having Marko languish in jail over Christmas. This holiday means a great deal to him. Therefore, I am determined to exonerate him before the day is over tomorrow. In all probability, I can accomplish this only if two of our assumptions are correct: first, that the man who killed Rusterman is the same hoodlum that's harassing Dopplemeyer; second, that you bring him to me tomorrow. Otherwise, I shall look like a complete witling to the law and everyone else. More important, we shall have failed. Archie, I am counting on you."

I assured him I'd do my best, and went back to my rooming house. I needed a good night's rest.

XVIII

Friday. Christmas Eve. What a way to spend it! Yet, it was filled with anticipation. Although I had promised Dopplemeyer no involvement on his part, it wasn't quite working out that way. However, as he could see the possible end to his trouble, he didn't seem to mind. In fact, if anything, he had begun to overcome his fear.

Saul was already parked across the street when I arrived at the delicatessen. As we waited through that long day, time seemed to stand still. There were few customers, most evidently busy with last-minute Christmas shopping. The few who did come in were usually after a last-minute bottle of Christmas cheer.

As the clock wound down toward closing time, I retired to the small back office where I would be out of sight but still able to keep my eye on the front door. I thought it best for Frieda to come with me. Ordinarily I would have welcomed the close quarters away from the watchful eye of Dopplemeyer, but my mind was on other things. At 4 o'clock, Dopplemeyer closed and locked the door, pulled down the shades on the windows that fronted the street and dimmed the interior lights. Still we waited. Five o'clock. Six o'clock. Seven o'clock. The tension mounted with every slow minute.

Suddenly, the silence was shattered by a loud knocking at the door. In the stillness and semi-darkness, it sounded like thunder. The figure outlined in the doorway couldn't have been more unexpected, even if it was Christmas Eve. I nodded to Dopplemeyer to open the door. Santa Claus walked in!

As he entered, I could see that Saul was crossing the street. Santa swaggered in, reeling slightly. He evidently had a head start on the Christmas cheer. He took a small sack from his shoulder and held it out toward Dopplemeyer.

"Ho! Ho! Ho!" he roared. "It's old Santa. This old Santa don't give no presents. This old Santa takes. Time to pay old Santa for whiskey and protection. Time to fill up the old sack. Hurry!" I felt a tingling up my spine as I recognized the voice.

Dopplemeyer played his part well. He mumbled that he had to open the cash register. As he moved toward the counter, Santa turned to accompany him. That's when I broke quickly from the office, gun in hand. At the same time, Saul rushed in through the front door. Old Santa didn't stand a chance. I jammed my gun, none too gently, into his back. Saul quickly frisked him and retrieved a fully-loaded revolver and a wicked-looking knife. I reached over, pulled off his whiskers, and grinned at Saul. "Saul, meet Santa Claus, otherwise known as Mike Jablonski!"

Jablonski didn't recognize me at first. Then it dawned on him.

"Goodwin!" he exclaimed.

"Yeah!" I replied. "That hick hayseed from the country! Let me assure you this gun is in perfect working condition. I have a score to settle with you, and I'd like nothing better than to put a slug in your fat gizzard right here and now. Make just one funny move and you're gone!"

I told Saul to keep him covered. Then I went to the phone in the back room and made two calls. The first was to a number I had locked in my memory. The second was to Wolfe. I filled him in quickly. For the second time since I'd met him, I heard one word, "Satisfactory."

By this time, the street was pretty well deserted. Making sure no one saw us, we hustled Jablonski into Saul's car. Dopplemeyer and his daughter came with us. In a few minutes, we pulled up in front of the old brownstone. Fritz let us in. As instructed, Saul led Jablonski into the front room and closed the door behind them. The Dopplemeyers and I entered the office.

Quite a sight greeted us. Wolfe, seated at his desk, loomed like some Far Eastern Sultan holding court. Seated in yellow chairs before him were Barber, Vukcic, Morley, Rowcliff, Cramer, Stebbins, Felix and Antonio. I finally admitted to myself that Wolfe must be a genius to get this gang there on Christmas Eve.

(And don't think he ever let me forget it, as he frequently reminded me, on the many occasions he gave me the impossible task of getting people to his office for one of his charades. But that was in the future.)

As soon as Vukcic saw me, he jumped up and embraced me like a brother.

I made sure that Dopplemeyer and Frieda were comfortable, then took the chair at the empty desk. Wolfe made the introductions: Nothing like old world courtesy when you're after a murderer!

The introductions, however, were the full extent of courtesy, old world or any other kind. From here on in, Wolfe was in complete control and he let everyone know it. "With the exception of those kindly assisting me in this case," he began, "I make no apologies for this gathering on Christmas Eve. Each of you here tonight is motivated by one reason only, that of self interest.

"One who has been outrageously accused and imprisoned is as innocent as that Babe who was born nearly two thousand years ago tonight, and who was later just as falsely accused and crucified. Even after that mockery of a trial so long ago, it seems that civilization has progressed no further. A man must prove his own innocence rather than rely on the wheels of justice to provide proof beyond any doubt of his guilt.

"This farce has gone on long enough, Tonight I intend to prove conclusively that Marko Vukcic is innocent of the ridiculous charge of murder. In doing so, I shall provide sufficient evidence for the arrest of the culprit who did kill Mr. Rusterman. I warn you, this session may last well into the night. I have many questions to ask and will not desist until I have satisfactory answers to them all."

Here Rowcliff intervened. "I wish to state unequivocally that this is not an official investigation. It is not sanctioned by the Police Department or by the District Attorney's office. No one is under compulsion to answer this man's questions and you are all free to leave at any time."

There was a general stirring among the group, but no one made any move to leave.

Wolfe glared at Rowcliff. "Thank you, Lieutenant," he said with thinly disguised sarcasm. "I was about to add that clarification. May I point out that the freedom to leave applies most sincerely to yourself."

Rowcliff started to reply. I put in my two cents worth. "L-l-lieutenant,' I drawled, "Sh-sh-shut up!" He turned almost white with rage but he had the good sense to shut up.

Wolfe then continued, "I understand that the evidence against Mr. Vukcic consists primarily of the flimsy motive of greed and the testimony of a so-called eye witness. Neither of these is valid. The supposed motive of greed is so absurd that it hardly needs examination. Let us dispense with it once and for all. "Marko," he asked, "what is your position at Rusterman's?"

You could sense the roar of the cornered lion behind Marko's response. "Nero," he growled, "you know very well that I am Master Chef and also Manager of the restaurant."

"And do you consider yourself well-paid?"

There was the hint of a sob in Vukcic's voice as he answered calmly but proudly. "Herman Rusterman was the most generous man I have ever known. My salary as Master Chef was as high as any of those in the largest restaurants in New York! When old age prevented Mr. Rusterman from continuing active management, he insisted on, what you call, profit sharing? This more than doubled my salary. I have all the money I need."

"And now that he has so sadly left us," continued Wolfe, "I understand that his will bequeathed ownership of the restaurant entirely in your hands. How does this affect your position and income?"

Vukcic looked at Wolfe with amazement. "Why, of course, I continue as Master Chef and Manager. That's all I ever wanted. I do not need ownership. Believe me, I would rather have his friendship and guidance. He was an old man, with not much longer to live. But he should not have died in this way!"

His voice broke and a lone tear rolled down his cheek. No one in that room could doubt his sincerity. Wolfe allowed the silence to remain unbroken for a full minute. "I believe we can now dispense with greed," he continued in a voice so low it was almost a whisper. He slowly looked around the room. No one uttered a word. Abruptly, he turned his icy glare on Antonio. "You," he snarled, "tell us exactly what you claim to have seen the night Mr. Rusterman was killed."

Antonio's shifty eyes darted around the room as if seeking help. He got none. He wet his lips and, without looking at Wolfe, began almost in a monotone. "I am cleaning in dining room when I hear sound of loud argument upstairs. I go up to see what is happening. Door to Mr. Rusterman's office is part open. I hear Mr. Vukcic make threats. I stay back in hall where I am not seen but can peek in. I see Mr. Vukcic take out gun and shoot Mr. Rusterman."

Wolfe regarded him coldly. "That," he remarked, "is a most interesting story, especially considering that every word you uttered is a blatant lie."

Wolfe turned to Felix and asked, "From the dining room downstairs, is it possible to hear anything in the floor above?"

"Absolutely not," replied Felix. "If that were possible it would disturb the diners. We cannot have that. The walls upstairs are soundproof. And the door from the stairs is always left closed. Furthermore, no one except myself is ever allowed upstairs under any circumstance. Antonio lies."

Wolfe turned again to Antonio. "Is it not true," he continued, "that you were recently given your notice for incompetence and insubordination? That you held Mr. Vukcic responsible? That you saw the shooting as your opportunity to get back at him? That . . ."

Antonio kept interrupting each question with "No! No! No!" But each answer carried less conviction. He kept looking at Felix with both resentment and fear.

Finally, Felix spoke directly to him. "Antonio," he said quietly, "you are no damn good. You know perfectly well that Mr. Vukcic ordered me to fire you two weeks ago. I should have kicked you out right then. Instead, in the spirit of the Christmas Season, I said you could stay until the end of the year. This is the way you repay!"

As Felix was speaking, Antonio had shrunk further back in his chair. Wolfe's steely glare pierced him like a pin through an insect. "There's no place to hide," he declared. "Admit your malfeasance!"

Antonio had enough. With downcast eyes, he stammered, "Yes, yes! I lied."

"So much for your eye witness," Wolfe said with disgust. He addressed the District Attorney. "Inasmuch as his accusations were not made under oath, I suppose you can't charge him with perjury. Archie, get him out of my sight, and bring in the guest in the front room."

I grabbed Antonio and propelled him into the hall, handed him his hat and coat, and booted him out the front door. Then Saul and I brought Jablonski to the office. As soon as we entered, Vukcic jumped to his feet and shouted, "That's him! That's the scum who murdered Mr. Rusterman! Let me at him!" He lunged forward and it took both Cramer and Stebbins to hold him back. We seated Jablonski away from Vukcic. Saul remained standing behind his chair. I returned to the desk.

Wolfe continued, "Gentlemen, and Lady," he conceded, "in spite of the gay red and white costume, this is not Santa Claus. Rather than a saint, it is a devil named Michael Jablonski. He attempted to murder Mr. Goodwin. He attempted to extort money from Mr. Dopplemeyer." He paused. "And he murdered Mr. Rusterman."

The proverbial pin dropping would have sounded like a thunderclap in the deadly silence that pervaded the office. There was not only a complete absence of sound but also of movement. Both were finally broken by Rowcliff. He stood up and sputtered,

"Those are serious charges. If any of them are true, you are guilty of withholding evidence and obstructing justice. I'll have your license!"

"Pfui!" interrupted Wolfe. "Sit down. All we have done is unearthed evidence and identified a criminal, something the police should have accomplished long ago."

District Attorney Morley spoke for the first time. "This is all very interesting, Mr. Wolfe, but you still haven't proved any of these charges."

"Must I do everything?" growled Wolfe. "Archie, is this the man who gave you a defective gun and set you up to be killed?"

I assured him it was.

"Mr. Dopplemeyer," he continued, "is this the man who tried to extort money by threatening the life of your daughter?"

"Ja!" was the answer.

"Mr. Vukcic, is this the man you encountered in Mr. Rusterman's office moments after he was murdered?"

"Just let me at him!" roared Vukcic.

Wolfe spoke to Morley. "There are three legitimate eye witnesses," he declared.

He then turned to Jablonski. Unlike Antonio, Jablonski stubbornly maintained his innocence. The warehouse robbery? He had no idea the gun he gave Mr. Goodwin was defective. The delicatessen? He was simply on a mission of good will in the spirit of Christmas. Mr. Rusterman? He never heard of him! He even had the audacity to accuse me of kidnapping him!

No matter how hard Wolfe pried, he couldn't shake him. Finally, the District Attorney intervened.

"Mr. Wolfe," he said quietly, "you have certainly provided enough evidence to charge Mr. Jablonski with extortion. I'm not sure there's enough evidence on the warehouse. As for the murder of Mr. Rusterman, we have only Mr. Vukcic's word. This is neither sufficient to charge Mr. Jablonski, nor to exonerate Mr. Vukcic."

Jablonski sat there smirking. I felt like taking a poke at him and beating it out of him. But after having seen Wolfe in action, I knew he hadn't even begun. Like a maestro leading a symphony orchestra to a crescendo, he started probing, almost softly at first, then with increasing tempo and volume. Questions came thick and fast. You could sense Jablonski's confidence beginning to wane. Beads of sweat broke out on his brow. He started to hesitate more and more with his answers. Gradually, his shoulders slumped. His jaw started to sag. His lips quivered. His voice grew hoarse. Before our very eyes, he became a different person, obviously cracking under the strain of a master interrogator. Clearly, it was only a matter of time before he broke.

However, just as it seemed to everyone that Wolfe was about to administer the coup de grace, the doorbell rang. Having arranged previously with Fritz, I went to answer it. I pulled back the curtain in the door window and peered out. I smiled to see not only The Angel but also Tweedledee and Tweedledum! I opened the door and spoke briefly to the two goons who immediately left.

The Angel brushed aside my offer to take his hat and coat. I ushered him into the office. All eyes turned towards us.

XIX

The party was finally over. The minions of the law left with Jablonski in tow. The DA seemed pleased with the result. The Homicide cops were just pleased to get out of there. Vukcic, with bear hugs all around, couldn't wait to get back to his beloved restaurant to make sure it survived his absence. He left with Felix. Barber, who had performed a minor miracle in getting Vukcic, the DA, and the cops out on Christmas Eve, hurried to his own celebration. Saul said he'd drive the Dopplemeyers home. As Fritz and I escorted each group to the door, I could see it was beginning to snow. Perhaps Nature would cover the sins of the city for one brief period in time.

As the Dopplemeyers started the Auf Wiedersehens, the clock began to strike twelve. We all just stopped and listened to the chimes usher in Christmas day. Mr. Dopplemeyer paused and, with slight embarrassment, stammered that he and Frieda always followed an old German tradition at Christmas. He put his arm around his daughter. Shyly, but with growing confidence, in a clear, sweet soprano voice, she began the most beautiful Christmas Carol in the world. The strains of "Stille Nacht" echoed throughout the hall. Dopplemeyer's tenor provided perfect harmony. I have never heard a more lovely rendition. It touched us all.

As I was helping Frieda on with her coat, she handed me a package. "Special Christmas strudel," she smiled.

On impulse, I asked if she had a date for New Year's Eve.

She smiled again and answered, "Nein."

I couldn't resist hamming it up. "Nine?" I exclaimed. "You have nine dates?"

She shook her head. "Nein. No. Is verboten. By der poppa."

Der poppa, taking it all in, grinned broadly and said, "Mit Mr. Archie, is OK."

So Frieda and I agreed to see in my first New Year in New York together.

Wolfe, standing in the hallway, didn't miss any of this. When they had left, he remarked, "Archie, you seem to have a way with young women." Then, almost to himself, "That could be an asset. Then again it could be a distraction."

He continued, "Archie, your performance for the past few days has been satisfactory, with the exception of withholding information about that character you call The Angel. I don't like surprises. However, for the most part, you have acted reasonably. In time, with your native intelligence supplemented by experience, you might become quite useful.

"I need an assistant. Saul is the absolute best at what he does. But what he does isn't what I need full time. Besides, I do not believe he would want to relinquish his other clients completely. I am willing to offer you the position. We can agree on an adequate salary. The position would include the best meals in New York, served by a master chef, namely Fritz. Also, you could move into the spare room upstairs. I'll order furniture right after Christmas. In the meantime, you could stay in the guest room."

"No, Sir," I replied firmly.

"You do not accept my offer?" growled Wolfe.

"Mr. Wolfe," I replied, "I would indeed enjoy working for you. In addition to the leg-work you require, I can see several ways I could be helpful in the office. And while I am with you, I guarantee complete loyalty. At the same time, always remember that I am my own man, free and independent. For example, I shall select and pay for my own furniture. I shall choose what I want, not necessarily what you want. That way, too, you'll have to pay me at least enough to take care of the installments. If, to use your own word, this is satisfactory, you have an assistant. Otherwise, I might just marry Roly, or Frieda, and live on love and strudel."

Wolfe carefully removed his seventh of a ton from his chair, approached me and looked closely into my eyes. "Archie," he said, "I can predict some stormy days ahead in our relationship.

Nevertheless, I believe it can be mutually beneficial." He extended his hand and we shook warmly.

That brings me to the beginning, how it all started. But there were still a couple of surprises in store that I might as well share. Wolfe reached into his desk drawer, removed a brightly wrapped package, and handed it to me. I opened it carefully to expose a brand new Wembly automatic and shoulder holster plus a license for the gun. Wolfe said, almost apologetically, "I realize that this hardly seems appropriate in the spirit of Christmas. Yet, in the future, it might help you keep the peace."

He then handed me an envelope. Inside was a private investigator's license issued by the State of New York in the name of Archie Goodwin.

Wolfe explained, "Normally, there are tangled ribbons of red tape and interminable waiting periods in order to obtain a license for guns, even longer for a private investigator's license. I seldom ask for favors, especially from politicians. I despise bureaucracy. However, a powerful Tammany Hall district leader, a smart Irishman named Rowan, owes me several favors. In anticipation of your acceptance of my offer, I prevailed on him to cut through the red tape and procure these licenses."

I thanked him, then asked him to wait a moment while I went to the kitchen. When I returned, a smiling Fritz was with me, carrying a tray with glasses and a huge pitcher filled to the brim with beer. He carefully deposited it on the desk in front of Wolfe.

That was one of the few times I ever saw Wolfe show surprise. He looked first at Fritz, then at me, then carefully poured beer into a glass and watched the foam settle to just the right level he liked. He raised the glass and drank deeply, wiped his upper lip, closed his eyes, leaned back in his chair and sighed.

"There's a keg cooling in the cellar," I explained. "The two goons with The Angel brought it tonight. Seems like we're both calling in favors. You see, The Angel was grateful to me, first for preventing the robbery of his warehouse, and, second, for locating Jablonski and helping to make sure he'd end up in the pokey. He insisted on returning the favors. A fresh keg will be delivered here each week. And, as I'm sure you've discovered, this is the real stuff, not some watered down slop."

Fritz, having been told I didn't much care for beer, had brought a bottle of pre-prohibition brandy. Wolfe insisted on pouring a drink for both me and Fritz. I opened the strudel. It tasted swell with brandy. It didn't seem appropriate with beer, but Wolfe put away his share and suggested that Fritz obtain the recipe.

Wolfe raised his glass and remarked, "This has been a most satisfactory case. It is the first one I've ever undertaken where there was no fee involved. Yet even without a fee, I have received the rich harvest of barley and hops. And while I am always willing to give Uncle Sam his due," he made a sound that must have been intended for a chuckle, "I do not see how I could possibly list bootleg beer under "Income" on my tax form. "There is an old German proverb," he continued, "which, loosely translated, proclaims, "In Heaven ain't no beer — gotta drink it here." The grammar in the English translation is so atrocious it actually pains me — but the sentiment is sound. This is probably the nearest I shall ever get to Heaven.

He continued, almost dreamily, "I am not inclined to wax sentimental or to conjure up symbols where none exists. Yet my dearest friend is home for Christmas. We have had a visit from an angel, albeit hardly one of the celestial variety. My cup runneth over with a hearty brew that to me is more valuable than frankincense or myrrh or even gold. It would not strain credulity too much to assume we are Three Wise Men, although with varying degrees of wisdom. And among our blessings, there is plenty of room for all three of us here at the Inn. So, I say unto you, Merry Christmas!"

Fritz solemnly echoed, "Joyeux Noel!"

Wolfe continued, "While Peace on Earth may be an impossible goal, let us fervently hope that together we can at least bring some small measure of that priceless ingredient to our own little corner of the universe."

Looking back, I guess we accomplished that goal. But in so doing, we more often than not shattered the peace in the old brownstone. And I fervently hope we'll keep right on doing so.

****

ACKNOWLEDGMENTS

William S. Baring-Gould, *Nero Wolfe of West Thirty-Fifth Street*
Ken Darby, *The Brownstone House of Nero Wolfe*
Sir Arthur Conan Doyle, *A Study In Scarlet, A Scandal In*

Bohemia, The Adventure of the Empty House

The Rev. Frederick G. Gotwald, *The Nero Wolfe Handbook, The Nero Wolfe Companion*

Clive Hirschmann, *The Warner Bros. Story*

Joel Levy, *The Gazette*

John McAleer, *Rex Stout: A Biography*

George T. Simon, *The Big Bands*

"The Smithsonian Magazine," *Dr. Goddard and the Magic Rocket*

Rex Stout, 73 novels and short stories

Barbara Burn, with Rex Stout, *The Nero Wolfe Cookbook*

Time-Life, *The Fabulous Twenties*

The Burns Family, 3 generations: for their interest, encouragement and critique

MEMO FOR MURDER

by Greg Hatcher

ONE

I NEVER thought I'd see the day when any woman would use Nero Wolfe to crack a smile, but Karen Merriman did it. Not that smiling at Karen Merriman was an implausible idea — far from it. I've been smiling at pretty girls since before I was old enough to shave, and a leggy redhead like Karen Merriman certainly qualified for special attention. I flashed her a good big one as I helped her off with her coat and showed her into the office where Wolfe spends most of his life sitting and drinking beer and reading and doing crossword puzzles and even occasionally doing a little detective work. I spend a lot of time there as well, me being Wolfe's confidential assistant, stenographer, book-keeper, errand boy, saddle burr, and goat. I detect sometimes, too, but Wolfe's the one who's the genius, and he's the one people come to see. Nevertheless, I gave Karen one of my best grins as I ushered her in. You never know which one you meet is going to be Miss Right, and anyway, a man has to keep in practice. She smiled back, a nice enough smile, not exactly full of promise but not just politeness, either.

Apparently she had done some reading up on Wolfe, because she had doused the grin by the time I had her settled into the red leather chair. She nodded gravely at Wolfe's seventh of a ton and said, "Thank you for agreeing to see me, Mr. Wolfe. I know you don't shake hands. I understand that you may not be able to help me. Archie made that clear on the phone; however, I hope you won't think I'm just trying to flatter you if I say that if you can't, then I'm lost."

So far so good with Wolfe. The surest way to butter him up is to explain that you're not. I wasn't sure how I felt about already being just Archie, though.

Wolfe inclined his head an eighth of an inch, acknowledging the tribute. "You say the police are harassing you, Miss Merriman. If that is your difficulty, I am afraid I cannot help you. The police harass everyone. They often harass me in the course of my business. In a case of murder it cannot be prevented and should be expected —"

He stopped because she had started to giggle. It put some color in her cheeks and lit up her eyes. I decided being just Archie was okay. "I'm sorry," she gasped after a moment. "Truly. It's just . . ."

"Archie," Wolfe snapped at me, "Is she hysterical?"

That was a silly question from him, because he thinks all women are hysterical. "No," I said cheerfully, "but she's been under a strain. Miss Merriman? Would you like a glass of water? Or something stronger?"

"No. I'm all right. I'm not hysterical." She smiled at me, and this one was full-on. With that much dazzling wattage trained in my direction I decided being just Archie would only do until she changed it to My One And Only. "It's just — here I am, about to be arrested for murder . . . and you're both calling me Miss Merriman. It's so adorable. Mostly everyone calls me Karen."

"I call no women and few men by their first names." Wolfe raised a hand, palm out. "As for the abominable locution `Ms.', I see no reason to concede personal preference to fashion. Nor will I abandon a courteous formality for counterfeit intimacy, so `Miss' it shall remain — as long as it is accurate," he amended. "You are unmarried?"

"Very. That's how it started." Karen turned the smile from me to Wolfe, only now it held a hint of danger. "But — you said `Ms.' is just a fashion. Don't you believe in female equality?"

"I do not." Wolfe's voice was matter-of-fact. "I believe in female superiority. All of human history backs that belief. I maintain this household as a fortress against surrender to it. No, please refrain from commenting; such a debate should be reserved for leisure, and you have little, with the police hounding you."

"Hounding isn't the word." Karen's voice turned sour. "It's way beyond that. They had me at the precinct house until six this morning. I went home and had a shower and called in sick to work, and then I thought about it and finally I called you. Or Archie, rather." She swiveled to nod at me and I nodded back with courteous formality. Her eyes returned to Wolfe. "The thing of it is, I can't answer their questions. I don't know why Peter Ford called my house four times that night. I didn't even know he worked for the government. I'd only given him my number that afternoon . . . what?"

"Please." Wolfe was wiggling a finger. "Even granting you are not hysterical, your thoughts are not ordered. Are we to understand that you had not known Peter Ford previous to that day?"

"Of course you're to understand it, it's the truth." Karen looked peevish. "I meet a lot of men at my job, I meet a lot of all kinds of people really, and most of them are pretty nice. I mean, sure, there's a few sleazebags, that's part of the package working at a downtown copy shop that's open twenty-four hours. But you look confused," she said, and stopped.

Wolfe started to speak, but I cut in. "He's not confused, exactly," I explained. "It's just that he never leaves the house on business and has no idea what kind of place it is that you're talking about. It's the store on Second Avenue where they bind the germination records for the orchids," I told Wolfe. "I've been down there a couple of times. It's crowded. More like a supermarket than a bookbinder's."

Wolfe grunted. "In Bari, when I was a boy, the bookbinder's shop was staffed only with an old man named Vasily and his nephew." He made a face. "No matter. Let us see if I can clear away some of the brush, Miss Merriman. You met a man the afternoon of August tenth at your place of business and gave him your phone number. That evening he was found dead in the street two blocks from your home, a victim of a hit-and-run, and the only item found on his body was the slip of paper with your telephone number. The body was soon identified as Peter Ford of the U.S. State Department, and that he had been entrusted with highly sensitive and valuable documents. The police examined the phone records and found he had placed four calls to your home between six and eight o'clock that evening. The body was discovered at eight-forty. You have given the police no satisfactory explanation of why he was found so near to your home, nor why he had your number and nothing else, nor what the calls were regarding. Nor have you been able to account for your movements between eight and eight-forty. The documents were with him at five o'clock, according to witnesses, and now are missing. Is it any wonder the police regard you with keen interest?"

"I know how it looks," Karen said, with an impatient toss of her hair. "I'm not an idiot. But the plain fact is that I don't know any of the answers they want. I don't have an alibi because I didn't go anywhere. I was at home reading a book. I had the ringer on my phone turned off."

"Really'?" Wolfe regarded her with something like approval. He hates the phone. "Why?"

"Because — " Karen sighed. "I go out on the weekends, sure, but what I really like best is to just curl up at home with something to read. This was a work night, and I just wanted to settle in with my book and be left in peace."

Now Wolfe's approval was open. To have three of his favorite prejudices confirmed in less than two minutes — hatred of the phone, preferring to stay home, and a love of literature — had earned Karen Merriman huge points with him. I bet myself a finif that I knew what his next question would be, and I hid a grin when it came.

"What was the book?" he asked her.

"*Jane Eyre*. It's an old favorite of mine."

That was what got Nero Wolfe's smile. In fact, looking back on it, I would almost bet that it made the difference whether or not Wolfe took her case. If she'd said Danielle Steel or John Grisham her goose would have been cooked for sure.

"I share your admiration," he told her. For Wolfe that was backslapping enthusiasm. He caught himself smiling and glanced at me. Seeing my grin, he sighed and decided there was no help for it now, and returned his gaze to her. "But what about the calls? Do you have an answering device? Were they recorded?"

"Yeah, but they were just hang-ups. I erased them. Of course the police are suspicious of that, too." She leaned forward, her eyes glistening. "It's so goddamn frustrating. It looks so incriminating. and I swear it wasn't. He was just a cute guy and I gave him my number and — now this. I don't know what to do. Please, you have to help me. There's no one else."

There was no mistaking the sincerity of the appeal. Wolfe's mouth twitched. I watched in fascination, thinking that if he actually smiled at her again it would shatter all precedent. He didn't, but he didn't admonish her for her profanity, either. Normally he would have. She certainly had hooked him good with the book thing. He said, not harshly, but matter-of-fact, "The only way to relieve the police's attention from you is to catch the real murderer, with evidence to convict. Is that what you are engaging me to do?"

"I don't — yeah. I guess. Whatever it takes." Karen looked

near tears, then shook herself. Suddenly she unleashed another one of her megawatt smiles at Wolfe. "You know, you have a cute smile," she said. "I — never mind. Thank you, thank you both," she added, turning to me. "Thank you for listening. Even that's more than the police did."

I smiled back, not wanting to shatter her illusions. We needed the case and I was all in favor of Wolfe going to work, but he wasn't doing it for her. He was doing it for *Jane Eyre*. Cutie pie or not — I reserve judgment on that, he's the genius, but in that office, I'm the cute one — but in any case, he would never be swayed by a woman's plea. But a chance to rescue a Bronte reader who just wanted to be left in peace with her book hit him where he lived.

"I trust we can do more than merely listen," Wolfe told her. "Did the police give any indication —"

The front door buzzed and I went down the hall for a quick look. Seeing a face I knew, I spun and headed back to the office. "The man about the chair," I told Wolfe.

Wolfe scowled at me — he always wants to shoot the messenger — and turned to Karen. "Miss Merriman. Give me a dollar."

"Huh?" Karen stared.

"Inspector Cramer of Manhattan Homicide is at the door," Wolfe told her. "I daresay you were followed from the police station . . . and the officer assigned to tail you must have telephoned Mr. Cramer when he saw you arrive here. Mr. Cramer has a history with this establishment and no doubt he wishes to secure you before that history entangles him again. If I am to act in your interest I need a retainer. Give me the dollar."

When push came to shove she had sand. She didn't comment but simply handed Wolfe a dollar bill. Wolfe took it and nodded at me. I went back to the door and opened it a crack, leaving the chain on. "Come for another lesson?" I asked Cramer brightly through the opening. "Mr. Wolfe is engaged at the moment but I think we could fit you in by the twenty-eighth of — "

"Can the clowning," Cramer growled. The summer heat made his beefy red face even redder than usual. "I've got a warrant here for Karen Merriman. Are you going to deny she's here?"

"I deny nothing," I told him. "I just — "

"What has she told you?"

"Just talking books. She and Mr. Wolfe have a mutual love of the writing of Charlotte Bronte. Oh, and she says we're cute." The history of our establishment being what it was, I felt justified in including myself in the appraisal.

"I'll say you're cute. Open up, Goodwin."

"Sure. In a moment. What's the charge?"

"Murder." The look in Cramer's eyes had hardened into an expression I knew better than to defy, and I took the chain off and let him in. He blew past me to the office in such a rush the back-wash of it would have taken my hat off if I'd been wearing one. By the time I got there Cramer already had the cuffs out and was saying heavily. "Do you understand these rights as I have read them to you, Ms. Merriman'?"

Karen looked at me with wide, trapped eyes. I started to speak but Wolfe got there first. He said icily, "Miss Merriman, keep silent! Mr. Cramer, this is an outrage. This woman is no street hooligan to be hauled away in irons. For you to come in here in such a manner forfeits all right to civilized discourse. Miss Merriman, I advise you to stand mute until we can secure your release. Archie, get Mr. Parker."

I nodded, thinking that even for a fellow book lover Wolfe was really giving it the full treatment. Nathaniel Parker was one of the best lawyers in New York and the only one Wolfe can stand to have at his dinner table, and I knew that Parker's retainers ran a lot higher than a dollar.

"Now look here," Cramer began in what he thought was a peacemaking tone. "I have a warrant and she's . . ."

"Pfui! Swallow it, sir!" Wolfe manipulated his bulk upright. "You barge in here barking about threats to national security from this young woman as though she were some terrorist! Very well, take her, you have the force of law, and once you have removed this deadly menace from this office," his voice dripped with contempt, "taken her downtown and incarcerated her, I assure you that you will be releasing her on bail within a few hours, accomplishing what? Nothing, save to annoy me and disrupt my place of business, and for no reason other than to strut and pound your chest like some aboriginal — "

"There's been a new development," Cramer barked, inter-rupting. "I know no client of yours has been convicted of murder, but there's always a first time. One of the missing documents has turned up and it's got Karen Merriman's fingerprints on it. Explain that."

It brought Wolfe up short. "I can't," he admitted, still smoldering. "Not yet. But I will. To your everlasting sorrow," he added, with renewed fierceness. By God, he was going to come out of this with his shield or on it. "Archie? Have you got Mr. Parker?"

I had already talked with Parker and given him the bare bones while Wolfe was calling Cramer a strutting aborigine. "On his way," I told him, but I was looking at Karen. She was shaking. I told her, "It's okay. We're on it. I'll see you in a few hours."

She nodded, biting her lip. "I . . . okay. That's the last thing I'm going to say," she added, defiantly glaring at Cramer.

"Have it your way." Cramer grunted. "Let's go."

They went. I glanced at Wolfe. "Pfui." he said.

"I agree." I said. "In spades."

TWO

IT LOOKED bad from any angle. and from the expression on Wolfe's face I could tell he thought so, too. It was all very well to extend a little courtesy to a lover of literature, but now we were out on a limb and Cramer looked like he had all he needed to saw it off. I dropped back into my desk chair and spun to face Wolfe. He was still scowling at the door through which Cramer had departed with our client, his finger tracing little circles on the arm of his chair. That usually was the prelude to an explosion, and he was so mad at Cramer there was no telling what he'd do. I thought I'd better try to head it off.

"Look," I said in a placating tone, "I know you would rather eat oysters with horseradish than let Cramer take a trick, but this is a special case. You were bedazzled. You were so overcome with the idea that you'd finally met the woman of your dreams that you lost your head. I admit she is a looker, and I probably would have been dazzled myself at the idea of having her stay home and read *Jane Eyre* to me every evening, but — "

"Archie. Stop prattling."

"Yes, Sir. Also. it's not as though there's a big fee at stake. One dollar. If you're short, I can spot you a dollar, even considering my measly salary — "

"Shut up." Wolfe glared at me. "There is something at stake besides the fee. Our honor. I gave Miss Merriman my word. Also my pride is wounded. Mr. Cramer knew he had a trump card for once and played it. He did not put on that barbarous display with the handcuffs and the Miranda recital for Miss Merriman's benefit, but for mine. He was gloating. I will not permit his petty triumph to stand, at least not until we have no choice." He paused. "You are quite correct that I am not thinking straight. I am in a rage. Therefore I appeal to you and your expertise with women. Did she kill that man?"

"Sure, put it on me." I sighed. "I'd like to see what Cramer's got, but provisionally, no. It might be possible that she would commit murder for reasons of jealousy or passion, but then where are the documents? Also, I don't think it would be hit and run. A girl like that would want to look the guy in the eye and make him squirm first."

"Very well." Wolfe sighed the way he always does when it looks like he'll have to go to work. "Instructions. We will have to — what the devil?"

It was the front door again. I ducked out for a quick look and reported back. "It's Carpenter and some bird in a black suit I don't know. Probably they heard Karen was here and came to search the place for documents."

Wolfe scowled so furiously at the idea of any further violations of his sanctum that I almost regretted saying it. Lord knows we didn't need any more outbursts today. But all he said was, "Confound it. Bring them."

I went, not with enthusiasm. General Carpenter owed us a couple since Wolfe had bailed him out of some tight jams during the war, when Wolfe and I had been on special assignment to Military Intelligence. But I knew he wouldn't let that get in the way of his duty, and if he decided that duty meant Karen Merriman was going to do hard time, well, no amount of goodwill would stop him. Black Suit was an unknown quantity, but I bet myself two-to-five that he was with one of those alphabet agencies that swatted private detectives like flies. And with Wolfe already committed to the lady's honor, it was a cinch they wouldn't leave happy. Not only that, but Wolfe had already got me on record saying I thought she was innocent, so when Carpenter threatened to send us to Leavenworth he would be able to blame me. The big fat bum.

"Major Goodwin," Carpenter greeted me with a smile as I opened the door and escorted them to the office. Black Suit was silent. I put Carpenter in the red leather chair since he was a general and the other guy probably wanted to lurk in the background, anyway. He had that look.

Wolfe regarded them, not with hostility, but his face was set and I knew that he had reached the point where an H-bomb wouldn't move him. "General Carpenter," he said, and inclined his head forward a fraction of an inch. It was Wolfe's idea of a bow. "To what do we owe this visit? We haven't seen you since the war."

You had to give him credit for slipping in that reminder of our patriotism right away. Carpenter smiled back at Wolfe. and gave me a friendly nod to show I was included, too. "I haven't forgotten what you did for us." he said. "Both of you. I was hoping your sense of duty hasn't faded since then. I understand you have a client, Karen Merriman."

There went our one-in-a-million chance he was here on an unrelated matter. Not only was Cramer all set to hang us out to dry, but Carpenter was going to hold his hat and coat for him while he did it.

Wolfe said dryly, "I am flattered at the speed of your arrival. Miss Merriman retained me in her interest less than an hour ago. "Then she is your client."

Wolfe sat up a little straighter. He was getting riled again. "General Carpenter. This is absurd. Though we are no longer under your command, Mr. Goodwin and I are civilized men who hold you in some esteem. There is no need to tiptoe. If you have a question to ask, then ask it. We may well answer." He turned his gaze to the man in black, and then back to Carpenter. "Speaking of civility, you have not introduced your companion. Or is it colleague?"

Carpenter started to reply, but the other man cut him off. "I'm Smith, with the State Department," he said. I thought, Sure, and I'm Jones with the Mounties. He went on, "I agreed to let Carpenter do the talking, since he's dealt with you before. But let's cut to the chase. Where are the documents Karen Merriman took from Peter Ford?"

Wolfe sighed. "I should have qualified it. We may answer a sensible question. But you are a witling to ask that and I would be an even bigger one to attempt an answer."

"But you admit that Karen Merriman is your client." Smith hissed it, adding to the vaguely reptilian impression I already had of him.

Calling a statement an admission is a shabby trick, implying guilt. I admit nothing. However, I will state that we have accepted Miss Merriman as a client, and I see no reason to feel guilty for doing so." Wolfe's shoulders rose a millimeter and lowered again.

"What did she hire you to do?"

"We agreed to represent her interests." Wolfe's tone was silken, but I knew he was boiling. "General Carpenter, I appeal to your good sense. Unlike your colleague, once upon a time you demonstrated that you had some. Surely you know I would never agree to act on behalf of a traitor, let alone one who was also a murderer."

"Not knowingly," Carpenter said, in what he probably thought was a soothing tone. "But with the new evidence Cramer's men uncovered at the copy shop- "

Wolfe glared. "Pfui. So I am only a fool and not a traitor. Am I such an imbecile that I could be gulled by a mere shopgirl? Admittedly, a literate one." he added hastily, "but still, the idea is preposterous. If you had any real evidence Miss Merriman is embroiled in some espionage plot — "

"We'd had our evy on Ford for a while," Carpenter said. "There have been — well, leaks, let's say. Ford's department was the most likely source. He's made several trips in the past few months and . . . well, I can't go into detail, but the documents Ford had on him were part of an ongoing negotiation that has to be kept quiet. We've already had some serious exposure on this and we think Ford was the source. Now he's dead. It's not implausible that Karen Merriman was his contact and somehow the deal went wrong."

Wolfe raised his eyebrows. "So Peter Ford was already under suspicion of espionage? That detail obviously was omitted from the newspaper accounts," he said. "Was Ford under surveillance?"

"Yes. He shook our man at five p.m. the night of the murder — and it was after that he started trying to phone Karen Merriman. You can see why we want her." Carpenter was more sure of his ground now that he'd sketched it for us. and I had to admit it looked bad. All we had to put in the plus column was Charlotte Bronte and Wolfe's cute smile.

Still, Wolfe wasn't going to go down easy. "But without any hard evidence of espionage —" he began.

"We've got evidence," Smith gritted. "Homicide detectives obtained search warrants for Karen Merriman's home and also for the store where she worked. There are employee lockers there in the lunch room, in the rear of the store. No one but employees have access to that room. A page from one of the documents Ford was carrying was found in Karen Merriman's locker and it has her prints on it. That was enough for us to pick her up."

Wolfe sat back in his specially-constructed desk chair and shifted his eyes. His lips pushed out, then in, then out again. "Indeed." he said after almost a minute, addressing no one in particular, then fell silent again.

Carpenter started to say something, but I shushed him. Not that it would have mattered. When Wolfe gets like that it wouldn't matter if you threw a vase at his head. Abruptly he opened his eyes and nodded at Carpenter. "I do not apologize for my earlier remarks," he told him, "but nevertheless we are in your debt. You have suggested a line of inquiry that had not previously occurred to me. I think you will find that your best course of action right now would be if you leave me to it. I will notify you if I deem it necessary."

Smith burst out, "Of all the high-handed, arrogant — "

Carpenter waved him to silence. He knew Wolfe well enough to know what the lip exercise meant. "You'll notify me? Your word of honor?"

"If you must have it, then yes. My word of honor." Abruptly Wolfe sat up and leaned forward. "Confound it, the longer you remain, the longer you delay me, and your agitation tells me that delay is the last thing you want. You've muddied the waters enough already, heaven knows. Go!"

I knew what was eating him. It was almost lunch time, and Wolfe wouldn't be able to go have his lunch with the two of them badgering him. Sometimes guests were invited to join us, and Carpenter alone might have qualified, but Smith, never. Normally I might have just sat back and enjoyed Wolfe's discomfiture, on the theory that a little hardship is good for his soul, but I'd had about enough of Smith, too. After all, if Wolfe was a traitor, then so was I. So I stood up and gestured at the door. "You heard the man. C'mon, on your bikes. I'll show you out."

They didn't like it, but they went. When I got back to the office Wolfe was leaning back in his chair, looking as self-satisfied as I'd ever seen him — and that's a lot. I sat down and swiveled to face him, crossing my legs, which annoys him since he can't do it comfortably. I'm not a genius but I am not without talent, which is something I think he needs to be reminded of now and then. "Okay, I admit it," I told him. "Usually I'm panting along right behind you, but I'm up a stump. What got you so revved up?"

"Archie." I hate it when he uses that tone. "Surely it was obvious. The location of the document the police found was extremely suggestive." The bell rang for lunch and Wolfe rose to go to the kitchen. "Highly satisfactory. I had feared that we might well have placed ourselves in an untenable position, but this new information changes matters considerably, and we didn't have to humble ourselves before Mr. Cramer to obtain it from the police files. Coupled with what you suggested earlier . . ."

"What did I suggest'?"

"Your memory is trained better than most," Wolfe said. "I see no need to remind you of something so obvious." He started for the kitchen, his nostrils flared for an anticipatory sniff of the aromas emanating from there. "I admit to being relieved. I had thought this bother would spoil my appetite."

Nuts. As if anything could spoil that appetite. He was just showboating. I rose and followed him out, only because I couldn't think of anything to throw at him.

THREE

I HAD wanted to call Parker and see how he was doing with getting Karen sprung. but Wolfe said no. after lunch was fine. Normally I don't like missing one of Fritz Brenner's lunches, either, and the roast duckling and candied pineapple was superb, as it always was. Nevertheless, I was worrying about Karen and sore at Wolfe, so the duckling was wasted on me that day. Wolfe never permits business to be discussed at mealtime, but I could tell our predicament was on his mind as well — he held forth on the social changes that literacy had brought to the masses with the advent of the printing press. I sometimes will take a contrary position just to see how he'll take it, but I was already sore at him and didn't feel like playing along that day. It didn't faze him. He argued it up one side and then back down the other all by himself. Like I said. Showboating.

Fritz pulled me aside as we were going into the office with our coffee. "Archie, Is it a case? That woman?"

He looked vaguely worried as he said it, and I could guess why. On the one hand, a case was good news because it meant that Wolfe would be able to pay our bills, which are considerable, when you consider what it takes to finance Fritz's salary and the meals that he prepares with such artistry, not to mention the ten thousand orchids in the plant rooms on the roof and Theodore tending them, plus all the rare books Wolfe is always having shipped to him from hither and yon. and the other four hundred expenses a month. most certainly including the weekly check for yours truly, and I don't come cheap, either. So a case was good news.

However, a case also meant all sorts of disruptions to the meal schedule, and I mean all sorts — in the past we'd had bombs go off in the house. police showing up with search warrants, once a person was strangled in the office, and then there was the time someone had tommy-gunned the plant rooms . . . well, you get the idea. Just that morning we'd already had Cramer making a pinch in the office and then the general's visit. All of this had not gone unnoticed by Fritz. Plus there had been a woman in the house, which always worried Fritz because he suspects every woman visitor of trying to get hooks in Wolfe somehow.

All of which explains why he looked so upset when he asked me, and why I took pity on him and lied cheerfully. "Oh, yeah, a nice big one. Client's already paid us a retainer. Mr. Wolfe thinks he'll be ready to tie a bow on it by this time tomorrow."

Fritz shook a spoon at me and said, "You are a bad liar, Archie. You are worried. I can tell because you did not enjoy lunch."

I spread my hands. "What the hell, I'm always worried, Fritz. He seems to think it's all wrapped up, and he's the genius. I'll let you know." I went on in to the office with my coffee, trying not to feel guilty about Fritz's long face in the kitchen behind me. It was a good thing he didn't know about the puny retainer we'd gotten or he really would have been beside himself.

By the time I reached the office Wolfe was already settled into his chair, his custom-built special one from Meyer that will accommodate up to five hundred pounds. It's the only chair in the world he really likes. He's not at the weight limit yet, but he gets closer every year. I plopped into my standard-issue desk chair and swiveled to face him. Wolfe already had his current book open. *The Portable Dorothy Parker.* I got my notebook out of my desk and slammed the drawer with more force than necessary, which made him look up.

"Instructions?" I said, brightly. "I recall you had some before we were so rudely interrupted by the general and his friend Smith-orJones-or-whatever."

"The situation has changed," Wolfe grunted. "Now we must await events. I must speak with Miss Merriman, and we are hamstrung until she is released on bail. Confound it, don't rattle your papers at me." He sighed and put the book down. "Very well. Get Saul. If he is available, we need him here by three o'clock. If not, try Fred, but we would prefer Saul."

That took the wind out of my sails, which of course had been Wolfe's main idea. He hates to be nagged after a meal. Still, it brought me up short. Saul Panzer is the best freelance operative available north of the South Pole, who could easily have the most successful detective agency in the city if he didn't prefer working for himself. He asks $200 a day and gets it, which was what made me think Wolfe might really have something. Wolfe would never lay out that much lettuce just to shut me up. Of course, it did give him a ready-made excuse every time I started in on him — whenever I suggested that he might be more involved with Dorothy Parker than our client, all he had to do was say that he was working like the very devil supervising Saul and that I wasn't to worry about it.

Which is why, when I had Saul on the line and put him through to Wolfe, Wolfe gestured me out of the room. I went, not happily, but I was beginning to think Wolfe wasn't just showing off, he really had found a crack to get a wedge in somewhere. But it was obvious he wasn't going to spill it, and be damned if I'd ask him.

I thought about going into the kitchen, but then I'd have Fritz asking me more questions, so I stayed in the hall for a moment. Which is how I happened to be standing so close to the front door when the bell rang. Through the one-way panel I saw a young guy with a blue work shirt and tan slacks, no tie. He looked barely old enough to shave. I opened the door and grinned at him. "What can we do for you?"

"I . . ." He stopped and swallowed. "I just — is it true? Did you have Karen arrested?"

"Now hold on," I protested. "Introductions first. How do you even know —"

I stopped because he swung at me. Normally I am a peaceful man, but I was having a bad day and this bird had picked the wrong moment to get physical. I ducked it without having to breathe hard and pistoned a right into his soft middle, which folded him neatly in half and left him gasping. I swung a left uppercut that straightened him back up again and he staggered back and fell, landing flat on his back at the bottom of the stoop. I stood, waiting, but he didn't get up. I grinned. I couldn't help it. I hadn't realized how good it would feel to sock somebody until presented with the opportunity.

"What the devil is going on out there?" Wolfe emerged from the office to glare at me.

I hooked a thumb over my shoulder at the fallen champion. "Apparently Miss Merriman seems to have another knight fighting for her honor. Who knows, the city's probably full of 'em. You should all get together and start a book club."

Wolfe stepped forward and looked with distaste on my assailant, who was sitting up, unsteadily, and fingering his chin. "Is this flummery?"

"Just the book club part. He showed up asking about Karen and when I didn't answer fast enough he got rough. So I cooled his ardor."

Wolfe made a face. "I suppose it was necessary."

"He started it." I said, annoyed. "I should let him just take a poke at me?"

Wolfe shuddered. He hates physical exercise of any kind and the idea of fisticuffs makes him nauseous. However, he decided there was no point in making an issue of it, and instead addressed the man sitting on the stoop. "Sir! Are you demented? What do you mean by coming here and assaulting my assistant?"

"I'm sorry about that," the man wheezed, and scrambled to his feet. "Sorrier than I thought I was going to be," he added wryly. "That's the hell of a left you got there, mister."

"Clean living. You heard the man, what's the story?"

Wolfe had already turned and strode back to the office. I helped our visitor dust himself off and escorted him in. I figured there was an even-money chance of Wolfe getting something useful out of him, and it was better than just letting Wolfe go back to his book.

Wolfe had to have known I would bring him, but even so he scowled at me. "Must you?"

"You said we would await events. Here's an event." I parked the champion in the red leather chair and circled to my desk.

Wolfe turned the scowl on our visitor. "Very well. You have succeeded in disrupting our afternoon. Our attention is yours. Justify it. What do you want?"

"I'm here to ask you about Karen Merriman," the man said. "I think she's in trouble."

"We will answer nothing to an anonymous ruffian," Wolfe

replied, still scowling. "Your experience with Mr. Goodwin a moment ago should have taught you that. First we will want your name and a reason for your interest."

The guy considered it, then shrugged. "I guess you're right. Hell, I'm so wound up about this thing I'm not thinking straight. 1 probably shouldn't have —"

"Your name, sir," Wolfe prodded.

He grinned. "Sorry. Again. My name's Rodney Baird. I work with Karen down at the store. She's . . . a friend of mine. I heard from Kate that they were after Karen for this Ford thing, and then when the police came by the store this morning and emptied out all our lockers, well, I got really worried."

"So you came and assaulted Mr. Goodwin," Wolfe said, with asperity. I thought, my God. he's madder about that than I am. Baird held up a hand and let out a rueful laugh. "I said I was sorry. I just snapped, I guess. I know you work for the police and when I heard on the news that Karen had been picked up from here, well . . ." He sighed. "I'm an idiot, that's all. That's what a woman does to a man, makes him an idiot. I don't know what I was thinking." He turned and smiled at me, as if to say it really hadn't been his idea to jump me, it was those crazy womenfolk making him do it. I nodded back, willing to let bygones be bygones, but personally, I like to take responsibility when I decide somebody gets a poke in the snoot. It was preferable to have relations on a friendly basis, though, so I kept the sentiment to myself.

Wolfe sat back and regarded him with interest. "You may be right," he said. "Certainly history is on the side of your argument. I presume it is Miss Merriman who has provoked your idiocy? How so?"

"Well — nothing she did, exactly." Baird sighed. "I got to know her from working at the store with her, and we went out on the weekends a couple of times. Nothing big, just dinner and dancing. I was hoping . . ." He stopped and sighed again. "Look, it's just me, okay? I know Karen doesn't think much of me, but I thought if 1 could help — I don't know what I was thinking," he finished miserably, and stared at the floor.

"You were not thinking at all. obviously," Wolfe said. "For one thing, while I occasionally cooperate with the police, I do not work for them. For another, if it was gallantry you wished to demonstrate, Miss Merriman would not have witnessed it. However, you may yet be of assistance. To begin, let me be clear on this. You have occasionally alluded to the possibility of romance between yourself and Miss Merriman but never claimed it outright. What is the situation, sir? Do you have a romantic attachment to Miss Merriman? Yes or no?"

Baird snorted. "No. I just leave it at that. No."

"I cannot leave it at that, Mr. Baird." Wolfe had been inclined to be patient before, when Baird was talking about how dangerous women were, but now he was getting annoyed again. "I have engaged to represent Miss Merriman's interest and clear her of these charges. The engagement requires that I ask questions you may deem impertinent. If you truly wish to help her you will answer them."

Baird nodded. "I — okay. It's just so damn embarrassing."

"Murder often requires us to air our linens before they are laundered. Bear in mind that I am trying to assist Miss Merriman. So. You say it was not romance. What was the situation between you?"

"Wel l —" Baird considered it. "I'm not sure there's a word, really. We're friends. I care about her. We've been out a couple of times, but Karen . . . likes to play the field. And it got a little awkward, us both working at the store. So we settled into a sort of, well, call it a flirtatious friendship. I probably think more of it than she does. That's nothing against her, you understand," he added stoutly.

I thought, Brother, you've got it bad.

Wolfe made a sour face at Baird's description of these grisly male-female rituals, but manfully pressed on. "Tell me more about the situation at your workplace. Are there others who share your attitude toward Miss Merriman?"

"Well — the guys all like her. I don't think she's dated any of the others but me." Baird rubbed his jaw — thoughtfully this time, not in pain.

"And the women?"

Baird shrugged. "Oh, well, you know women."

"I do not," Wolfe said flatly. "Be specific."

Baird blinked, and glanced at me as if to say, Is he for real? I nodded to show he was. Baird shook his head and said. "Well. am time you get a pretty girl — I mean, Karen gets propositioned a lot. Naturally the other girls down there are going to get a little miffed about it. Kate especially gets a little sharp about it sometimes. Thinks it's unprofessional. But, you know . . . I mean, all women are at war all the time."

"Just so." Wolfe nodded, accepting it for the time being. "Now, Mr. Baird. Describe the operation of the store to me. Miss Merriman's duties, yours, all that goes into the daily operation."

That took a lot of time and carried me through six pages of the notebook. Not that any of it was really helpful. For example. I found out that the copy store was part of a larger corporation that was about to go public. I found out that the total crew complement was twenty-three, and that there were as many as ten on the shop floor at the peak hours during the afternoon, down to a low of two during the night shift. All twenty-three had access to the employee locker room, occasionally coming in after their regular shift for one reason or another, and it was not unheard of for friends or family members to wait for them there. I found out that the store grossed as much as a quarter-million dollars' worth of volume in a month. That made Wolfe sit up a little straighter.

"Preposterous," he said, almost involuntarily. "At less than a dime per copy? It would be bedlam."

"Oh, don't think it isn't. It gets crazy." Baird grinned. "We get people going off with other people's jobs, people getting all hysterical and threatening to sue, people who are just plain nuts. I mean, we advertise quick turnaround, twenty-four hour access. So our customers tend to be frantic." He spread his hands and shrugged. "It goes with the job."

"Mmmph." Wolfe looked vaguely revolted. "To think that the craft that began with Blake and Gutenberg has degenerated to this. Were you working the day Peter Ford came in?"

"I was, but I was in the back, working at the bindery. Karen and Kate are the only ones that really deal with customers. They're at the front counter. The rest of us work production." Baird looked up as Wolfe winced. "What."

I could have told him. It was his grammar, or lack thereof. As Baird had been speaking, he had grown more relaxed, and so had his manner of speaking. I could tell that Wolfe had been restraining himself heroically from correcting him first on "turnaround," which is not a noun in that house, and then "work production." Instead, Wolfe said, "Was there anything about Peter Ford's visit to the store that you remember? Anything at all? Was there, for example, a difficulty with his job such as the ones you described?"

"No, no re-do on that one. He was running his stuff in Express, by himself." Baird wrinkled his brow, concentrating. "I think Karen had to show him how to work the machine. That was how they got to talking, and then Kate was all 'oh, you just wanted to get his number,' and Karen was kinda being all, 'well, if you got it, flaunt it,' but that was all."

Even I had to admit to a little trouble translating that. Wolfe closed his eyes for a martyred moment, then continued, "If I am to understand you, Peter Ford operated the photocopy machine himself? Is that correct?'"

"Yeah, he was in Express. Self-service," he added. at Wolfe's expression.

Wolfe leaned forward. "Was there any indication that Miss Merriman had handled Peter Ford's papers?"

"Well, sure. I mean, I didn't actually see her, but she had to, getting him all set up. The big collating copiers, they scare people. We usually have to talk 'em into the idea that they're user-friendly." Baird shrugged. "I mean, we handle all kinds of *stuff*. The store makes us sign a non-disclosure agreement when we're hired, but really, we never look at the stuff. It's just copies."

Wolfe nodded. "Just so. Very well, Mr. Baird. you started bad, but in spite of it all you have indeed been helpful." He glanced at the clock on the wall. "May I have the full names of all those who were on duty during the period that Peter Ford was in your establishment?"

"Um. Let's see. Well, there was me, Karen. Kate —"

"I said full names," Wolfe snapped. I hid a grin. He was close to the edge, what with Baird's mishandling of the language.

"Oh, yeah. Okay. Well, there's me, Karen Merriman on counter. Kate Ryan at cashier, Greg Huser the manager. Roger York at key-op. Kohen Burrill in color, and Michael Persons on the computer. That's it."

Wolfe nodded. "Can you have those people here at eleven o'clock tomorrow morning?"

"Uh — all of them? Here?" Baird looked doubtful.

"Yes. It is vital." Wolfe was unwavering. "Mr. Baird. You expressed a desire to help Miss Merriman, a desire so profound that it earlier moved you to violence. Now let it move you in a more useful direction."

"Well — sure." Baird squinted. "Only — I mean, they won't come just on my say-so. Maybe if you called the store —"

Wolfe nodded. "Archie. Your typewriter. Take a letter, on our stationery. Address it to Mr. Huser. 'Dear Sir: I request the attendance of yourself, Mr. Roger York, Miss Kate Ryan, Mr. Rodney Baird, Mr. Michael Persons, and Mr. Kohen Burrill at an informal meeting this Wednesday at eleven o'clock a.m. to discuss the implications of a lawsuit Karen Merriman is considering bringing against your corporation to compensate her for harassment and lost wages following her wrongful arrest in the matter of the death of Peter Ford. This is only a preliminary discussion and an attorney should not be necessary. Regards, Nero Wolfe.' Two carbons, Archie." He returned his gaze to Baird. "Will that do?"

Baird goggled at the two of us. "You're kidding! Karen's going to sue? But —"

"Mr. Baird. Control yourself." Wolfe's patience was used up. He glanced at the clock, saw that it was close on to three o'clock, and nodded at me. I peeled the completed letter out of the typewriter, stood and handed Wolfe the original to sign, then proffered it to Baird. He took it and I shooed him out, with him still shaking his head and muttering.

I returned to the office and grinned at Wolfe. "I'll be damned. Okay, I admit it, you bowled out the fingerprint thing pretty neatly, but how did the paper get from the copier to her locker? And why was Ford copying such top-secret stuff in that shop, anyway? All you've proved now is that Karen had access to the papers, which Cramer was assuming, anyway, and if all Karen's co-workers are as dense as that guy, you're going to have a job getting anything at all out of them. Not that I'm complaining, you understand. I can see you're really slaving away on this. But what can you do with —"

"Archie. Saul will be here shortly. Now would be a good time for you to see Mr. Parker and check on our client. We need Miss Merriman here, tonight if possible." Wolfe sat back and pointedly picked up his book.

I growled, but there was no point in berating him. So I simply nodded and got my coat and headed for the door.

FOUR

NORMALLY when I leave the house on any errand associated with a murder case I slip my Marley .32 into my coat pocket, just as a precaution, but this time I vetoed it on the grounds that I didn't want to go through the whole routine at the courthouse entrance of explaining who I was and showing my permit and all that associated annoyance. If we ran into trouble I would just have to depend on my wits.

But there was no trouble, at least not that kind. Parker's secretary told me that Parker was at the courthouse, and that Karen's arraignment had been set for 2:30. I had known Parker would put pressure on, but it was still good news — I had thought there was a better-than-even chance Karen would have been held over-night, and a night in the Manhattan hoosegow is not something I would wish on my worst enemy, let alone a comely young Bronte reader. In fact, I thought it was the first real item of good news that day, because privately I didn't put a lot of faith in Wolfe's 'new line of inquiry.' I had seen him pull some pretty fancy rabbits out of some pretty bedraggled hats, but so far nothing seemed to justify the smug attitude he'd had ever since our morning visit from the Pentagon.

But it wouldn't do to show any doubts to the client, so I did my best to look solid and reassuring when Karen and Parker emerged from the courtroom. Karen took one look at me and flew into my arms, muttering, "Thank God, thank God."

I did my best to return her embrace with the attention it deserved, which took a moment or two. Over her shoulder I saw Parker's sly smile, and I raised an eyebrow. "Some men just have it, I guess," Parker said and let out a mock sigh.

"Yeah," I told him. "Those of us who aren't rich lawyers have to skate by with talent and charm. You should try it some time just for the experience."

Parker said a word that I would not have expected to hear from an uptown lawyer. I ignored it and disentangled Karen from my chest. "Don't go getting any ideas," she said in an arch tone. "I just wanted you to hold me for a moment. Oh, Archie, it was so awful."

"I bet. Don't worry about me getting any ideas. That's Mr. Wolfe's department. Did you say anything?"

"Not a word," she assured me. "All I told them was that Mr. Parker was my attorney and Mr. Wolfe would be acting for me from this point on. But they just kept at me — there was this one lieutenant —"

"Rowcliff?"

She nodded. I grimaced. Rowcliff is the one Cramer sends when all he wants is a piece of somebody's hide. "Well, with any luck you won't be seeing him again. Mr. Wolfe has had a busy morning. Right now his idea, him being the idea man, is that he needs to see you. Right now. Do you need anything?"

As I said it I was hustling her out on to the sidewalk, Parker following close behind. Karen ran a hand through her hair, an involuntary reflex. "Well — I mean, I should go home and change, I must look awful."

"You look great," I told her gallantly. "Dazzling. Anyway, Mr. Wolfe won't care, he's only interested in your literary mind." I glanced over her shoulder at Parker. "What was the price tag, anyway?"

"Fifty thousand." Parker's mouth twisted in a sour grin. "Of course, probably at least ten thousand of that came from the knowledge that she was Nero Wolfe's client, but I didn't think it would be politic to point that out, with the judge being so willing to accede to my demand for an immediate bail hearing."

"We're good for it. Anything else?"

"Not right now, not unless Mr. Wolfe has plans."

"I'm sure he does, but he didn't mention them to me. So I guess you're free for the afternoon."

"I'll go home and practice my charm." Parker raised his hand in a wry salute and went on down the street. I turned to the curb and waved down a taxi.

In the cab Karen snuggled in close to me and I let her. "It's so damn cold in that place," she said. "I know this probably seems terribly wanton, my draping myself all over you like this. It's just —"

"Forget it. I have that effect on women. It's a burden, but I try to bear it with a smile. Anyway, we have more important things to worry about. Do you know a man named Rodney Baird?"

"Rodney?" It shocked her into sitting upright. "But — what does Rodney have to do with anything — ?"

"I don't know. That's why I'm asking. That's what detectives do, ask things. He showed up at our place a little while after you were hauled off in irons. He had the mistaken impression that we were somehow responsible and I had to correct his thinking a little."

"Oh. my God," Karen was appalled. "Did he try and start a fight? He did, didn't he? Oh, God. I am so sorry . . ."

"It wasn't anything," I said. "Once I straightened him out we got along fine. Mr. Wolfe has asked him to line up a little gathering at the House tomorrow." I explained what Wolfe had told Baird and the letter, and I was pleased that she didn't protest or demand explanations. The latter was especially nice since I didn't have one. Of course there was always the old standby that Wolfe was a genius and geniuses never explain themselves. but that one was wearing thin even with me.

By the time I had finished we were at Thirty-Fifth Street. I paid the hackie and escorted her up the stoop. It was just shy of five o'clock, which meant that Wolfe would still be upstairs with the orchids. Civilization might be crumbling about us, but it would take a lot more than that to disrupt Wolfe's schedule — from nine to eleven in the morning and four to six in the afternoon he was in the plant rooms with Theodore. I am not supposed to interrupt him during that time but I thought he'd want to know that our client was loose, and anyway I figured it wouldn't hurt to give Wolfe a little reminder that we were no longer hamstrung by Miss Merriman's unavailability and it was time he went to work.

Fritz met us at the door, looking furtive. The chain bolt was on, which was more or less standard when I was out, but Fritz replaced it the second we were inside. I raised an eyebrow. "I was only gone a couple of hours. Are we under siege?"

"Dieu." Fritz rolled his eyes. "There have been many phone calls. Lawyers insisting on speaking with Mr. Wolfe. The police. That general. He would not speak to any of them. He said to bring you and Miss Merriman immediately."

So it appeared a reminder wouldn't be necessary. I told Fritz to keep his chin up, and led Karen up the three flights of stairs to the plant rooms at the top of the brownstone.

No matter how dire the crisis, I usually slow down a little as I pass through the rows of orchids; the sudden blaze of color is that overwhelming, and it deserves a look. I had underestimated the effect it would have on Karen, though. As we passed from the cool room to the medium and then the tropical, I slowed down a little, as usual, but Karen actually stopped twice to look around and try and take it all in. You can't, of course, not in one look, but still, I had to hand it to her. She was operating on maybe three hours' sleep and had spent most of the last twenty-four hours being barked at by city employees, including Lieutenant Rowcliff, which all by itself was enough to qualify anybody for hazard pay. But she still had enough left to take a moment to admire the beauties of nature.

I let her have her moment, then gestured at her to follow me. We found Wolfe in the potting room, attacking a pile of osmundine with a hand trowel, Theodore cowering off to one side. Wolfe's face was screwed up into a fearsome scowl as he jabbed the trowel into the stuff, and I could only conclude that the osmundine was serving as proxy until the real irritant showed up. I bet myself five-to-two it was Cramer, since no one else can put Wolfe in that state, not even me. With him in such a fury there was no telling how he'd react to having a woman interrupt his playtime with the orchids, but there was no help for it, and anyway he'd asked. So I soldiered on ahead. "Reporting as ordered. Karen followed instructions and didn't give them so much as a squeak."

Wolfe turned to face us, and then for the second time that day precedent was shattered because of Karen Merriman. She said, "I know we have other things to talk about but I've got to tell you. Mr. Wolfe, this is the most amazing greenhouse I've ever seen. It's extraordinary. Like an arboretum. I would think it would be this that you would be famous for, not your detective work."

And by God, as quick as that, Wolfe's bad temper was gone. He had been gathering himself for an explosive rant, and instead he swallowed it and just nodded in acknowledgment. "Not truly an arboretum," he said, mildly. "An arboretum implies a single cultivated forest environment. 'Greenhouse' is adequate, but I prefer 'orchidaria,' since technically there are three linked rooms with a different environment for each."

"It's incredible." Karen shook her head. "Do you give tours?"

"Not usually, but I often accede to a private request. I'm sure Mr. Goodwin would be happy to escort you." Wolfe glanced past Karen to me and saw me staring at him in slack jawed astonishment. He sat up a little straighter and handed the trowel to Theodore, who took it and disappeared with relief into the tropical room. Wolfe surveyed Karen and said politely. "I appreciate the compliment, Miss Merriman, but there are indeed other matters of concern. There have been some developments. I hesitate to ask you to endure further hardship, but I must ask you to remain as our guest until at least noon tomorrow. Have you eaten?"

Of course Wolfe would ask that. Karen sighed and said, "Oh. God. I can't remember the last time — they gave me this crappy sandwich at the jail. but I couldn't even look at it — I've been so — "

Naturally, for Wolfe this crisis outweighed all others. He stood up and snapped, "Archie. Take her to the kitchen at once. Fritz of course has discretion but I would suggest the smoked sturgeon and perhaps some of the ham. You can see to her other needs. We'll put her in the south room. Miss Merriman, I will need to speak to you after you have eaten, in my office at six o'clock." With that, he turned back to the osmundine and started scooping it into a pot.

I was dying to ask him about the various calls that had got him so wound up while I was gone, but when he takes that tone there's no arguing with him. And anyway, Karen had looked so grateful at the prospect of real food I took pity on her and decided I could stand it another hour or so. So I simply bowed and gestured her towards the door, and downstairs we went.

She did have to stop on the way out and look at the medium room one more time, but it was only once. Watching her, I made a mental note to arrange the tour as soon as it would be feasible. Wolfe can have the orchids, but I have my own ideas about beauty, and the way Karen's face lit up looking at those flowers was it.

FIVE

"OH, GOD." Karen took another bite of the ham and rolled her eyes skyward in pleasure. "Fritz, this is so awesome. I can't believe this is just leftovers."

Fritz blushed, and I winked at him. He had been hovering over the two of us, wanting to know the details about our current problem but too much the gentleman to ask. I was seated across from Karen at the kitchen table, not eating, though I had taken a glass of milk just to be sociable.

The phone had rung twice, but since Fritz had tipped me the word that a state of siege was in effect I didn't bother to answer. After the second caller's eleventh ring I stood up and went over to the phone and turned the ringer off. There was no point in answering until we had spoken to Wolfe, and if I had put the call through to the plant rooms Wolfe would have just told them he was unavailable until six and hung up on them, and then taken it out on me. So I decided to just let them all stew until after six.

But I couldn't help wondering. It had to be the letter Wolfe had given Baird that lit the fuse, though I was a little taken aback at the speed and fury of the response. Never underestimate the effect of the word lawsuit on a business. Cramer was another story, though. With Cramer on the warpath again, sooner or later Wolfe was going to have to show his cards, and from what I could tell we didn't even have a pair of deuces to bet with. Of course, there was always Saul's chore, whatever that was.

Remembering Saul, I excused myself and went to the office. Sure enough, there it was in the expense book, in Wolfe's tidy handwriting: Panzer $1000 8/18, Flight 107 5pm US Air.

So Saul had been sent on a trip. I chewed on that one for a few minutes, then gave it up. Whatever had bit Wolfe that morning, it was beyond me. I didn't mind so much not being able to keep up, that was all right because Wolfe was a genius, but I get irritated when he leaves me out entirely. He says it's because he doesn't like to tax my powers of dissimulation, but it's really just because he can't stand the idea that someone might figure out the plot before he's ready to raise the curtain. The reason it gets my goat is because there's nothing wrong with my powers of dissimulation and he knows it.

Anyway, whatever had him going, it must have been good because he was spending money like water. Even though we were already in the eighty-percent bracket for the year and it was all deductible, Wolfe would never let go of that much dough without something concrete in mind. The thought cheered me a little, though I still thought it was even money whether or not Carpenter would have the two of us sharing a cell in Leavenworth by the end of the week.

The sticking point for me was the missing documents. That was what had Carpenter and his buddy in black all steamed up, and they had no doubt brought all that pressure on Cramer to wrap it up quick. Murder wasn't even their primary consideration, they'd made that clear this morning: the fact that Ford was dead only made it more complicated. But what stuck in my craw was that Wolfe wasn't looking at Ford or anything to do with documents or espionage. Instead he had cooked up this charade about suing the copy store and gotten a whole new set of people mad at us, including a couple of corporate lawyers. What the hell was that all about?

I was still sitting in the office worrying at that when I heard the rumble of Wolfe's elevator descending from the plant rooms at 6:02. When he entered the office a moment later, he nodded at me as cool as could be and settled himself into his chair. Apparently Karen's swooning over the orchidaria had been enough to calm his temper for the time being. He took in a bushel of air and let it out again, then rang for beer. Fritz appeared with two bottles and a glass on a tray, and Wolfe took it, poured and let the foam settle before he asked Fritz, "Has she eaten?"

"Yes, sir. She says to thank you especially for the ham."

Wolfe grunted in appreciation. It was the special peanut-fed Virginia ham that a farmer out there raises to his specifications.

"Very well. Bring her in half an hour. Oh, and dinner at eight-thirty tonight, Fritz. Even a snack should have a little time to settle. We can stand a small delay, and the kidney should not —"

The phone rang, since I had switched the ringer back on as soon as I heard the elevator. Wolfe scowled at me as I picked it up and said cheerfully, "Nero Wolfe's residence. Archie Goodwin speaking."

It was a woman's voice, edgy. "Mr. Goodwin, this is Sharon Buhammad. I am an attorney representing King Photocopy Corporation. I wish to speak to Mr. Wolfe."

"I'll see if he's available," I said, and pressed the hold button. "Corporate attorney, female," I told Wolfe. "Name of Sharon Buhammad. Probably not carrying roses. Is the siege lifted?"

Wolfe growled. "Pfui. If I could have contrived another stratagem — never mind. I'll take it." He picked up his phone and I stayed on mine as I punched the button that would open up the line. "Miss Buhammad, this is Nero Wolfe. May I assume you are calling on behalf of the photocopy establishment at Second and Union?"

"I'm calling on behalf of the corporation that owns that establishment." From her tone of voice it was obvious that corporation was second only to God himself in power and influence. "You may not be aware that all legal matters are handled through our head office in Ventura. As the corporation's legal representative, I must ask you to suspend —"

"No. Not possible." Wolfe was polite but firm. "This is a case of murder and my client remains in some peril. Tomorrow's interview is merely a preliminary meeting, and as yet no proceedings have been instituted against your corporation. It is my hope that after that meeting with the store employees no such proceeding will be necessary. But if you balk at such a meeting I will have no choice but to pursue this by other means."

The edge was back in her voice. "I hope that's not a threat. Mr. Wolfe. If it is, I warn you —"

"No threat was implied, madam. I hope for a speedy resolution of the matter and an interview with that store's employees should facilitate that. Some of those employees have information regarding a murder and I must have that information. As their de facto attorney I would think that you would advise them that the sooner this matter is cleared up the better, for them, for you, and for your corporate employer, as well as my client. Delay benefits no one."

"What information could they possibly have?"

"I cannot answer that until I have spoken with them. Possibly none, though I think that unlikely. The sooner I see them the sooner I can shift from operating on a speculative basis to a factual one. I leave tentatively scheduled a meeting at eleven o'clock tomorrow morning. Unless as their attorney you expressly forbid them to attend I see no reason for them not to be here. I would prefer to resolve this on an informal basis outside of a courtroom, as you would as well, certainly." Wolfe put suavity into it. He can be suave when he wants to, though it's almost never with a lawyer. "Well, madam? Surely an informal interview presents no mortal threat."

"I don't think so." She sounded mollified. "All right, they'll be there at eleven, though I reserve the right to have representation present for them as well."

"That is their right, of course, madam." Wolfe said it as though granting a boon. "If there is any difficulty you will of course notify me."

"I'll have Mr. Huser call you if there's a snag," she said, and hung up. I racked the receiver and grinned at Wolfe.

"Too bad she has no idea it's just a fancy bluff," I said. "You were so smooth you almost had me believing it. If any of those copy shop kids has information —"

"Pfui. One of them does. Manifestly. If the document was planted in Miss Merriman's —"

The phone rang again, interrupting him. I grimaced and picked it up. "Nero Wolfe's residen —"

"I want him, Goodwin. Now."

"I'll see if he's in," I said, and looked at Wolfe. "Cramer."

Wolfe didn't growl this time, just picked up. Once again I held the line. "Mr. Cramer. Good evening."

"My ass." Cramer was sore as a boil. "I had a call this afternoon from the manager of that copy shop. You've got them all in a panic. What the hell is this about wrongful arrest? If you bring suit against the department I'll make you eat it."

"Mr. Cramer. Calm yourself. The lawsuit has not yet been brought, and if it is, the corporation that employs Miss Merriman will be named as defendant, not your department, though of course your testimony will be material." Wolfe was openly enjoying himself now. "However, it may be that —"

"Balls. What have you got?"

"A hypothesis," Wolfe replied, almost smug. "I plan to test it tomorrow morning at eleven. If you wish to attend —"

"I'm coming down there now."

"If you do you will not be admitted without a warrant." Wolfe's voice sharpened. "Confound it, you would not be calling me if you hadn't already begun to have doubts about Miss Merriman's guilt. Tomorrow morning at that meeting I have every intention of exposing a murderer and I have invited you to attend. I am extending this courtesy to you despite your colossal jackassery this morning because I wish to see your face when you apologize to Miss Merriman. However," he raised his voice over Cramer's sputtering, "I am not yet ready to act and your coming here this evening would accomplish nothing. Need I remind you, sir, that I warned you that you would regret your precipitous action? This morning it was only a surmise now it is a near-certainty. I am only awaiting one or two small details and as yet I do not have them. Tomorrow I will. No, there will be no further discussion. Good night, sir." Wolfe hung up without giving Cramer a chance to reply, not slamming it down but not daintily, either, and there was nothing for it but for me to hang up as well.

I looked at Wolfe sourly. "Well, that's torn it. I assume the one or two details are what Saul's gone after. What if he doesn't call?"'

"He will."

I snorted. "I'm glad you're so sure. What if the plane crashes?"

That got him. Wolfe's fear of all machinery more complicated than a can opener is the main thing that keeps him indoors, and he considers getting on an airplane an act of sheer madness. Knowing Saul, I figured he probably would deliver the goods, but I didn't like the way Wolfe had taken us past the point of no return with Cramer and thought it would do him good to be reminded that even a genius can't plan for everything.

As for me, my main worry wasn't about the safety of air travel so much as it was that even someone as good as Saul might not have it by eleven tomorrow. Whatever it was. I was about to open up on Wolfe about that when the phone rang again. "Nero Wolfe's residence, Archie Goodwin speaking."

"Saul, Archie. Was the phone turned off before?"

"It was. I hope to hell you've got some good news, because Mr. Wolfe's stirred up a hornet's nest here." I looked over at Wolfe and opened my mouth to say "Saul," but he was already on the line. Since he didn't wave me off I stayed on.

"Saul. Did you get confirmation?"

"I did, sir. Three people identified a photograph and I got signed affidavits from all of them. I can bring the witnesses back with me if you want but I'd need more funds for their tickets."

"The affidavits should suffice. Satisfactory." Wolfe was practically purring. "Well done, Saul. Can you be back here by eleven in the morning?"

"I'm already booked on a red-eye tonight at midnight. It should be no problem."

"Very satisfactory. I apologize for the necessity of putting you on an airplane twice in one day but the situation here is exigent. Be here at ten tomorrow with the affidavits — no, nine. If you would like breakfast."

"From Fritz?" Saul chuckled. "You don't have to ask twice. I'll be there."

"Very well. Again, Saul, extremely satisfactory."

We hung up. I sighed and spread my hands. "All right. You win. I assume it's all locked up. If the damn plane doesn't crash. You have often told me that I am to rely on intelligence guided by experience. My intelligence tells me that there's going to be a murderer here tomorrow at eleven and my experience tells me I better know who he is ahead of time so I can frisk him for guns or grenades before you hand him over. I won't make a move before you say the word, but, damn it, I ought to know in advance so you don't get killed while you're showing off."

Wolfe grunted. Apparently he decided I had suffered enough. "Very well. Bring Miss Merriman, because she should hear this also and I don't wish to expound it twice. We should be through in time for you to telephone General Carpenter before dinner. He should be here tomorrow as well." He rang for beer.

SIX

THE NEXT morning, Wednesday, was a busy one for all of us. Wolfe had sketched the program for Karen and me the night before, and I was kept hopping making sure everyone and everything would be ready by eleven.

Wolfe, of course, breakfasted in his room, as always. Since he didn't buzz me on the house phone for a conference I assumed that there were no changes in the plan, so when I rolled out at seven-thirty I shaved and showered in a hurry and then hotfooted it downstairs to the kitchen, where Fritz had a plate of eggs au beurre noir and toast waiting for me along with the

Times. Usually I like to take my time over breakfast while I get caught up on current events, but that morning the only event that interested me was the one coming at eleven. So I didn't dawdle over the eggs. While I chewed I asked Fritz, "Is she up?"

"Yes. I took a tray up half an hour ago." Fritz paused, then asked, "Archie — ?"

"Don't ask. I still don't know. But I can tell you it's looking a lot more rosy than it did yesterday. Too soon yet to break out the champagne, though."

"Nevertheless, I will have some chilled and ready by noon," Fritz said firmly. "You should have faith, Archie."

"Nuts. If there's anything we've got too much of around here it's faith. Mr. Wolfe has enough faith in himself for both of us and plenty left over."

Fritz giggled and made a French movement with his hand that I had learned over the years to translate as oh, go on with you, before turning back to his pots and pans. Fritz is the only man I know who can giggle without making you wonder about his fundamentals. Maybe it's because he's Swiss.

Saul Panzer arrived at nine precisely. Fritz showed him into the kitchen just as I was taking care of the last of my eggs, and Saul grinned at me. I grinned back, thinking for the thousandth lime how unlikely-looking he was for the best private op in North America. With his face that's all nose, his clothes that always look slept-in, and his battered old watch cap that looks like a missionary barrel reject, Saul doesn't quite look like a bum, but he doesn't look classy, either. But there's no area of the detective business where he isn't the best, whether it's tailing someone, digging up background, or . . . whatever, you name it, he's the best. Even Wolfe admits it.

"What's the plan?" he wanted to know.

"Breakfast first. I think Fritz may have a crust of bread for you. Afterward, I'll take you upstairs and introduce you to the client. You'll like her. She's literary."

"I think you mean literate."- Saul pulled up a chair to the table just as Fritz arrived with a plate for him. "Thanks, Fritz. You're the only one in this den of thieves I can count on."

"You're welcome. Mr. Panzer." Fritz isn't quite as touchy about using first names as Wolfe is, but he has his own odd ideas about it. He's known Saul as long as I have and is perfectly willing to refer to him by his first name when he is absent, but to his face it's always 'Mr. Panzer.' Saul finally gave up trying to talk him out of it a couple of years back. "We may be running short of eggs but there are griddle cakes with honey."

"Whatever," Saul said. "After nothing but airline food yesterday I'm sure it'll be ambrosial. Bring it on."

While Saul ate I filled him in, and after he had finished, the two of us went up two flights to the south room where I had installed Karen the night before. I knocked. "Are you decent?"

"I don't know about that," came Karen's voice archly, "but I'm dressed. Come on in."

I opened the door and went on in, Saul a discreet few steps behind. Karen turned from the window and greeted me with a warm hug and a kiss on the check. "One of you is a perfect angel, washing and pressing my clothes in the middle of the night like that," she said. "It's no wonder there are no women in this house. No woman could stand the competition."

I grinned down at her. "I would love to take credit, seeing how grateful you are and all, but honest and true-blue American lad that I am I have to admit that it was Fritz who took care of your clothing. Seeing as how we abducted you from the courthouse yesterday without even letting you go home and pack a bag, it seemed the least we could do."

She leaned back and raised a playful eyebrow. "Okay. So Fritz does the cleaning and the housework and cooks those incredible meals and Theodore tends the orchids, and Mr. Wolfe does the detective work. What do you do?"

"You got me," I admitted. "Not much except the occasional bit of heavy lifting. I'm also the hell of a dancer, but there's not much call for that around here since Mr. Wolfe always wants to lead. Miss Merriman, allow me to introduce Mr Saul Panzer, who is also a first-rate detective, though he is a lousy dancer."

"How would you know?" Saul shot back, and then stepped forward and held a hand out to Karen. "Miss Merriman."

"Mr. Panzer," Karen said gravely, then burst into giggles as, instead of shaking her hand, Saul raised it to his lips European-style. He then swept off his frayed old watch cap and with the same motion bent over in a formal bow that could have easily passed muster for style and execution in a British royal throne room. "Oh, my God. You all are just too much," Karen said, still giggling.

"I thought you two would get along," I said. "Saul, you two are going to be at the hole. Ringside seats. Until show time you call hide out in the front room and play pinochle or something."

"Maybe Miss Merriman could teach me to dance," Saul said, with a twinkle in his eye.

"Oh, I'm sure Archie would be a much better teacher."

"I've tried." I said. "He's hopeless. Come on, I'll show you the hole, Miss Merriman. Saul?"

They followed as I led them downstairs to an alcove in the hall. From the hall it just looks like a phone nook with no phone in it, with a cabinet set at eye level against the back. But if you open the cabinet you are looking at the back side of a painted gauze picture of a waterfall, translucent . . . and through the gauze you have a fairly good view of Wolfe's office. Of course you can hear, too. From the office it just looks like a framed painting of a waterfall. A few years back it had been a picture of the Washington Monument at the hole, but for some reason people in the office paid more attention to that, which is not what you want people doing to your spy-hole when you are spying on them through it. After some trial-and-error Wolfe and I had settled on the waterfall picture as being anonymous enough to escape scrutiny, and the soft pastels it's painted in are easy to see through.

It had been a bone of contention last night with Karen, talking it over with Wolfe. She had wanted to be present at the conference and Wolfe had said flatly nothing doing, he wanted a free hand and the temptation for Karen to interrupt would be too much for her. Wolfe didn't actually come out and say so, but I knew a large part of his reluctance was his basic unwillingness to believe that a woman can keep silent for any length of time for any reason.

I hoped he was wrong as I told Karen, "The important thing for you to remember is that when this cabinet is open, they can't see you, but they can hear you. You have to remain absolutely silent or you'll blow the whole thing. Understand?"

"I understand," Karen said, a little pettishly. "1 understood last night."

"I know, but I want your promise. If you can't keep quiet you'll have to wait it out upstairs. Okay? Promise?"

"I promise." She smiled. "Really, Archie. I'll be quiet."

"Okay, then. Saul, you entertain her in the front room. Fritz will come and get you when it's time." I left them in the hall and hoofed it to the kitchen, where Fritz was putting together a tray of liquids to have ready in the office at eleven. That had been another bone of contention, serving refreshments. This time it had been me who disagreed with Wolfe on it. I had pointed out that we would have a killer in the room and I didn't fancy the idea of having to watch out for a doped drink, but Wolfe had said pfui, the chance was infinitesimal and the others present who were not murderers were his guests and would get refreshment if they wished. So then I tried flanking him by suggesting that we at least have Fritz serve people but Wolfe had vetoed that, too, pointing out that the office was already going to be uncomfortably crowded and it was unfair to Fritz. So I gave it up and just resolved privately to keep my eyes open.

Fritz had the drinks situation under control, as always, and Karen and Saul were in the front room. Wolfe was still up with the orchids. There was nothing for me but to arrange the office and wait for our guests. So I started bringing chairs in and setting them up, and after a while Fritz came in to help with that, and by 10:25 we were all set. Now there was nothing but waiting.

By 10:45 1 was wound up so tight that I was considering rearranging all the chairs just to have something to do, but I was saved from that by the sound of the doorbell. Our guests were arriving.

First was Carpenter, who didn't look too happy with us. I didn't get the friendly smile today, but merely a grunt as I took his hat and coat and ushered him into the office. He declined my offer of a drink and then the bell rang again, and this time it was the copy shop employees, all in a bunch. I was kept busy taking coats and showing them into the office, but I did take a moment to size them up as I was getting them all settled.

Greg Huser, the manager, was a serious-faced man in his thirties with thinning blonde hair. He nodded politely at me as I showed him into the office and put him in the red leather chair, but his eyes kept traveling around the room with a worried look.

Kohen Burrill, on the other hand, didn't look like he'd ever worried about anything in his life. He was the youngest, maybe twenty-five, and when I offered him a drink he accepted beer. When he saw the label on the bottle his eyebrows rose and he nodded at me. "Right on!"

"Mr. Wolfe agrees with you," I told him. Behind Burrill were Roger York and Michael Persons, both of whom declined drinks. York was a pleasant-faced man in his forties with a blonde streak in his hair that I suspected came out of a bottle, but then we detectives are the suspicious sort. He looked around the office with interest before sitting down behind Burrill. Persons, the computer operator, was a thirtyish man with spectacles and a neatly-trimmed goatee. He wore the supercilious expression of distaste that I had come to associate with self-important concierges and government clerical workers, but I had never seen it on the face of a computer whiz before. Not only did he decline a drink, but he looked so disgusted with me as he said it that if he had accepted one I'd have been tempted to spit in it first.

Kate Ryan, the only woman, looked distressed, pale, and underfed. I knew she would be trouble. Wolfe hates people who look as though they don't get enough to eat, and then she compounded it by asking for a gin and tonic, which Wolfe says is the most destructive thing one can do to the palate. Now he would really have it in for her.

Bringing up the rear was Rodney Baird, who offered me a strained grin but no comment as I took his coat and set him in the chair closest to my desk, where I could reach him easily if he took a notion to get physical again. I didn't expect him to, but as Wolfe often says, the only thing you can expect from a dunce is the unexpected, and I figured better safe than sorry.

Last to arrive was Cramer, who scowled at me when he saw that I had given the red leather chair to Huser, but didn't make an issue of it. He settled himself on the end of the yellow couch in the rear of the office just as the rumble of Wolfe's elevator signaled his descent from the plant rooms. It was 11:00 precisely. I was just getting seated at my desk as Wolfe entered and inclined his head at the assembled throng.

"Good morning," he said, getting his bulk adjusted comfortably in his oversized chair. "I thank you for coming. You will have noted the presence of Inspector Cramer, whom some of you have —"

"I did notice that," Huser cut in. "We talked it over and decided we didn't need a lawyer, but now, with the police here —"

Wolfe held up a hand. "Please. This will go much faster if you allow me to proceed. As I was about to say, you will all have noted the presence of Inspector Cramer of the New York Police Department, and 1 would also like to introduce General Carpenter, representing the U.S. State Department." Heads turned to gawk at Carpenter, who nodded. Wolfe continued, "These men are here at my invitation, but this is not an official proceeding. I am engaged privately to protect the interest of your co-worker, Miss Karen Merriman."

"I reserve the right to intervene, if necessary." Cramer growled. "If you get too — "

"Of course," Wolfe said, with exaggerated patience. "But until that time, should it arrive, may I proceed? Thank you. This may take a while. Are the refreshments suitable?"

Various nods. Burrill said, "This is great beer, man."

"Thank you, Mr. Burrill. Now then, to begin, of course you are all aware that one of your store's customers. Mr. Peter Ford, was murdered by a hit-and-run driver on the evening of August tenth and Miss Merriman was the chief suspect. The reason for this was twofold: Mr. Ford's body was discovered close to Miss Merriman's apartment, and Mr. Ford had been trying to reach her by telephone until shortly before his death. Therefore it was a natural assumption that a relationship existed between Ford and Miss Merriman. Yes, Miss Ryan? You have a comment?"

Kate Ryan had let out a snort. "Just that there isn't a male customer that came in that Karen didn't have a relationship with. Of course it was a natural assumption."

Baird bristled. "Oh, come on, Kate — "

"Mr. Baird." Wolfe snapped. "I'm talking. The police had a further reason to be suspicious, one that has not become public knowledge. Peter Ford was under surveillance, suspected of espionage. He had documents with him that have since gone missing, and it was only after he evaded the agents tailing him that he began trying to telephone Miss Merriman. This was what made the case against Miss Merriman so damning. I confess that I myself thought it looked as though Miss Merriman was guilty when she came to me yesterday morning and engaged my services."

Huser was scowling, not at Wolfe, but just in concentration. He said. "But — excuse me — if Karen's guilty, what's all this about wrongful arrest? Where do we come in?"

"I'm coming to that, Mr. Huser. Please bear with me. Miss Merriman came to us yesterday morning after spending the entire night before being questioned by the police. She was desperate and deeply frightened. After speaking with her I decided that it strained credulity too much to suspect her of putting on an act for our benefit. If she was truly guilty she would have sought a lawyer's aid, not mine. Therefore she was telling the truth when she claimed to be innocent. At least that was my working hypothesis, and Mr. Goodwin concurred." Wolfe paused and took a swallow of beer. "However, I had no starting point from which to test that hypothesis. Ironically, it was the overzealous actions of Mr. Cramer that supplied one. Frantic to secure the missing documents, he obtained search warrants for Miss Merriman's home and her place of employment, the copy store. At the store, in the employee locker room, a page of one of the documents in question was found in Miss Merriman's locker, with her fingerprints on it."

"But, damn it, Wolfe —" Cramer said.

"I'll do the butting, Mr. Cramer," Wolfe said sharply. "Had you the wit of a common mollusk you would have realized that instead of sealing Miss Merriman's doom, the sudden appearance of that single page proclaimed her innocence. Miss Merriman could not possibly have placed that page there. If she was guilty and had chosen the locker as the hiding place for the documents, all of them would have been found, not just a fragment of one. If, then, she was not guilty, she would have told me yesterday morning about the page in her locker. Finding such a potentially damaging item would have placed her in mortal fear, for she would have had no explanation for its presence. When she asked me for aid, she placed all the facts she had at my disposal and that would have been first on the list. But she didn't mention it, didn't even know it existed. Therefore it had been planted there, within the last twenty-four hours, since she would have discovered it otherwise, but as I said, she did not go to the store yesterday at all. She spent the night being questioned at the police station, went home and telephoned the store to say she would be absent, and then came here. She was here when the page was discovered and Mr. Cramer took her into custody — with far more force than was necessary or advisable, I might add."

"But —" This from Michael Persons. "You say it was planted. That just isn't possible."

"It is the only conclusion, Mr. Persons, unless you allow for the possibility of thaumaturgy, and I do not."

Persons wasn't going to be brushed off that easily. He smiled at Wolfe, as though he were speaking to a foolish child. "But then that means that one of us put it there."

"Yes. Precisely, Mr. Persons. That is exactly what I am saying." Wolfe was offhand. "As I would have told Mr. Cramer, had he not so belligerently —"

But nobody heard him because the room erupted in bedlam. Burrill was shaking his head and saying, "No way," and York and

Huser were both on their feet. Kate Ryan sat and glared at Wolfe as though if she stared hard enough he might shrivel up and die on the spot.

It was Cramer who put a stop to it. "Sit down and shut up!" he roared. "All of you!"

Slowly they all settled down again. Cramer waited until they were quiet, then scowled at Wolfe. "If you try and interrupt he'll prolong it just to show you. Let him finish. All right, Wolfe, go ahead. You just better not screw up —"

"I shall endeavor not to screw up. Mr. Cramer. Very well. As I was saying, the discovery of the missing page in Miss Merriman's locker not only satisfied me of her innocence, but it also led me to a conjecture." Wolfe had finished his first bottle of beer and opened the second. He poured, waited for the foam to settle, then continued. "Since it had to have been planted by a fellow employee of Miss Merriman's, I wondered, what if the killer of Peter Ford had no interest in the documents at all? What if the motive for his killing had not been political, but personal? It was Mr. Goodwin who suggested the possibility, and I decided to explore it. I already had formed the provisional theory that the killer bore an animus not just towards Peter Ford but toward Miss Merriman as well."

"What's 'animus' mean?" Kohen Burrill blurted.

"Antagonism. Dislike. Hatred." Wolfe paused to make sure everyone got it, then went on, "General Carpenter had already informed me that Ford was under suspicion of attempting to pass the documents on to an enemy agent. As part of his plan, he took them to the copy shop and had them duplicated, counting on the fact that no one would suspect him of using such an obvious venue for doing so to shield him. Even so, he took the precaution of making the copies himself, but he required Miss Merriman's assistance to operate the machine. In the course of getting him started she handled the documents and thus left fingerprints on them. Mr. Baird told me yesterday that during such a procedure on a normal workday it would be a common occurrence. During this period Miss Merriman and Peter Ford had a friendly exchange which resulted in Miss Merriman giving him her telephone number. Later, when Ford planned to rendezvous with his contact, he divested himself of identification but forgot the slip of paper on which Miss Merriman had written her number, which is why it was the only thing he had on him when his body was discovered."

"Who was the contact?" Carpenter barked.

"I don't know." Wolfe raised a hand as Carpenter started to splutter. "It's not material. Ford never made the rendezvous. When he shook the surveillance team he discovered that some of the copies were missing. Panicked, he remembered Miss Merriman and tried to reach her by telephone, but since she had her ringer turned off he assumed she was absent. He determined to go to her apartment and wait for her on the assumption that she had taken the copies for some reason of her own, but he never reached it. He was killed two blocks away."

Wolfe paused, but no one interrupted this time. Satisfied he had their complete attention, he went on. "Even at this point I still had nothing specific on which to base a suspicion. I knew the guilty party had to be someone at the copy shop who was working the same shift as Miss Merriman, but who? It could have been any of you. I had taken the matter thus far when we were visited yesterday by Mr. Rodney Baird. He —"

"I didn't do it," Baird burst out. He was pale and sweating. His left arm twitched and I tensed, thinking I might have to restrain him, but he stayed in his chair, his eyes fixed on Wolfe.

"Don't squeal before you're hurt, Mr. Baird. Allow me to finish." Wolfe glared at him. "As I was about to say, Mr. Baird provided the final pointer I had been lacking. After an initial intemperate scene during which Mr. Baird had to be restrained by Mr. Goodwin, he actually proved quite informative. He told me that copy jobs are occasionally mislaid or lost during the busy times of the afternoon, which satisfied me as to what must have happened later that evening, but more importantly, he mentioned a fellow employee and her dislike of Karen Merriman." Wolfe's eyes swiveled to fix on Kate Ryan. "Specifically, he mentioned you, Miss Ryan."

"You're crazy," Kate Ryan spat. She gripped the arms of her chair so tightly her knuckles were white. "Greg, tell him."

Huser merely shook his head and said, "Shut up, Kate. It's not like he's telling a secret. I'd like to hear the rest of it, Mr. Wolfe."

Wolfe nodded. "There is little left to tell. So far what I had I got simply by the process of ratiocination. There was still proof. One or two little items struck me as suggestive. First, that it was only Miss Ryan and Miss Merriman who had opportunity for interaction with customers, and thus with Ford, stationed as they were at the front counter. It would have been a simple matter for

Miss Ryan to shuffle a few of the documents into some place of concealment for later use in some scheme to embarrass Miss Merriman. It was only upon later examination of those papers, highly sensitive state documents, possibly stamped TOP SECRET or some such designation, that she discovered the potentially explosive nature of her petty act of vengefulness, and thus she decided to return the pilfered copies to Ford via Miss Merriman. I can only speculate, of course, but such must have been her thinking. It was that evening, on her way to Miss Merriman's apartment, that she saw Peter Ford and something provoked the murderous impulse that caused her to swerve her vehicle and kill him." Wolfe paused and raised a quizzical eyebrow. "What was it, Miss Ryan?"

Kate Ryan hadn't moved. She was still gripping the armchair. Her face was a taut skull. "I don't think —" She stopped and swallowed. "I don't think I'm going to say anything."

Wolfe nodded. "Wise," he agreed. "So far I am still only speculating. But the extrapolation was enough to turn my eye on you and to investigate the possibility of previous contact between you and Peter Ford. Therefore I dispatched an operative in my employ to Ford's home town, Washington, D.C. after he had provided himself with a photograph of you. Saul? The affidavits?"

On cue, Saul Panzer appeared at the office door, a sheaf of papers in his hand. "Three people identified a picture of Kate Ryan," he said. "A clerk at a Motel Six Ford was known to frequent, a nurse at an abortion clinic, and the doorman of Ford's apartment building. The nurse said —"

"That's enough, Panzer." Cramer was on his feet. "I want those affidavits, and the names of those —"

Carpenter was on his feet as well. "What about the papers?" he barked. "Wolfe. damn it. you can't just —"

Wolfe held up a hand, his gaze still fixed on Kate Ryan. "Well. Miss Ryan?" he inquired. "Manifestly you are doomed. Given this information, the authorities will soon have all they need to indict you on a murder charge. A laboratory examination of your car alone, along with testimony from the three witnesses Mr. Panzer has located just in the last twenty-four hours. There will be others, once Mr. Cramer's army of investigators is unleashed on you. Your only hope for leniency is to surrender the —"

But Wolfe never got to finish, because Kate Ryan exploded into a blur of motion, smashing her glass on the desk and using the jagged shards to go for Wolfe's face. I was up and moving in the same instant, but Baird was faster. He grabbed her shoulder and spun her around so fast she went sprawling. She tried to scramble up, but by then Cramer had her in a firm grip.

"He didn't even recognize me," she spat. "It had only been two years since that bastard knocked me up and lied to me and used me like his whore, and he didn't even recognize me. He only had eyes for that slut Karen — even when I saw him on the way to her building — he didn't —" Suddenly she slumped and burst into tears.

"Well, Mr. Cramer?" Wolfe glared at him. "If you must advise someone of her Miranda rights, I think now would be the time."

Cramer merely shook his head and hauled Kate Ryan to her feet. Wolfe addressed her. "Miss Ryan. Peter Ford was indeed a liar, a cad, and a traitor. But Miss Merriman? What was her crime?"

She just shook her head, and Cramer escorted her out. Suddenly everyone started talking at once. Carpenter was loudest. "Damn it, Wolfe, what about the docum —"

"I suggest you start with a search of Miss Ryan's home, since she did not have them at the store," Wolfe said. "Confound it, must I do everything for you?"

He would have added more, but Carpenter was already headed for the door. I went with him to make sure he got his hat and coat, and by the time I got back to the office Karen was there as well. She was saying to Huser, "No, of course I'm not suing anybody. Get a grip. It was just something Mr. Wolfe was using to get everybody —" She was interrupted by a popping sound from the door to the dining room.

It was Fritz, with champagne. I looked at the clock on the wall and saw that it was noon, straight up.

SEVEN

A FEW weeks later, the day after Kate Ryan had been sentenced to twenty years for second-degree murder, Karen Merriman arrived at precisely 11:05, carrying a brown paper bag. We exchanged pleasantries as I escorted her into the office, and Wolfe favored her with a small nod as I seated her in the red leather chair. "Good morning, Miss Merriman," he said politely. "I trust you have had no further difficulties with the police."

Karen blushed. "No, no, nothing like that. I just well, I felt bad, you and Archie going to all that trouble for me for just a dollar. I've been waiting for you to submit some kind of a bill, but when I called this morning Archie said there wasn't going to be one."

"That is correct, Miss Merriman." Wolfe was gruff. "The scope of my engagement was set by me and so was my fee. Mr. Cramer provoked me into an intemperate decision before we had a chance to discuss it fully, but that onus rests with me, not you. I set a price and you paid it."

Karen frowned. "Well okay. But still, I thought you should have something." She pulled a book out of the bag and proffered it to Wolfe.

"Jane Eyre," Wolfe said. The corners of his mouth started to pull up and I thought he might actually smile at her again, but he controlled himself. "Thank you."

"I hope it's okay," Karen said, a little breathlessly. "I mean, you probably already have a copy, but this is a nice hardcover, I had a guy in the Village bind it special —"

"Miss Merriman." Wolfe raised a hand. "The gesture is noble, and appreciated. There is no need to besmirch it with an apology. I say again, thank you." He paused. "Was there anything else? Did you wish to see the orchids?"

"Um no, not today. I've got to get to work. Thank you, though. I mean, for everything." There was an awkward silence. Karen rose. "I better get going."

I rose and followed her to the door. At the vestibule she paused and pressed an envelope into my hand. "I didn't want to give you this in front of Mr. Wolfe," she said. "Open it later."

I raised an eyebrow. "What is it? Secret documents?"

"Sort of." she said, with a mischievous smile. "I — oh, hell, I better go." She was out the door and out on the sidewalk before I could reply.

I shrugged and went back into the office. Wolfe was paging through the book, eyes half-closed, his expression one of serene satisfaction.

"Nuts," I told him. "It's nice, sure, but you've already got that British first edition Jane Eyre that Hitchcock shipped last —"

"Archie. You have no soul." He was purring. Seeing there was no possibility of getting a rise out of him, I grinned and opened the envelope. Inside was a card with a picture of an orchid on the front. Inside it had Karen's phone number and the inscription:

I'm a hell of a dancer, too. Call me sometime and I'll

show you.
Love,
Karen

Which just went to prove what I said all along. No smile at a pretty girl is ever wasted.

A SONNET TO WEST 35TH STREET

by John McAleer

Rain beats down at dusk on a brownstone house.
Within, sage Wolfe adjusts his Mauro chair,
Alert for Archie's tread upon the stair,
And an impending meal of choice blue grouse.
Now Archie enters, wearing his broadest grin,
And says he'll wed Lily the very next day.
He gives the Gouchard globe a sudden spin
And asks for a substantial raise in pay.
Wolfe sighs for his orchideous concubines.
A girl arrives, distraught, her fate unsure.
Trim ankles, Archie notes, and eyes azure.
Fritz simmers sauces, and decants white wines.
Eyes shut tight, Wolfe moves his lips in and out.
How grand and glorious, this world of Rex Stout.

December 2, 1978